Secret Sanction

Secret Sanction

A novel by
Brian Haig

ORION

First published in Great Britain in 2001 by Orion
an imprint of The Orion Publishing Group
Orion House, 5 Upper St Martin's Lane, London WC2H 9EA

A CIP catalogue record for this book is available
from the British Library

ISBN (cased) 0 75284 662 0
ISBN (trade paperback) 0 75284 663 9

Printed and bound in Great Britain by
Clays Ltd, St Ives plc

For Lisa, my love
also Brian, Patrick, Donnie, and Annie

Acknowledgments

Special thanks to Linda Janklow, who gave me this chance, and Luke Janklow, who gives the words "agent" and "friend" the highest connotations. And Chuck Wardell and Pete Kinney, two great former soldiers who were the inspiration for Sean Drummond. Also special thanks to Rick Horgan, the editor who struggled to wring out all my bad jokes and mushy ideas. Those that survived are not Rick's fault; they are reflections of my own literary shortcomings and bad taste. Finally, thanks to all the wonderful people at Warner Books, especially Mari Okuda and Roland Ottewell, who did the painful but, in my case, very necessary task of making this book readable.

But my greatest thanks goes to the men and women of the United States Army and the allies who serve beside them. They are out there upholding our most laudable ideals.

Secret Sanction

Chapter
☆ ☆ ☆ 1

Fort Bragg in August is so hellish, you can smell the sulfur in
the air. Actually, though, it's not sulfur, it's 98 percent humidity,
mixed with North Carolina dust, mixed with the raunchy bou-
quet of about thirty thousand men and women who spend half
their lives scurrying about in the woods. Without showers.

The moment I stepped off the plane, I had this fierce urge
to call my bosses back in the Pentagon and beg them to re-
consider. Wouldn't work though. "Sympathy," the Army likes to
say, is found in the dictionary between "shit" and "syphilis," and
regarded accordingly.

So I hefted up my duffel bag and oversize legal brifcasc
and headed for the taxi stand. Of course, this was Pope Air Force
Base, which adjoins Fort Bragg, which makes it all one big, happy
military installation. No taxi stand, and shame on me for not
knowing that. I therefore marched straight to a payphone and
called the duty sergeant at the headquarters of the 82nd Airborne Division. These are the same men and women who make
their living flinging themselves out of airplanes and praying their
government-issued parachutes open before their fragile bodies
go splat. Mostly their prayers work. Sometimes not.

"Headquarters of the 82nd Airborne Division, Sergeant Mercor," a stern voice answered.

"Major Sean Drummond, here," I barked, doing my finest impersonation of a bitchy, obnoxious bully, which, by the by, I always do pretty well.

"How can I help you, sir?"

"How can you help me?" I demanded.

"Sorry, sir, I don't get it."

"That's pretty damned obvious, isn't it? Why wasn't the duty jeep waiting for me at the airport? Why am I standing here with my thumb up my ass?"

"We don't send jeeps out to the airport to pick up personnel. Not even officers, sir."

"Hey, Sergeant, think I'm stupid?"

I let that question linger a moment, and you could almost hear him grinding his teeth to keep from answering.

Then, much friendlier, I said, "Look, I don't know if you weren't properly instructed, or just plain forgot. All I know is, the general who works upstairs in that building of yours promised a jeep would be waiting when I arrived. Now if it were to get here inside twenty minutes, then we'll just write this off as an inconvenience. Otherwise . . ."

There was this fairly long pause on the other end. The thing with Army sergeants is that they have incredible survival instincts. They have to. They spend their careers working under officers, some of whom happen to be pretty good, but plenty of whom aren't, and a man must be pretty damned artful to treat both with perfect equanimity.

"Sir, I . . . well, uh, this is really irregular. No one told me to have a jeep there to meet you. I swear."

Of course nobody told him. I knew that. And he knew that. But there was a world of daylight between those two facts.

"Listen, Sergeant. . . . Sergeant Mercor, right? It's ten-thirty at night and my patience wanes with each passing minute. What will it be?"

"All right, Major. The duty driver will be there in about twenty minutes. Don't be screwing me around, though. I'm gonna put this in the duty log. The colonel will see it in the morning," he said, making that last statement sound profoundly ominous.

"Twenty minutes," I said before hanging up.

I sat on my duffel bag and waited. I should've felt bad about fibbing, but my conscience just wasn't up to it. I was tired, for one thing, and royally pissed off for another. Besides, I had a set of orders in my pocket that assigned me to perform a special investigation. In my book, at least, that entitled me to a special privilege or two.

Private Rodriguez and the duty jeep showed up exactly twenty minutes later. I was pretty damned sure Sergeant Mercor had instructed Rodriguez to get lost, or drive around in circles, or do about any damned thing except arrive one second earlier than twenty minutes. That's another thing about Army sergeants. They're woefully vengeful little creatures.

I threw my duffel into the back of the humvee and climbed in the front.

"Where to?" Private Rodriguez asked, staring straight ahead.

"Visiting Officers' Quarters. Know where they are?"

"Sure."

"Good. Drive."

A moment passed before Rodriguez sort of coughed, then said, "You assigned here, sir?"

"Nope."

"Reporting in?"

"Nope."

"Passing through?"

"You're getting warmer."

"You're a lawyer, right?" he asked, glancing at the brass on my uniform that identified me as a member of the Judge Advocate General's Corps, or JAG for short.

"Rodriguez, it's late and I'm tired. I appreciate your need to make conversation, but I'm not in the mood. Just drive."

"Hey, no problem, sir."

Rodriguez whistled for two minutes, then, "Ever been to Bragg before, sir?"

"Yes, I've been to Bragg before. I've been to every Army post you can name. I'm still not in the mood to talk."

"Hey, sure. No problem, really." Then, only a few moments later, "Y'know, personally, I really like it here."

Poor Private Rodriguez either had short-term amnesia or he'd been ordered by Sergeant Mercor to find out everything he could about me and report back. That's another thing about Army sergeants. When they're curious, they get fiendishly clever.

"So why do you like it here?" I wearily asked, not wanting his ass to get gnawed into little pieces on my account.

"My family comes from Mexico, right? And we settled in Texas, so I like the warm weather. Only they got trees up here, and it rains more. And I love jumpin' outta airplanes. You know that feeling, right? I see you got wings."

"Wrong. I went to jump school and did the five mandatory jumps required to graduate. But I'm not Airborne. I hated it. I was scared as hell and couldn't wait for it to be over. I'll never jump again. Never."

"You're a Ranger. Not many lawyers are Rangers."

"I'm the most reluctant Ranger you ever saw. I cried and whimpered the whole way through the course. They gave me the tab only because they feared that if they failed me, I might have come back and tried again. They hated me."

"You got a Combat Infantryman's Badge," he said.

Private Rodriguez, annoyingly clever fellow that he was, kept adjusting the rearview mirror to study the various items on my uniform. In civilian life, nobody wears nametags or badges or patches, or any other kind of silly accoutrement that advertises anything about you. In the Army, the longer you're in, the more your uniform resembles a diary. It's a wonder the old-timers can even walk under all that weight.

"I used to be infantry," I admitted.

"And you went to combat."

"Only because they shipped me off before I could figure out how to go AWOL. I spent the whole time huddled in deep foxholes, praying nobody noticed me."

"No offense, sir, but why would a guy wanta stop being an infantry officer just to become a lawyer?"

That's another thing with the Army. What's important on the inside can be quite a bit different from what's important on the outside.

"Someone gave me a test and, wouldn't you know it, turned out my IQ was over twenty. Bastards said I was too smart to be an infantry officer anymore."

"No shit?" he asked, quite sincerely, too, which tells you miles about infantry officers.

"Yeah. Not a lot above twenty, just a little. You know the Army, though. Rules are rules."

"You go to law school and all that?"

"Yeah, I went to law school and all that. You done asking questions?"

"No, sir, only a few more. Why you here?"

"Passing through, Private. I thought we already covered that."

"Passing through to where?"

"To Europe."

"Would that be . . . uh, Bosnia?"

"That's where it would be."

"Then what you doing here?"

"I'm supposed to catch a C-130 that leaves Pope Field at seven o'clock in the morning, and military air bases don't exactly run like civilian airports, with connecting flights and all that stuff. As a result, I have to sleep here."

A more truthful reply would have included the fact that I had an appointment in the morning with a general named Partridge, and only after he was through with me was I allowed to head for Bosnia. But Private Rodriguez, and thereby Sergeant Mercor, did not need to know all that. In fact, nobody but the general, myself, and a few very select people back in Washington needed to know all that.

"VOQ just ahead," Private Rodriguez announced, pointing out the windshield at a bunch of long blockhouses.

"Thanks," I said as we pulled into the parking lot, and I retrieved my duffel from the rear.

"No problem. Hey, one thing, sir. That Sergeant Mercor you spoke with, well, he really is a prick. If I were you, and I didn't really have permission from the general, I'd get my butt on that airplane as early as I could."

"Thanks for the ride," I muttered.

That's how business is done in the Army. I scratched his ass, so he scratched mine. Sounds simple, but it can be very protean in practice. I left him there and walked into the VOQ, checked in, and found my room. In less than a minute I was undressed, in bed, and asleep.

It didn't seem like a full five hours later when the phone beside my bed rang and the desk clerk informed me that General Partridge's military sedan was waiting in the parking lot. I showered and shaved with dazzling speed, then rummaged through my duffel for my battle dress and combat boots. This was the only appropriate attire when meeting with Clive Partridge, who truly was one of the meanest sons of bitches in an institution not known for producing shrinking violets.

The drive out to the John F. Kennedy Special Warfare Center, which is, among other things, the headquarters for the United States Army Special Forces Command, took slightly shy of thirty minutes. General Partridge's driver, unlike Private Rodriguez the night before, said not a word. I chalked that up to his being grumped up about having to chauffeur a lowly major, instead of the four-star general he worked for. Headquarters guys get real fussy airs that way.

A sour-faced major named Jackson met me outside Partridge's office and coldly told me to sit and wait. I reminded him that I had to be on a seven o'clock flight to Bosnia, and he reminded me that four-star generals outrank majors. I gave him a fishy-eyed look and instantly decided that maybe General Partridge deliberately surrounded himself with nasty people.

Twenty minutes later, Major Jackson stood up and led me to the hand-carved door that served as the final line of defense into General Partridge's office. The door opened, I passed through, and marched briskly to the general's desk. I stopped, saluted crisply, and introduced myself in that strange way Army guys do.

"Major Drummond reporting as ordered, sir."

The general looked up from some papers, nodded slightly, popped a cigarette between his lips, and calmly lit it. My right hand was still foolishly stuck to my forehead.

"Put down that hand," he grunted, and I did. He sucked in a roomful of smoke, then leaned back into his chair. "You happy about this assignment?"

"No, sir."

"You studied the case already?"

"A bit, sir."

"Any preliminary thoughts?"

"None I would care to expose at this point."

He sucked hard on the cigarette again, so hard that nearly half of it turned into ash. He had thin lips, a thin face, and a thin body, all of which looked nicely weathered, very taut, and almost impossibly devoid of both body fat and compassion.

"Drummond, every now and again there's a military court

case that captures the attention of the great American public. Back when I was a lieutenant, the big one was the My Lai court-martial, named after that village in Vietnam where Lieutenant Calley and his guys butchered a few hundred defenseless civilians. Then came Tailhook, which the Navy botched past the point of redemption. Then the Air Force had that Kelly Flynn thing they dicked up in spades."

The general surely knew that all military lawyers had these cases tattooed on their brains. He obviously was taking no small delight in bringing them up.

"It's your turn, Drummond. You screw this one up, and generations of future JAG officers are gonna be sitting around in classrooms, scratching their heads and wondering just how this guy Drummond managed to mangle things so bad. You thought of that?"

"It has crossed my mind, General."

"I imagine it has," he said with a nasty grin. "You decide there's not enough grounds for a court-martial and you'll be accused of shoving the Army's dirt under a rug. You decide there *is* sufficient grounds, then we'll have us a nice little brawl in a courtroom with the whole world watching."

He stopped and studied my face, and I was not the least bit sure which of those two options he wanted. I had a pretty good idea, I just wasn't sure. He had that kind of face.

"You got any idea why we picked you?"

"Only a few vague suspicions," I cautiously admitted.

This, actually, was my sly way of saying that I wanted to hear his opinion, since his was based on the fact that he helped select me. Mine, on the other hand, was the bitter rumination of a guy who thought he was being tossed into an alligator pond.

He lifted three fingers and began ticking off points. "First, we figured that since you used to be an infantry officer and you actually saw a few shots fired, you might have a little better understanding of what these men went through than your ordinary, run-of-the-mill, snot-nosed attorney in uniform. Second, your boss assured me that you come equipped with a brilliant legal mind and are independent by nature. Finally, because I knew your father, served under him, hated his guts, but he just happened to be the best I ever saw. If you got even a fraction of his gene pool, then there's an outside chance of your being pretty damned good, too."

"That's very kind, sir. Thank you very much, and the next time I see my father, I'll be sure to pass on the general's regards."

"Don't blow smoke up my ass, Drummond. It's not a good idea."

"No, sir," I said, watching him suck another mighty drag through those thin, bloodless lips.

"I'm treading on quicksand here. I'm the commander of the Special Operations Command, and am therefore responsible for those men, and for what they did."

"That's right, sir."

"And when you're done with your investigation, your recommendation on whether to proceed with a court-martial will come to me. Then I'll have to decide which way to go."

"That is the correct protocol, sir."

"And you and I both know that if I say anything to you, even a whisper, that indicates anything but a neutral predisposition on my part, I can be accused of exerting command influence into a legal proceeding. That, we both know, would get all our butts in a wringer."

"That is a proper reading of military law, sir."

"I know that, Drummond. And I'd be damned appreciative if you'd withhold the commentary," he barked.

"Of course, sir."

"So the reason I had you fly down here," he said, pointing toward a tiny tape recorder on the corner of his desk, "is to ask you two questions."

"Fire away, sir."

"Do you believe that I, or anyone in your chain of command, has a predisposition, or have any of us, in any way, tried to influence you, prior to the start of your investigation?"

"No and no, sir."

"Do you believe you are being given adequate resources to perform your duties?"

"I have ample resources, sir."

"Then this interview is hereby terminated," he said, reaching down and turning off the tape recorder.

My right hand was just coming back up to my forehead when those thin lips bristled with another nasty little smile.

"Now, Drummond, since we have all that recorded for posterity, it's time for some real guidance."

"I am all ears, sir."

"This case is an embarrassment for the Army, and it will only get worse. But there are several types of embarrassment. There's the kind where some soldiers did a bad thing and the public wonders just what this barbaric Army did to these fine young boys to transform them into such awful monsters. Then there's the kind where the Army gets accused of covering up, and that is the worst kind, since it brings in lots of hungry politicians who are eager to help us sort fact from fiction. Finally, there's the kind where everyone believes that the Army is just too damned ignorant and heavy-handed to handle such delicate situations."

"Sounds accurate to me, sir. From my limited experience, of course."

His eyes fixed my eyes with an uncompromising stare. "This time it's gonna be up to you to decide which of those embarrassments we have on our hands. Don't be naive and think there's any way you can win. Got my drift?"

I certainly did get his drift, although I was just naive and arrogant enough to believe I could pull this out and walk off into the sunset looking good. That wasn't something I was going to admit to him, but that's what was on my mind. Shows how stupid some guys can be. Him, that is, not me.

"I believe I have a firm grasp of the situation, General."

"Well, you're wrong, Drummond. You think you do, but you really don't."

"Begging the general's pardon, but is there a point to this?"

The general's eyes blinked a few times, and I was instantly reminded of a lizard contemplating a fly and considering whether to lash out with his long tongue and have himself a happy meal with wings. Then he smiled, and I'd be lying if I said it was a friendly smile.

"All right, Drummond, you're on your own."

Now, the general might've thought he was making some kind of theatrical point here, but the truth is, he was the fifth high-ranking official in three days to use one of those damned tape recorders as he offered me a little on- and off-the-record guidance. I was actually getting pretty used to watching these guys cover their asses and prod me along my way.

In the old Army, a man who was about to be executed was marched down a line of his peers and a slow drumroll was sounded to accompany him to the gallows. The modern version of this death march, I was learning, was to stand in front of a bunch of powerful desks listening to lots of windy lectures, all timed to the beat of tape recorders being flicked on and off.

Chapter
☆☆ **2**

As a burly Air Force tech sergeant ushered me through the aircraft doorway, I immediately spotted Captain James Delbert and Captain Lisa Morrow waiting for me in the cavernous rear of the lumbering C-130. The first thing I noticed, though, was that the C-130, which is a cargo plane, was indeed packed to the gills with cargo. So much for my putative sense of importance. It was worse than that, though. The aircraft was stuffed with feminine hygiene products in OD green boxes.

A thousand wicked wisecracks crossed my mind, and maybe if Captain Morrow had been a he, instead of a she, I might have let loose. But fifteen years of ingrained sensitivity training stilled my tongue. It's dicey to tell a risqué joke in front of any female soldier. It's often suicidal in the presence of a female lawyer.

The second thing I noticed was that both Delbert and Morrow had sour faces. Whether that was because of me or the accommodations, or the fact that, without warning, they'd both been ordered to drop everything and meet me on this airplane was as yet unclear.

Neither had been told why they had to be here, but both were ridiculously clever and probably had some strong suspicions. For three days, headlines and talk shows around the world had focused on nothing but this case. It wasn't hard to deduce that a gathering of the Army's top lawyers on an airplane headed to Europe had something to do with the massacre. They both stood as I worked my way past four massive cartons marked TAMPON, 1 EACH.

"Delbert, Morrow, good to meet you," I said, thrusting my hand forward and awarding them my most winsome smile.

"Good to meet you, too," said Delbert, a fine-looking soldier, who smiled even more winsomely as he pumped hands with holy fury.

"No it's not," complained Morrow, whose sourpuss gained a few more creases.

"You're not happy to be here?" I asked.

"Not in the least. I was right in the middle of an armed theft trial that has now had to be declared a mistrial."

"Were you going to win?"

"Absolutely."

"Bullshit," I told her.

"What do you know about it?" she asked, becoming instantly suspicious.

"I know your client was charged with two counts of breaking and entering and one count of armed theft. The breaking and enterings you might've managed, but the armed theft? Seven witnesses identified him, the MPs had the weapon he used, his fingerprints were all over it, and he confessed right after he was picked up. Your client should've stuck to second-story jobs. He was a complete klutz as a holdup guy."

"You checked into my case?" she asked, and it was hard to tell if that made her angry or surprised.

"Sure."

"And you second-guessed me?"

"No. The trial judge, Colonel Tompson, he second-guessed you. He said you were doing a masterful job. He also said it was hopeless. His exact words were that you were 'doing a very stylish breaststroke in quicksand.'"

"So you knew you were pulling me away from my client?" she demanded, nodding her head to punctuate each word.

And in that instant it was easy to understand why this woman was such a successful attorney. She played for keeps. After eight years of trying cases, she still took it personally. She wasn't hardened or cynical, not one bit.

"That's exactly what I did," I told her. "I pulled you out of a trial that concerned one soldier and his pissant crimes to put you on the biggest, most important Army case in three or four decades."

Now this was the point where we could have launched into one of those libertarian debates that lawyers just love, about how unjust I'd been, about how the rights of one man were every bit as insistent as the needs of the Army. But what would be the point? She might score a nice philosophical victory, but it wasn't like she could climb off this plane and return to her client's side. Besides, I had just confirmed what she and Delbert had previously only suspected, and that's a little like getting hit by a bus. Took the air right out of her lungs.

The two-star general in charge of the Army's JAG Corps had told me I could have as many of the Army's top lawyers to serve on my investigating board as my heart desired. Being one myself, I know that the more lawyers you gather under one roof, the more the situation gets to be like a barroom donnybrook. The rate of progress is nearly always commensurate to the scarcity of lawyers. I therefore informed him that I only wanted two lawyers: one prosecutor and one defender.

I decided that because there are two ways to look at any case: from the standpoint of guilt, and from the standpoint of innocence. One, obviously, is through the eyes of the prosecutor who must gather the facts, then persuade a board of officers and soldiers that the man at the defense table is not only richly guilty, but deserves to be hung from the highest yardarm. Then there's the defense side, which understands that American law, even military law, is, at its core, highly procedural: that the rights of the accused *always* outweigh the needs of justice. Any good defense attorney pays as much attention to the way the culprit was caught, and how the catchers did their job, as to the facts of the case itself.

Prosecutors are the spoiled stepchildren of the law. They get to decide which cases they'll try: If the facts don't favor them, or they detect any infringements on the rights of the accused, they simply take a pass. Defense attorneys are eternally cursed. They get appointed only *after* a prosecutor has decided there's at least a 99 percent chance of a conviction. There are plenty of prosecutors who win almost all the time. There is only a small handful of defense attorneys who win even half the time.

Lisa Morrow was the exception. After eight years as a defense attorney, she had won 69 percent of her cases. She'd defended murderers, rapists, thieves, child molesters, and about every other assortment of bad guy imaginable. But, she had never defended anyone accused of violating a rule of the Geneva Convention. For that matter, neither had I. For that matter, neither had anyone; at least anyone who was still wearing a uniform.

James Delbert had a 97 percent conviction rate and even by the lopsided nature of the way the law is stacked in his favor, that's pretty damned striking. Even the best prosecutors sometimes get tripped up by things beyond their control, such as witnesses who fall apart on the stand or aren't terribly convincing, or a court-martial board that just acts in wild-assed ways that are contrary to all logic. Even the most brilliant prosecutor is still going to occasionally lose.

Before this moment, I had never met either of them. They were handpicked because I told Major General Clapper that I didn't want just any couple of attorneys. I wanted the prosecutor and defense counsel with the best win-loss records in the

Army. He picked them, then gave me copies of their military files. And I must admit that I spent considerably more time with my nose stuffed inside Morrow's packet than Delbert's. There was this great picture of her in there, standing stiffly at attention in her dress greens, and that picture offered my only hope that this investigation might have a few good angles. Or curves. Or whatever.

Nor did it take more than a quick glance to see why so many juries and boards had fallen under her sway. I don't know that I'd describe her as beautiful, although she certainly was that. She just had the most sympathetic eyes I ever saw, which as I mentioned before is not a real popular emotion in the Army, unless, that is, it happens to be pasted on a gorgeous female face. Then exceptions get made.

Delbert, on the other hand, looked every bit the soldier. Trim, fit, handsome, with straight, dark hair that sat perfectly in place without a single stray strand. He had one of those razor-sharp faces, and eyes that looked ready to pounce. I could see where a jury or a board would look at him and think only of their duty.

I would have liked to have talked with them, but the thing about riding in the rear of a C-130 is that once the engines kick in, the racket gets simply awful. Unlike civilian airliners that are packed with sound insulation, the Air Force saves money on all that crap by simply requiring its passengers to wear earplugs the whole trip. Pretty slick, if you ask me: Even if it is brought to you by the same fellas who are known for buying three-hundred-dollar hammers and five-thousand-dollar toilets. But like I said earlier, what's important inside the military machine ain't always the same as what's important on the outside.

The thing about a transatlantic plane ride is that it gives you plenty of time to read and digest. And while I had assured General Partridge that I'd already familiarized myself with the particulars of this case, the truth is that in the past two days, between meetings with lots of very important Army officials, a meeting with a very antsy aide from the personal staff of the President of the United States, and assorted others, I barely had time to breathe.

I knew little more than had been described to me by these Washington people, and the interesting thing about that was that all of them seemed to be convinced these nine men had done nothing wrong. Nobody had said that outright, because that would've infringed on the code of neutrality the law demands in these things. But I'm a careful listener; I can sniff a subtlety or a nuance from ten miles away. If I was the more suspicious sort, I might even believe that all those powerful people in Washington knew something I didn't. And I do happen to be the more suspicious sort.

My legal case was stuffed with a number of news articles, a few preliminary statements given by the accused, and a long-winded statement written by a Lieutenant Colonel Will Smothers, who was the direct commander of the accused.

I dug into them, and the facts were these. A Special Forces A-team comprising nine men from the Tenth Special Forces Group had been assigned to train a group of Kosovar Albanians who had been driven from their homeland by the Serbian militia. It was part of the effort to build up the Kosovar Liberation Army, or KLA. They spent seven or eight weeks training their recruits, then were given secret orders to accompany the unit they trained back into Kosovo.

A week later, the Kosovar unit attempted a raid on a village and all of them were killed. The A-team, against orders—make that *supposedly* against orders—took it on their own to seek vengeance, or justice, or something. They set an ambush on a well-known Serbian supply route and unleashed blistering fury on a Serb column containing thirty-five men.

The next Serb column to come down that route discovered their slaughtered brethren, found lots of expended American munitions and several pieces of discarded American equipment, informed their superiors, and, after several very dramatic press conferences, the international media became persuaded that some American troops must've done a terrifically bad thing.

The Army put two and two together and arrested the entire A-team, who were currently being held in detention at an air base in Italy.

Now here's where the case gets both real interesting and real mawkish. The United States and NATO were bombing the hell out of the Serbs in a desperate attempt to coerce them into changing their stance toward Kosovo. As much as this sounded like war, and I'd bet it sure as hell felt like war, at least to the folks being bombed, the legal nicety of a state of war had not been declared. The rules of the Geneva Convention are written to cover a state of war, so exactly what laws were supposed to govern the behavior of these soldiers? Some lawyers love those kinds of questions. Others loathe them. I, for instance, fall squarely into the loathing category. I happen to be pretty simpleminded. Black and white are my favorite colors. Gray just doesn't suit my mental complexion.

The second thing was that there were no survivors from that Serb column. Thirty-five men and not one survivor. Now those who know a little about land warfare know that for every man who gets killed in battle, there nearly always are one or two who get wounded. Believe it or not, there are people who actually study and compute these grisly things, and that's how it comes out. There was a very nasty implication here.

Finally, the talk show pundits around the beltway were in high dudgeon. This was just the kind of incident that got them standing in long lines at TV studios, and they were trotting out all kinds of theories, from the frivolous to the absurd. The big question was what orders that A-team had been given. Every time the Pentagon spokesman got asked that question, or what limits were set on their behavior, he suddenly got deliciously vague and evasive, in the way all good spokesmen are trained to do. All he'd admit was that the name of the mission was Guardian Angel and that it was some kind of humanitarian thing. Jay Leno couldn't resist that one. In one of his opening monologues, he awarded it the Most Regrettable Misnomer of the Year prize. The team had obviously not *guarded* their Kosovars real well, and it didn't sound like the nine men in that A-team acted the least bit like *angels.*

As I read through the documents, I could almost hear the jaws of the alligators snapping in hungry anticipation.

I read each document, then passed them on to Delbert. He read them, then passed them on to Morrow. We were becoming a smoothly oiled team. A regular lawyers' production line. By the time we landed at Tuzla Air Base a nice tidy pile of papers was stacked on the seat next to Captain Morrow, and all three of the Army's top legal guns were snoring loudly.

Chapter ☆☆ 3

This time there actually was a vehicle waiting by the ramp to transport us. In fact, there were two humvees; except that one was already filled with this huge brigadier general, in battle dress, with a natty little green beret tucked neatly on top of his head.

He was about six foot five, and anybody in uniform would recognize him instantly. He'd been an All-America tackle at West Point, first in his class, a Rhodes scholar, and was at this moment in time the youngest brigadier general in the United States Army. That's a hell of a lot of ego-enhancers for any one man, if you ask me. It's amazing that he could look in the mirror and not faint. The sum of my own lifelong distinctions was that I once got elected treasurer of my third-grade class. Unfortunately, my triumph was short-lived, since the election got overturned by the principal as soon as it was learned I had a D in math. I don't mention that second part to too many people. I just let them keep thinking I served out my term with honor and distinction.

The guy in the jeep didn't have to mislead anybody about anything. His name was Charles "Chuck" Murphy, and every few years or so, *TIME* or *Life* or *Newsweek* did a nice little feature article on him so that every American could track the career of their army's most dazzling boy wonder.

At that moment, though, his face was clouded with anxiety. Or, as my mother would say, he seemed to be "brooding." I always liked that word. It's so much better than "anxious" or "unsettled" or "agitated." When someone broods, it seems to me there's a bit more inner turmoil, and it sinks a little deeper.

Anyway, anybody with any sense knew why, because the A-team that was in detention worked for him, which meant his fabulous career was now up for grabs.

It was obvious that he was about as happy to see me as he would a big-fingered proctologist, but there was nothing he or I could do about that. I therefore walked right up to him and gave him the same kind of snappy salute I'd given General Partridge, his four-star boss, only twelve hours before back at Fort Bragg.

"Major Drummond, sir."

He actually returned the salute. "Welcome to Bosnia, Drummond. How many lawyers are with you?"

"Three of us, sir."

"That's it? Just three?"

"We're heavy hitters," I announced, giving him my most overconfident smirk.

"Okay. Stow your gear in the other humvee and follow me."

We did, and we peeled out of the airfield about thirty seconds later. We drove past about a mile of large tents built on concrete slabs, large metal containers, and a bunch of prefabricated wooden buildings. Tuzla Air Base had been made the supply and operations center for the Bosnian mission, and, when the situation in Kosovo boiled over, the military decided that it made sense to use it for that purpose as well. And if there's one thing the military is really good at, it's creating large, sprawling, impromptu cities out of thin air. Tuzla was a case in point. The place was laid out, dress-right-dress, with long, straight streets and none of that urban clutter or disorder you find in real cities. Lots of soldiers and airmen were walking around or lying around or doing minor chores, and a lot of them stopped and gawked as our procession drove by. Maybe I was imagining things, but I had the feeling we were expected. I had another feeling, too, because the looks we were getting weren't real warm and friendly.

We finally came to a two-floored wooden building with a couple of flags out front. This was a signal that it was being used as a headquarters of some sort. Our humvees stopped and we all piled out and walked inside, where lots of soldiers were scurrying about frantically, or posting things on maps hung on walls, or jabbering on phones, or doing about anything to look busy, because the general was here and only a damned fool would choose this moment to look bored or idle.

We ended up in a meeting room in the back of the building with a large wooden conference table surrounded by some fancy faux leather chairs. General Murphy told us to sit, so we did.

His eyes marched across our faces and I guessed he was wrestling with how to approach us. Friendly or cold? Informal or stiff? One way or another, his future might well rest in our hands, so this was one of those momentous coin tosses you so often hear about. Should he scare the crap out of us, or make us love him?

He finally broke into what I would call a charmingly disarming smile. "Well, I can't exactly say I'm happy to meet you, but welcome anyway."

This struck me as a pretty ingenious compromise. "Thank you, General," I said on behalf of the group.

"I've been told to offer you whatever assistance or resources you need. We've arranged a private tent for each of you. I've also had a building cleared for your use. Five legal clerks arrived last night from Heidelberg, and they're busy preparing your facility as we speak. Is there anything else you need at this moment?"

"Nothing I can think of," I answered. "Although if anything comes to mind, I'll be sure to contact you."

That was a wiseass crack, but I'd made my choice on how to approach him. Friendly just wasn't in the cards.

His lips tensed ever so slightly. He studied my face, made an assessment, then got up and walked to the door. He opened it, and in marched a lieutenant colonel, a tall, lean, handsome sort with a nice little green beret perched on his head as well.

The general said, "Let me introduce Lieutenant Colonel Will Smothers, commander of the First Battalion of the Tenth Special Forces Group. Will's going to handle your needs from day to day."

Which was a very slick way of saying that he, General Murphy, wasn't going to fetch any damned thing for me. It was masterfully done. It almost worked, too.

I said, "Excuse me, General. That won't be acceptable."

"I'm sorry?"

"As the battalion commander of the accused A-team, Colonel Smothers is a possible suspect in this case. Please arrange another liaison, so there's no possibility of polluting our investigation."

Now here's where it gets important to understand that Army lawyers aren't held in particularly high esteem by *real soldiers,* which is to say those soldiers who serve in combat branches. Warfare is the business of soldiers, and lawyers talk a lot but don't shoot a lot, so we're seen as an inconvenience or an annoyance, or an evil, but certainly not as part of the brotherhood. Make that ditto with an exclamation point when it comes to Green Berets, who are a little more clannish and lofty than about anyone else in uniform. It's a very rare day when you see a couple of lawyers and Green Berets standing at a bar knocking down a few brews and sharing a few yucks. Come to think of it, I've never seen that happen.

There were a few coughs and a bit of awkward foot-shuffling because this lieutenant colonel was suddenly being told right to his face that he might be a suspect. He might have been dimly aware of that possibility before that moment, but nobody had actually confirmed it. Nor was it too hard to extrapolate that General Murphy, the walking accolade, also might become a suspect.

This silly, oversize frown instantly erupted on Murphy's big-jawed, handsome face. He said, "You think that's necessary?"

"In my legal opinion, absolutely."

"Then I'll appoint a new man."

"Thank you," I said.

"You're welcome," he said. It didn't sound real sincere though. In fact, by the time he said it, he had turned about and was halfway through the door. Actually, he kind of mumbled it. In fact, it might not even have been "You're welcome." It was two words though. And there was a "you" in there somewhere. I'll swear to that. I did have the impression he wasn't going to invite me over for drinks anytime soon.

My two legal colleagues wore befuddled expressions as a result of this swift display of one-upmanship, but this was neither the time nor the place to make my explanations. We got up and left the building and, after a short humvee ride, were deposited at another wooden building. This one was somewhat smaller than General Murphy's headquarters. Actually, it was considerably smaller, since the military places a high premium on symbolism.

We strolled in and there were indeed five clerks frantically buzzing about, moving a desk into this or that corner, setting up computer workstations, testing phones, and hefting large boxes of legal-size paper to be positioned at strategic locations throughout the four rooms that constituted the interior of the building. Legal clerks are known for being brainy but not overly industrious, so somebody had evidently scared the crap out of them.

A female soldier wearing the stripes of a specialist seven, which is a very high rank in the specialist field, immediately dropped two boxes of paper and rushed over to greet us.

Her name was Imelda Pepperfield, which is a pretty odd name for a Black, female, noncommissioned officer who was short and squat, had tough, squinty eyes that peered out from a pair of gold wire-rimmed glasses, and who made it clear from the opening shot exactly who was in charge of this legal compound.

A finger popped up and began waving like a fencing foil. "Keep them duffel bags out of my entry. Store them in your offices, or carry them back out to that damned humvee. Doesn't make a damn to me, just don't trash up my entry."

"Good day to you, too," I said. "You might find this hard to believe, but I'm actually supposed to be in charge of this investigation."

The finger instantly shifted to my face. "Nope! You're in charge of doing the legal work of this investigation. I'm in charge of the investigating team, and the building, and every damn bit of work's gotta get done. And don't any of you forget that."

"Perish the thought," I said, brushing past her. "You wouldn't happen to have been kind enough to allocate a little space for us useless officers, would you?"

Captains Delbert and Morrow were standing with their jaws hung a bit loosely, so I figured the time had come to do a little explaining. I swung my arm through the air in a gesture for them to follow me. Specialist Seven Pepperfield interpreted that to mean her, too, so she trailed along as we filed into one of the offices. A desk had already been set up, with five chairs arrayed around the front, and we all picked our seats. I took the chair behind the desk, of course. Rank doth have its privileges.

"Imelda," I said, "I'd like you to meet Captain James Delbert, and Captain Lisa Morrow."

She stared fiercely at both of them.

I turned to the other two. "Imelda and I have worked together about a dozen times the past few years. She's the best there ever was. She runs a tight ship and demands that we all be at work every morning at six o'clock sharp. She'll make sure we're fed and bathed and coffee'd and carried out to our cots at midnight, after we've all passed out from sheer exhaustion at our desks. She is remarkably resourceful. Her only requirement is that we work our asses off and do everything she tells us to do."

Imelda was glaring at me and nodding furiously. I'd been trying for years to ingratiate myself with her, which was a little like Napoleon trying to knock that guy Wellington off his hill.

She smacked her lips once or twice, straightened her glasses, and announced, "You got that right."

She then got up and stomped out of the room.

Captain Delbert was staring at me like I was getting things all wrong. You're not supposed to be rude to generals and take guff off of sergeants. As for the expression on Morrow's beautiful face, well, as a highly polished defense attorney, she was used to being around scoundrels.

Now that we had our own office, with a little privacy, and without the roar of four big C-130 engines in our ears, I figured the time had come for us to get better acquainted.

I leaned back in my chair, folded my hands behind my ears, and plopped my feet on my desk. "Congratulations to you both. You've been selected to make legal history. What we have here are nine good, clean-cut, wholesome American soldiers accused of murdering thirty-five men. Against orders, no less. They were led by an Army captain, with a chief warrant officer as his assistant, and the rest were all noncommissioned officers of varying grades. This was no group of youngsters, but a team of hardened professionals. Now, most Americans want to believe that this was just a mistake, a mix-up, or that these were just some group of green, frightened soldiers who simply broke under pressure. That ain't so. What we have here is mass murder under very questionable circumstances."

"You're talking like they definitely did it," Morrow said, instinctively jumping to the defense.

"They did," Delbert politely corrected her.

"The odds are they did," I corrected them both.

"Why us?" Morrow logically asked.

"Well, that's an interesting question. I was selected because I'm very good at what I do, but I don't exactly fit into the system real well, if you hadn't already guessed. I think the powers that be looked at me and said, hey, this guy Drummond, he's perfect. He's a great lawyer, but he's also a bit of an odd duck. Pick him. He's expendable."

This was a pretty frank admission on my part, but I believe in getting everything on the table.

"Then why us?" Delbert asked, by which he really meant why him, because he obviously believed the handsome piece of meat stuffed inside his combat boots was not the least bit expendable.

"Well, Delbert, in your case, because your record says you're maybe the best prosecutor in the Army. And Morrow, you just might be the best defense attorney. It's a yin and yang kinda thing."

"There's lots of good defense attorneys," Morrow said, which was true and, no doubt, left her suspecting that her sex and looks had something to do with her being picked. She must've had some bad experiences before. That, or she was reading some of the seamier corners of my mind, which was a disturbing thought. I willed myself to think, of course, that her sex and looks had nothing to do with it.

What I said was, "Yes, but I don't believe the Army considers either of you expendable and so, frankly, I was hoping to bask in your protection." Oops, another bald admission on my part.

"How very noble of you," she said, and at this point even Delbert was looking at me askance and wondering what he'd done to deserve this.

"Okay, let me elaborate a bit more. Aside from your sterling case records, you both took the mandatory classes in Law of War and the Geneva Convention when you went through the JAG School. You're probably unaware of it, but you got the second and third highest grades ever awarded. Colonel Winston, whom you'll remember taught both courses, described you as the two best minds he ever saw. Next to the guy who scored first, of course."

"And was that you?" Morrow asked.

I shrugged and gave them my aw-shucks grin, and they both appeared suitably awed.

But, no, it wasn't me. Not by a long shot. The same Colonel Winston called the Chief of Staff of the Army and bitched like a banshee the second he learned I'd been picked for this assignment. His exact words were that he remembered me as the biggest dunce he ever taught. But why discourage my troops before we even got our feet wet? Besides, another thing about lawyers is that they are eternally competitive creatures. Delbert was a grad of Yale and Yale Law, and Morrow went to UVA, then Harvard Law. It don't get much more competitive than that. Wasn't their fault, really—they were just that type.

Morrow's eyes flicked nervously in Delbert's direction before she coughed a little, then said, "By any chance, would you happen to remember which of us was second?"

See what I mean?

"Perhaps I should make one other point," I said, and they both fidgeted with frustration because they really did want to know who was second. "At the moment, we are surrounded by the enemy. All these soldiers and airmen running around here, they're wearing our uniform, but they're different from us. They're gonna smile and be real nice and polite, but don't be fooled. They don't like what we're here to do, and they don't like us. Those nine men sitting in that prison are their brethren. We're outsiders who've been brought here to decide whether they should be tried and lynched. Also, there may be more men walking around this compound who might be implicated in this thing."

"I think you're overstating it," Morrow said.

"Actually, I'm not. There are men on this base who wouldn't mind if we got lost in the woods and gave them a chance to shoot us in the back of the head. And you know what? They could come back here, brag about it to everyone on this base, and be admired for it. As such, I will require each of you to carry a loaded pistol at all times."

Morrow was looking at me incredulously. She was the dissenting type. I could tell.

I said, "You do know how to use a pistol, don't you?"

"I fired expert with the pistol and every other weapon," she starchly replied, and I can't say that came as any surprise.

"Of course you fired expert as well?" I asked Delbert.

"Of course," he said, nodding very energetically.

"Good. Personally, pistols scare the hell out of me. I can't hit anything farther than two feet away."

The two of them chuckled at my little joke and seemed to admire me for my self-deprecating humility. But it wasn't a joke. I was dead serious. I think I was born with one of those hand-eye coordination problems. Anyway, I chuckled along with them. If they didn't want to believe me, that was their problem.

"The point is," I continued, "we're completely on our own. There's not a soul we can trust except one another, so carry yourselves accordingly. You're already unpopular, so you've got nothing to lose. We've been given twenty-one days to get to the truth of what happened here, and more likely than not, it's a very ugly tale."

They didn't believe me. They swallowed a few times and gave me a few false nods, but you could see it in their eyes.

Big deal. They'd learn.

Chapter
☆ ☆ ☆ 4

I had fourteen years in the Army—the first five in the infantry, then three years at law school, six months at the JAG School, then the rest practicing military law. I'd prosecuted and I'd defended, and I'd developed the opinion that the best place to begin a murder investigation is at the morgue. There's something about a pale body lying on a cold slab that gets your attention. It reminds you of the solemnity of your purpose. Somewhere connected to that body are a family and friends, and they miss the spirit that once inhabited that flesh. The lawyer is their last and only hope for justice. The body can't vocalize, but it cries out for justice, plainly and dramatically.

I'd told them back in Washington that my investigating team was going to visit the morgue on the outskirts of Belgrade where the bodies were stored, only this turned out to be not quite so simple as it sounded. The problem was that the bodies were in Serbia, and we were still dropping lots of large metal canisters filled with explosives on that country's villages and cities. So there were a few understandable complications.

I met with two stiff-necked foreign service officers back in Washington who lectured me like I was some kind of idiotic novice in international affairs. Well, I am a novice, but I am also a lawyer, and a stubborn one, and I was not about to back off. This was a case that crossed international boundaries, and I really didn't care if the Secretary of State herself had to get on a phone and plead with Bad Boy Billy Milosevic himself to get us in. He'd let Jesse Jackson in. So why not us?

Well, there were a lot of peevish faces, but I guess I knew a little bit more about this stuff than those two State Department jerks, because a UN diplomat asked Milosevic if we could come, and he did not even hesitate.

He said yes. Of course he said yes. I knew he was going to say yes. See, he knew that our word was infinitely more credible than his, and he wanted more than anything for my team to verify that there were in fact thirty-five slaughtered bodies in that morgue. Still, his assent had its worrisome aspects. If he was willing to let us come see the bodies, then he must've been pretty damned sure that our boys killed them.

We all got a good night's rest, and at five in the morning on day two of our investigation, Captains Delbert and Morrow, myself, and a pathologist, who'd flown in from Frankfurt the night before, all climbed aboard a snazzy Blackhawk helicopter and began our flight. The pathologist was sort of an odd-looking duck with a misshapen head, pale, almost translucent skin, and these hyper-looking, bulgy eyes. Appearances aside, I'd been assured he was one of the best.

The flight took about three hours, and we had to land and refuel once. The guys who refueled us were Serbian soldiers, and I won't say they seemed too happy to see us. I didn't take any offense, though. After all, our airmen were at that moment pounding the bejesus out of some part of their country.

Two sedans with Serb military drivers awaited us at the Belgrade International Airport. No one said a word as we drove through the city, going straight to the morgue. It was not the fancy-type morgue like you so often see back in the United

States. In fact, it was a pretty grim, ramshackle, dilapidated old building, and I have to admit that seemed fitting, because most of the inhabitants were past caring about their accommodations.

A Serbian doctor named Something-o-vich met us at the entry and escorted us through a series of dark and dirty hallways, down some stairs, and into a gloomy cellar. American morgues are normally so clean and sterile you really could eat off the floors, if you were inclined to do such a ghoulish thing. This morgue stunk of rotting cadavers and was filthy from the rafters down.

The basement was cold and dank and had the kind of dim hanging lamps that tall people bang their heads against. I, thankfully, am a nicely compact five foot ten, so I survived right nicely. Poor Delbert is about two inches above six feet and he walks like he's on a parade ground, with a stiff rod jammed up his you-know-what, so he picked up some nasty lumps on his forehead.

We took a left at the end of the hallway, and you knew by the way our footsteps echoed that we'd just entered a very large room. The doctor reached over and flipped a switch. Ten long fluorescent bulbs flickered, and crackled and popped, then finally illuminated everything.

A lot of thought had gone into the arrangement that stretched before us. Thirty-five nude bodies were neatly arrayed in four long columns. Somebody had gone to the trouble of placing props behind the backs of the corpses, so that they all sat up, perfectly erect. It looked ghastly and made it impossible to ignore their faces, although there were a few who were missing faces, or only had parts of them. We all froze in our tracks and there was the sound of a few deep gasps.

A perfectly prone body can still be an impersonal object, but a body that sits up and stares at you, almost as if it has been resurrected—that's damned impossible to ignore. The first of us to recover was Dr. Simon McAbee, our friendly pathologist, who rushed forward with his doctor's bag and a savory gleam in his eyes. He began strolling around like a cavorting housewife in a grocery store meat selection, squeezing this one, prodding that one, trying to decide which was the choicest cut.

Delbert and Morrow fell in behind me as I began walking the columns, pausing at each body for only a few seconds, no longer than it took to determine what specific trauma caused the death. The bodies had been cleansed, which made it fairly easy to interpret the wounds. I couldn't be absolutely certain in every case, but what I saw generally met my most dismal expectations.

Some of the corpses were horribly mangled, but it seemed every single one had been shot in the head. One corpse, though, had no head at all, just an ugly, hacked-on stump at the bottom of the neck. Some of the head entry wounds were from the back or the front, but most were from the side. The entry holes were small, about the size that would be made by a 5.56mm round, which just happens to be the size bullet fired by an M16 rifle, which just happens to be the standard-issue weapon for American troops. The exit holes were large. This, again, is characteristic of the M16 bullet, which tends to tumble once it strikes hard objects, like skulls and bone, collecting a lot of tissue as it speeds through the body, making an ever-widening path and a big, ghastly exit wound.

At least half the bodies were so seriously mangled, and the nature of the wounds so severe, that they had obviously been hit by mines. It was the kind of mine, though, that intrigued me. American troops are issued something called a claymore, which is an upright mine that sits above the surface, planted on a pair of tiny metal tripods. The great virtue of the claymore is that it is a directional mine. It has a rectangular, curved shape, and the explosives are packed into the concave hollow, while the outward half is packed with thousands of tiny pellets that are propelled forward with great force. It's a highly favored weapon in ambushes. The mines are triggered by an electric pulse, and the technique of choice is to connect several of these nasty little things together with commo wire into what is called a daisy chain. That way, once the electric charge is triggered, all the mines appear to go off at once. The time it takes for the electric charge to travel the wire actually means the explosions are not precisely simultaneous—there's a few milliseconds of lag—but, as soldiers are wont to say, it's close enough for government work.

The half of the bodies that were badly mangled had lots of little pellet holes. Mysteriously, though, all of the wounds seemed to be somewhere in the back, which implied several possibilities, most of which were damned ugly.

After the first pass, Delbert, Morrow, and I gathered in a small knot in the back corner and whispered among ourselves. Dr. McAbee and Dr. Whatever-osovich continued to traipse around and pick at pieces of wounded flesh. The Serb was obviously a pathologist, and the two of them were rubbing chins and chatting amicably, just having a gay old time.

"What do you think?" I asked Delbert and Morrow, waiting to see who would answer first.

Morrow quickly said, "It's sobering."

"*Very* sobering," Delbert quickly one-upped her.

And indeed it was sobering. Both Delbert and Morrow had been through morgues before, so these were certainly not the first corpses they'd seen. Still, it's a very breathtaking thing to see thirty-five of them all at once. I had the advantage of having been to war once or twice, but I'll admit that the sight of lots of dead bodies still taxes my soul in strange ways.

"It doesn't look good, does it?" Delbert asked.

"No," I grimly admitted. "We won't know for sure till McAbee's done, but I'd guess most of the damage was done with M16s and claymores. There was a machine gun or two involved as well, but I can't even hazard a guess what kind."

"Some of them were little more than boys," Morrow said.

"Right."

"A few were just sprouting pubic hair," she continued, not as a matter of prurience, but because it exacerbated the seriousness of this. Killing grown men was one thing. Killing teenage boys took it to another level.

On my first sweep through, I had deliberately ignored the faces. I had focused only on the wounds, because I didn't want my reason clouded by emotion. Now it was time to go back and look at each corpse anew; to think of them as human beings rather than as butchered slabs of meat filled with clues. Perhaps some of these corpses had done some very nasty things to the Albanians they were herding out of Kosovo; still, I had to remind myself that they were also human beings. Besides, at issue here was not what crimes some, or maybe all, of these men had committed, but what crimes might have been done to them. So I spent another twenty minutes wandering through and trying to order my ever-pliant conscience.

Dr. McAbee had collected a number of specimens and was now taking photographs of each corpse. He worked efficiently and professionally and completed his work even before I was done.

He finally walked over to me. "It doesn't look good, Counselor."

"I can see that."

"Our host gave me a collection of projectiles removed from the corpses."

"Did you personally remove any?"

"A few."

"And?"

"The bullets are 5.56. The pellets appear to be claymore."

"So all the wounds were made by American weapons?"

"With thirty-five bodies, it would take three X-ray machines and a team of three assistants a full week to prove that beyond any shadow of a doubt."

"But is that your general impression?" I asked him.

His bulgy eyes fixed mine, and he seemed to sigh. "Every wound I saw appeared to come from an American weapon."

"What about the head wounds?"

"Most were shot from a distance of less than two feet. These fools washed the bodies, but I still found some gunpowder samples in their hair."

"And how would you guess that happened?"

"That's obvious, isn't it? Someone walked through and made sure there were no survivors."

"Nothing's obvious," I chided. "Be careful about assumptions."

"Of course, you're right," he said, although we both knew that it still appeared obvious.

"Did you tell that Serb doctor to maintain these bodies until we're done?" I asked him.

"I did. But he said he can't."

"Why not?"

"Milosevic has ordered a large state procession where the families of the dead are to be honored for their sacrifices. After the ceremony, the bodies are to be returned to their families for funerals."

"Then the Serbs will create a vast problem for us and themselves."

"Why's that?" he asked.

"If I was the defense attorney for the accused, I would insist on equal right to examine the corpses."

"Well, the corpses have now been examined by me."

I gave him my best cross-examining look. "And could you tell me, Doctor, with complete certainty, exactly how many of these men were killed with American weapons?"

"We already went over that."

"You'll go over it on a witness stand, too. If the members of that A-team are charged with murder, how many counts do we charge them with? You have to list those things. Then you have to be able to prove that was exactly how many people they murdered."

"Of course," he sheepishly said. "I'm sorry. I've never handled a situation of this magnitude."

"None of us have. But think this way from now on. What I want you to do is classify each corpse. I want to know how many died immediately, and how many were initially wounded, and then dispatched. Can you do that for me?"

He nodded. "I'll do my best."

"Good. Now, as the coroner of record, is there anything else you need from this place?"

"I'd love to have a couple of these bodies to carry back, so I can determine the exact circumstances of death, but that's not going to be possible."

"All right, the first thing you do when we get back is file an official request for just that. I'll file one, too. We'll inform Washington that this case could be jeopardized if we don't have a few bodies."

Chapter

☆ ☆

☆ 5

We arrived back at Tulza shortly after three. Our stomachs had gone from queasy to growling, so I asked Imelda to scramble us up a meal. Sounds easy, but you have to remember that this was the Army, and the Army has mess halls, and the Army tells you when you can eat and not eat. Three o'clock is one of those "not eat" periods. But you also have to remember that this was Imelda Pepperfield, who can make rocks cry.

She came huffing back into my office, followed by two of her female legal clerks, both of whom were strikingly deficient on the looks side but undoubtedly had stellar clerical skills. Imelda snorted a few times as her assistants plunked down several trays loaded with meatloaf sandwiches and mashed potatoes larded with a thick, pasty, gravy.

"Any trouble?" I asked.

"Nope. That mess sergeant tried to say no, so I kicked his butt a little, and he snapped to."

The thing about Imelda is that she was raised in the rural backcountry of Alabama and has all the inflections and manners of a poor, uneducated southern Black girl. And if you are too stupid for words, you buy into that act. I could have looked up her IQ in her military records, but I never bothered. The truth was I never wanted positive confirmation that she is much smarter than me. I did know one of her secrets, that she'd earned two master's degrees, one in criminal justice and the other in English literature. She never went anywhere without a few thick books hidden in her duffel, usually written by some of those Russian writers with long, impossibly tongue-twisting names.

Delbert and Morrow were eyeing the meatloaf sandwiches with pure disgust, while I launched in with gusto.

Imelda gave them a speculative glance, then flapped her arms once or twice. "You got some kinda problem with that meal?"

Delbert very foolishly said, "Actually, I do. I like to eat healthier."

Imelda bent toward him. "You're not one of those health food pussies, are you?"

"I try to take care of my body," Delbert replied stiffly.

"This is Army-issued food. If Uncle Sam says it's good for you, it's good for you."

"It's greasy. And it clogs the arteries."

Morrow was watching this exchange, and I saw her quickly grab a sandwich and start chomping. Smart girl, that one.

Imelda straightened back up, and her eyes turned into blazing hot lasers that bored searing holes into poor Delbert's forehead.

"Okay, fancy pants, I'll remember that. I've got your number."

Delbert's eyes shifted in my direction. Unsure of her connection to me, he was imploring me to either intervene or give him a signal to fire at will. Like I'd be stupid enough to step into the middle of this.

"Who are you looking at?" Imelda barked. "Don't you look away when I'm talking to you. You either eat that food or you're gonna get bone-ass skinny these next few weeks."

"I like salad," he said with almost pitiful politeness. "Could you get me a salad?"

"Salad?" she roared, as though he'd asked for a plate of pickled horse manure.

"Yes, please."

"I don't fetch rabbit food."

"Then I'll get it myself," he announced, then stood up and left.

Imelda flapped her arms a few more times, grumbled something that ended with one of my favorite anatomical organs, then stomped from the room herself.

Visibly relieved, Morrow placed her half-eaten meatloaf sandwich back on the plate. "Who won that round?" she asked.

"Who's fetching the rabbit food?" I answered.

"She's the real McCoy, isn't she?"

"Last of the breed," I replied, reaching over for my third sandwich.

"Did Delbert just start a war?"

"Hardly. She was only checking his mettle."

"How'd he do?"

"Not bad. She saw you pick up that sandwich, though."

"Was that a mistake?"

I scratched my nose. "Hard to say. Time will tell."

These two thoughtful creases appeared between Morrow's eyebrows. The truth is what I just said made absolutely no sense. Took her a moment, but she figured that out.

"You run a loose ship, don't you?" she complained. "She was very disrespectful. I would have thought a former infantry officer would instill a little more discipline in the ranks."

Did I mention before that Morrow is an astonishingly beautiful woman? Well, if I didn't, she is. And there's nothing like having a great-looking woman challenging your manhood, which was exactly what she was doing. Her perfectly shaped eyebrows were arched up, and her lips were kind of pointing downward, and the average guy would choose just that moment to flex his muscles and mutter something tough and virile to confirm he had something inside those jockey shorts.

I said, "That's why stereotypes don't come with guarantees."

See, Captain Lisa Morrow was obviously scared to death of Specialist Seven Imelda Pepperfield. She just wanted to shame me into protecting her. Like I said, she's a smart girl.

I finished my third sandwich and glanced at my watch. Unless I missed my guess, there should've been a witness waiting outside our door. It actually wasn't a real hard guess to make, though, since that morning, before we'd left for the morgue, I'd asked Imelda to contact Lieutenant Colonel Will Smothers to request his presence at 1530 hours, which, to the uninitiated, is pretty much the same thing as 3:30 P.M.

I walked over and opened the door. In fact, Smothers was standing there. And surprise, surprise, a bespectacled, slightly overweight, bookish-looking captain wearing JAG insignia stood slightly behind him.

"Please come in," I told Smothers.

He walked by, and I quickly stretched my arm across the doorway, blocking his lawyer, whose nametag read Smith. "You won't be needed," I told him.

Smothers spun back around and faced me. "I want him here."

"No," I said. "This is just an interrogatory. I won't be reading you your rights, and therefore nothing you say in this session can be used against you. This is merely a background session."

Captain Smith screeched in a high-pitched whinny, "If he wants me along, I'm coming in."

"Wrong. I'm the chief investigating officer. And if I say no lawyers, there'll be no lawyers."

There was a moment of wordstruck confusion as Smith and Smothers exchanged bewildered looks, both obviously wondering if I could do this. Frankly, I had no idea, but what the hell.

"No lawyers," I said, grabbing the door and closing it in Smith's stricken face. "Please have a seat," I said as I turned around and faced Smothers.

The thing about interrogatories with potential suspects is that you lose if you don't have the upper hand. Smothers out-ranked me, so I had to make up some lost ground. Besides, lawyers only get in the way. I know. I am one, and I'm always getting in the way.

I sat behind the desk, and Morrow and I stayed perfectly still. Smothers was trying to compose himself, which wasn't easy because I had just torn the guts out of his game plan. Finally I withdrew a tape recorder from the desk drawer and turned it on. That's always great for the nerves, too.

"Colonel, could you please state your full name and describe your relationship to the accused men?"

He squared his shoulders. "My name is Will Smothers. I'm their commanding officer."

"Could you be more specific?"

"I'm the commander of the First Battalion of the Tenth Special Forces Group. The A-team commanded by Captain Terry Sanchez was assigned to my battalion."

"Command? Elaborate on that word for me, please. What is your understanding of it?"

His brow became furrowed for a moment or two. "I guess . . . well, it means they work for me. That I'm responsible for them."

"That's a good definition. How long have you been in command?"

"Nearly two years."

"How long was Captain Sanchez one of your team leaders?"

"Maybe half a year."

"So you've only known him half a year?"

"No. He was on my staff before that. He worked in the operations office."

"Was he in the unit when you arrived?"

"Yes. I think he got here about six months before me."

"So you've known him two years?"

"Yes, two years. That's about right."

All of this was just a warm-up. Always start an interrogation by asking for simple, noncontroversial facts, to get the subject into the mode of answering quickly, almost automatically. Now it was time to dig for a few opinions.

"Would you say you know him well?"

"I suppose."

"Who made the decision to place him in the team leader position?"

"Me. It had to be approved by the group commander, but I recommended him."

"The group commander would be . . . ?"

"Brigadier General Murphy."

"Is Sanchez a good officer?"

"Uh . . . yes. A, uh, well, a very good officer," he said, suddenly appearing eminently thoughtful. "In fact, outstanding in every way."

"What ways?"

"Well . . . uh . . . he's very competent. He leads by example."

I gave him a ridiculing smirk. "He leads by example? That's pretty thin gruel."

"What do you want to hear?"

"You tell me. Was he a strong leader? Did he compel his men to follow him or try to convince them? Was he smart? Did he have backbone?"

"All the above."

This was getting a bit much, so I switched back to facts. "How old is he?" I asked.

"I don't know exactly. About thirty. Maybe a few years past thirty."

"How many years does he have in?"

"Ten, I think. Maybe eleven, maybe twelve. He's a senior captain. He should be up for major this year."

"He needed the team leader job to get promoted, right?"

"He's an outstanding officer. I've never looked at his record, but I'm sure it reflects that."

"But the Special Forces branch ordinarily requires an officer to be a team leader before he makes major, right? Promotion boards want to see if he can hack it in a demanding field job, right?"

"Usually, yes. It's not a requirement."

"Were you ever a team leader?"

"Yes."

"Do you know any Special Forces battalion commanders who weren't?"

"No."

By this time Smothers had caught on to where I was going and was therefore picking and parsing his words very carefully. As he had admitted himself, he was responsible for Sanchez's A-team and everything they did. Of course, a battalion commander with a lot of teams under his command can't be everywhere at once. What he can do is pick competent, reliable subordinate officers. In fact, the Army fully expects him to. If the team led by Terry Sanchez slaughtered thirty-five men in cold blood, then, de facto, Terry Sanchez was not up to the job he'd been given. That meant Will Smothers had made a mistake. That's why he was suddenly so frugal with the truth.

He'd worked closely with Sanchez for two years, yet could not tell me his precise age, could not describe his command style, could not describe his strengths and weaknesses. He knew the answers; he just wasn't going to tell me.

"So, tell me," I said, changing tack, "exactly what were Sanchez's orders when he was sent into Kosovo?"

"Well, he and his team had spent two months training a ninety-five-man Kosovar guerrilla unit. Since the Kosovars were still very green, Sanchez's team was ordered to accompany them back in and continue their training."

"Isn't that an odd mission?"

"No, it's a very common mission for Special Forces. Training indigent forces is exactly what we're organized and trained to do."

"I'm not talking about the training part, Colonel. I'm talking about the part where Sanchez's team followed them back into Kosovo."

"I wouldn't call it unusual, no."

"Really? What exactly were his instructions?"

"To continue training the Kosovars."

"Was he supposed to become involved in the fighting?"

"Absolutely not. Everybody here knows the rules, Major."

Morrow said, "Tell me about that."

"There's no ground war."

Then she said, "But we're bombing the Serbs in Kosovo. Hell, we're bombing the Serbs in Serbia. How do you keep it straight?"

"Special Forces aren't idiots, Captain. We may not be law school grads, but we understand what's happening here."

"Do you like it?" she asked.

"Like what?"

"The mission. What you're here doing."

"What's to like or dislike? It's a job."

I asked, "Were Sanchez and his people allowed to assist the Kosovars in planning their operations?"

"Yes and no."

"That answer doesn't count, Colonel. Yes *or* no."

"We're not combatants. So no, Sanchez and his people were not supposed to help them plan their operations. But if, for example, the Kosovar commander asked for advice, they could offer it."

"Pretty sketchy line, that one."

"I don't make the rules."

Morrow leaned back and hammered at her point again. "Were Sanchez's people supposed to accompany them into combat operations?"

"No. Absolutely no. A secure base camp was established, and Sanchez's team was required to remain at that camp."

"Say Sanchez and his people were attacked by a Serb unit. Were they authorized to shoot back?"

"Yes. Self-defense is authorized. If they were detected, they were supposed to extricate. If that required them to fight their way out, that was acceptable."

"Who wrote these rules?" I asked.

"I don't know who wrote them. Some staff officer somewhere, I guess. But I believe they were approved by the Joint Chiefs of Staff themselves."

"Why do you believe that?"

"Because they usually are."

"Usually?"

"The rules of engagement used in Mogadishu and Haiti and Bosnia were all approved by the Chiefs. I think it's a logical assumption these were, too."

"Thank you, Colonel," I said.

He looked surprised. "Thank you?"

"Right. You can go now."

He regarded me for a moment with a kind of slack-jawed look, like what the hell happened to the hard part. I just stared back. The hard part would come. Just not yet.

As Smothers walked out, Delbert walked back in.

"Enjoy your lunch?" I asked.

"Uh, yeah, sure." He rubbernecked around and watched Smothers's retreating back. "What was that about?"

"Colonel Smothers was kind enough to stop by for a little interrogatory. It was a very interesting session."

"Why didn't you wait for me?"

"Because you decided to run off and eat."

"But I had no idea this was scheduled."

"Imelda knew. That's why she was kind enough to fetch us some food."

"Why didn't she say anything?"

"I don't think I heard you ask her."

"Why didn't you say anything?"

"I don't think I heard you ask me, either."

I could see this was getting very frustrating for poor Delbert, and I'd be a liar if I didn't admit I was enjoying his discomfort. He might be the best prosecutor in the Army, but he was still a prig.

"Don't sweat it," I said reassuringly. "It's all on tape. Listen to it tonight after we close shop."

I then turned to Morrow. "Any thoughts?"

"He's an impressive officer."

"Special Forces battalion commanders usually are."

"He's worried."

"Was he telling the truth, though?"

"Was he being truthful? Maybe. Was he being open? No."

"About what?"

"About what he thinks of Sanchez. About what he thinks about the orders he's operating under. About what he thinks about anything."

"Why do you think that is?"

"Because you told him yesterday that he might be a suspect. It might've been better if you'd held off on that. You antagonized him."

Even Delbert, who'd missed the interrogatory, was vigorously nodding that he agreed with her on this issue.

I grinned and didn't say anything. If they didn't comprehend the way my brilliant legal mind worked, then I wasn't about to enlighten them. Besides, as I said earlier, these two were hungry thoroughbreds, and if they thought, even for a fraction of a second, that they could get a nose ahead of you, you'd spend the rest of the race staring at their fannies. That was a halfway pretty good proposition, but I didn't relish the thought of ogling Mr. Delbert's little tightass one bit.

The door suddenly crashed open and Imelda bustled back in with three legal clerks in tow, all carrying heavy boxes overflowing with documents.

"What's all that crap?" I asked.

"All the operations orders and the duty communications log, and the personnel files of the accused."

"I don't remember asking for that."

"And what are you gonna do without it? You're not going to get any further on this case unless you go over all this."

"And who signed the requisitions?"

"Don't be gettin' stupid on me, Major. I know your signature by now."

This caused more dropped jaws from Delbert and Morrow, because forging an officer's signature is a fairly serious military offense. It gets glacially serious when classified papers such as operations orders and operational duty logs are being requisitioned.

I turned to Delbert and Morrow. "By the way, make sure Imelda has good, legible copies of both your signatures before the end of business. By tomorrow, mark my words, she'll be able to fool your own mothers."

Imelda smacked her lips a few times and mumbled some unintelligible curse, which is kind of her way of expressing gratitude. Then she marched back out, shooing her three assistants ahead of her.

We each took a box, then spent the next eight hours trading files back and forth, reading furiously, saying little, and making our first real acquaintance with the nine American soldiers who were accused of mass murder and exactly what they'd been ordered to do across the border in a land called Kosovo.

Chapter

☆☆☆ 6

I had two phone calls that night. The first came from a general in the Pentagon and went something like this:

"Drummond, that you?"

I squeezed and pinched myself. "It's me, Drummond."

"General Clapper here."

"Morning, sir."

"It's not morning here. It's eight o'clock in the evening."

"That right? So that's why it's two o'clock in the morning here."

A mighty chuckle. "How's it going?"

"How's what going?"

"The investigation, Drummond. Don't play dumbass."

"Sorry, it's this two o'clock in the morning thing. Try me again at eight, when my mind works like a Cray computer."

"Am I hearing the sounds of whimpering?"

"Yes. Go away and leave me alone."

Another chuckle, which was easy for him because it was early evening where he was, and he still had a sense of humor. "Okay, give it to me."

"Well, we went to the morgue at Belgrade yesterday and spent some time with about thirty-five corpses. The pathologist is still doing his report, but the preliminary isn't good. All the perforations in the bodies appear to have been made by American weapons."

"We expected that."

"Yeah, but I'll bet you didn't expect this. Somebody shot each corpse in the head."

"All of them?"

"Well, a few didn't have much left for heads, and one didn't have any head at all, but from what we could tell, yeah, about all of them."

"Why didn't Milosevic and his people make hay of that in the press conferences?"

"You'll really have to ask him, General. I do recommend, however, that you wait until it's morning over here. From what I hear, he's not as nice a guy as I am."

"That's a debatable point. Are you getting sufficient cooperation?"

"Sure. They love us around here. We got the best tents in the compound."

"We got your request for Milosevic to postpone his state funeral and hold on to the bodies."

"Good. The coroner's sending one through his channels, too."

"Won't make any difference. I took yours over to the State Department and got laughed out of the building."

"Did you meet with these two guys, one real tall and skinny, and one real short and fat?"

"Sounds like them."

"Likable couple, aren't they? The Laurel and Hardy of international diplomacy."

"They liked you a lot, too. They studied your request and the words 'fat chance' and 'fathead' got mentioned a few times."

"A fella can't ask for much more than that, can he?"

"How damaging will it be if the request is denied?"

"It creates an opening for a good defense attorney to poke a few holes."

"Well, nothing more to be done about that. Need anything else from me, Sean?"

"No, sir. But thanks for asking."

He hung up, and I hung up, and it took a few minutes before I dozed off again. Major General Thomas Clapper was the closest thing to a friend I had in this case. He had taught me military law way back when he was a major and I was a brand-new lieutenant going through my basic officer's training. If I wasn't the worst student he ever had, the other guy must have been a stone-cold putz. One can only imagine his dismay when, four or five years later, I approached him to ask if he would sponsor my application to law school and the JAG Corps. I've never understood what went through his brain at that instant, but he said yes, and the rest is legal history.

Unlike my own lethargic career, Thomas Clapper was always on a fast track. He was now the two-star general who headed up the corps of Army lawyers. This is the largest law firm in the world, with offices spread around the globe, handling everything from criminal to contracts to real estate law. It is a corps of over a thousand military lawyers and judges and more than twice as many legal specialists of various varieties. It is a corner of the Army few people know exists, filled with grating personalities, oversize egos, and rawly ambitious lawyers. It takes an iron-fisted tyrant to keep all those egos in check, although Clapper was seen as a benevolent dictator, and thus was very beloved by the rank and file. Although not by me. Not at that moment. Clapper just happened to be the guy who threw my name into the hat to head this pre-court-martial investigation, and I knew he was calling to assuage his guilt. I wasn't about to offer him any clemency. I wanted his guilt to be so massive it gave him walloping headaches.

The next call came about an hour and a half later, and the

caller identified himself as Jeremy Berkowitz. Even at 3:30 A.M., I recognized the name. Berkowitz was a reporter for the *Washington Herald* who had earned a handsome reputation by exposing lots of embarrassing military insights and scandals. That call went something like this:

"You're Major Sean Drummond?"

"Says so on my nametag."

"Heh, heh, that's a good one. My name's Jeremy Berkowitz. A common friend gave me your number."

"Name that friend, would you? I'd like to choke him."

This resulted in another nice chuckle, and it struck me that everyone in that time zone back in Washington was filled with good humor that day.

"Hey, you know the rules. A good reporter never discloses his sources."

"What do you want?"

"I've been assigned by the *Herald* to cover the Kosovo massacre. I thought it would be a good idea for us to get to know each other."

"I don't."

"You ever dealt with the working press before?"

"A few times."

"Then you should know that it's always a good idea to cooperate."

"And in turn, you'll cooperate with me, right?"

"Exactly. I'll make sure your side of things gets printed, and I'll make sure you're well treated in our stories."

Click! Oops, the phone accidentally fell into the cradle.

Actually, it landed in the cradle because I don't like being threatened, and if you read between the lines that was exactly what he was trying to convey. Of course, it was a dumb, petulant thing to do. On my part, that is. I should've soft-pedaled and let him down gently. But then I would have had to act like a tease, because I wasn't about to leak any damned thing.

Not that I have anything against reporters. The military needs good watchdogs for it to remain the marginally healthy institution it is, and the press happens to fulfill that function. It doesn't pay to antagonize or mistreat them, but like I said, I was tired and not thinking straight.

My mood had not improved when, at 6 A.M., I entered our wooden building, where Captains Delbert and Morrow were hovering over a couple of steaming cups of coffee and awaiting my arrival. Both looked bright-eyed and bushy-tailed, and I resented that.

"Morning," I said, or barked or growled. Whatever.

"Ouch," said Morrow.

And wouldn't you know that at just that moment the phone rang again.

"Hello," I said, lifting it up.

"Major Drummond, this is Captain Smith. Remember me? We met yesterday."

"Yeah, I think I remember you. You're the short, chubby guy with the screechy voice, right?"

"I called Colonel Masterson, the military judge with jurisdiction over this command. I told him you blocked me from representing my client and asked for his judgment on this matter."

"And he said?"

"That if you ever do that again he will personally register a complaint with the District Court back in D.C. and seek to have you disbarred."

"I'm deeply ashamed of myself," I boldly admitted.

"You should be. Now my client told me you taped the interrogatory. I would like a copy delivered to my office first thing this morning."

"Did the judge say I had to do that?"

"I didn't ask him. I will, if you insist."

"I insist."

"Have it your way," he said, almost choking with anger, and then hung up.

Now it might sound perverse, but Smith's call really brightened my mood. The thing about big investigations like this one is that you have to get people's attention. You have to show people you're a rampaging barbarian, and then anybody with any inkling of guilt immediately starts racing for the nearest lawyer and looking for protection. Lieutenant Colonel Will Smothers had done exactly that. His troops watched him like a hawk and by now there were very few people on this compound who did not know he'd been called in and interrogated. And Captain Smith was now doing more of my work, making sure the local legal community was aware that I play hardball. Pretty soon, everybody around here was going to be walking on eggshells. And when people walk on eggshells, if you listen real close, you can hear all those little cracking sounds.

"What was that about?" Delbert asked.

"Wrong number," I said.

The door crashed open and in came the mobile hurricane known as Imelda, followed by two more assistants carrying trays piled high with steaming eggs and bacon, and something the troops disparagingly call shit-on-a-shingle, which truly does resemble its namesake but is actually a dried-out muffin covered with greasy gravy and chunks of ground beef. In the entire arsenal of Army foods, this is the one most likely to get you a quadruple bypass.

Imelda gave Delbert and Morrow a dreadful look and had her assistants carry the trays to a conference table that had been set up in a spare office. Morrow and Delbert traded conspirational glances, and I could tell they had cooked up something the night before. Wasn't all that hard to figure out, either. They'd obviously considered the proposition that a unified front might be enough to overpower Imelda. She stared back at them through her gold wire-rimmed glasses and said not a word, but her tiny little fists began clenching and unclenching. It was kind of a watered-down version of the OK Corral.

I walked to the table and launched voraciously into my Army-prepared breakfast, watching out of the corner of my eye to see who'd crack first. Actually, that's not true. I knew damn well who'd succumb. I just wanted to see how long it took Delbert and Morrow to figure that out and how ungracefully they extricated themselves: with their tails stuck between their legs, or dripping blood all the way to the conference table.

Imelda said, "Are you two gonna eat those damned breakfasts, or act like a coupla spoiled pussies?"

The good defense attorney acted as though she were speaking to nobody in particular. "I usually have yogurt, oatbran muffins, and juice for breakfast."

Imelda said back to her, "You want me to tell that mess sergeant to whip you up a cup of that latte crap, too?"

Delbert started to open his lips, wisely thought better of it, and just stood there shuffling his feet.

Morrow's eyes darted down in time to see Delbert's feet do their little retreat dance, and then she covered her own defeat with a halfhearted, "But there was a time when I really loved eggs and bacon."

"Then you learn to love it again, because that's all that mess sergeant makes."

Not two seconds later, Delbert and Morrow were seated beside me, taking mighty bites and silently praying Imelda would go away and die.

"What's on for today?" Delbert asked, diverting his eyes from Morrow's, which were at that moment bathing him with a world-class gutless weasel look.

I said, "I thought we'd spend our morning talking with the group chaplain, then the group commander."

"The chaplain?" Morrow asked, still staring at Delbert.

"Sure."

"Why the chaplain? When are we going to talk to Sanchez and his men?"

"Soon enough."

They both nodded. They didn't agree, but they nodded. That's one of the things I love about Imelda. She sucked all the feistiness right out of them.

The chapel was located in a large tent, long and broad enough to hold about forty chairs. The group chaplain, Major Kevin O'Reilly, was actually on his knees, praying, when we came in. We waited patiently for about three minutes while he finished up, then he walked to the rear of the tent where we were gathered.

As one might anticipate from a Special Forces chaplain, he didn't look much like a priest. He had a broad face, a pugilist's nose, and big, strong hands that squeezed painfully when we shook and introduced ourselves. I couldn't imagine that people were inclined to act real sinful in his presence. I didn't want to even imagine what kind of acts of contrition he exacted in his confessions.

"Father, thanks for agreeing to meet with us," I said.

"Would you like to do this here?" he asked, waving around the chapel.

"No. Why don't we walk around?"

"Fine."

So we began strolling through the dusty streets of the big Tuzla compound, where several thousand soldiers and airmen were at that moment in a frenzy of cleaning up and preparing for another day of waging a nonwar against the Serbs.

"How long have you been with the unit?" I asked.

"Four years."

"That's a long time. You must like it."

"Sure."

"What do you like about it?"

"These are good boys, Major. There's an image out there of

Special Forces troops being wild, rowdy hooligans that's completely out of character. Most of these men are good family people."

"I guess Captain Sanchez is Catholic, isn't he?"

"Yes, he is. A good one, too."

I had already known his religion from his personnel file but wanted to lead into this obliquely.

"You know his family?"

"Very well. His wife, Stacy, and both kids. Mark is seven, and Janet is two. I baptized her."

"Have you heard from his wife?"

"We've talked a number of times these past few weeks. It's very troubling having Terry's name splashed across the front pages as the man who commanded a massacre."

"I imagine so," I said, and I meant it.

"Three other members of that team were Catholic also, so I've been busy with all the families."

"Of course. Now, Father, if you don't mind, I'm going to ask a few questions. If you feel they're too sensitive or I'm infringing on your clerical confidences, please feel free to tell me."

"Okay, that's fair," he said.

"How would you describe the command environment here in the Group?"

He contemplated that a moment, and I sensed that his hesitation wasn't obfuscation but because he wanted to get this just right. He finally said, "On the whole, pretty good. Special Forces soldiers, you know, are older than you find in regular units, and the men are rigorously tested before they get to wear the beret."

"And if you could only use one word?"

"Gung ho."

I smiled, then he smiled. I said, "How about another word?"

"Okay, troubled."

"Why troubled?"

"Because these are can-do men with strong consciences. It's

very taxing to be around all these Kosovar refugees. Back in America, you see the images on TV, but it's very rending on the nerves to have to witness firsthand what's happening on the other side of that border."

"Right, of course. I imagine that has a dampening effect on morale."

He gave me a very trenchant look. "Dampening? Major, some of these men can't sleep at night."

"Have you had to do a lot of counseling?"

"We've had one suicide and one attempted suicide since we've been here. My days are filled with counseling."

"So you'd say the men are frustrated?"

"I suppose that's as good a word as any."

"Did you have to counsel Terry Sanchez or any of his men?"

He stared off at a lumbering C-130 that had just taken off from the airfield and was beginning its climb to altitude. Finally he said, "I'm afraid I'd be uncomfortable answering that."

"Okay, do you think the frustration you referred to might have caused that team to crack?"

"That's really just the same question parsed a little differently, isn't it?"

"Father, I'm asking off the record, one soldier to another."

"Okay, I don't believe Terry's boys did it. However, the pressures are certainly there."

Like hell, he wasn't saying they did it. That was exactly what he was saying, although I couldn't tell if he knew that for a fact, or just suspected they had and assigned it a reason, like everybody else in the world was doing.

"What can you tell me about Smothers's battalion?"

"It's a great unit. It should be, though. He's a first-rate commander, and there's a lot more veterans in his unit."

"Veterans?"

"Yes, you know. A lot of his men saw duty in the Gulf, Somalia, Haiti, Bosnia."

"Why so many veterans in his battalion?"

"As I said, it's a very good unit, very reliable."

"I'm sorry, I still don't get it."

"How much do you know about the Special Forces culture?" he asked.

"Just hearsay."

"Well, it's very inbred. The Tenth Group has a European orientation, so the men have specific language skills and regional training. You don't take a man from the Tenth Group and move him to say, the First Group, which specializes in Asia. Many men spend their whole careers in this unit."

"But is there something special about Smothers's battalion?"

"The men call it the old-timers' club. There's sort of an unwritten tradition in the Group that after five or ten years in another battalion, a lot of the sergeants put in for transfer to Smothers's battalion."

"Why would they do that?" I asked. I thought I knew the answer, but it never hurts to ask.

"Camaraderie, I suppose."

We had arrived back at the chapel tent, and I could see several soldiers gathered and anxiously waiting. Father O'Reilly obviously had priestly things to do, and I'd heard everything I wanted to hear, so I thanked him and we parted ways.

As soon as he was gone, Delbert said, "That was really helpful."

"Yeah? Why's that?" I asked.

"He was trying to communicate motive. He's the confessor of four men in that team, and he was trying to offer us their motive."

"Maybe," I said, looking over at Morrow.

"Is there something we didn't hear?" she asked.

I pulled on my nose a bit. "That old-timers' club thing. That bothers me."

Delbert said, "Sounds like a good idea to me. Sort of a grouping of the elite of the elite."

"Maybe."

"You think there's more?"

"Depends."

"On what?"

"This is a combat unit, Delbert. A battlefield veteran is a very different breed than a green buck sergeant who might be highly trained but has never been truly tested. It's the green guys who can get you killed. They might break under pressure. They might make mistakes, like maybe put a blasting cap in the wrong way, or use incorrect radio procedures and give away your position."

"I still don't get it," Delbert said.

"The old-timers' club sounds like a survivors' union. A guy spends five or ten years, and he becomes eligible. He gets to spend the rest of his career with seasoned, battle-tested pros, the kind of guys who don't make mistakes."

"And something's wrong with that?" Morrow asked.

"Maybe not. Your chances of survival go way up, since I'd suspect the First Battalion is very choosy about who it takes and who it turns down."

The two of them nodded, and I decided not to expose everything else I suspected. Like General Partridge mentioned earlier, I'd done time in the infantry, whereas Delbert and Morrow put on their JAG shields straight out of law school. Some things you just gotta be there to learn.

We arrived at General Charles "Chuck" Murphy's wooden building about ten minutes later. I could have ordered Murphy to come to my building, but there were limits to how much I wanted to shove people around. There's a fine line between being a legal barbarian in search of the truth and being a spoiled brat, and I've always been a stickler for nuances.

Actually, I wouldn't know a nuance if it hit me in the face, but I didn't want to push my luck with Murphy. At least, not yet I didn't.

As it was, Murphy actually met us at the door, which made me damned glad I hadn't ordered him to come see me, because this courteous, meeting-us-at-the-door thing sort of evened it out.

I said, "Morning, General."

He said, "You look like crap, Drummond. What's the matter, not sleeping well?"

I put on my bitchiest pout. "It's the damned accommodations here. I'm used to an air-conditioned hotel room, with a well-stocked bar and a big double bed. These damned tents and cots are killing me."

He emitted a very manly, contemptuous chuckle, then led us inside and up some stairs to the floor where his office was located. A burly sergeant major, who looked as though he lived in a weight room, growled something as we walked by. I kept a wide berth and hoped he didn't bite.

The general's office was fairly spartan for a man of his rank, containing a long field table that was being used as a desk, two smaller field tables, two metal file cabinets, and two flags, one of the American variety and the other red in color, with a big white star in the middle. A visitor was supposed to be impressed by the austere, abstemious furnishings and believe that they somehow reflected on the humble nature of the man who worked in this office. I might've bought it except for the two silver-framed photographs carefully arrayed on the smaller field tables: One showed the President of the United States himself pinning a general's star on Murphy's shoulder, and the other a much younger Chuck Murphy in a football uniform, holding a ball, kneeling beside the Heisman Trophy and grinning like a kid who was cocksure the world was his oyster.

Five chairs had been neatly arranged in the middle of the floor, and he directed us all to have seats. With some difficulty, he lowered his large six-foot-five-inch frame into one of the chairs, crossed his legs, and folded his arms across his chest. It was a big chest, but he had long arms.

The empty chair was kind of mysterious, and I guessed that at one point he must've intended to have counsel there to represent him, then thought that might imply he had something to hide and therefore decided against it.

"I apologize," he said. "I can only give you ten minutes this morning. We have an important operation going on, and my presence is required in the operations center."

"No problem, General. You're a busy man. We'll make this quick."

"Thank you."

I paused briefly, then asked, "How long have you known Captain Sanchez?"

"I've commanded the group the past eighteen months. Terry was here when I arrived."

"You approved his appointment as a team commander?"

"Yes, but it was a pro forma thing."

"Why pro forma?"

"There are four battalions in Tenth Group. It's hard enough to know all the colonels, lieutenant colonels, and majors. I recognize the names of most of the captains, but I'm afraid I don't know them well."

Now, if I was a more suspicious guy, I might have considered that a Rhodes scholar who'd graduated first in his class from West Point ought to have a more impressive memory than that. I might also have suspected that the general was a smart guy, and just like Will Smothers, also had caught a sudden case of selective amnesia.

I gave him a dubious look. "But was Sanchez maybe one of the ones you know well?"

"Not really. I'd recognize him on a street, but not much more than that."

Delbert said, "Sir, could you tell us how much more than that?"

He scrunched up his face as though he had to go bottom-fishing to come up with anything. Finally, he said, "I know he's married. I remember meeting his wife at a few of the Group functions. I know he did a good job on a few exercises, and I think I visited his team a month or two ago, before they went into Kosovo."

Frankly this didn't wash. And he apparently sensed our doubts.

"Look, if you'd like," he swiftly added, trying to sound and appear gracious, "I'll ask my adjutant to go through my log and see how many times I've met with Sanchez over the past six months."

I wasn't nearly as gracious. "That would be very kind, General, but why don't you tell your adjutant to provide us the log and we'll do the checking?"

He said, "That log is classified and can't be released."

"General, we all have top secret clearances with lots of strange little suffixes that allow us to look at whatever we want to look at. Right now, I'd like to look at your log."

He appeared flustered for a moment or so, before that strong jaw pushed forward an inch or two. "If you don't mind, Major, I'd like to talk to legal counsel before I comply."

"Actually, sir, as the investigating authority, I am within rights to sequester that log. It is military property, and if I believe it is relevant to this investigation I can order you to turn it over."

"I'd still like to seek advice."

"Okay, do that, sir. But do it quickly, because I'd like to have that log before close of business today."

His eyes got like little round ice cubes, but his lips were still smiling. "Any other questions?"

Morrow inched forward in her chair. "Could you tell us why the First Battalion is called the old-timers' club?"

The general's right eyebrow sort of notched up. "That? Well, it's an old tradition with some of the sergeants in the Group. It's harmless, really. It's kind of a natural evolution to want to move up to a unit that has a little higher standards, that's a little more challenging."

"Is this encouraged within the command?"

"It's sergeant's business, handled by the sergeant majors within the Group. There's no official policy on it."

"Is it a good thing?" she asked.

"I think it has its advantages, yes. The men seem to like it. And I can tell you from my perspective, it's a damned good thing to have one unit that's totally reliable, that you can put in to handle the really tough missions."

She shot me a quick sideways glance, a kind of triumphant look.

Delbert, the prosecutor, took his shot. "Sir, could you tell us who ordered the arrests of Terry Sanchez and his men?"

"I did."

"What chain of events led to that decision?"

"When Milosevic and his people began holding daily press conferences, we realized that something had happened."

"But how did you narrow it down to Sanchez's team?"

"Simple, really. The corpses were found inside what we call Zone Three. That's where Sanchez's team was operating."

"Did you order his team out?"

"I didn't have to. They had extricated three or four days before I ordered their arrests."

"Why did they extricate?"

"Because the Kosovar unit they were training were all dead."

"How long had they been dead?"

"Three or four days."

"When their Kosovars were killed, didn't they report that immediately?"

"I believe they did. I'd have to check the operations logs to see exactly when they reported it, but I think so."

"Then why weren't they ordered to extricate at that point?"

"Because I made a decision to leave them in place."

"Why?"

"Because, after their Kosovars were ambushed, Terry automatically relocated his team to a new base camp, one known only to his team. Their safety wasn't at issue."

"I'm sorry. I don't understand."

"We're training more Kosovar guerrilla units, and when we infiltrate those units into Kosovo, we might have wanted to use Sanchez's team to perform the same Guardian Angel function with a new team. I hadn't made a decision yet. I was keeping my options open."

I said, "How is morale in the unit, General?"

"Great. In fact, as high as I've ever seen."

"Why so high?"

He offered us a very humble smile and genuflected ever so slightly. "I'd like to take credit for it, but the truth is that soldiers are always happiest when they're in action."

"No disillusionment with the mission?"

"These are soldiers, Major. They don't question the mission."

Like hell they don't. Personally, I'd never met a soldier yet who didn't spend every waking hour dissecting every aspect of the mission and moaning miserably about the complete idiots who designed it. Anyway, I said, "I heard you've had a suicide and an attempted suicide."

"Every unit has suicides."

"True, but you've had one successful and one attempt in only a few months."

His eyes got real narrow. "Look, Major, the Group hadn't had a suicide for three years. Our number came up. I don't mean to sound cavalier, but go study any unit and you'll see we're way below average."

"You must've investigated the causes of the suicides?"

"An investigating officer was appointed in the case of the successful one."

"And what did he find?"

"The man was a staff sergeant with serious marital problems. He had a son with Down's syndrome. He had a drinking problem, and his peers afterward described him as a borderline manic-depressive."

"And the attempted suicide?"

"There was no investigation, but the unit commander told me that the man suspected his wife of cheating while he was stuck here."

The general then looked down at his watch, and a pained expression instantly popped onto his face. "Listen, I've got to get down to the operations center. We're doing two insertions today, and I have to be on hand."

"Of course, General," I said. "Sorry to take so much of your time."

I was lying, of course. I would love to have had this guy in a room for about twelve hours, with a few hot klieg lights and some small pointy objects to jam under his fingernails. Sometimes you can just smell a lie. If anything he said was true, it was an accident.

Then again, maybe I was just jealous. Here sat this hulking Adonis, a Rhodes scholar, the youngest general in the Army, a guy people had been predicting would be a four-star ever since he wore diapers. And here was me, a run-of-the-mill major, whose bosses considered him expendable, and, believe me, there'd been no crowd of adoring fans crammed around my crib talking about the glorious future that lay ahead of me.

What I found intriguing was the gap between the time when Sanchez's team reported that their Kosovars were all dead and when they extricated. Murphy really didn't seem to have a good explanation for that. Give him a few days and I was sure he'd think one up, though.

I turned to Morrow right after we got out of the building. "I don't see why the press always writes him up as such an attractive guy. I didn't think he was so attractive, did you?"

She gave me an amused smirk. "Oh, I don't know. Some women might find him attractive."

"Some women?"

"Blind ones might not notice, but the rest of us would probably say he's pretty cute."

I had to think about that a minute. I mean, get real. How can a six-foot-five, 240-pound former right tackle be called cute?

"So what do we know?" I finally asked.

Delbert rubbed his chin and said, "We know Sanchez's team was the pick of the litter."

"Right."

Morrow said, "We know that all of a sudden nobody seems to know Terry Sanchez very well."

I said, "Yeah, a little odd, isn't it? All of a sudden, he's a leper."

We all thought about that, then Delbert said, "So, what's on for this afternoon?"

"We're going to Albania to visit a refugee camp."

"Why? When are we going to see Sanchez and his men?"

"Look, Delbert, consider that it's a near certainty that Sanchez and his team killed thirty-five men. Worse, somebody went around afterward and did the coup de grâce, perhaps out of spontaneous rage, or perhaps in a more premeditated way to ensure there were no witnesses. Do we all agree with that?"

"Of course," Delbert said, with Morrow nodding along in a very thoughtful way.

"We've got corpses, and we've got weapons, and we've got suspects in detention. What don't we have?"

"Motive," Delbert said.

"Right," I said, playing the obnoxious law professor to the full hilt.

Chapter

☆☆☆ 7

The flight to Albania took about two hours. We had to wind
down the coastline of Bosnia, then veer sharply to the left. Albania itself is a small place, very poor, filled with dilapidated
Stalinist architecture, which never was known for its splendor
or its charm, and lots of shabbily dressed people. The Albanians
are called the Bird People because they live largely in mountains. They're known pretty much throughout Europe as somewhat touchy folks, particularly since they have this quaint old
custom, called a blood feud, which dictates that if anyone kills
an Albanian, then the family of the victim inherits an obligation
to start knocking off the killer's family. Sometimes these blood
quests pass down through five or six generations, and I figured
there must be something in the mountain air, because to me
that sounds an awful lot like West Virginia.

At any rate, aside from this sedulous custom, the Albanians
are not known for a heck of a lot. They invented the necktie.
They were led before World War Two by a guy named King Zog,
who, as his name implies, was not your ordinary run-of-the-mill
royalty figure, but a guy with a big handlebar mustache who
rode around the country with bandoleers strapped across his

shoulders, marrying exotic foreign beauties and doing pretty much what he wished. Then they were led, during the cold war, by a guy named Enver Hoxha, who was so obnoxiously paranoid that he built concrete pillboxes on nearly every single acre in the country and placed long upright poles in all the fields to keep assaulting helicopters or parachutists from landing. More bizarre still, he actually allied Albania with Red China, which had to be one of the most moronic geostrategic gestures in history. Not surprisingly, Albania ended up the poorest and loneliest country in Europe.

But, in spite of all this, or maybe because of all this, the Albanians are a fairly tough and hardy folk. They don't mess with others, and they don't expect to be messed with in return. They're surprisingly hospitable folks, too. And brave and determined as well, which was partly the cause of the current difficulty, because the shaky history of the Balkans being what it is, lots of Albanians ended up living in other places, like Macedonia and Kosovo.

Kosovo is kind of a Serb's Jerusalem, filled with old Orthodox shrines and historically significant places, and although only some 10 percent of the people who live there could claim even a drop of Serbian blood, selfish old Billy Milosevic had decided to rid the land of Albanians, either by killing them or driving them over the mountains into neighboring Macedonia or Albania.

We landed with a mighty series of whumps on a roughed-in airstrip about fifteen miles south of the Kosovar border. Once again, a humvee was standing by when we climbed off the plane, and a Special Forces major named Willis was waiting in the front seat to escort us to a refugee camp, inelegantly named Camp Alpha.

This wasn't my first introduction to refugee misery. I'd seen similar sights after the Gulf War, when thousands of Kurds and Shiites fled south into Kuwait to try to escape the wrath of Saddam's Revolutionary Guards. Delbert and Morrow, however, developed an instant case of the wide-eyes, as the troops call it. The wide-eyes are about 30 percent horror, 30 percent pity, and the rest pure guilt.

"You get used to it," Major Willis said as we drove past row after row of hastily constructed tents, crammed with mostly old men, old women, mothers, and young children. There were very few young men, and many of those we saw were either wearing bandages or missing limbs. Everybody, young and old alike, looked gaunt, hungry, and unhappy. Judging by the smell in the camp, it seemed obvious that two things they were woefully short of were showers and toilets.

"How many are in here?" Delbert asked.

"We're not sure," our guide answered. "It kind of shifts from day to day. Sometimes it goes up by a few hundred, sometimes a few thousand."

"How do you know how many to feed?" Morrow asked.

"The UN caregivers handle all that. There's no science to it, though. They adjust up as a result of how many people are left in the chow line when the food runs out. You'll meet the lady who's in charge of all that. Later."

We pulled into a small compound surrounded by barbed wire, with two armed guards at the front gate. They recognized Willis and immediately waved us through.

"Our training compound," Willis announced.

We dismounted and walked into a large tent, where a mixture of Green Berets and Albanians in makeshift uniforms were running what appeared to be an operations center. Willis led us over to a table in the rear and offered us coffee, which we naturally accepted, because real soldiers live on coffee, and we didn't want to be mistaken for lawyers or anything as shameful as that.

"This is one of three operations centers we've set up for training the Kosovar Liberation Army," Willis said. "The KLA was already fighting the Serbs before NATO started its bombing campaign, but the Serbs rolled right over them. Frankly, the KLA was pretty small, since lots of Kosovar Albanians thought it was doing a lot more harm than good."

"Why was that?" Morrow asked.

"One of those lamb-being-led-to-the-slaughter things. Like the Jews before the Second World War, you know, kind of hoping the wolf wasn't really as bad as all that. Lots of Kosovar Albanians thought the KLA fighters were agitating Milosevic and his boys, so they just wanted 'em to stop."

"Were they?"

"Nah. They were hardly more than a nuisance, but Milosevic was exploiting them to justify his ethnic cleansing. After what he and his thugs did in Bosnia, you wouldn't think anyone would've fallen for his lies, but hope always springs eternal, right?"

"How large is the KLA now?" Delbert asked.

"Maybe five or six thousand, all told."

"Only five or six thousand? That's hardly a pinprick."

"Right, well, the Serbs have been real selective in the way they've done their cleansing. About any Albanian male who looks old enough to hump a gun, they take 'em into the woods, shoot 'em, and bury 'em. Real practical, those Serbs. Guess they figure that if they wipe out this generation of Albanian men, they'll get a bye on vengeance till the next crop gets old enough to fight. Anyway, we try to recruit whatever eligible survivors make it out."

"That hard to do?" Delbert asked.

"Nope. Hard part's keepin' 'em here long enough to teach 'em a few things before they go runnin' back into Kosovo to start killin' Serbs. They're pretty stoked up with hate when they get here."

"Do they make good soldiers?" I asked.

Willis glanced furtively around the operations center to be

sure he wasn't overheard by any of the Albanians working there. "The Serb army's been fighting about nine years now and understands this kind of war pretty good. Most of these Albanians haven't got a clue. A few months ain't much time."

We all pondered that a moment.

"Tell ya what, though," he added, "guts ain't the problem. The American press don't know much about what's happenin' on the other side of that border"—he pointed his hand in a northerly direction—"but lotsa these Albanians we're training are dyin' up there."

"Did Sanchez's team operate out of this camp?" I asked.

"Nope. Sanchez and his guys worked out of Camp Charlie, maybe forty clicks east of here. All the camps are pretty much alike, though. Seen one, seen 'em all." He looked at his watch. "If you wanta spend a little time with the UN folks, we'd better get moving. Only free time they got's between meals."

We walked out of the operations center and clambered back into the humvee, then drove by more tents to another fenced compound. This one had no flags or guards, just a tiny little sign that said UNHCR, which was the acronym for the United Nations organization that shifts around from one disaster area to the next, trying to care for the world's most miserable people.

A wiry, birdlike woman about fifty waited for us by the front entrance. She climbed in beside us as we pulled up, then directed the driver to take us back to the middle of the camp. She spoke English with a heavy French accent, and Willis told us her name, but the only part I caught was her first name, which was Marie.

She and Willis seemed to know each other pretty well. The two of them sat comfortably side by side without saying anything, like an old married couple who're content to just quietly enjoy each other's company, particularly in the presence of strangers. That was what they were like.

Delbert and Morrow still had the wide-eyes, which in most

cases I'd seen tends to last up to a week. After that, the sight of such omnipresent misery becomes just an everyday fact of life, and the nerves sort of get all the oxygen sucked out of them. We finally came to a bunch of tents that were encircled by wire, and there was a big red cross in front. We got out of the crowded humvee and stood there.

Marie said, "New refugees are brought first to this station for medical processing. To get across the border and reach this camp, they must complete a very dangerous and arduous trek across the mountains. At this time of the year, many arrive with frostbite and mild hypothermia. Also, many have wounds inflicted by the Serbs."

She turned around and led us into the first tent, talking as she walked. A long line of doleful-looking Albanians waited by the entrance, and as we walked in, we saw five or six stations where doctors were inspecting people using stethoscopes and prods and various other medical implements.

"This is the processing tent. Here our doctors inspect their wounds and sort them out for later treatment," she said as she led us over to a little girl who was lying on a cot. The little girl was filthy, her clothes ragged and torn. A woman who looked about fifty, but on closer inspection was probably just a hard-lived thirty, was huddled over the child, while a doctor made notes in a journal of some sort.

Marie and the doctor exchanged words in French for a minute or so, while all of us stared at the little girl, who seemed to be in a waking coma, wide-eyed but unseeing.

"The girl is twelve," Marie finally turned and explained to us. "Her mother says a Serb militia unit came to their house late one night about a week ago. Her mother recognized two or three of the men from the village, men she had known from her own childhood. They broke down her door and dragged her little girl and her two sisters from the house, out into the yard. They raped them. She says the rapes went on for hours, about twenty men taking turns. This little girl screamed through the first five men, then fell silent as they kept coming. When they were done, they shot her sisters. The mother does not know why they spared the little one, but they left her there, with her mother, and gave them two days to be gone, or they promised they would come back and do it again."

We then moved to the next doctor. He had a stethoscope on the chest of an old man whose feet were wrapped in rags but who was sitting on a metal table, stoically enduring his checkup. Again, Marie and the doctor exchanged words, while we stood there trying our best not to appear like a bunch of pathetic Peeping Toms in the midst of these suffering people and those who ministered to their horrors.

Marie again turned to us. "This man was swept up by the Serb police about three weeks ago. They imprisoned him with about two hundred other men for about fourteen days. Then they began taking them out, one by one, for interrogation. He said that for several days he could hear the sounds of horrible screams before his turn came. He was led into the basement of the police station. The walls were covered with blood, and a pile of body parts, fingers and toes, had been swept into a corner. He said that nobody cut anything off him. He was lucky, he said. They took heavy metal truncheons and beat him for an hour or two. He says he knew nothing. They knew after the first few minutes that he knew nothing, but they kept beating him anyway."

As Marie spoke, our eyes were fixed on the old man, who coughed a few times, and we could see blood drip through his fingers every time he tried to cover his mouth.

"The doctor says it's a miracle he made it out alive. He and the other prisoners were finally taken out to the woods. A machine gun was set up and the bodies began falling all around him. He grabbed his stomach as though he had been shot and flung himself backward, landing among a bunch of bodies, then used his hands to scoop some of their blood onto himself. When the Serbs came through and began killing the wounded, he fooled them. He crawled off after it became dark, then walked for three days until he arrived here."

She then led us out of the tent, and we paused before the next tent. In a matter-of-fact tone she said, "The old man won't last another two days. He has severe internal bleeding. His left arm is broken in at least three places, there is a hole in his lungs, and there is a very good chance a kidney is burst."

"What will you do with him?" I stupidly asked.

"We will move him into a tent we reserve for the dying. We will give him morphine shots and try to make his death as pleasant as possible. He has a fever of 41 degrees, probably because of internal infections. He knows he is dying. He suffered terribly to come this far so he could die with his own people."

"What about the little girl?" Morrow asked.

Again matter-of-factly, she said, "We have a rape counselor, but that girl would require years of intensive treatment with real professionals to heal. Girls raised in such rustic circumstances mature much faster than in our societies, so there's a possibility she's pregnant, too. At least we can do something about that. Her mother asked us to examine her and perform an abortion if there's a fetus."

And so it went for the next hour as we wandered through tent after tent, dropping in on one godawful case after another, and I have to confess that I felt like some kind of a shameful voyeur, spying on these people's miseries and horrors.

Marie then walked us back outside the medical compound, said she had to return to her duties, and profusely thanked us for coming. My mouth almost dropped when she thanked us.

We all piled back into the humvee, and Willis asked, "Anything more you'd like to see?"

The three of us looked at one another, and we all kind of blushed, since none of us felt all that proud of ourselves at that very moment. Willis seemed to sense that and told the driver to take us back to the compound.

"You said you get used to this," Morrow said to Willis. "How long does that take?"

"Forever," he said with a very wooden smile.

"She's a very impressive woman, isn't she?" Morrow asked, watching Marie's back retreating down the dusty street.

Willis said, "I worked with her in Mogadishu and Bosnia. She's been doin' this twenty years. You'd think that someday she'd just go home and put a shotgun to her head."

"She must feel proud about all the lives she's saving," Morrow replied.

"Not actually. When you get flooded with refugees like this, all you can do is triage. You know, separate the ones you can save from the ones you can't. The ones you end up thinking about are the ones you toss on a trash heap, like that old man."

Sometimes you meet someone who just makes you feel really tiny and selfish, and Marie was one of those people. I also have to admit that after seeing that little girl and that old man, I wasn't feeling real sympathetic to the Serbs right at that moment. The whole flight back to Tuzla the three of us hardly said a word.

Chapter

☆☆
☆ 8

Imelda and her assistants waltzed in carrying trays of eggs, bacon, and shit-on-a-shingle. Again, she looked primed for battle, her little body tensed and coiled, her eyes expectantly awaiting a challenge from Delbert or Morrow or both. Neither said a word. They exchanged brittle looks, then picked up their knives and forks and immediately began eating off the trays, listless and indifferent. Imelda watched them through narrowed, distrustful eyes, just sure this was some kind of slick new tactic cooked up by the pair. She didn't get it. After an afternoon at Camp Alpha, even the most chauvinistic health nut knew it would be cosmically wrong to complain about a little too much cholesterol.

When the English first came to Ireland, they built this real deep trench around the castle in Dublin where they established their rule. That trench was called the Pale. The Irish, back then, were a real wild and barbaric people, and the English, who always were known to be pretty snobbish and condescending, used to sit inside that castle and describe the unruly, irascible ways of the Irish as being "Beyond the Pale." Well, we'd just got-

ten a long, hard glimpse of things that went way beyond the
pale.

I had lain awake nearly the whole night, unable to sleep
while an old man was dying from the wounds of a brutally
senseless beating and a little girl with cold eyes was reliving
nightmares inside her head and dying in her own silent, tortured
way. From the dark circles under Delbert's and Morrow's bleary
eyes, I guessed they'd had the same nocturnal visitors.

Imelda finally mumbled some unintelligible curse, which I
knew from experience was sort of her version of a victory grunt,
then stomped out of the room, headed off, I was sure, to ter-
rorize somebody, somewhere. She just had a biological need to
start every day by dancing on somebody's forehead.

Delbert, Morrow, and I at least now had some kind of moral
compass to begin this investigation. Murder, in a situation like
this, wasn't likely to be the result of an evil or reckless impulse.
Back in America there were lots of folks who murdered just to
see what it felt like, or as revenge for a nasty childhood, or because of some dark vision they saw on TV or read on the Internet or heard in the lyrics of a rap song. But when nine
American soldiers did a heinous deed in a place such as this,
their motives were likely to be grounded in far sturdier stuff.
We still had no precise idea what those motives were, but now
we at least knew something about the environment in which
they were concocted.

"I think it's time to take a trip to Italy to visit our prisoners. I think we're ready to start interrogating the suspects," I announced.

Morrow's beautiful eyes got crinkly at the corners. "How do
you want to approach it?"

"I haven't really made up my mind," I admitted in a rare burst
of uncertainty.

Delbert perked up for the first time since I'd met him, apparently sparked by my rare lack of resolve.

"I'd start with the three senior guys first," he boldly suggested.

"Why would you do that?" I asked.

"Because it seems likely the leaders of the team made the decisions."

"Would they be most likely to spill their guts, though?"

"I think there's only one way to find out," Delbert said.

"He's right," Morrow chimed in. "The big point in question is motive. We'll only get that from the leaders."

This was too much for me to resist. I said, "That would be a huge mistake."

There was a sigh from Morrow. "I thought you didn't have a plan."

"I changed my mind. I do. I thought we'd jointly interrogate Sanchez, then split up."

"Okay," Delbert said, seemingly resigned to the fact that nearly anything he suggested was destined to be spurned.

"And do you have some line of questioning in mind?" Morrow asked, wisely trying to avoid stepping into another trap.

"Actually, I do. I don't think it's time to go for the jugular yet. What I'd like to accomplish in this round is just to hear their version of what happened."

The ever-efficient Imelda had arranged our flight the day before. A fresh C-130 was at the airstrip, this one packed to the gills with boisterous soldiers and airmen waiting to go to Italy for a little R&R. When the three of us walked in, the back of the plane suddenly grew very still and quiet. We found seats together and, excepting a lot of sullen and acrimonious glances, were ignored the entire flight.

Mercifully, the flight was brief. It took only an hour and a half before we found ourselves at a modern, perfectly flat airfield located in northern Italy. Imelda had also lined up a military sedan, and the driver was waiting for us at the flight building. We weren't hard to pick out. We were the only folks who marched off that plane wearing barely worn, hardly faded, stiffly starched battle dress. That's the thing about lawyers. Even when we try to blend in, we stick out like sore thumbs.

We drove for about ten minutes and went straight to a small three-floor hotel located on a hilltop that gave us a stunning view of long, stretched-out plains that were dotted every now and again by tiny hills with castles or palaces mounted atop nearly every one. This being Italy, it was a wildly romantic setting. Aviano Air Base, where our suspects were being held, was three miles away.

Delbert and Morrow immediately broke out their running togs and loped off down the road. Now that we were back in civilization, they meant to make immediate amends for all the carbohydrates and cholesterol they'd sucked down as a result of Imelda. I put on a bathing suit and went to sit beside the pool. This was the kind of place where I normally did my best thinking. It helped that several Italian women were lounging around in some of those half-an-ounce-of-cloth, let-the-cheeks-hang-out bikinis, which for me had a certain restorative effect.

I had closely studied the file of Captain Terry Sanchez, the team leader, and was actually curious to meet him. What I had learned was that his mother and father were Cuban immigrants, part of the vast tidal wave who fled from Fidel Castro and settled in the lush cities of southern Florida. I was only guessing, but most sons of that wave were raised to be intensely patriotic, to have an almost surreal hatred of Fidel, and to try to lead their lives according to the macho mores of the Latin world. I hate to stereotype, but stereotypes have their use, especially those of the cultural variety.

Sanchez was thirty-two years old and a graduate of Florida State University. He had earned his way through on an ROTC scholarship. His file contained an official photo, which showed him standing rigidly at attention in dress greens with a perfectly blank expression—the expected look of all military file photos, because the Army takes a dim view of smiley faces. He was medium height, medium weight, with dark hair, and eyes that struck me as sorrowful.

His commander, Lieutenant Colonel Smothers, had described Sanchez as an outstanding officer. But like the rest of the performance reports in Sanchez's packet, the two signed by Smothers put Sanchez squarely in the middle of the pack. So much for open disclosure.

After I'd been sitting beside the pool for an hour, I saw two bodies steaming up the road, their arms flailing wildly and their legs kicking up and down with great fury. Morrow was in the lead, and the closer they got, the more wildly Delbert's arms fluttered and whipped, as though he could pull himself through the air to catch up with her. Like I said, these two were very competitive creatures, and both were heaving like draft horses by the time they finally made it to my lounge chair beside the pool. Morrow had on a pair of those skin-hugging nylon runner's pants, and I have to be honest, she fit into them like they were meant to be fit into. If I were Delbert, I would've stayed right behind her the whole way, simply because the view was majestic. But that was me. Delbert was too pure for that kind of stuff.

"Have a nice run?" I asked.

"Yeah," Morrow heaved out. "Jus'"—puff, puff, puff—"great."

Delbert was bent over beside her and looked about ready to spill his guts.

"How about you, Delbert?" I asked.

"Nah"—puff, puff, puff—"I . . . uh"—puff, puff.

"You what?"

"Torn hamstring"—puff, puff.

"Ah, I see. A torn hamstring, huh? Could that be why Morrow beat you?" I said, saving him the trouble of having to spell it out, which it didn't seem he was going to be able to do for the next few minutes.

Puff, puff—"uh-huh."

Morrow made no reply, only straightened up and made a very exerted effort to get her breathing under instant control. This took her only about six or seven seconds, and then she was standing there perfectly erect and composed. I guess she figured that if Delbert wasn't going to accord her a legitimate victory in the race, the least she could do was win the post-run-regain-the-composure contest.

I checked my watch. "We've got about thirty minutes before we're supposed to meet our first suspect."

The two of them headed upstairs to their rooms, while I loitered beside the pool for another fifteen minutes before I went upstairs to climb back into my uniform.

The Air Force detention center at the air base put the Army to shame. It was damned close to being a luxury hotel, with cable TVs in the cells, separate showers and toilets, and a nice, modern eating hall. I'd seen Army barracks housing innocent soldiers that looked like rickety slums compared to this.

The warden, a chubby Air Force major, met with us before we were permitted to interview his prisoners. He seemed like a nice, amiable fellow and had a double chin that vibrated as he talked. He had lots of kind things to say about Sanchez's A-team. They had been model prisoners, very polite, very soldierly, very well behaved.

I told him I was sure he had kept the team separated since their detention. He said something real evasive and instantly tried to change the subject, so I got real close to his face and asked him. "These prisoners have been quarantined from one another, haven't they?" He said no, that the team members were allowed to exercise together, and that three hours a day they were allowed to commingle in the common room. I asked him what idiot had allowed them to commingle. He blushed deeply and said that privilege had been specifically authorized by the Tenth Group commander, General Murphy.

Sanchez's team was being investigated for conspiracy, among other charges, and any penologist would know that standard procedure called for co-conspirators to be kept strictly separate, so they can't connive on their alibis. The Air Force major knew a very serious taboo had been violated, and after his blush gained a few shades of darkness, he asked me if I wanted to see a copy of the authorization order from General Murphy. This was his way of covering his ass and staying out of deep doo-doo. I said that I sure as hell did, that I wanted the original, that it had better be waiting for me when I was done, and that I was hereby countermanding the order.

What I really wanted to do was kick the crap out of this chubby little Air Force major, who had just given Sanchez and his team an extra week to mature a common alibi, and thereby made my job about a hundred times harder.

We were then led to a room where we were asked to wait. About three minutes later, Captain Terry Sanchez was led in. He wore battle dress, without manacles or restraints. The Air Force sergeant who led him in then discreetly disappeared.

Sanchez stood frozen beside the doorway as though his feet had sunk into the concrete floor. He studied us like we were lions who had come to devour him. He looked thinner than he had in his photo, and his eyes were harder, less sorrowful, almost tight. Being accused of mass murder can have that effect.

"Captain Sanchez, I'm Sean Drummond, chief of the investigating team, and these are the other two members, James Delbert and Lisa Morrow. Please have a seat," I said, indicating for him to sit across the table from us.

He walked wordlessly across the floor and fell into the chair.

"This is just a preliminary interview," I said. "We've been told you waived the right to have counsel present. Is that correct?"

"That's right," he answered, and his voice broke a little.

"How's your family doing?" I asked, trying to help him relax.

"They're fine."

"You getting to talk to them regularly?"

"Often enough."

"How are you being treated?"

"They're treating me fine, Major. Why don't you cut the crap and get to your questions."

There was no anger on his face, but he was tightly wound up, like a man being led to the scaffold who just couldn't bring himself to exchange pleasantries with the crowd.

I smiled back nicely. "Okay, we'll get right down to business."

"Good."

"We have just a few opening questions," I said, placing the tape recorder on the table between us. "If, at any point, you don't want to answer a question, that's your right. I must warn you, however, that this is an official investigation, and if anything you say turns out later to be false, that can result in additional charges."

Delbert and Morrow shot me a pair of "that was a fairly stupid thing to say" kind of looks. The man was already facing thirty-five charges of murder, among sundry other serious offenses, and here I was threatening him with chump change.

Had Sanchez been anything but an officer in the United States Army, then Delbert and Morrow might have had a point. But he was. And he therefore was likely to feel a certain stiffening in his backbone from my warning. An officer's integrity was still a cherished relic.

"I understand," he said.

"Good," I said. "Please start with the mission of your team when you went into Kosovo."

He leaned forward and cupped his hands tightly in front of his lips, which any professional interrogator will tell you is exactly the kind of gesture a man might make when he's preparing to tell a few whoppers. So much for my warning.

"We were part of an operation called Guardian Angel. The

KLA company we'd trained was being put into operation. Our job was to accompany them and provide assistance."

"Assistance? What kind of assistance?"

"Continued training, help with planning operations, that kind of thing."

"Weren't they well trained enough to handle themselves?"

"No."

I withdrew a piece of paper from my bulging legal case. "I have here a copy of the evaluation you gave that team when their training ended. That's your signature, isn't it?" I asked, pointing at the tight, almost childlike scrawl at the bottom of the page.

He barely glanced at it. "Yes."

"You said here they were ready."

He stared coldly at the paper. "What I said was that they met the minimal standards each KLA company had to attain before they were certified."

"Was something wrong with those standards?"

"Yes. Those standards are slightly below what a basic trainee gets in our army. We taught them just enough to get them killed," he said with obvious bitterness in his voice.

Anyway, I moved on. "How was your relationship with your KLA company?"

"What do you mean?"

"Was it friendly? Professional? Personal? Impersonal?"

"Professional."

"Could you elaborate?"

"We were told to train them, so we did. It was a job and they were part of it."

"Did you feel responsible for them?"

"No, I didn't. It's not our war, it's theirs."

"Good point," I said. "Still, I'd think it would be awfully hard not to develop some feelings for them. Living and working together, exchanging stories about families, and—"

"Major, we both know where you're trying to go with this."

"Where am I trying to go?"

"That when the KLA company got slaughtered, we went on some kind of bloody rampage and took revenge. That's not what happened."

"No?" I said, interested that he chose the word "slaughtered," which carried interesting implications. I mean, there're words like "were shot," "died," "got killed," "were wiped out," any of which connoted a milder fate than the words "got slaughtered," in the food chain of death.

"Look, that's what the press is reporting, but that's not the way it happened."

"No? Then tell me what happened."

"After our KLA company got, uh, wiped out, we reported that back to Tenth Group headquarters. We were told to relocate our base camp and await instructions. So we did. We'd been there about two days when we suspected our new base camp was compromised, so we—"

"Why did you suspect that?" I interrupted.

"Because Sergeant Perrite and Sergeant Machusco detected a Serbian patrol that appeared to be surveilling us."

"When was that?" I asked.

"The afternoon of the seventeenth. Maybe three o'clock, maybe a little earlier."

"I don't remember seeing that in the communications log at the Tenth Group ops center."

Sanchez seemed to chew on his tongue a moment. "I didn't report it."

"Why? I'd think you'd report that immediately."

"Maybe that's because you're a lawyer and you've never been in that kind of situation before."

I had most definitely been in that kind of situation before but wasn't about to tell him that. Sanchez was giving me the cover he and the rest of his team had concocted, and for the time being, the best path was to hear the entire tale before I looked for ways to tear holes in it.

"What did you do, then?" I asked.

"We grabbed our equipment and ran. We could have been attacked at any moment, so we reverted to an escape and evasion plan we'd planned two days before."

I thought I saw where this was going. "And were you followed?" I helpfully asked.

"Yes."

"How did you know?"

"Because we laid trip flares on our trail."

"How many went off?" I asked.

"I don't remember exactly. Maybe one, maybe two."

"Was it one, or was it two?"

"Maybe two. My memory could be wrong, though."

"What kind of trip flares were they?"

"Star clusters with a string on the pin."

"How many did you set?"

"I don't know exactly. I was preoccupied with leading the team out. The trailman was laying the flare traps."

"What kind of string did he use?"

"I don't know. Commo wire probably."

One of the tricks when you're investigating a conspiracy is to ask detailed questions and just keeping asking for more and more details, because usually the conspirators have only agreed on a broad cover, and it's the details that get them in trouble. The topic of trip flares was just the kind of detail that was liable to get Sanchez and his team stuck in quicksand.

"So you didn't feel you had time to make a radio call to the ops center, but you had time to set warning flares on your escape route?"

"It was a matter of priorities. A radio call wasn't going to do us any good, but warning flares would at least tell us if we were being followed."

"Then what happened?"

"Our E&E plan called for us to move straight south and cross the border into Macedonia. I became worried that the Serb team tracking us would just call their headquarters and have an ambush set up ahead. I decided to shift our direction to the east."

"Did you discuss that with anyone in the team?"

"Not that I remember."

"Is that a definite no?"

"I can't remember every detail I said to everyone. We were being stalked by a large Serbian unit. Things were happening fast."

"A large Serbian unit? I'm sure you said it was a small surveillance team. How did it suddenly become large?"

"I made a reasonable assumption. We knew we'd been detected, and it just seemed logical that the Serbs would've thrown more men into hunting us down."

"Why?"

"Because the Serbs would've loved to kill or capture an American A-team. The whole focus of America's strategy in this thing is to avoid losing any men. Everybody knows that. The Serbs sure as hell know it. The American people have a very low interest in what's happening here. Casualties would wreck everything. Look what happened in Somalia."

I couldn't argue against that. "How far behind you was the Serbian unit?" I asked.

"How would I know? They were behind us, that's all I knew."

"But you said several trip flares went off. If the flares went up into the sky, you must've been able to judge the distance they were behind you."

He looked at me a moment before he answered. Like most folks, he wasn't used to being interrogated and obviously wasn't enjoying the experience.

"I didn't see them go off."

"You didn't?"

"No. I was busy leading the unit. I was reading the map and compass and watching ahead."

"Then how did you learn the warning flares went off?"

"Someone told me."

"Who told you?"

"I don't remember."

Now it was my turn to stare at him. I worked my face into as much disbelief as I could summon and stayed silent. He stared back until he grew uncomfortable.

He finally said, "Look, the word was passed up the file, I guess. I don't remember exactly who told me."

I stayed quiet another moment, but he decided not to embellish any further. "Okay," I said, "what did you do then?"

"We walked the rest of the day, zigzagging so our route wasn't predictable. We could see dust columns over the treetops, and occasionally we heard the sounds of vehicles off in the distance."

"And what did you interpret that to mean?" I asked.

"The Serbs were moving mobile forces around to try to trap us."

"Did you discuss that with any team members?"

"Yes."

"Who?"

"I remember discussing it with Chief Persico, my team deputy."

"But you still didn't make any radio reports back to Tenth Group headquarters?"

"No."

"Why not?"

"We were moving fast. Things were happening quickly. Besides, what could they do about it?"

"Provided an aerial recon to let you know your situation. Offered you air cover. Maybe even mounted an aerial extraction to get you out of there."

He had not expected me to answer that question so spontaneously and appeared nettled for a moment. Then he shrugged. "Look, I'll admit I wasn't thinking that clearly at the moment. I was just trying to get my team out alive."

"Maybe," I said back, just to let him know I wasn't buying it.

"Besides, I was worried about the Serbs intercepting a radio transmission. They would've vectored in and known exactly where we were."

"I thought they already knew exactly where you were. You were being followed, right?"

"No, I said I assumed they knew where we were. I was told trip flares had gone off, but that didn't mean they knew exactly where we were."

The expression on Sanchez's face was becoming flustered. All of these questions about flares were obviously beginning to unhinge him. Which was exactly what I wanted. If I could divert him away from the canard he and his team had obviously prepared, and force him to start ad-libbing, we'd have our opening.

"Okay, go on," I told him.

He took a moment to compose himself, then said, "We kept running all day. I hoped that after it grew dark we could turn south again and try and head for the border. Around midnight we drew into a perimeter. We could still hear vehicles moving on the roads around us, so we knew the Serbs were intensifying their search. Then, at around two, another trip flare went off, about a mile away. That's when I decided."

"Decided what?" I asked him.

"We had to ambush a Serb column."

"And why did you decide that?"

"Because we had to get the Serbs' attention. We couldn't outrun them. They were building a noose around us. We had to force them to be as cautious as they were forcing us to be. Do you understand that?"

"No," I said. "Please explain it more clearly."

"Look, this was their territory. They felt safe. They were moving around at full speed, chasing us on foot, trying to block us with men in vehicles. If I didn't find some way to make them slow down, they were going to get us."

"And you figured what? An ambush would make that happen?"

"Sure. They had to know we were dangerous. If they kept acting sloppy, we'd make them pay for it."

"Didn't your orders say you were only allowed to kill in self-defense?"

"This was self-defense," he insisted, like it was indisputable.

"So you set an ambush?"

"Right. I decided to hit them at first light. I used the map to pick a spot on the road where there was a double curve with hills on both sides. We moved for about another hour and were in position by around four in the morning. Then we set up the ambush and waited. Every now and again a vehicle passed by, but we let them go through. Then, around six-thirty, a column with about six vehicles came into the killzone and we unleashed."

"Why did you pick that particular column?"

"Because it was larger. I wanted the Serbs to think we were bigger than an A-team. I wanted them to think there were maybe thirty or forty of us. If we only hit a single vehicle, they might have realized they were only dealing with a small team."

"But if they'd already spotted you, and they were following you, don't you think they already had some idea of the size of your unit?"

"That's exactly the point. I believed they did, and I wanted to make them question that. They had no way of knowing if there was one team or three dozen teams operating in our sector. I figured that if we took on a large column, they might think there were more of us than they'd originally thought."

"And how long did the ambush take?"

"I don't know for sure . . . maybe five minutes, maybe a little longer."

"Describe it."

"It was just a standard L-shaped ambush. We planted two command-detonated anti-armor mines in the road to blow the lead vehicle and stop the column. We set up a daisy chain of claymore mines along the opposite side of the road that we blew after the troops emptied out of the trucks and were taking cover behind their vehicles. Then we raked the column with M16s and machine guns for a few minutes. Then we left."

That answered why so many of the corpses back in Belgrade had their backs shredded with claymore pellets. It was a relief to hear, because the alternative was that Sanchez and his people cruelly blew off a bunch of claymores at the backs of a retreating enemy. If he was telling the truth about this, then he'd at least negated one element that took this beyond a simple fight and onto the precarious grounds of a shocking atrocity.

"Were there any survivors?"

"Yes."

"How do you know?"

"Because they were still shooting when we left."

"Was the return fire heavy or light?"

"Not heavy, but there was enough of it."

"How many survivors would you say there were?"

"There were probably four or five who were still firing. And there had to be a fair number of wounded."

"You know the Serbs are claiming there were no survivors?"

"That's a lie!" he shouted with evident outrage. "There were men still alive on that road when we left."

"I've examined the corpses," I said. "Thirty-five of them."

At that point our eyes met and we just sat and stared at

each other for a moment. Sometimes, when you're being bombarded with lies, a tiny morsel that sounds like the bald truth works its way into the conversation. Your ears almost tingle from the fresh sensation. And this was one of those moments.

I finally asked, "What did you do next?"

"We continued our E&E. I figured that once the Serbs found their column, that would slow them up for a while. So I began leading the team southward again. We were about fifty clicks from the border. I figured we could make it that night if we moved fast."

"Were you still being followed?"

"I don't know. We didn't set any more flares, so there was no way to tell."

"Why didn't you set any more flares?"

"I think we were out of them."

"You think?"

"I didn't ask for a count, but I remember thinking we'd used our last one in the ambush."

"Did you report to headquarters?" I asked, knowing damn well he had, because his report was noted in the communications log.

"Yes."

"Did you report the ambush?"

"No."

"Why not?"

"Because I didn't want anyone second-guessing me."

"I'm sorry, could you explain that?"

"I guess I knew they weren't gonna be too happy about what we'd done. I just didn't have time to get into all of that with them."

"So what did you report?"

"That we were extricating."

"Did you explain that you were being followed, that Serb

columns were on the roads around you, that you felt your team was at risk?"

"No."

"Why didn't you?"

"I thought I had things under control. I figured the ambush bought us enough time to get out of there."

"And you still didn't report the ambush after you returned. Why was that?"

"Look, I made a mistake there," he said, looking suddenly repentant. "I admit that. I figured that no harm had been done, and I really didn't see any reason to have to report it."

I turned to Delbert and Morrow, both of whom were sitting with their chins resting on their hands, listening raptly to Sanchez's tale. The underlying concept of the cover story was damned good. You could split hairs over what constituted self-defense, but the notion of a desperate team trapped behind enemy lines, surrounded by bloodthirsty Serbs—the same fellas who'd ambushed and shot down Scott O'Grady, who'd snatched three American peacekeepers in Macedonia—that was likely to elicit a sympathetic response from anyone.

"Do either of you have any questions?" I asked Delbert and Morrow.

They both shook their heads. Like me, they could spend hours interrogating Sanchez, but that would come later. First we needed to interview some other team members, look for incongruities, and then we'd come back.

Sanchez was still sitting with his hands folded in front of his mouth. His fingers were squeezed tightly together, desperately tight, like if he didn't press them together they might fly off and start doing funny things on their own. I guessed he was feeling some tremendous anxiety over how his performance had gone over with us. I stared back expressionlessly.

"Thank you for your time, Captain Sanchez," I said, turning

off the tape recorder and putting some papers back in my over-size legal case.

He stood up and pushed his chair back into the table. He waited there, looking awkward, almost helpless. "Hey, Major," he finally said.

"What?" I answered, standing and preparing to leave.

"We didn't murder those Serbs. I swear we didn't. When we left, there were still some of them alive."

I nodded. It wasn't a nod of agreement, just acknowledgment.

Chapter

☆ ☆ ☆ 9

An envelope had been slid beneath the door to my room when we returned to the hotel, and that irritating little red message light was blinking on the phone. I opened the envelope as I dialed the number for my messages, which was no easy thing with only two hands.

The envelope contained a fax that had been forwarded by Imelda. She had appended her own little note, which read, "Bastard!!" I couldn't tell if that was directed at me or mankind in general, so I read on.

The fax was a copy of a *Washington Herald* story from the day before. It was written by none other than Jeremy Berkowitz, the same fella I'd hung up on, and it exposed the shocking revelation that the Army had turned over the investigation of perhaps the most serious criminal case in its history to a lowly Army major and two captains. The implication was that if the Army genuinely wanted to get to the bottom of this case, it would have appointed some heftier, more qualified officials to handle the investigating. My name was even mentioned a few times in the story—spelled wrong, which struck me as adding insult to injury.

Now I could've decided that Jeremy Berkowitz was a vindictive prick who was trying to get even with me for hanging up on him, but that would've implied a disturbing lack of professionalism on the part of a very famous journalist. And as it was, the story was pretty weak. I mean, really, who cared if the Army appointed a major to head up this investigation? If that's the best Berkowitz could do, then bring him on.

There were three phone messages. One was from the same pushy, antsy special assistant to the President I met before I left Washington, and the second was from General Clapper, the chief of the JAG Corps. I was not about to call the White House operative. The way those guys are, you call them once and they never get off your back. Like a bad date that just won't go away.

I asked the operator to connect me to General Clapper's number immediately. I didn't really want to talk with him, either, but if I didn't I was likely to get another of his late-night, cheery calls.

His dry-voiced, ever-efficient secretary answered on the first ring, and a moment later I heard his voice.

"How's it feel to be famous?" He chuckled, which was easy for him, because nobody had bent him over and let him have it on the front page of a national newspaper that morning.

"I liked it better yesterday, when nobody ever heard of me."

"What did you do to piss Berkowitz off?" he asked in an impressive display of worldliness.

"Does hanging up on him count?"

"It's not the way I would've recommended you handle him."

It wasn't the way I wished I'd handled him, either, but I wasn't going to admit that. Only the communists practiced public confessions, and look where it got them.

"So how's the weather in Washington?" I asked.

There was a brief pause, then, "Hot as hell, frankly. Some folks are having second thoughts about having you head up this investigation. Nothing against you personally, Sean, but Berkowitz's article struck home in certain quarters."

"Anybody in particular having second thoughts?" I asked, biting my lip.

"I haven't talked with him directly, but I'm told the President read the article and had to be peeled off the ceiling."

"Oh, him," I said with as much phony sangfroid as I could muster. "Anybody else? I mean, anyone important?"

"The Chairman of the Joint Chiefs doesn't sound too happy, either. And him, I did talk to."

The phone went silent, and there was one of those long pauses that could only be termed as strained. Apparently Berkowitz had fired a much better-aimed shot than I'd thought. The moment of silence dragged on a little too long, until I finally figured out that it was Clapper's subtly polite way of allowing me to make the choice of voluntarily turning over the reins of the investigation to someone else, presumably someone with a little more consequence on their shoulders. And I have to admit I seriously considered it, because no matter how you looked at it, there was no upside for me in this thing.

I couldn't tell what Clapper was thinking, but I knew what I'd be thinking if I were him. I'd be praying the guy on my end of the line would say, hey, look, maybe this thing is a little over my head, and I've given it the old college try, but don't you think it might be time to appoint a whole new posse, possibly headed by a general with lots of high-ranking deputies. Clapper, after all, was the poor sap who'd recommended me. It didn't take a genius to know he was probably getting his ass whipped pretty hard right about now. To put it another way, General Clapper's career was suddenly in my hands, and I can't imagine that was a very reassuring thought for him.

Finally, I blurted out, "Look, General, I've started this thing, and I'd like to see it through."

Without pause or hesitation, he said, "All right, we'll try it that way. One thing, though, Sean. You work on how you deal with the press."

"That's fair," I said, wondering why I hadn't gracefully backed out. Berkowitz had unconsciously given me a painless opportunity, and it was a sure bet that no more of that variety was going to come along.

The next phone call was the one I least wanted to return, but I knew I'd better. I asked the operator to dial the number, and it was answered with "Drummond speaking," in his normal, gruff voice.

I said, "Hello, Dad."

"How ya doing?" he asked.

"Fine," I answered very simply. "Just fine."

"Saw your name in the paper."

"I figured you would."

"I didn't know you'd been appointed to head the investigation," he said, and while there was no recrimination in his tone, the statement stood on its own merits.

"I guess I forgot to tell you. I've been kind of busy."

"Want some advice from an old soldier?" he asked.

"I guess that can't hurt," I said, which was a bald-faced lie. His advice usually stung like hell.

"Don't lead with your chin. Oh . . . and watch your flanks."

"Yeah, sure, Dad," I said. This is the way Army fathers speak to their kids, in soldierly parables that actually sound kind of ridiculous.

"Well, I gotta run," he grunted. "Your mother wants me to cut the lawn again. Third damned time this week." Then he hung up.

Maybe I should explain a little bit about my father at this point. My mother didn't want the grass cut. No way in hell. My father mowed and trimmed his lawn at least three times a week. He treated it like a brigade of little green troops that required his unyielding attention. It was the best-tended lawn in the neighborhood, if not the universe. If so much as one weed appeared, he pruned it out like an unruly soldier just begging for discipline. If even a single blade of grass had the temerity to rise above the others, the whole lawn got a punishing shave, with a pushmower.

He had been a hell of an officer in his day. He was tall and handsome and manly, and Jesus, was he tough. When I was a kid, even on Sundays and holidays he rose every day at five o'clock sharp, did about two hundred push-ups and sit-ups, ran about five miles, then made sure his larynx was in good working order by bellowing at my brother and me. He then marched purposely out of the house for another day of soldiering. There were years when we never saw him, like when he went to Vietnam, not once, not twice, but three times, which could only happen to a guy who was screaming and begging to go back there. Every time he left, a huge vacuum was created, which was instantly and happily filled by Mother, my brother, and myself. A year later he'd return, his chest heavier with more medals, and bludgeon his way back into the family.

It seemed to be commonly agreed that he was on his way to becoming a four-star general when cruel fate intervened in the last week of his third tour in Vietnam. He was a colonel by then, and was leading his brigade on a sweep, when he bent over to pick something up, and, no kidding, got shot right in the ass by some Vietcong with a nasty sense of humor and a crossbow.

Sounded kinda funny, but the doctors didn't think so. He spent a year in the hospital as the doctors kept chasing infections and trying to repair the various internal canals that had been punctured. When they were done, his insides had been rearranged in some pretty nutty ways and his military career was over. No more punishing early-morning runs. No more daily dozens. No more troops to push around or medals to be earned.

He wasn't bitter, though. He took a job selling cars, because he needed the kind of work where he could dash off at least once an hour to purge in a bathroom. And damn, did he sell lots of cars. He spent fifteen years pushing autos and crapping his brains out, until he ended up owning three dealerships and being worth a small fortune. His dealerships were something else, too. They were the tidiest, most orderly car lots anybody ever saw. Every car was spit-shined daily and lined up, dress-right-dress. The salesmen popped to attention and nearly saluted anytime they approached a potential buyer. I always got nervous when I stepped on one of his lots, but most customers seemed to like it.

My brother, who was a year older than me, knew from birth he didn't want to be like my father. He grew his hair long, registered as a Democrat when he was only six, got tattooed, wore earrings, and was in trouble with the military police almost habitually. About three years ago, he sold the Internet company he founded and retired at the ripe old age of thirty-seven. He has about a hundred and fifty million in the bank and spends every day sitting in the backyard of his huge house, which overlooks the Pacific Ocean, smoking dope nearly every waking hour and laughing his ass off at the way it all turned out.

I was smarter than him. I followed in my father's footsteps. I took an ROTC scholarship and chose a career that paid squat, that treated its people like cannon fodder, that had no qualms about ending a career over a stupid thing like a reporter with a nasty grudge against a tight-lipped Army lawyer.

I hadn't had a good strong drink in over a week, and things being what they were, very badly wanted that rectified. Tout suite, as they say. I lifted up the phone and asked first Delbert, then Morrow, if they wished to join me downstairs in the bar.

Delbert begged off, saying he wanted to prepare his questions for tomorrow.

Morrow said, "Sure, be down in ten minutes."

I'd be lying if I said this was a disappointing outcome.

I was on my first scotch on the rocks when Morrow arrived in tight jeans and a loose-fitting knit shirt. I decided on the spot that if this woman ever wanted to get out of the legal field, she could make a pretty good go as a model. Or, better yet, in my suddenly frenzied imagination, as a stripper. I wasn't the only one who noticed, either, because there were lots of Italian men in the bar, and Italian men aren't exactly reticent about show-ing their admiration of the opposite sex. They sure as hell weren't pulling their punches when they saw her.

"So what will you have?" I asked as she slipped into the chair across from me, trying to act oblivious to the drooling fools who were whistling and catcalling in some strange tongue. I halfway expected her to order an Evian bottle with a twist of lemon or some such obscenely healthful drink.

"Scotch on the rocks," she said, which nearly threw me off my chair.

I stuck my finger up for the bartender to send over one of the same, then turned back and decided it was time to reap-praise Miss Morrow. I sniffed the air once or twice and the odor of lilies filled my nostrils. We were dealing with an oxymoron here. A man can always tell a lot about a woman from her choice of perfumes, and lilies are something I always associate with the wholesome, midwestern variety of her gender. The ones who stay virgins till they're twenty-one. The ones who call their moth-ers every week and still send money to their old 4-H clubs. The ones who don't go near scotch.

"That your normal drink?" I asked.

She sort of smiled. "No. Usually I'd just order an Evian with a twist of lemon, but I wanted to surprise you."

I guess I blinked once or twice, and she giggled, apparently delighted that she'd beat me at my own game.

"Yeah, I usually drink Evian, too," I finally said, thinking I was being witty.

"No, you usually drink scotch. In fact, I'd be willing to bet that you've never taken a sip from a bottle of Evian in your life."

"And why would you bet that?"

"Because. Want to play a little truth or consequences?"

If I weren't such an overconfident guy, I would've said no, right then and there. Instead, I stupidly said, "Sure. What's the stake?"

"Point-by-point loser chugs a shot of scotch. Overall loser pays the tab."

"All right," I said, withdrawing a quarter from my pocket and flipping it. "Heads or tails?"

"Heads," she said, and it came down heads, and I should've quit right then and there.

"Okay." She smiled. "What's your father do?"

"He's a hairdresser," I said. "Lives in San Francisco and works at one of those men's hair parlors frequented by gays. He's kinda fruity, too, but he had this one-time fling with a woman, and I was the result."

"Drink!" she ordered me. "Your father is ridiculously heterosexual. In fact, if I was to guess, I'd say he was career Army."

I wiped a few drops of scotch off my lips, stuck my hand up for the bartender to send over another, and did my best to hide my shock. "Why'd you guess that?" I finally asked, hating to think I was that easy to read.

"I wasn't guessing. I was making a reasoned deduction. Sons of strong-willed men often become very rebellious and act like wiseasses. I know. A lot of them end up as my clients."

"Okay," I said, wanting an early victory to even the score, "where are you from?"

"Ames, Iowa," she said. "I grew up on a farm, spent my childhood milking cows, plucking eggs from underneath hens, and praying desperately that I'd get into law school."

"That's true," I declared. "Drink! And don't forget the part about how you were crowned homecoming queen and almost married the captain of the football team."

"You drink," she ordered. "I've never been to Ames, Iowa, in my life. I'm from the Northeast, was born and raised in a city, and the closest I've ever come to a cow is digging into its broiled carcass on my plate."

My mouth kind of fell open as I reached down for my shot glass. "Really?" I asked, dumbfounded.

"Really," she said with a vague smile. "And for your information, I went to an all-girls' private school. We didn't have homecoming queens. Or a football team, either. We had a field hockey team, and I didn't date the captain, because I was the captain."

I gulped the scotch and considered the proposition that she had schemed on playing this game before she ever came down here. She must have deliberately doused herself in that lily-smelling perfume just to throw me off her scent. No play on words intended.

She still hadn't touched a drop of her scotch. She grinned, then said, "Okay, why'd you leave the infantry and become a lawyer?"

I stared at the new shot glass that had just appeared and thought about that a moment. Finally, I kind of shrugged and admitted, "I guess I got tired of killing people. I went to war a couple of times and decided I really didn't like it all that much."

She studied me a moment, staring deeply into my eyes, and her face suddenly became very soft. Her eyes, which I already mentioned were abundantly sympathetic, acquired a few more notches of compassion. "Drink," she said, almost remorsefully.

"Nah, you drink!" I shot back. "I had a great time at war. In fact, I nearly cried when they were over."

Which actually was true. And which actually was why I became a lawyer. I developed this huge phobia that I would end up like my father, in love with combat. And maybe I'd end up just like him in another regard, too, with an arrow stuck in my rear end. Metaphorically speaking, of course.

"All right," I asked, relishing my victory, "were you ever married?"

"That's too personal."

"No limits to this game, lady. This is a blood sport. Answer the question."

"Okay, I was. My husband was also an Army lawyer," she said and seemed suddenly very sad. "One day I came home early from a trip, and there he was, in bed with a twenty-year-old paralegal."

"How long were you married?" I asked. Although the game has a one-question rule, I was taking advantage of the most supreme rule: to wit, that higher rank doth make its own rules.

Her eyes seemed fixated on something inside her tiny shot glass. "Three years. We met in my second year of law school and got married right after it was over. I guess I blame myself. I've always worked too hard and I . . . well . . . I, uh, I guess he felt neglected."

"Drink!" I barked.

She looked at me in shock. "What?"

"You heard me! Drink!"

She gulped it down, then gave me this really cute, really spiteful look. "How did you know?"

"You said too much. You're the type who likes to keep everything private."

"All right. Were you ever married?" she asked.

"No."

"Were you ever in love?"

"One question to a turn."

"You asked two the last time."

"Okay. I was in love once."

"And why didn't you marry her?"

"You're over your limit."

She gave me a pleading look. "I'll drink the scotch and cede the round. Please. Just answer."

"Drink first," I insisted, and she did. "Because you can't marry your dog, no matter how much you love her," I said, giving her a perfectly evil smile.

She frowned. "That sucked."

"So did the lily perfume," I said, which nearly made her fall off her chair, she laughed so hard. "By the way," I added, "it's three to two, my favor. You pay for the drinks."

She stuck two fingers up, the bartender grinned, and two more drinks instantly appeared. The bartender was Italian, and he obviously thought I was trying to get her drunk as hell before I took her upstairs and screwed her lights out. In America, that's considered caddish behavior, bordering on rape. But this was Italy, where the rules are different. Here it's considered delightfully good form, since nearly anything that results in a roll in the hay is probably good form. He gave me this fawning, jealous smile as he brought the drinks, and I gave him a manly nod of acknowledgment.

"What did you think of Sanchez?" she asked.

"Seemed a nice enough fella," I admitted.

"I thought so, too."

"Was he what you expected?" I asked.

"No. Not at all what I expected."

"What did you expect?"

"I don't know. I've defended a number of killers. He didn't strike me as the type. Too soft maybe. Not aggressive enough."

"He might not be a killer."

"How do you get that?"

I sipped from my fourth glass of scotch in only twenty minutes and felt it starting to do fuzzy things to my brain. "I'd guess that something very strange happened out there among those nine men."

"Strange like what?"

"Well, you need to understand something. This wasn't combat like in Vietnam or Korea or World War Two, where whole units sometimes snapped and went into some kind of killing frenzy. Sanchez and his guys were under a very different type of strain."

"So you don't think it happened the way the newspapers are reporting?"

"No, I don't. I don't think it was anywhere near that uncomplicated."

"Why?"

"Because they didn't kill the Serbs right away. Because they waited two days after Akhan's guys were killed, which was enough time for their emotions to cool. Because there were nine men in that team, and nine men don't universally decide to do a rotten thing. Because when things like this happen, there's nearly always circumstances lurking underneath that are damned hard to fathom if you weren't there."

"So what do you think happened?"

"I really don't know."

She paused for a moment and took a large sip from her scotch. "You were in combat. Did you ever feel the urge?"

I thought about that a moment. "Once, I guess."

"What caused it?"

"It was a few days after the Gulf War ended. Saddam's Guards had escaped the net and started slaughtering the Kurds and Shiites, whom our government had encouraged to rise up against the regime after we'd promised we were going to destroy Saddam's military. It turned out we lied."

"I think I remember something about that."

"Yeah, well, it didn't make big news in America. What happened was, they rose up and suddenly the Revolutionary Guards appeared. They never knew what hit them. Thousands of Kurds and Shiites, lots of women and children, began getting slaughtered. The survivors fled the carnage and headed south, into

Kuwait. We set up camps and did the best we could to mend their wounds and care for them, and that only made us feel more miserable."

"So you wanted to avenge them?"

"Nope. We wanted to appease our guilt. Our government had done a very dishonorable thing and these people were paying for it. Only Uncle Sam wasn't around, having to look them in the eye."

"So you think that's what happened here?"

"Nope. That's not at all what happened here. See, we wanted to, and God knows we talked about it a lot. But talk was all we ever did."

She drained the last of her scotch, and she looked a little tipsy, and her lips looked kind of moist. I felt kind of frisky, and our eyes came together and met. Then came this long awkward moment.

Chapter

☆☆
☆ **10**

The way that look ended was her telling me to get my big shoe off her sandaled foot. She then paid the bill and we parted ways at the elevator, since she wanted to limp the two flights upstairs to her room, while I insisted on ascending in comfort. The last I saw of her, she was careening between the rail and the wall, stumbling occasionally on the steps and trying to appear graceful. Some girls really should stick to Evian water with a twist.

The next morning, my head throbbed ever so lightly on the car ride to the Air Force holding facility, although poor Miss Morrow obviously got the full, vituperative brunt of the scotch. She spent half the ride with her fingers plugged into her ears, trying to protect her addled brain from the raucous roar of six pistons pumping up and down and from Delbert, who seemed in a remarkably chipper and garrulous mood.

This was the day when we would split up and each take different team members to interrogate. If we limited ourselves to two hours with each of the remaining eight team members, then by midafternoon we'd be done. I decided to handle Chief Warrant Officer Mike Persico, Sergeant First Class Andy Caldwell, and Sergeant First Class François Perrite.

Michael Persico was forty-six years old. He was a former staff sergeant who'd applied for warrant officer training and been accepted. Every A-team has a chief warrant officer. They are the technical experts of the teams, the masters of every function of the other members, from weapons to communications to medical. Persico had been with the same team the past eighteen years. He was the "old man" of the team, meaning he was like the living, breathing heritage. He had earned a Bronze Star for valor in Somalia, and a Silver Star for valor in the Gulf.

I'd read the citations and was impressed. In the Gulf War, he had helped lead the team deep into Iraq's desert for a little Scud-hunting. They found one Scud missile, directed an airstrike that annihilated the missile and its launcher, then lost two team members fighting their way back out. In Somalia, Persico and his team had been committed to help save the Ranger company that got bushwhacked trying to nab Aideed. One of Persico's team members got wounded and he risked his own life to dodge through a hail of Somali fire to save him. Persico was a brave man, there was no question of that.

I studied him closely when he was led into the room. He was average height and build. He looked leathery and tough, with mostly gray hair and harshly weathered skin that had left deep creases on his face, particularly around his mouth. His eyes were gray, like a wolf's. He moved confidently, like a man who'd gotten most of what he wanted out of life.

He brought a lawyer into the play, a female captain named Jackie Caruthers, who resembled a middle linebacker, only a little bigger, and with a face that looked like it had been kissed by the bumper of a speeding Mack truck.

"Please have a seat," I said to both of them, and they sat straight across from me.

"You've informed your client of the rules?" I asked Caruthers.

"I have," she said.

"Then if you don't mind, I'd like to get right into it."

Persico's pale gray eyes were taking my measure, like he would a foe on a battlefield.

"Fine with me," Caruthers answered for him.

I ignored her and looked straight at Persico. "Chief, could you explain the series of events that led to the destruction of the KLA unit you trained?"

He glanced at his lawyer, who nodded.

"All right. The KLA company commander was named Captain Kalid Akhan. He came to us on the afternoon of the thirteenth and said he planned to do a raid on a Serb police compound at dawn the next morning—"

"Did he plan the raid?" I interrupted.

"Yes, sir, he did. He said he had heard from some locals that the police compound was poorly guarded, that the Serbs spent most of their days drinking, and torturing local citizens."

"And did he have any help from you or your team?"

"No. He pretty much decided what he wanted to do on his own."

"Pretty much?"

"Completely."

"Did you like his plan?"

"Looked okay to us. Based on what he said about the Serbs, it sounded like kid's play."

"Could you describe that plan for me?"

"Sure. The police station was located in the middle of a village named Piluca. Captain Akhan had ninety-five men. He planned to break 'em into three elements and hit at first light. One element was to go into the village and isolate the police station from the other houses. The second was to build a security screen along the main road that led into the village from the north. The third was the assault element. It would take down the police station."

"And what did they plan to do once they took the police station?"

"Well, you gotta understand a few things about that Piluca station."

"Like what?"

"Like it had a real nasty reputation."

"Why so?"

"The Serb captain who commanded it, he got put there about a year before by the authorities in Belgrade. He'd done some time in Bosnia and was regarded as something of an expert on ethnic cleansing. He even had a nickname: the Hammer."

"Why that nickname?"

"That was like his signature. He always carried around a hammer in his belt. He liked to use it to bash fingers and toes and testicles. Apparently, he was a real sadist."

"Did he have a large force?"

"About thirty Serbs were under him, give or take a few. They'd pretty well terrorized that little town for the whole year."

"So Akhan's team wanted revenge?" I asked.

"There was probably some of that, but what Captain Akhan figured was that the Piluca station was a symbol. Knocking it off would show every Albanian Kosovar in our sector that the Liberation Army had balls and could actually accomplish something."

"What do you mean by 'knocking it off'?" I asked, genuinely curious.

"They'd take it over for an hour or two. Maybe take the Serb captain prisoner, and certainly take all the weapons."

"*Maybe?* Did they or didn't they intend to take him prisoner?"

"Okay, they did. Him and as many other Serbs as they could get."

"And what did they plan to do with the Serbs they took prisoner?"

"We didn't ask."

The funny thing is, he was looking me straight in the eye

as he said that. Funnier still, he apparently expected me to be-lieve it. This Captain Akhan was talking about taking prisoners, only prisoners are pretty damned inconvenient when you're op-erating behind enemy lines, moving base camps every few days, and trying to save your ass from marauding Serb hunter-killer teams.

It seemed much more likely that Akhan and his crew planned to slaughter whatever Serbs they could get their hands on. And if I was right about that, then Sanchez and his team, in obliging that kind of thing, had already taken the first deadly step over that thin line that separates warfare from atrocity—even before Akhan's company were killed.

"But what did you assume they were going to do with the prisoners?" I asked.

"I assumed the captain planned to turn 'em over to UN au-thority so they could be tried for crimes against humanity."

"And how did he plan to do that, given that you were be-hind enemy lines, at least a two-day march from Macedonia, and the capturing of the Serb police surely was going to lead to a manhunt?"

"I just trusted they would," he said very simply. "Captain Akhan wasn't the type to commit murder."

"Did you report the planned KLA attack to Tenth Group headquarters?"

"No."

"And why didn't you?"

"We didn't have to. We had authority to approve Captain Akhan's operations."

"You had authority? I thought you were there in an advisory capacity."

He never blinked. "That's right. I misspoke."

"You're sure you misspoke?"

"Yes. It was just a slip of the tongue. The truth was, Captain

Akhan had the authority to decide on the attack himself. It was what he wanted to do, and we had no right to stop him."

"So what happened?" I asked, filing away that line of inquiry for later.

"Usually a few men stayed behind with us, maybe a few sick guys. Not this time, though. Everyone went. They left about two in the morning, figuring to hit the station at first light. Like I said, the Serb police were known for getting drunked up every night, so Captain Akhan figured they'd be sleeping it off. We don't really know what happened after that. Maybe they were expected, or maybe it was just bad luck and the Serb police garrison got reinforced the day before. Anyway, they got down to Piluca, and the crap hit the fan."

"Could there have been a security leak?"

He appeared thoughtful and scratched his jaw for a few moments, which I considered a bit of theatrics for my benefit, because he and the rest of the team must already have spent a considerable amount of time trying to figure out why Akhan's plan turned into a disaster.

Finally, he said, "Probably a pretty good chance that's what happened. The Serbs ain't stupid. We've suspected that they've been sending agents south to infiltrate the Kosovar camps and try to get into the KLA. Sometimes they're holding a guy's family and he's got no choice but to work for 'em. We try to be careful when we recruit, but you gotta expect a few turncoats or spies to get through."

"Were you in radio contact with Akhan's company?"

"No."

"Isn't that unusual?"

"No. The SOP was to maintain radio silence."

"Even if things went wrong?"

"Sure. Wasn't like there was anything we could do about it. We weren't there to fight."

"So what happened?"

"What happened? Well, it went to shit, and they were all wiped out."

"Every man?" I asked.

"A few of 'em were captured, then immediately executed."

"How did you find that out?"

"Around ten or so, when they still weren't back, we sent a recon team to check on 'em."

"Who was in that team?"

"Perrite and Machusco. They snuck into the village and checked it out."

"And how did the members of your team react to that news?"

"Shit happens. It's war. Guys get killed."

"Weren't you disappointed?"

"Not enough to go out and kill a bunch of Serbs."

"Did you feel a sense of personal loss?"

"Look, Captain Akhan and his company were pretty good guys. But we weren't real close or any of that shit. We kept to ourselves; they kept to themselves."

"Why was that?"

"Because we were different. Most of them didn't speak any English, and only two of our guys speak Albanian. Also, Captain Akhan's guys were real tight."

"Tight how?"

"Most of 'em grew up together, or at least knew each other before. Also, the captain did a pretty good job of keepin' 'em together."

Lots of folks give off clues they don't mean to. Persico was making what I regarded to be a very enlightening mistake. Warrant officers are notoriously disrespectful. They're bred that way. They occupy an awkward position in the Army, caught in a netherworld between the enlisted ranks and the officer ranks, accepted by neither. Like porcupines grow spines, they respond with a slouchy grouchiness toward any but their own kind. Persico's constant referrals to Akhan as *Captain* Akhan was a sign of respect, if not outright reverence. I didn't buy the breezy indifference.

"How was your relationship with Captain Sanchez?" I asked, changing tracks.

"Great."

"Was he a good team leader?"

"Yeah, fantastic."

"Could you please describe what you did for him?"

"I was his deputy. I was responsible for the training and professional competence of the team. He led, and I made sure the men who followed knew their jobs."

"Did you share operational responsibilities?"

He gave me a withering look, as though that were a particularly dumb question. Which I suppose it was. "The Army don't believe in sharing responsibilities. He was in charge, and I followed."

"Was there any friction between you?"

"None. We got along real well."

"How did he perform his duties while your team was in Kosovo?"

"Great. What are you angling at?"

"Nothing. I'm just trying to figure out how an A-team works, how you two functioned together."

"Look, Major, I've known Sanchez two and a half years. We ain't drinking buddies, but we get along. As I said, I *liked* the way he ran the team."

"Could you please describe the events on the day of the seventeenth when you believed your team had been discovered by the Serbs?"

"Okay, sure. We were in our base camp, and Sergeants Perrite and Machusco were pulling perimeter security. Perrite came running back from his outpost and reported that he and Machusco had seen some Serbs up on a hilltop observing us. Then—"

"Did anybody else verify that?"

"Nope. Nobody needed to. Perrite and Machusco ain't rookies."

"How many Serbs did they spot?"

"A few. He said they didn't get a real good look at 'em, but there was a few."

"So what did you do?"

"Sanchez gave the order for everyone to get their gear together and book."

"Did you have a planned E&E plan?"

"Of course. We'd built one the day before that called for us to move almost straight south."

"Is that what you did?"

"For a while. Perrite was in trail and was laying trip flares every mile or so, and a few of 'em went off, so Sanchez decided to deviate."

"How many went off?"

"I dunno. Maybe two, maybe three."

"How far away were the Serbs when they went off?"

"I'd guess about two miles."

"The same distance each time?"

"About."

"Where were you in the column?"

"The middle. We've got a movement SOP. Perrite and Machusco handle rear security, Sanchez handles the map and compass stuff, while I make sure the team's following good procedures."

"If you were in the middle, then I assume you and Captain Sanchez weren't discussing his decisions?"

"Not all the time, but we talked once or twice."

"What did you talk about?"

"We talked when we knew the Serbs was following us. I recommended we change course to a zigzag and start moving eastward, since I figured the Serbs would deduce that we'd move south, straight for the Macedonian border."

"And when was the next time?"

"That night. We took a halt, about midnight, and formed a perimeter. We could hear convoys and see dust columns all day, so we figured the Serbs were trying to box us in. We knew we had to do something. We decided the best idea was to hit the Serbs with an ambush to make 'em slow down."

"Whose idea was that?"

He paused for a moment and I could see he wasn't prepared for that question. Then he said, "Might've been mine. Or maybe Machusco or Perrite. We all thought it was a pretty good idea, though."

"So it wasn't Captain Sanchez's idea."

"No, but he bought into it right away. Why not? Wasn't like we had another option."

"Where were you positioned at the ambush site?"

"The middle."

"Did the Serbs return fire?"

"At first, no. The lead vehicle blew and they were in shock. They were unloading out the back of the trucks and running around like a buncha ants, scrambling for cover behind their vehicles. Then we blew the chain of claymores, and that set 'em back a bit, too. Took 'em two to three minutes before someone on the ground got 'em organized and they began returning fire."

"Describe the fire. Was it heavy or light?"

He sort of smiled at that question. "From my experience, anytime more than one person's shooting at you feels like heavy fire."

I did not smile back. "How many people would you estimate were returning fire?"

"At first maybe ten or so. By the end, maybe four or five."

I stared at him hard. "So how many Serbs do you think were still alive when you and the team departed?"

"I don't know. At least the four or five who were shooting at us. Probably a fair number of wounded, too."

"How do you think they all died?"

"My guess would be that the Serbs killed their own people."

"Why would they do that?"

"Maybe to punish 'em for being caught like that. Maybe just to make it look a lot worse than it was. Seems to have worked, too."

"Why is that?"

"Because the Army and the press all believe we massacred those guys," he said. Then his gray eyes bored into mine. "You believe we did it, too. Don't you?"

I wasn't about to answer that. "Did you?" I asked.

"No. We was just trying to escape."

I reached over and turned off the tape recorder, placed my note page back in my briefcase, and stood up as though I were ready to leave. Persico coolly watched all this, and his attorney sat perfectly still.

I walked toward the door, then turned around. "One other question, Chief. After the ambush, when you all were making time back to the Macedonian border, do you remember how many trip flares went off?"

He stroked his chin a few times. "Yeah. Two, I think."

Chapter
☆☆☆ 11

We broke for lunch at noon, right after I'd finished with Sergeant First Class Andy Caldwell, who turned out to be a well-meaning, jocular soul, and who struck me as intellectually modest and not a very meticulous observer of his environment. He was definitely not one of the leaders of the team. He was the team's heavy weapons expert, and from the best I could tell, this was the limit of his passions and talents. Everything he said closely mimicked everything Persico had said. I regarded it as a fairly useless session.

We ate in an Air Force dining facility that had a well-stocked salad bar, and Delbert and Morrow made three trips each, apparently having experienced withdrawal from the leafy stuff as a result of Imelda. Delbert had spent his morning with Staff Sergeant George Butler and Sergeant Ezekial Graves, the team medic, who was coincidentally the youngest team member. Morrow had interrogated Sergeants Brian and James Moore, twin brothers who had been with the team for six years. Next to Graves and Sanchez, this made them the team's third and fourth most recently added members.

My eager-beaver associates not only taped their interrogations, but also scrawled lots of lengthy, detailed notes on yellow legal pads. Law schools emphasize that technique, and I somehow wasn't surprised that Delbert and Morrow proved to be such conformists. The truth is, when you're busy making notes, you're not paying attention to the subject, who could be transmitting thousands of nonverbal clues, which are completely wasted on an attorney whose eyes are glued to a yellow sheet of paper. Some day, when I get to be dean of Harvard Law School, I'm going to start a movement to put an end to that stupid advice.

"Did you hear anything exciting?" I asked Delbert, who of course had to review his notes before he gave his summary.

"I spent two hours with Butler, and one hour with Graves. Both were cooperative and open. Their testimonies corresponded in nearly every way. However, neither Butler nor Graves were involved in any of the key decisions. They were essentially along for the ride."

I was astounded that he had to check his notes to make that summary. "Did they contradict anything Sanchez said?" I asked.

"Not in any significant way." Delbert studied his notes again. "Graves said he didn't see the ambush. Because he was the medic, he was positioned about a mile south of the ambush. He said he heard about seven or eight minutes of intense fire, including a couple of large explosions, but he wasn't a direct witness."

"That would make sense," I said.

According to the laws of war, medics have to act as noncombatants unless they are killing in self-defense.

"That limits what he can be charged with," Delbert continued. "Conspiracy, at most, maybe obstruction, but not murder or manslaughter."

"How'd they strike you?"

"Oddly enough, Graves was the tougher of the two. Butler is your good ol' southern boy, nice-looking, but there's something soft about him. Maybe even a little effeminate. Personally, I'd love to get him on a stand."

This is the kind of macho side comment some prosecutors are wont to mutter. Sort of like professional boxers at those orchestrated press conferences doing all that bombastic posturing about how they can't wait to get their opponent in the ring so the whole world can see who the real man is. From a purely technical standpoint, since boxers hurl big, beefy fists at each other, that brand of bellicosity might require a modicum of real guts. Delbert sounded more like a castrated squirrel mumbling about going out and finding some nuts to chew on.

"How about you?" I asked Morrow. "What did you get from the Moore twins?"

She twiddled her pencil and very conscientiously refused to study her notes. "It was weird," she answered. "I did Brian first, and when James walked in, I thought somebody screwed up and brought me Brian again. They're completely identical, even down to their voices. It was uncanny."

"And did that carry over to their statements?"

"Yes, but again, like Butler and Graves, neither was involved with the decisions. All they could do was describe the events."

"All right," I said, "here's what we're gonna do. This afternoon, I'm gonna take Perrite, while you two double-team Machusco. Perrite and Machusco were the eyes and ears of the team. They seemed to have been involved in everything."

We then quickly finished our meals, dashed off, and got ourselves repositioned in the interview rooms.

Sometimes you look at a man and just know he's a killer. That was François Perrite, a lean, swarthy Cajun with the most frigid eyes I ever saw attached to any breathing thing. Added to that, there was no break between his eyebrows. It was just one long streak of dark hair that stretched completely across his narrow forehead, running almost perfectly perpendicular to the thick black mustache above his lips. Hollywood would take one look and immediately typecast him as a bloodthirsty buccaneer.

He moved so quietly that I didn't even hear his footsteps as he walked in. I think he knew the effect he had on people, because there was this slight upward curl on his lips, like a taunting sneer.

He came without a lawyer, which I guessed was because he considered himself to be the strong, self-reliant type.

"You know the rules of this session?" I asked.

"No, tell me," he ordered as though he were talking to a waiter.

I didn't answer, but just stared at him coldly, hoping to make him uncomfortable. I didn't. He just stared back, even more coldly. I wasn't going to be able to rival those eyes of his. A man is born with eyes like that.

I very politely said, "Let's start over, Sergeant Perrite. I'm Major Drummond, the investigating officer. I'm used to being addressed by my title, or as sir."

"And I guess that's rule one, right?"

"You're catching on. Now rule two stipulates that anything you say can be used against you in a court of law. That extends to any mistruths, as those would fall under the heading of obstruction of justice and lying in an official investigation. Are you sure you don't want an attorney present?"

"I'm sure. I don't really like lawyers . . . sir."

"No? And why's that?" I asked, instantly wishing I could take that question back.

"Because they're mostly a bunch of overeducated, lying fat-asses who'd diddle their own mothers just to be able to brag they got laid once in their life."

Well, I'd asked the question, and I'd gotten a frank response, so I really had no reason to take offense. Besides, I knew my ass wasn't fat. Women were always telling me it was skinny, in a cute little way.

I leaned toward him and smiled. "Now rule three. Don't screw with me, Perrite. You're implicated in the possible murder of thirty-five men, so park your macho horseshit in a box."

I'd like to say Perrite turned red or shuffled his hands, or blinked a few times. He didn't. He gave me this look I knew I'd seen somewhere before. It took me a moment to place it. It was that squinty tightness a sniper gets just before he pulls the trigger.

I continued. "Let's start with the seventeenth, when you and Sergeant Machusco reported that you saw Serbs watching your team. Could you describe that event?"

He leaned back with an amused expression, but his lips stayed tightly shut.

I leaned toward him. "Oh, did I forget to mention rule four? This is an official investigation and I am ordering you to answer. So far, you've been convicted of nothing, but if you refuse to answer my questions, I'll convene a summary court-martial tomorrow and convict your ass for refusing a lawful order. Then we'll just start over."

He casually scratched his chin, a facile motion meant to communicate he really didn't give a damn about my threat.

But he apparently did, because he then leaned forward and planted his elbows on the table. "Machusco and I were on security for the team, and we saw a bunch of Serbs on a hill staring down at our patrol base."

"And did the Serbs see you and Machusco?"

"No."

"Why didn't they?"

"'Cause Machusco and me don't make stupid mistakes," he replied, which I guessed was probably true.

"How many Serbs did you see?"

"A few."

"Was that two? Three? Four?"

"Maybe three."

"Was it maybe three, or was it three?"

He gave me the kind of shrug a man might give who wanted to get under your skin. "Make it three . . . but then again, it might've been two . . . or four."

"And what were they doing when you spotted them?" I asked, pretending his smart-assed response didn't bother me, which fooled neither of us.

"Watching."

"Watching your team's patrol base?"

"Right."

"How far away were you?"

"'Bout a half mile. Maybe a little more."

"How do you know they were watching your patrol base?"

"Because they was staring in that direction."

"Staring with binoculars? With the naked eye?"

"Just staring."

"Were they wearing uniforms?"

"Yes."

"What kind of uniforms?"

"Camouflage."

"Who did you report that to?"

"Chief Persico."

"Why him? Why didn't you report it to Captain Sanchez?"

"Because."

"Because why? Sanchez was the team leader, wasn't he?"

"Because I couldn't find Sanchez."

"Wasn't he in the base camp?"

"I just told you I couldn't find him," he said, grinning like I was a simpleminded idiot. "How the hell do I know where he was?"

I grinned back. "Persico testified that when you told him about the Serbs, you admitted you didn't get a good look at them. His impression was that you only got a fleeting glance. Are you sure they were watching your base camp?"

"I didn't walk up to them and say, 'Yo, you assholes, you wouldn't happen to be staring at my base camp, would you?' But that was sure as shit the direction they was looking at."

"Okay. Now while your team was escaping and evading, what were you doing?"

"Machusco and I handled rear security, like always. We hung back, 'bout half a mile behind the team, puttin' down trip wires along our route."

"How many did you set?"

"I don't know. A lot."

"How did you happen to have so many flares with you?"

"Because we're the security team. We always bring lots of 'em wherever we go."

"Like how many?"

"Like about ten or fifteen each."

"Doesn't that take up a lot of room in your backpack?"

He gave me this mocking look. "Don't all them law books take up a lot of room in your office?"

"I don't have to carry my office around on my back."

"And Machusco and I get the whole team killed if we don't bring the right equipment."

"That's a good point. Now while your team was moving, were you being followed?"

"Yeah."

"How do you know that?"

"Because the Serbs kept setting off trip flares."

"How many times did that happen?"

He seemed to hesitate a moment, then gave me what I'd call a screw-off grin. "I don't rightly remember."

"You don't remember?"

"That's what I said."

"Give me a ballpark. Was it once? Was it ten times?"

"I told you I don't rightly remember."

"Captain Sanchez said it happened five times," I lied.

"Okay. Sounds about right to me."

"Persico said it happened eight times," I lied again.

"Well, Persico's miles smarter than Sanchez, so make it eight. Yeah, it was eight," he said, obviously lying right back at me.

"I'm sorry. Persico's smarter than Sanchez?"

"That's what I said."

"Smarter how?"

"Smarter like he's been in lotsa tight situations and knows what he's about. Sanchez couldn't wipe his ass without Chief's hand back there scraping away."

A very interesting observation, I decided, and one I would definitely file away for later. I wasn't going to delve into Perrite's personal likes and dislikes at this moment, however, because he struck me as the type who had lots of dislikes and rather enjoyed talking about them. He disliked lawyers, for instance.

I moved on to the next field of inquiry. "How was the decision made to execute the ambush?"

"I dunno."

"Weren't you involved?"

"No, I wasn't involved. I guess it happened sometime after we drew into a perimeter that night. Sanchez and Chief huddled together for a while, then the word got passed around to check weapons and ammo, because we were gonna ambush some Serbs. That's all I know."

"Was there anything specific that triggered that decision?"

"Yeah."

"What?"

"What? Man, ain't you been payin' attention? We was being tracked by a bunch of pissed-off Serbs who wanted to friggin' rip our guts out."

"Did more flares go off that night?"

"I don't remember."

"Come on, Sergeant. You were in charge of security for the

team, and you're trying to tell me you don't remember if any more flares went off?"

"That's right."

I opened my briefcase, withdrew a yellow legal pad, and acted like I was reviewing some notes. After about twenty pensive seconds, I said, "Captain Sanchez reported that three more flares went off, and Persico agreed with that number."

"Okay, that's right," he said. "Now that you've refreshed my memory, it happened three times."

And now that we'd confirmed he was still lying his ass off, we continued.

"Who provided the security element for the ambush?"

"I did."

"Where were you positioned?"

"I put myself about half a mile east of the ambush site. I picked a place on a hillside where I had visibility for about a mile."

"So was it your job to notify the team which column to hit?"

He nodded.

"Did you have any instructions to follow?"

"Yeah. They wanted me to pick a nice big fat column without any armored vehicles in it. I let three or four minnows pass through before I found one that was just right," he said. His eyes were lit up, the way most people would get if they were remembering the taste of a thick, cold milkshake on a hot summer's day, or their first roll in the hay with that big-bosomed high school sweetheart.

"Did you participate in the ambush itself?"

"No. I stayed in my position, watching to see if any more Serb columns or vehicles was coming. If that happened, I was supposed to warn the team that it was time to disengage and pull out."

"Then I guess you don't know what happened at the ambush site itself?"

He gave me a sharp shrug of disappointment. "I heard shots and explosions, and I heard stories afterward, but I didn't see nothing. When the ambush was over, I rejoined the rest of the team at the designated rally point, about a mile south of the ambush site."

"And then you continued your E&E?"

"That's right."

I turned off the tape recorder and shoved my papers back inside the briefcase. Perrite watched this with his deadly little eyes and his taunting grin.

"Thank you, Sergeant," I said in my most civil tone. "You've been extremely helpful."

"How helpful?" he asked, studying my face.

I shrugged. "Extremely."

For the first time, he appeared to lose his composure, and I departed with a smug sense of self-satisfaction. The truth was, he hadn't been the least bit helpful. The bigger truth was that I wanted him to stay awake in his cell all night, worrying that he'd given me some earthshaking revelations.

Chapter ☆☆ 12

Imelda and two of her most homely assistants flew in that afternoon to begin the process of preparing written transcripts of the taped interviews. She booked a room at our hotel that she and her crew turned into a makeshift office.

Delbert and Morrow were not expecting to see her, and both involuntarily gasped when we walked into the room and there sat her two aides deliriously pounding away on their transcribers, with Imelda hunched over behind them.

Imelda glanced up and smacked her lips a few times in anticipation. "Well, well," she loudly declared, "if it isn't the yuppie lawyers. Hmmph! You've been here two days—three lawyers—and all you've got is ten hours of tape. What the hell have you been doin'? Drinkin' and screwin' off?"

Morrow shot me a fast, sheepish look, since Imelda obviously had half her story. Too bad about that other half, I thought to myself. Delbert drew himself upright, and a pained expression popped onto his face.

"Look," he said, bleeding wounded dignity all over the floor, "we've been working around the clock. You don't just walk into interrogatories without preparation. Since you aren't an attorney, I wouldn't expect you to know this, but every hour of questions takes at least three hours of preparation."

Imelda slid her gold-rimmed glasses down to the tip of her short nose, and had I been more merciful, I would've found a way to warn Delbert that this apparently innocuous gesture was akin to a gunslinger unclipping his holster. She lowered her head and peered long and hard at Delbert. I edged away from him, because I sure as hell didn't want to get hit by any stray shots.

"Okay, smarty pants, are you gonna try to tell me you spent twenty hours preparing to ask a few questions? What kind of fool do you take me for?"

"I did," Delbert staunchly insisted. "And although I certainly don't have to prove anything to you, I can show you the notes I made to prove it."

She gave him this careful examining look. "Notes?"

"Yes. That's right. I always make notes."

"What's it say in those notes?"

"I list questions I intend to ask. I draw pert charts . . . uh, flow diagrams, if you will, of the directions the interrogatory might take, and how I should respond."

"I know what a damned pert chart is, fancy pants. You actually read those notes when you're interrogating?"

"Sure. That's the whole point. That's how I stay ahead of the man I'm interrogating."

A huge guffaw exploded from Imelda's throat, and she wiggled around in her seat and nodded at her two assistants, both of whom chuckled a few times as well.

"What's so funny?" Delbert demanded.

Imelda shook her head. "Damn, I should have guessed."

"Guessed what?"

"Nothing."

"No, tell me," Delbert beseeched.

"That's why your tapes sounded that way."

"Sounded what way? What's wrong with my tapes?"

Imelda just kept shaking her head in disbelief. Poor Delbert was nervously wringing his hands. Finally he looked over at me.

I shrugged. "Sorry, Delbert, I haven't listened to your tapes. I haven't got a clue what you screwed up."

He spun back to Imelda. "Did I do something wrong in my interrogatories?"

She kept shaking her head. "Notes. I should have guessed. No damn wonder," was all she said.

Delbert stormed over to the table where his tapes were neatly stacked, grabbed them, and stomped from the room. As soon as he was gone, Imelda cackled a few times, then got up and rejoined her girls, both of whom were quaking with repressed giggles. Morrow and I walked out right after Delbert.

Morrow looked at me in complete confusion. "What the hell was that about?" she asked.

"What? That?" I asked, trying to pretend innocence.

"Tell me. Did Delbert do something wrong?"

"Why? Don't tell me you prepare notes, too?"

"Of course I do. Is something wrong with that?"

I smirked, but said as sincerely as I could, "No. Nothing. Really. It's a very admirable trait."

"Then what was that about?"

"It's Imelda's law. She opens every reunion by gnawing your ass for not working hard enough. It only lasts a few seconds, and it's harmless. The approved response is to wince slightly, nod humbly, and swear to do better. The cardinal sin is to argue, or try to justify."

"I still don't get it."

"What do you think Delbert's going to do with those tapes?"

"Figure out what he did wrong."

"Yep. He's going to stay up all night, listening over and over to those tapes. By morning, he will have dissected his own performance to pieces. He's going to be a nervous wreck. He'll be wondering about every question he asked. His confidence will be shot."

She didn't believe me. "Imelda's not that devious, and he's not that stupid."

"Yeah, you're probably right," I lied. Imelda was beyond devious. The woman could give Machiavelli lessons. What I was interested to see was whether Morrow was going to inform Delbert that Imelda had only been screwing with him.

The three of us got back together at seven and spent three hours reviewing what we'd heard, as well as what we'd learned, which, from my viewpoint anyway, wasn't anywhere near the same thing as what we'd heard.

Delbert and Morrow's session with Sergeant Machusco apparently went a lot like my session with Perrite, which is to say that Machusco also proved to be about as charming as a rattlesnake in heat. Morrow described him as a sinister-looking Italian boy from south Brooklyn who, if he wasn't in the Army, would probably have been back on the streets of New York knocking off hits for the mob. And doing really well at it, too.

A-teams, like most Army units, start with a raw mixture of men who eventually organize themselves into an operating entity. Those men with average talents tend to be made into common riflemen whose sole responsibility is to shuffle along with the flow and act when told. Most freeze with fear the moment the bullets start flying. They contribute nothing to the battle. That's why, in the old days of Napoleon and Frederick the Great, they used to post all these big, gnarly sergeants in the rear ranks, where their job was to put a musket ball into the back of any man who failed to methodically load and fire his weapon in the face of withering enemy fire. Today's average soldier knows there's no bloodthirsty, implacable sergeant in the rear ranks. He also knows somewhere deep inside that he is average, and he isn't about to risk everything to prove that he is anything more than that.

The most deadly men, the ones who are able to kill with re-
flexive skill, who are natural woodsmen, who can think on their
feet in the most taxing circumstances, usually are the ones made
responsible for those special functions upon which the survival
of the unit depends. That was Machusco and Perrite.

"They're scary," Delbert said.

I nodded. "Every army, from the beginning of time, has attracted men like them. It's a good thing, too. If there wasn't an
army for them to join, they'd be out on the streets looking for
blood. This way, at least, they kill for the good of the country
and for their comrades in arms."

"How reassuring," Delbert said with a really irritating, prig-
gish twang.

"Actually, it is," I told him. "That Desert Storm image of all
those nice little knights in shining armor always was pure
horsecrap. Nearly all the best soldiers out there, if you scratched
the surface, they all had a little bit of psychopath hidden somewhere in there. With some of them, you didn't have to scratch
the surface real deep. A completely sane and balanced man is a
fish out of water on a battlefield."

Morrow coughed a few times, which was her subtle way of
intimating that it was late, and all this philosophical talk was
great, but did it really have anything to do with completing this
investigation? Women hate it when men talk about cars and
broads and war.

"Did any of us hear anything today that contradicted their
main defense?" she asked, trying to steer us back on course.

"I didn't," Delbert said.

"That depends," I replied. "They're all vomiting out the same
general concept, but they're walking all over each other on the
details."

Delbert gave me a speculative look. "Maybe, but I sure wouldn't
want to try to prosecute them."

"No?" I asked.

He began ticking down fingers. "One, they have a splendid justification for what they did. Two, they were the only witnesses. Three, as you admitted, they're all telling the same story. Four, and most ominously, it's an incredibly believable story."

I said, "Then you think they've got a good defense?"

Delbert nodded, while Morrow said, "No, Major, not a good defense. They've got a great defense."

"Aha, haven't you overlooked one inconvenient little fact? What about those little holes in the heads of the Serbs?"

Morrow said, "Maybe Persico was right. Maybe the Serbs did it themselves to fabricate an atrocity."

"Then why haven't the Serbs blown the whistle on it?" I asked.

Delbert quickly said, "I don't know. Maybe they're just waiting to see what we do. Maybe they're keeping that revelation in reserve, just in case we conclude that Sanchez's ambush was justified."

"Like blackmail?" I asked.

"Sure. It's brilliant, if you think about it. We recommend against charging Sanchez's team, then the Serbs convene another big press conference. They hand out the close-ups of the holes in the head and announce what our troops did to their people. We'd be stuck looking like we tried to cover it up. Better yet, the Serbs now know that we know. That's probably why Milosevic was so willing to let us visit the morgue."

"So you think that's it? A setup?" I asked.

Delbert stood up and began pacing, a very distracting habit that seems to be common among lawyers. For some reason, many can barely utter a word unless they're on their feet. It's like the blood has to rush out of their brain before their lips can move.

"Who knows?" he said, gesturing with his arms as though this were a courtroom. "Maybe they were polished off by a roving band of Albanians who heard the shots and made it to the ambush site before the Serbs. The corpses were shot with M16s. The Kosovars are armed with U.S. weapons."

"I suppose that's another possibility," I admitted.

"The problem is that all the possibilities are just conjecture. The most critical fact is that Sanchez and his team are the only surviving witnesses."

"And the inconsistencies don't bother you?" I asked.

"You mean that flare thing you keep bringing up?"

"Yeah. How about that flare thing?"

"To be perfectly honest, I don't understand why you keep focusing on it. I don't wish to be offensive, but I think it's asinine. First of all, it's completely irrelevant. Second, under similar circumstances, I doubt I could recall how many flares were set, and how many went off. I think those men were scared witless, running for their lives, physically and mentally exhausted, and in the midst of everything else, nobody was keeping a running diary of how many flares went off."

"He's right," Morrow said. "Any experienced defense attorney would turn you into hamburger if you tried to bring that up in a courtroom."

"You don't think it impugns their integrity?"

"No, I think Delbert's right. I think we can keep probing at little details, and we'll find all kinds of tiny incongruencies, but it has to be something that's tangible, something germane. On every important thing that happened out there, they're in total agreement. And they are the only living witnesses. You can't prosecute without witnesses."

"So you believe they're innocent?" I asked them.

Delbert said, "I believe we have to strongly consider that possibility. I've seen nothing that indicates otherwise."

I looked at Morrow.

"Let's just say I'm a lot less convinced they murdered those men than I was two days ago, before I heard their side. Don't tell me you aren't, too."

I looked from her to Delbert. They expected me to say I thought the men were guilty as hell. So far I had not agreed with either of them on anything and, judging by their peevish expressions, they weren't anticipating a precedent.

"What I believe is that every man I've talked to so far has lied to me. Some in small ways, others in large ways. Men lie for a reason. They had a week together to cook up a common defense. Hell, maybe they cooked it up while they were still out there and just improved on it in detention. Something doesn't smell right."

"You can't convict a man on smell," Delbert said.

"Well, yeah, actually you can," I said, vaguely recalling the case of a notorious rapist who wore a mask, and although none of his victims was able to visually identify him, the fact that he had earned the nom de guerre of "Stinky" proved enough to undo him.

I stared at Delbert. "Have you ever had a near-death experience? Maybe when you were driving and someone ran a red light and nearly plowed into you?"

"Sure, everybody has."

"Describe it."

"It happened a few years ago. I was driving down 95 to Florida when a semi crossed lanes and came at me head-on."

"Day or night?"

"Daytime."

"Did you honk your horn?"

"It happened too fast. There wasn't time."

"What did you do?"

"I swerved hard to the right and went off the road."

"Did you hit another car?"

"No. There was no other traffic."

"Did you hit any trees?"

"I almost did, but I steered hard to the left and avoided them."

"What kind of trees?"

"Scrub pine."

"What color was the semi?"

"Red."

"You remember all that clearly? There's still a clear picture in your mind?"

"Yes, but I don't agree with the point you're trying to make."

"That's because you haven't been in combat. Your senses become razor-sharp. Why do you think all those old World War Two veterans can still sit around telling fifty-year-old war stories and recall every detail vividly, like it happened only yesterday, when most of them couldn't remember a single word their wife said at breakfast that morning?"

Delbert said, "Nobody listens to their wives at breakfast. Besides, I'd love to get nine of those veterans on a witness stand and see how well their creaking, antiquated memories really correspond."

"You'd be surprised," I told him. "I can recall almost every waking hour that I was in combat. The exhaustion, strain, and fear don't dull your senses. Your brain has to work in overdrive just to function. You don't forget things like how many flares went off or who told you the Serbs were following you, or how many Serbs were on the hillside looking down on your position. It's like Sam Peckinpah has taken hold of your mental faculties."

Delbert said, "I'll take your word for it. But I also know that nine sets of eyes, collecting images from nine different perspectives, then shoving them across nine different sets of synapses and neurons, are apt to process things a bit differently. Any experienced attorney or investigator knows that."

"What about the fact that Sanchez never reported the situation they were in, nor did he report the ambush, even after they'd extricated?"

"I don't know," Delbert said. "It's an intriguing question. Maybe he was worried about the repercussions. He's been passed over for major once. This year is his last chance. He's got a wife, two kids, and a file that's borderline. He'd be dead in the water if someone decided they didn't like how he got his team out of there."

Morrow, who had been idly watching us argue, tapped her pencil on the table a few times to get our attention. She was going to make a fine judge someday.

She stared at me. "I watched you with Sanchez. I thought you were bullying him."

"So you thought my interrogation technique was flawed?"

"It *was* flawed. You browbeat him into making inaccurate statements. I haven't listened to the tapes, but maybe you did that with the others as well."

"Come on, Morrow, these are battle-hardened veterans."

"And this is the Army, and you've got those big, shiny, gold major's leaves pinned to your collar. Most of them are noncoms, and now you're wondering why they lied about how many flares went off."

"You think I badgered them?"

She gave me an exasperated look. "I think you're predisposed. That's the way you come off. You made them nervous. I'm not saying they're innocent; I'm saying your approach was flawed."

"She's right," Delbert said.

I could've defended myself, but the truth is, they were right. I was predisposed. I believed in my bones that Sanchez and his men were lying. And if you could call dubious looks, eye-rolling, verbal baiting, and finger-pointing a bullying technique, then I was guilty. I'd used the authority of my rank and the odor of my official position to coerce them into answering my questions. I could see where Delbert and Morrow thought that I'd instigated the very inconsistencies, mistruths, and fabrications I was now complaining about.

These were seriously frightened men. On a battlefield, you

have about a millisecond to decide whether you want to be a hero or a coward. More often than not, you don't even decide, you just leap toward your fate.

Most of these men were as courageous as lions on a battle-field, but this was not a battlefield. Here they had time to weigh the repercussions and decide a course. And, in an odd sort of way, what could come out of this investigation was far worse than losing a leg or an arm, or even their lives. These men accepted the prospect of becoming maimed or even dead; they did not accept the loss of their honor. They had families and careers and reputations. They were facing humiliation and imprisonment. They were facing everlasting shame upon themselves, their Army, and their country.

I understood all that. I understood it before I ever asked my first question.

I smiled warmly at Delbert and Morrow, just to show them that I could take their criticism without any hard feelings. In my most penitent tone I told them, "You're right—both of you—and I'll try to do better next time."

It was a lie, of course. Something was seriously wrong with the story Sanchez and his men were telling. I'd break all their legs and arms if that was what it took to get to the bottom of it.

Chapter
☆ ☆
☆ **13**

Early the next morning, we all checked out of our rooms and trundled back out to the airfield. We climbed into another of those ubiquitous C-130s that, as I mentioned earlier, have no soundproofing. We all stuffed in our earplugs and felt grateful we'd been relieved of the obligation to converse.

Poor Delbert looked like death warmed over. There were dark shadows under his eyes. His hair hung limp and unwashed. At various times during the flight, I could see his lips moving as though he was rehearsing something over and over, like possibly the questions he had asked during the interrogatories. Imelda sat directly across from him and somehow maintained a perfectly straight face. I glanced over at Morrow, and she immediately tore her eyes away. Maybe she was worried that I still had a grudge from last night's session. Maybe it was because she hadn't informed Delbert about Imelda's devious bent and I'd just caught her in the act.

As soon as we landed, we went back to our little wooden building. Imelda and her girls began filing and faxing all kinds of things. There was a message for me to call General Clapper, so I went into my office and rang up the Pentagon.

Clapper's ever-efficient secretary answered on the first ring and put me right through.

"How was Aviano?" he asked.

"Nice place. Next time I do a crime, promise to lock me up in an Air Force facility. I smelled lobster and champagne on the prisoners' breaths. By the way, I see you're working early," I mentioned, since it was 6 A.M., his time.

"Just trying to catch up," he groused. "Spent nearly the whole damned evening over at the White House."

"They're not still talking about me over there?"

"Your name popped up a few times, but you're passé, no longer the topic du jour."

"What was the subject?"

"They wanted me to help brainstorm the options."

"Options? What options?"

"Option one is you recommend a court-martial. Option two is you don't."

"Don't they have better things to do, like feed the homeless, fix the interest rates, check out the boobs on the new crop of interns?"

"It's not so simple, Sean. The President's policy on Kosovo does not enjoy wide national support if you haven't noticed. Hell, it's not even being called our national policy. It's called the President's War. They're scared."

"Scared of what?"

"This thing's been presented as the first war fought solely on moral grounds. That's how they're justifying it. It's a war based solely on principle. So, let's say you go with option one. See any problem there?"

"No. The actions of a few men shouldn't undermine the moral underpinnings of the President's policy."

"That's because you and I don't live, breathe, and eat politics the way those guys over in the White House do. They're catching hell from some of our allies. Some of the Republicans up on the Hill are threatening to cut off all funding and hold hearings."

"So this is a battle for the high ground."

"You might call it that. Now the other alternative is you recommending that there's insufficient grounds for a court-martial."

"And what's wrong with that one?"

"Nothing, unless it's due to insufficient evidence. Here we are dropping bombs on a bunch of Serbs we publicly vilify as war criminals, and it turns out we have some of our own war criminals. Only thing is, we let them go scot-free. God forbid we ever eventually capture Milosevic and his bloodthirsty henchmen. The moment we attempt to try them for war crimes, we'll be branded the biggest hypocrites there ever were."

"Rules of evidence are rules of evidence."

"You know that, and I know that, because we're lawyers and knowing that's a condition of our employment. Joe Sixpack doesn't understand it, though. As for the rest of the world, they haven't got a clue what our crazy legal system's all about."

"So the only thing that works for them is if I say Sanchez's team acted responsibly and innocently?"

"Did they?" he asked a little too quickly, which was a good omen of where he was now coming from.

"I still don't know. They've got a good tale to tell. It just doesn't all add up."

"Does it not add up a lot, or only a little?"

"Depends who's listening. I think there's some gaping holes and inconsistencies that might collapse the whole thing."

"Can you prove that?"

"Not yet. Inconveniently, Sanchez's team are the only living witnesses."

"But their stories coincide?"

"Except for some details."

"Then maybe they're telling the truth."

"I don't think they are."

There was a moment of awkward quiet before Clapper said, "Sean, do you know my one reservation when I recommended you for this?"

"Reservation? I didn't know you had any reservations."

"Your infantry background. I was worried that you'd start trying to second-guess what Sanchez and his men did out there, the decisions they made, the way they handled themselves."

"What makes you think I'm doing that?"

"I'm not saying you are. I'm just warning you not to get all caught up in little details, like who held whose rucksack during the ambush."

"Thanks, General, I'll bear that in mind."

"Uh . . . there's another thing."

"Another thing?"

"A decision was made to shorten the time line. It's no longer twenty-one days."

I said, "You're kidding, right?" because I couldn't think of anything more clever to say.

"No. The White House thinks this is dragging out too long. They're taking ungodly political heat. They want it wrapped up in ten days."

"Ten? That's ten days from today, right?" I asked.

"That's ten from when you started. Six days from today."

"Any reason I should know about?"

"Sean, is this a problem? If it is, I can find someone to replace you."

"No, it's no problem," I said, trying to sound reasonable.

"Good. I know you're doing a great job, Sean. Just stay with it."

I chewed on my tongue for a moment, then very briskly said, "Right, thanks."

I hung up the phone. I took three deep breaths. I yanked the phone out of its socket, took careful aim, then flung it with great force against the wall. There was a loud, satisfying crash as the phone punched right through the wallboard and ended up with the base still in my office and the handpiece dangling through the hole.

One of Imelda's assistants rushed to the door and stuck her head in. It was the one whose head looked like a big, mottled grapefruit with tiny glasses. She took one look at my face, blinked once or twice, quickly backed away, then frantically scurried from desk to desk and warned everybody to stay the hell away from me.

Either Delbert or Morrow had ratted me out. Hell, maybe they'd both ratted me out. I could just hear their two voices on the phone, competing to see who could outrat who.

It's not that I expected loyalty, because most lawyers can barely spell the word. But there's disloyalty, and then there's something that flies unspeakably beyond those bounds. It was a really good thing neither of them were here at this moment. They'd look damned silly with a telephone sticking out their butts.

And why did I get this sudden feeling that Clapper had just subtly pressured me to declare these men completely innocent of all possible charges? I wanted to vomit—and I might have— except I'm too cool for that.

I had trusted Clapper completely. Worse, I owed him. This was the same guy who gave me my start in law, literally in a classroom at Fort Benning, then later when I needed the Army to sponsor me through law school. He was also the man who picked me for this job. Until now, I'd just assumed it was because I was the hotshot young lawyer he'd always wished he'd been. Okay, that's an exaggeration, but I at least thought he liked me.

Somebody at the White House must've really put his balls in an intolerable vise, because until this moment he'd been very high and mighty about seeking the truth. Or maybe he'd just been pumping me full of bullshit to prepare for this moment.

They say that the devil makes sure the wicked get more than

their share of luck, and just at that moment there was a timid knock on my office door. It slowly opened, and another of Imelda's assistants, the one who strongly resembled a saber-toothed tiger, cautiously stuck her long, narrow face in.

"Uh, Major . . . excuse me," she kind of whispered, like she didn't want to start an avalanche.

I looked up and tried to control my temper. "What?"

"There's a man here to see you. A civilian."

"Does he have a name?"

"I asked him, but he wouldn't tell me."

"Did you ask him nicely?"

She giggled a little too nervously, the way some people do when they're placing blasting caps inside C4 explosive. "If you'd like, sir, I'll tell him you're busy."

"No, show him in," I said.

For some reason or other, nearly all reporters, when they're in the field, like to wear those silly-looking tan vests. You know the type, the ones that have a dozen or so pockets, like bird shooters use, so they can have a handy place to tuck all that ammo they're going to use against all those vicious ducks and geese.

This man wore one of those vests, only it was a really big one, more like a tent with pockets. He looked to be about three hundred pounds. He was a little shorter than me and about thrice as wide. The word "lardass" instantly popped to mind, and I instinctively looked around to see if there was any chair in my office that was sturdy enough to handle him. There wasn't.

"Hi," he said, real friendly-like, as his beady little eyes did a quick inspection, apparently also seeking a chair. "You must be Major Drummond."

"Says so on my nametag," I replied, pointing down at my chest.

"Hah-hah," he laughed, waddling forward. "That's a really good one."

"Actually it wasn't all that funny the first time you heard it, and it hasn't improved with age."

His laughing stopped. "You know who I am?"

"Mr. Berkowitz, right?"

He gave me this ingratiating smile. "Hey, no hard feelings, right?"

"Hard feelings?" I asked with an inquisitive frown. "Why would I have hard feelings?"

"Come on."

"No, what?"

"You're screwin' with me, right?"

"I'm sorry, Mr. Berkowitz, we don't get the *Washington Herald* out here. Is there something I should know about?"

This sly grin crossed his lips. "Nah. It's just that some military guys don't like my writing slant very much. I always worry about it."

"Well, don't. I never read the papers. They make pretty good toilet paper in an emergency, but of course, then you end up with all this black ink stuck to your fanny, which is damned hard to explain to your proctologist."

He edged over and planted his big ass on the corner of my desk. "Hah-hah! That's a good one, too. By the way, call me Jeremy." He stuck out his hand.

"Nice to meet you, Jeremy. Call me Major Drummond."

"Okay, if that's what you're comfortable with," he said, becoming more amiable by the second now that he thought I didn't know he'd raped me on the front page of his paper.

"So what're you doing out this way, Jeremy? Checking out the good restaurants?"

"Hah-hah." He gave me another dose of that same phony laugh. "Actually, I'm doing a story on how the operation's going.

Of course, I'm also working on the ambush story, and I thought I'd stop by and see if you changed your mind."

"Changed my mind?"

"Yeah. About talking with me."

"Geesh, this is tough, Jeremy. I'd love to, I really would."

"Then what's stopping you?"

I rubbed my jaw a few times and gave him the squinty, calculating look people say makes me resemble a Turkish rug merchant. "Well, there's a certain amount of risk in it for me. I mean, what do I get out of it? I just don't see that it's worth my risk."

Jeremy stared at my desktop for a moment, contemplating this new twist. Then he tentatively said, "The paper provides me this very tiny pool of money for occasions like this. Perhaps a small emolument would be in order?"

I got rid of the rug merchant look and replaced it with my best "Gee, I'm shocked as hell" look. "Jeremy!" I yelled.

"Sorry," he declared, quite insincerely, "I didn't mean to insult you, but lots of you military guys insist on being paid."

"You're shitting me."

"No, really. I'm talking colonels, even some generals."

"Generals?"

"Greediest sons of bitches you ever saw."

"Was that how you got my name? Did you pay someone for it?"

"I didn't pay anyone, but that's as much as I'm gonna say."

I grinned. "Yeah, sure. More power to you. In fact, confidentiality was gonna be one of my requirements."

He gave me this real righteous look and sketched a cross on his heart. "They could stick hot pokers up my ass and I wouldn't divulge."

By the look of him I suspected he might be telling the truth. About the hot poker thing, anyway. But just wave one juicy Big Mac under this guy's nose and he'd be singing arias.

Then he said, "What other requirements you got?"

"I want a two-way street. I give you info, you give me info."

He actually looked relieved. "Just info? That's all? Hey, no problem."

"Okay, me first. What nasty rumors are you hearing back in Washington about the investigation?"

"I would've thought you'd know more about that than me."

"Well, I'm stuck out here, and like I said, I don't read the papers."

He grinned. "The stuff I'll give you, you won't find in the papers. Least, not yet."

"Like what, Jeremy?"

He bent toward me, very conspiratorially. "Well, did you know, for instance, that the President starts every day with a fifteen-minute update on your investigation?"

I tried my best not to look surprised. "Of course he does," I said, as though I already knew that, as though where else could the briefer possibly be getting his information, if not from me? Except that I hadn't given out fifteen minutes of information on the investigation since we started. Not to anyone, not even Clapper. So where the hell was the information coming from?

"They say this thing has him tied up in knots," he added. "The press secretary says that's because his conscience is eating him alive, that the thought that our soldiers—American soldiers—would massacre a bunch of Serbs has him begging forgiveness from the Lord every night."

"But you don't believe that?" I asked.

"The only time that son of a bitch prays is when a camera's around. And if he's got a conscience, it's news to me. News to his wife, too, I'd imagine."

"Maybe he's worried that this thing might erode support for the whole operation."

Berkowitz jumped off the desk and his whole body shook

like a bag of Jell-O that had been tossed out of an airplane. "Horsecrap."

"You don't think it would do serious damage to the cause if those men are guilty?"

"People ain't stupid, Major. Besides, what's there to erode? There is no support for this thing. Okay, my turn, right?"

"Shoot."

"What'd you do before you became a JAG officer?"

"I was an infantry officer."

"Where? What unit?"

"Bragg, with the 82nd Airborne. Hoorah!"

His arms reached out and his hands landed on my desk. He looked like a bent-over egg with a smug scowl. "Well, that's the interesting thing, Major. See, I got a copy of your personnel file from one of my buddies."

"Yeah?"

"And that's what it says in your file, so I called a buncha friends of mine who were in the 82nd at the same time. Now here's a coincidence. One of my buddies was actually a captain in the same battalion your file says you were in."

"So?"

"So he never heard of you before."

"That is odd," I said. "I mean, there's only like forty officers in a battalion."

"Yeah, isn't it."

"Either he was in a different battalion or you must've misread my file."

"Could be."

"Yeah," I said, "probably that's exactly what happened."

"So why do you think you were picked to be the chief investigating officer? I mean, no offense, but this is a pretty big one. Wouldn't you think the Army would pick someone more senior?"

"Gee, I don't know," I said. "Must be because I'm shit-hot and have ethics like a rock."

"I've got a more interesting theory."

"I'm not sure I want to hear it."

He took his hands off my desk and went over and stood by the wall to contemplate my face from a safer distance.

"There's this very special unit down at Bragg that's so outrageously secret that nobody's ever supposed to have heard of it. Anyone assigned to that unit, while they're in it, their files are separated from the rest of the Army's and are administered by a special cell. Of course, once these guys leave that unit . . . well, then they gotta have regular files like everyone else. So what happens is their files are filled in with units they never really served in."

"They really do that?" I asked.

"They really do," he said, grinning. "Nearly always they list units at Bragg. That way, if these guys are ever asked, they can at least sound like they know something about the base."

"Damn, that's really cunning of the Army," I said.

"Of course, those guys are never allowed to disclose they've been in that unit, or even that it exists. But it does. Kind of like Delta, that other unit that doesn't really exist, only the boys in this outfit are tougher, more deadly, and do more dangerous stuff."

"Isn't that something. Here I've been in the Army all these years and never heard of any such thing."

"Really something," he said. "Now, just for the sake of argument, let's say a Special Forces A-team went out and did a very bad thing while they were performing a very secret mission. Then, let's say, just for argument's sake, that the Army actually had a lawyer who used to belong to that special unit that doesn't exist."

"A guy could write a real great novel about something like that, couldn't he?"

"Or a few really good newspaper articles. I mean, why would the Army pick a guy like that to head up the investigation?"

"First, there would have to be such a guy. Personally, I did my time in an infantry battalion in the 82nd, and if you'd like, I'll bring you some witnesses—"

"Of course you did, Major. But what would worry me is that the Army might pick just such a guy because he'd be most likely to feel some sympathy for that A-team. Hell, after living in a secret world, where he's had to lie to everyone he knows about what he does, he might even be more inclined to help build a cover for that team."

I grinned at him, and he grinned back at me.

Then he added, "Of course, like I said, all of this was just for the sake of argument."

"Is there a point to this argument?"

"No, it's only academic. After all, you've already agreed to cooperate with me, so there's really no need for me to see how far I could go in checking this story."

"That's good, because it's all wrong," I said.

We both chuckled at the irony of that. There's nothing like starting a relationship of trust based on what we both knew was an outright lie.

"So," he said, "what's their story?"

"Their story is that they were detected by the Serbs and had to fight their way out. The team leader felt the Serbs were boxing his team in. He decided that ambushing a large column was the best way to make the Serbs believe his unit was larger than it was and to make the Serbs slow down and become more cautious."

Berkowitz let out a loud whistle. "No kidding."

"That's what they say."

"You believe 'em?"

"So far, sure. It meets with the facts, and all nine men are telling the same tale."

His eyes kind of lit up, and the letters PULITZER seemed to emerge on his forehead. "Jesus, what a great story line."

"Yeah, it really is, isn't it."

"Here these poor bastards were, trapped behind enemy lines, doing a secret mission this administration ordered them to do. They fight their way out, and instead of getting the medals they deserve, they get stuffed behind bars and investigated like common criminals."

"That about sums it up," I said. "Frankly, it's an embarrassment for me to be part of this. I almost can't stand to look those men in the eyes. I mean, these guys are genuine heroes."

"No kidding."

"Nope, no kidding."

His face got very serious. "You're sure you're not kidding, right?"

"God's honest truth. Left to me, I'd wrap this whole thing up in two days. Only problem is, one of the other investigating team members is a real prick and seems dead set on proving they did something wrong. He keeps nitpicking little details, even though all he's doing is making a damned nuisance out of himself. The rest of us are convinced he's an idiot and these men are innocent."

I could see he was now itching to race out of my office and file a story. The international press were all convinced these guys had committed a heinous crime, and now Jeremy Berkowitz was about to break the *real* story, that these men were not only innocent, but heroes to boot. He'd paint the administration as cruel and unfair for persecuting these poor, decent guys who were only doing their job the best they knew how. The story would play well. The President, everybody knew, was a draft-dodgin' lefty who once wrote a letter about how much he detested the military. He wrote that letter a long time before, in a very different era, but the opposing party had a copy of that letter engraved in bronze and kept shoving it in everybody's face every time the President did anything that could halfway be construed as antimilitary, or antidefense, or anti-American. According to the opposing party, about everything the President ever did fell into one of those categories, and now Berkowitz here was staring at yet another opportunity to remind the great unwashed public that the President once wrote such a letter.

He walked toward the door, then turned around. His feet did this little shifting thing. "You know I have to refer to you in the story?"

"Uh, actually, no," I lied. "I hadn't thought about that."

"I'd like to call you 'a source on the investigating team.' Anything more generic and the story loses credibility. My editors, and the public, they have to know this is coming from inside."

"I don't know . . . there's only a few of us . . . and, uh—"

"Hey, Major, I've never had a source caught. Trust me on this."

I let out a heavy sigh and scratched my head a few times. Finally, I reluctantly said, "If it's absolutely necessary, then okay."

I felt pretty smug when Berkowitz walked out the door. It isn't often when you get two vindictive retaliations for the price of one. Berkowitz would print his story, make a big splash, bask in his fifteen minutes of glory, then as soon as I proved that Sanchez and his team had cold-bloodedly murdered the Serbs, he'd look like a worldwide horse's ass.

The White House and Clapper would have no reason to suspect me of being the leaker. I had pooh-poohed myself in the story. Pretty slick that. Now Delbert or Morrow or whoever was leaking on me was going to be suspected of leaking to the press also.

About a minute after Berkowitz departed, the door flew open and in marched Imelda. She shut the door behind her, then plopped into a seat in front of my desk.

She snorted once or twice, then said, "That a reporter?"

"Yep."

"That the same reporter that wrote that shitty article?"

"One and the same, Imelda."

She seemed to consider that a moment. She played with her hair and fiddled with the rim on her glasses. Then she gave me this stern, disapproving glare, which, given that this was Imelda Pepperfield, could burn paint off walls.

"You sure you know what you're doing?"

"No, I'm not."

"Reporters are nothing but low-life trash. Don't you let him come suckin' up here again, stinkin' up my building. Got that?"

"Sure, Imelda. And thanks."

She pushed herself out of her chair, grunted something brief that sounded either like, "You're really very welcome, sir, and I admire the hell out of you," or "Frigamugit," then shuffled back out.

In her inimitable way, she was warning me that the surest way to get caught leaking to the press was to allow Berkowitz to show his face here again. What a woman.

Chapter
☆☆ 14

Henry Kissinger once said that just because you're paranoid doesn't mean they really aren't trying to get you. Suddenly I was beginning to think it was true, he was right, and he'd been talking about me.

Someone inside my organization was leaking things to somebody who worked for the President of the United States, who, for some inexplicable reason, spent his early mornings listening to someone talking about me. One, or maybe both, of my co-investigators was spilling their guts about how incompetent I am to the chief of the Army's JAG Corps. A ruthlessly ambitious reporter knew something very dangerous about my background, and to top everything off, the very same general who got me this assignment had suddenly developed a severe case of character deficiency.

That's a fairly long list of crappy things to discover in only one day. The problem was, like most paranoids, I wanted someone to lash out at. But who?

There were Delbert and Morrow, neither of whom I knew anything about. That is, aside from what I'd read in their legal and personnel files. Of course, those files came from Clapper's office, and I suddenly found myself wondering if they were authentic. As Mssr. Berkowitz had discovered, not all Army files are what they purport to be. Then there was Imelda's chorus of four legal assistants, any of whom could be passing information along.

I kind of wanted the mole to be Delbert, since I didn't like him all that much. He struck me as an uptight pretty boy who would put a shiv in his own mother to get ahead. I was praying it wasn't Morrow. She was gorgeous and had those sympathetic eyes, and I really wanted to see if the body underneath those running pants matched the fervid extremes of my imagination. I'd already built myself this nice little scenario where I cracked the case, got the pretty girl, and rode off into the sunset. I love Imelda, but she was a little too old and gnarly to be climbing up on the back of my horse. It had to be Morrow or nobody. The problem was that Morrow was every bit as scheming and ambitious as Delbert, and as I'd already discovered, she could run circles around him in the sly and devious categories. Sly and devious just happened to be the traits of whoever was ratting me out.

Then just as I'm about to nod off, a new hallucination slowly interrupted my progress. If these guys in Washington were going to all this trouble, they must know something. Something really awful. Like maybe this was one of those White House conspiracies they always make such great movies about, the ones where all these guys in Brooks Brothers power suits get together and start manipulating the organs of government in sinister ways to . . .

This was when I decided that I was going way too far. The problem with paranoia is that it sneaks up on you. You start by wondering why the guy next door didn't invite you to his barbecue. Then you're convinced the whole neighborhood's in on the conspiracy. Then you're passing out literature about the Trilateral Commission. Then before you know it there's a high-powered rifle in your hands, and you're on a rooftop, and there's a bunch of angry cops scurrying around who really are trying to get you.

Maybe Clapper just guessed that I was getting bogged down in details. Maybe he really was concerned about my unique background and how that might make me inquisitive about all sorts of innocuous little things that really have nothing to do with guilt or innocence. And now that I thought about it, he never actually came out and asked me to give Sanchez and his crew a clean slate. He just hinted how convenient that would be. What the hell? That was nothing more than a harmless restatement of the obvious. And how did Jeremy Berkowitz know what the President did every morning? Hell, the President's own wife didn't know all the things he was doing in that round office.

I awoke the next morning feeling game and fresh. I actually sang while I showered, until the guy two stalls down hurled a bar of soap at me. By the time I reached our little office building, I was actually thinking about being nice to Delbert for a change, which only goes to show you how awfully guilty I felt about all those dark thoughts I'd had the night before.

I noticed when I walked in that everybody was sitting quietly and somberly at their desks. Somberly, like something was terribly wrong. Somberly, like something very distressing was going down. Quietly, like nobody was talking because nobody knew what to say.

I also noticed two big, burly military policemen sipping coffee and lounging by the entrance to my office.

"Excuse me, Major Drummond?" the bigger of the two asked, shoving himself off the wall. He wore captain's bars, and his nametag read Wolkowitz.

I said, "How can I help you, Captain?"

"We need to talk to you." He glanced around the office and his face acquired a very portentous cloud. "Alone, if you don't mind."

We walked into my office and I politely offered him and his

sergeant seats, which they both too brusquely declined. The sergeant pulled a small notebook out of his pocket, poised his pencil, and stared at me like I was the Boston Strangler. I knew this routine.

I sat behind my desk and tried to look relaxed.

Captain Wolkowitz said, "Could you tell us where you were between 2400 and 0500 hours this morning?"

"No, I cannot tell you where I was. I mean, I could, but you haven't given me any reason."

He gave me one of those "Oh brother, what have I done to deserve another smart-assed lawyer" kind of looks. All cops, even military cops, learn to master that look fairly early in their careers.

"Do you know a man named Jeremy Berkowitz?" he asked.

"Again, Captain, why are you asking?"

"I'm asking because Berkowitz was murdered last night."

I stared at him, and he stared at me.

Then he said, "Now, I'll ask you again. Did you know Mr. Berkowitz?"

"I met him here yesterday."

"And where were you last night?"

"I was on my cot, in my tent, trying to fall asleep."

"You share that tent with anyone?"

"No."

"Then there are no witnesses to corroborate your story?"

"Captain . . . uh, Wolkowitz," I said, pronouncing his name with exaggerated care as though I were committing it to memory, "do you have some reason to suspect me of murdering Mr. Berkowitz?"

He paused, and that was his first serious mistake.

I stood up and pounded a fist on my desk. "I asked you a question, Captain! You've got two seconds to answer or I'll press charges against you for refusing a lawful order."

He backed up a bit. "Sir, I—"

"What's your unit?" I barked.

"502nd Military Police Battalion. But, sir, I—"

"Are you gonna answer my damned question or do I need to pick up the phone and call your commanding officer?"

By this time he had backed up all the way to the wall. He obviously was not used to having his suspects, or whatever I was, explode in his face. "Sir, I—"

"You nothing, Captain! Obviously, you've already questioned my office staff?"

Like most people do when they get flustered, his eyes quickly darted toward the floor. Mistake number two.

I pounded the desk again and went down about three octaves and up about twenty decibels. "I can't believe this! See what's on my collar, Wolkowitz? You know why I'm here at Tuzla? The Secretary of the Army personally appointed me as an Article 32 investigating officer. And you come in here, without my permission, and interview my people?"

I was working up a nice head of steam, and it suddenly struck Captain Wolkowitz that I am a lawyer, and that means I'm genetically long-winded, and I could probably go on like this for hours. He made the wise decision.

"No, sir, you're not a suspect," he said, surrendering very nicely. "At least, not yet," he added, trying to recover at least a bit of ground.

"Then why are you asking me these questions?"

"We found your name in Mr. Berkowitz's notebook."

"Berkowitz was a reporter who covers the military. Probably half the names on active duty were written in that book. How many other names were in there?"

"A lot . . . but only a few of them are assigned here."

The golden rule of military tactics is that once you've taken the offensive, never hesitate or you'll find yourself in full-scale retreat.

"How did he die?" I demanded.

"He . . . uh . . ."

"How did he die, Captain?!!"

"Sir, he was strangled."

"How was he strangled?"

"With a garrote. His arteries were cut, but the actual cause of death was asphyxiation."

"And where did this happen?"

"He was staying at the press quarters inside the information officer's compound. He apparently got up in the middle of the night to go to the latrine. He was murdered right at the urinal."

"With a garrote, you said?"

"That's right."

"Homemade or professional quality?"

"It looked store-bought. A metal wire attached to two wooden handles."

"Who found him?"

"An AP reporter named Wolf. He had to catch a 5 A.M. flight. When he went into the latrine to clean up, he walked right into it."

I studied the two of them for a moment. Then I said, "Sergeant, please step out of my office."

He looked at his captain, who nodded for him to do as he was told. Then I stood up. I walked around the desk and leaned against it. The time had come to eliminate the barriers and restore relations with Captain Wolkowitz.

"You've already called the *Washington Herald*?" I asked in a much calmer, much friendlier tone.

"Yes, sir. They're real unhappy. This isn't going down well."

I chuckled at that. "Their star military reporter murdered while standing at a pisser at an American military installation. I don't blame them. That's a pretty hard headline to write."

Since poor Captain Wolkowitz was charged with the responsibility of maintaining law and order on this compound, he was having a bit of trouble seeing the humor in that.

I said, "Are you aware what Berkowitz was doing here?"

"The information officer told us he was working on a story about the bombing operation."

"That's only half of it. The other half was that he was working on a story about my investigation."

Wolkowitz scratched his head, then said, "The *Herald* told us he filed a dispatch at about 2330 hours last night. That's how we narrowed down the time of death. They didn't say what it was about, though."

This was where it was going to get tricky. As a lawyer, I've been trained to know it's never a good idea to lie to or mislead the police. Lord knows, I'd counseled enough clients to always tell the truth, because the mere act of lying is a crime. At least it is under military law, which is a bit stingier than civilian law. The trick was that I had to appear forthcoming without actually being all that forthcoming.

I said, "He came here yesterday to interview me. I had the impression he had an inside source and was ready to break something big."

"What gave you that impression, sir?"

"He alluded to the story a few times. He was obviously excited, like he was on to something. Hell, he as much as admitted he had an inside source."

"And what did he want from you?"

"I think it was just routine journalistic courtesy. He wanted to give me the chance to confirm some details."

"He gave you no hints or clues who his source was?"

I looked disgusted. "His exact words were that he's never had a source uncovered. He seemed very proud of that."

"Was this your only interaction with him?"

"No. He called me from Washington the other day."

"And what was that about?"

"I don't know. I hung up on him before he could get into it."

"Why did you hang up on him?"

"Because I think he wanted me to leak, and frankly, I found the idea repugnant."

So far, I'd managed to be completely truthful without being the least bit truthful. My law school professors would be abundantly proud of me. But if this conversation continued, then this big captain was liable to ask me a question or two I couldn't contort into a wholly wrong context. And I'd be breaking at least one or two laws.

I quickly said, "So . . . hey, what's your first name, anyway?"

"Paul. My friends call me Wolky, though."

I smiled warmly, like I was one of those friends. "Okay, Wolky. First, I apologize for my blowup. I'm sorry. It's just that . . . well, I've been under a lot of pressure. Coming in here as the investigating officer . . . you know, folks haven't been real friendly."

"Hey, I understand," Wolky said, and I was sure he did. Remember how I mentioned that lawyers aren't real popular in the Army? Well, military policemen are about ten notches down from that. The only reason Green Berets even allow MPs inside their bars is so they can have somebody to pound the crap out of when they get bored with the booze.

"No hard feelings?" I asked, still with that silly smile.

"Nah, 'course not."

"Good. Now I imagine you're bringing the Criminal Investigation Division into this?"

"A team's flying in from Heidelberg right now. They've asked me to begin collecting evidence and statements."

"Right. That's good. Never let the trail of evidence get cold. Now it's not that I have any reason to suspect that there's any connection between Berkowitz's murder and my investigation, but I'd like to play it safe. When CID gets here, I want them to stop by. I want to know everything you learn about this murder."

"You think there might be a connection?"

"Wolky, there are a million plausible reasons Berkowitz was

murdered. This guy made his living writing derogatory stories about the military. He's hated by about everyone who's ever worn a military uniform. Hell, he could've bought some dope from a pusher in uniform and was running delinquent in his payments. Maybe he was gay and got caught peeking over the urinal at the wrong guy's peepee. Wouldn't be the first time. At least three or four gays have been offed in military latrines over the past few years."

Wolkowitz was listening intently to my silly theories, as though what I was suggesting was perfectly lucid. A nice guy, but he sure as hell wasn't the brightest bulb in the hardware store. Of course Berkowitz's murder was connected with my investigation. I was sure of it. He'd wired back his story, gone to his room to get some sleep, was awakened by that tiny bladder, and somebody was either waiting for him or followed him into that latrine.

The garrote is no weapon for amateurs. It's a wonderful weapon to kill with, except it's so damned hard to use. You have to sneak up behind someone, then fling that little wire just right so it forms a perfect lasso around the neck. At the same instant, you have to whip the two handles in opposing directions with lightning speed and enough force to completely cut off the victim's airways. A killer who is untrained, or out of practice, gets the wires caught on the victim's nose or chin, or the victim's hand shoots up and gets in the way. It's even harder when the victims are erect, as Berkowitz apparently was. Then you have to get a knee firmly positioned in the small of their back, otherwise they are liable to kick out, or spin about and mess up the whole thing.

It's not the kind of weapon some homophobic warrior carries around in his pocket, just on the off chance that someone gets attracted to his willie in the potty. Nor is it the kind of weapon an angry drug pusher would use to punish a delinquent client. The garrote is an assassin's weapon. It's used for cold-blooded murder.

Regular Army troops wouldn't know a garrote from a carrot. However, garrotes are a highly favored weapon among Special Forces, who sometimes have need to kill silently. Whoever murdered Jeremy Berkowitz chose his weapon deliberately. He meant to leave a signature.

I said to my new buddy, "Wolky, listen, I got a few meetings I've got to attend. No offense, but I've got thirty-five possible murders on my hands, and the whole world breathing down my throat."

He gave me a hearty pat on the shoulder. "Hey, no problem, Major. I'll make sure the CID guys hook up with you when they get here."

Chapter
☆☆☆ 15

I asked Delbert and Morrow to join me in my office at noon. Imelda's minions were still abuzz about the morning's happenings. Only yesterday, they had all seen this big guy lounging around the office, and today he was snack food for worms. Actually, to do Berkowitz credit, he was more on the order of an eight-course meal.

Delbert came in first, then Morrow, who gave me a full dose of those sympathetic eyes. "Are you in any trouble?" she asked. "Is there anything I can do to help?"

"Nope, no trouble," I assured her. "The MPs heard I was the smartest guy on the compound, and they just wanted to stop by and see what I thought about that dead journalist." I looked down at my watch. "In fact, I'm expecting a call from CID any minute. It's really hell when everybody knows you're smart."

Delbert had this perplexed look on his face, like if the MPs and CID wanted to talk to me, then why the hell hadn't they dropped in to have a chat with him, too? He was the one who went to Yale. He was the one who had maybe the best prosecutorial record in the Army. Morrow, on the other hand, gave me the look all mothers award to their naughty three-year-olds.

"I've got some terribly good news," I quickly said to get the subject changed. "Because of the outstanding progress we've made, the Army has decided to shorten the time line of the investigation."

"To when?" Morrow asked.

"Four days, starting this morning."

"Wow, that *is* short," Delbert said, restating the obvious, which was yet another trait in his legion of bad habits.

I said, "If we had to vote today, where would we be?"

They stared at each other for a moment. Morrow scratched her chin, while Delbert pulled on an ear. Morrow scratched her chin some more, and Delbert nearly pulled the lobe off his ear.

"Hey," I said, very chummy-like, "this isn't that hard. You're not committing to anything. If you had to vote today, how would you vote?"

They both, at the same time, said, "No grounds for prosecution."

"Okay. So is that no grounds because you think they're innocent? Or is that no grounds because you think there's insufficient evidence to prosecute?"

"The former," Delbert said.

"The former," Morrow echoed. Then she added, "What about you?"

I said, "If I had to vote today, I would abstain."

"You can't abstain," Morrow said. "Our orders say we can only make two choices."

"Okay, I'd write a long letter and say I vote no, because there's insufficient evidence, but I don't feel this team had time to make a proper recommendation. Do the rules allow me to do that?"

We all knew that the rules did not mention anything about that. We also knew that if I did such a thing, it would invalidate the entire investigation. You can't really have the head of an Article 32 investigating committee expressing no confidence in the outcome and expect the report to carry even an iota of credibility. Not that either of them should really give a damn. I mean, it would be an embarrassment for the Army, which would then have to appoint a whole new investigating team and go through this whole routine again. But that should mean nothing to Delbert and Morrow, who would've done their jobs ably and to the best of their abilities. The thing was, they were both organizational creatures right down to their Army-issued green underwear, and the Army had appointed them part of a committee, and they just naturally felt it was their duty to bring home a unanimous verdict. They couldn't help it. They just were that way.

Morrow said, "Then we have four days to either change your mind or change our own."

"That's the way I see it," I admitted.

"What would it take for you to change your mind?" she asked, which told you exactly where she was coming from.

"I'd have to see some positive confirmation that Sanchez and his men aren't lying."

"There is no confirmation," Morrow said, quite painfully. "We've already been all through that. These nine men are the only living witnesses."

A strange expression suddenly came over Delbert's face. "Maybe there's an alternative to a living witness," he said, bouncing in his seat like an overexcited schoolboy who thinks he knows the answer to the teacher's question.

"What?" I asked.

"The NSA or somebody must have satellites orbiting over Kosovo. I've never personally seen a satellite photo, but from what I hear, they can read the print on a dime."

"Delbert, you little genius, you," I declared. "You're absolutely right."

I can't begin to tell you how painful that was for me to say. Not only because I had these vague ill feelings toward Delbert, but also because I wanted to give myself a good, hard kick in the ass. If anybody should have thought of this, it was the guy who spent five years living in the world of supersecret operations where we used up satellite photos like toilet paper.

I checked my watch. If I called right now, I could catch Clapper just as he arrives at the office. I dialed the number and waited. It took three rings before Clapper's secretary, Nora, picked up.

"Hello, Nora, Drummond here. What happened?"

"What?"

"You didn't pick up till the third ring. You're slipping."

"What?" she said again in her dry, humorless voice.

"Forget it," I said. I mean, why should I waste any more of my golden wit on this block of ice? "Is the general in?" I asked.

"The general's in a meeting and I should not interrupt him."

"This is brutally important."

"So is the general's other meeting."

"I'll bet mine's as important," I said.

"Major Drummond, I know who you are, and I know what you're working on, and I assure you this meeting is more urgent."

"Anything to do with a certain reporter who got strangled in a bathroom?" I asked, which really was more in the nature of a simple deduction than a blank question.

"I'll put you right through," she said.

A moment later, Clapper said, "Hello, Sean."

"Hi, General, having a nice day?"

"I haven't had a nice day since I took this job. You know, Sean, this town is full of big, glitzy law firms that pay a million dollars a year to their partners. One more thing goes wrong, and I'm gonna be banging on their doors."

"Geez, you really do sound depressed. Don't you think that's a little drastic?"

He did not chuckle, which I took as a bad sign. Either I was

not as witty as I thought or his mood was really sour. Had to
be the sour mood thing, of course.

"You've heard about this dead reporter?" he asked.

"You mean the guy who called me the other day?"

"Right. Did you actually meet with him?"

"He stopped by yesterday. We had some words. He went on
his way."

"The editor in chief of the *Herald* called the Chairman of
the Joint Chiefs. He's promising to raise hell until we catch whoever did this."

"I don't blame him. Poor guy's standing at a urinal and the
next thing he's pissing and bleeding all over the wall while
someone chokes him to death. What a world, huh? Listen, the
reason I called is we might have a breakthrough. Actually, Delbert thought of it. We'd like to see if NSA or any of those other
supersecret agencies might have any surveillance tapes or pictures of Zone Three that were collected between the fourteenth
and the eighteenth."

"It's a good idea," was all he said.

"Can you run the request, sir? You know those spook guys.
A request from a major isn't even going to make them peek inside their vault."

"I'll make the calls as soon as this meeting is over."

"Thanks, General," I said, then we both hung up.

I suppose I could've shared my suspicions of the Berkowitz
murder with General Clapper, just like I should've shared them
with Wolky. But the truth was, the moment Wolky said that
Berkowitz was dead, I instantly lost trust in everyone I knew. I
was sure Berkowitz's murder was somehow connected with me.
All that dark paranoia I'd managed to bury the night before came
rushing back like a tidal wave.

Also, I was having a lot of difficulty working up any compassion or grief for the so recently departed Jeremy Berkowitz.
The sum of my relationship with him was a smear job on the

front page of his newspaper and a very blatant attempt to black-mail me into becoming his stooge. I had no idea who killed him, but I wasn't having any trouble at all seeing why somebody would want him dead.

There were all these disparate dots out there; I had no idea how they all connected together, but some rotten sense told me they did. Besides, I figured that if NSA had overhead photos or tapes of what happened in Zone Three, then we were on the verge of a huge breakthrough. Personally, I was looking forward to getting copies of those pictures. Then I'd go back to visit Sanchez and crew. I was dying to see the looks on their faces.

There was a hard knock on the door, and I looked up to see Imelda enter with a piece of paper in her hand. She held it as though it were the holy grail.

"Hi," I said.

"Here's the damned bill to fix that damned hole you punched in the damned wall yesterday," she announced, flapping the paper in front of my face.

"Oh that," I said. "Clumsy me. That damn phone just flew out of my hands. I tried to grab it, but it was slippery as hell, and it just got away."

"Don't you smart-ass me, Major. You do the crime, you pay the fine," she said, throwing the paper down on my blotter and handing me a pen. This was one of her favorite sayings, I might add.

"Two hundred dollars!" I bellowed.

She actually smiled. "That's for the wall and to fix that damn phone."

I scrawled my name on the bottom of the charge sheet that Imelda would give the local supply sergeant, who would have my pay docked two hundred dollars to handle the damage. Imelda stood there, her face all scrunched up in triumph. She shared the old noncom's belief that Army property was sacred property. Those who defiled, damaged, lost, or misappropriated said sacred relics deserved to be stiffly punished. There was no use arguing or pleading.

I handed her back the charge sheet with a mutinous look on my face.

"By the way, there's two men in civvies waiting to see you," she said.

"CID?"

"Uh-huh." She nodded.

"Could you two please wait outside the office?" I asked Morrow and Delbert.

They left with Imelda, and were immediately replaced by two young, crew-cutted investigators, who, like most military men, wore cheap civilian suits and wore them badly. Their ties were something out of the *Twilight Zone*, and their shirts were polyester blend, no-iron specials; no doubt bought on sale at Kmart.

A pair of badges were flashed, and they quickly muttered their names. David something and Martie whatever.

"Sir, we were told by Captain Wolkowitz that you wanted to meet with us," said Martie whatever.

"That's right. Did he explain what I'm doing here?"

"Yeah."

"Then he must have mentioned that Berkowitz was writing about my investigation?"

"He did," said Martie.

"And as trained criminologists, I'm sure you recognize that's what we call a point of coincidence."

Martie, who sported a green paisley tie with a red-striped shirt, nodded thoughtfully, then said, "Speaking of points of coincidence, we understand Berkowitz did an article about you on the front page of his paper three or four days back."

"Yes, he did," I admitted. "And that's why I killed him."

Their heads snapped up in surprise.

"Just kidding," I said. "I mean, he misspelled my name, but otherwise the article wasn't objectionable. He expressed the view that the Army should have picked a more senior officer to head my investigation."

"Did that make you angry?"

"You're kidding, right? I wished I wrote it. Gentlemen, how would you like to be the one who has to decide what to do with those nine men at Aviano Air Base?"

"That bad, huh?" David asked. He was the nerdy one wearing spit-shined black Army dress shoes with a brown suit, bright red tie, and blue shirt. Positively hair-raising.

I looked at him like the good big brother he'd always wished he had. "David, I'll be honest, I'm not having much fun. It's a no-win situation."

"Pretty rough, huh?"

I shook my head in pure misery. "I found rotten cabbage in my sleeping bag last night. Rotten cabbage," I moaned. "Every night, it's something."

"Lousy bastards," he mumbled, referring to the Special Forces guys who were running all over Tuzla. Remember how I mentioned that lawyers aren't loved and MPs are despised? Well, CID investigators are legions below every other living creature on earth. They're known for planting informers and tattletales inside units, and for skulking around and doing the undercover dirty work. They are the closest thing to a Gestapo a democratic army is allowed to have. I'd known troops to actually paint CID badges on the chests of targets at rifle ranges.

"Now I know how you guys feel," I said with a commiserating headshake.

"Yeah, it's rough," agreed David, and Martie nodded along.

"If we get a chance," I said, "maybe you guys can join me for drinks. I'd love to get some advice on how you handle all this pressure and strain."

"Sure," said David, beaming like a poodle that just got its fanny licked by a big, handsome Great Dane.

"So," I said, reaping the treasures of my disgusting servility, "anything new turn up in the investigation?"

Martie said, "There's not much to go on."

I said, "Captain Wolkowitz mentioned that the garrote was manufactured. There are probably only one or two manufacturers who make them. If it were me, I'd get the name of that manufacturer and check to see who bought any in the past year or two."

"Speaking of the garrote," Martie said, "we're a little curious why the killer left it around the victim's neck."

"Hmm," I answered, trying not to appear too certain. "If it were me, I'd guess he knew that if he took it with him, he'd have to find a place to dispose of it. And he'd probably get the victim's blood spilled on his clothes. I assume there are no fingerprints on the handles?"

"Right. We're assuming the killer wore gloves. So you think the murderer left it there because it would be too hard to get rid of?"

"Hell, I don't know a lot about these things," I lied, "but I'd imagine a garrote is a lot like a disposable razor. I'd guess that was one of the reasons the murderer chose that particular tool. If he used a gun, there'd be the noise and some bullets left around and you could trace them back to the right gun. A knife, and you'd know what type and where to start looking. Besides, a garrote leaves a message. Maybe the killer left it as a warning."

"Makes sense," said David, who was taking a liking to me. I could tell.

"You ran traces for shoeprints?" I asked.

"We're still collecting molds. It was a latrine, though, with a lot of traffic."

"True, but this *is* the Army. And it's a public facility, one used by the press, and we all know how much the Army cares about its public image. I'd bet the place got a thorough scrubbing some-time in the evening. You might want to find out who cleaned it, and what time. Also, I think you can narrow it down to rubber-soled shoes. The killer had to sneak up behind him without being heard."

"Good point," said David, who had withdrawn a notebook and was scribbling in it. The same guys who teach lawyers must teach these gumshoes, too. I mean, what's so hard to remem-ber? Garrotes are disposable weapons, and the killer probably wore rubber soles.

"Was there a lot of blood around the body?" I asked.

"All over the wall, the urinals, and the floor. Looked like someone sprayed it on with a hose," Martie said.

"Yeah, cut arteries are messy things. If you're lucky, the killer got some on himself, too."

David added this to the list in his tiny notebook.

I said, "So, what do you figure? Was the killer waiting for him in the bathroom? Maybe hiding in a stall? Or did he just follow him in?"

They both scratched their heads.

I said, "Personally, I'd put my money on the killer following him in. I mean, maybe the killer guessed or maybe even knew that Berkowitz had a weak bladder. Berkowitz was a big boy, and it's a fairly common side effect of obesity. But, if the killer waited around inside the latrine, he might get noticed. I'd bet he waited outside, then followed him in."

"Think the killer knew him?" Martie asked.

"Hard to say," I replied. "You might want to question every-body who came in or out of the press quarters, or the latrine, say between ten and midnight. See if they saw anybody stand-ing around, waiting, or just watching the building."

Another note was scribbled in David's little book, then they both stood up.

"Listen, we gotta get runnin', Major. Hope you don't mind, but we got lotsa things to do. Mind if we call on you again?"

"On the contrary, I'd very much appreciate it. Maybe I can help."

"Sure," said Martie, obviously the leader of the two.

"And remember that offer for drinks," I called as they walked out. I said it loud enough for the whole office staff to hear. I wanted them to know this visit was friendly.

I doubted, though, that my new, abysmally dressed friends were going to get very far with their investigation. I had this strong sense that the man who murdered Berkowitz was highly trained and had killed a number of times before. If we were in Topeka, Kansas, knowing that much would actually be a lucky breakthrough. It would allow the police to trim their list of suspects down to a nice, workable number. At Tuzla Air Base, with the entire Tenth Special Forces Group in residence, you could throw a rock in any direction and hit a suspect.

Chapter
☆☆
☆ 16

General Chuck Murphy looked profoundly pissed off, and I guess I didn't blame him. Nobody likes to start their day inspecting a purple-faced corpse in a blood-soaked latrine, and it must have dawned on Chuck Murphy that his sterling career had just moved one notch closer to the ledge of oblivion. The Army expects its commanders to maintain law and order on their compounds. Dead, internationally renowned journalists littering up your latrines falls just a wee bit outside those parameters.

"Good morning, General," I said, falling into the seat across from his desk.

"Major," he replied, which I considered a notable response only insofar as he failed to wish me a good morning back.

"Hey, I'm sorry to bother you, sir. I'm sure you're having a real busy day, but I have a few questions I really have to get answered."

"My time is your time," he said, glancing impatiently at his watch.

"Okay, here's the thing. We've interviewed Sanchez and all his men. We've been through the operations logs. We've viewed the Serb corpses. I guess what I still don't get is what Sanchez and his guys were doing inside Kosovo in the first place."

"Haven't we been through this already? It's a classic military assistance action. We arm and train the Kosovars to fight their own battles."

"Whose idea was it?"

"Whose idea was what?" he asked in a very brittle tone.

"The whole operation. I mean, somebody somewhere had to say, 'Hey, I've got this great idea. We should use the Tenth Group to help the KLA.' Every military operation has a godfather. Who was that guy?"

"I'll be damned if I know, Drummond. These things usually just evolve. I'd guess this happened like that."

"Who gave you the orders, General?"

"My orders were signed by General Partridge, the JSOC commander."

"I'm sorry. I don't know much about these things. I would've thought you were working for the NATO commander in Brussels. I mean, isn't he the guy in charge of Europe and this whole Kosovo thing?"

"He is, but Special Forces rarely work for theater commanders. We usually get our marching orders direct from Bragg. The word for it is 'stovepipe.'"

"Really? Why?"

"Because of the special nature of our operations. Conventional force commanders aren't expected to understand our unique capabilities, how to properly employ us. This isn't unusual, Drummond. Check the record. They did it this same way in Mogadishu and Haiti."

"So then where does General Partridge get his orders from?"

"From the Joint Chiefs."

"Does he deal straight with the White House?"

"Why do you ask that?"

"Just curiosity," I lied. "I mean, I'm new to all this high-level stuff, so I'm trying to figure these things out."

He gave me a hard, discerning look. "Has this got something to do with your investigation?"

"Well, yes, but only in sort of a roundabout way. See, Sanchez and his men are saying their ambush was an act of self-defense. You see the problem there? I mean, some folks might say that's pretty convoluted logic. An ambush is a form of attack, right? I'm just trying to determine what constituted self-defense. To do that, I might have to interview the people who crafted this operation in the first place. You know, to find out their idea of what constitutes self-defense."

"It wasn't anybody at the White House, I can tell you that. General Partridge doesn't work for anyone in the White House. No . . . let me rephrase that. He, of course, works for the Commander in Chief, who happens to be the President, but everything is channeled through the Chairman of the Joint Chiefs."

"So maybe the idea for this operation originated with someone in the Pentagon, or maybe from General Partridge's staff?"

"That would be my guess."

"Do you have time for one more question?" I asked, since he kept staring at his watch to remind me how ridiculously busy he was.

"One more, Drummond. That's it," he said, shaking his head. "You might not believe this, but I'm actually a fairly busy man."

"Oh no, I believe that, General. I'm just thankful every day that I'm not the guy in your shoes," I said, and he looked at me with fire in his eyes, trying to figure what I meant by that. I continued: "So how often were Sanchez and his men required to give situation reports to your headquarters? I mean, you must have some kind of standard operating procedure that dictates that sort of thing."

"I'm afraid I don't know."

"Well, I just read the operations order for Sanchez's operation. According to that, he was supposed to provide a situation report twice a day. Once at dawn and once at dusk."

A quick snarl appeared on his lips, then disappeared almost as quickly. I'm sure he was thinking that if I already knew the answer, why was I wasting his time with the question? Old Chuck obviously didn't like to play lawyer games. In a thoroughly irritated tone, he said, "Okay."

"Well, according to the operations logs, Sanchez missed making his reports three times between the fourteenth and the eighteenth. What do you make of that?"

"Maybe he didn't miss making his reports. Maybe the ops center forgot to log it in. I think we run a pretty tight show here, but the ops center is run by soldiers, and soldiers are not perfect."

"Yessir, I sure understand that. But I imagine the reason all these teams have to report in twice a day is because they're operating behind enemy lines. I mean, aren't those reports really the only way you have to be sure they're still alive? Wouldn't some major alarm bells go off if they failed to report?"

"No, not necessarily," the general said. "In most cases, I think the ops staff would wait before pushing the panic button."

"Wait for what?"

"Say the team missed the morning report, they might wait until the evening report. Certainly, if a team missed making two sitreps in a row, then flags would go up."

"And what would that mean? What would happen if a team stopped reporting?"

"We'd increase the aerial recon over their sector. If that didn't get us anywhere, we might insert a recon team to see what we could discover. We know the locations of their base camps, so we've got a general footprint for a search."

"But none of that happened when Sanchez's team missed its reports?"

"No."

"Should it have happened, General?"

He gave me a royally pissed-off look. "Look, the team still made it out okay, all right? No harm, no foul. We haven't lost a team yet, so I guess we're doing something right."

Nobody likes being second-guessed, but General Chuck Murphy obviously liked it less than most people. That's the problem with being told all your life that you're something special. You might eventually start to believe it. That big jaw of his was now protruding like the prow of a battleship and his mood was very brackish. I could see I'd about worn out my welcome. Actually, that's not true. I hadn't really been welcome in the first place.

I looked at my watch. "Oops. Hey, sir, I really gotta run. I'm supposed to be taking another deposition."

That wasn't really true, either. I just couldn't resist giving him the bum's rush for a change. I left the way I came in and steered a wide path around that big, beefy sergeant major of his.

I hurried to the Operations Center, which was located in another of the ubiquitous wooden buildings, about five down from Murphy's headquarters. The guard at the entrance spent about thirty seconds trying to tell me why I wasn't allowed to enter this supersecret facility before I finally whipped out the nice little set of orders the Secretary of the Army had helpfully provided me. According to these orders, I could enter the White House situation room if I so desired. No kidding.

I followed a trail of stenciled signs that took me down a long hallway, then down a dimly lit stairway. In the basement there was another guard standing before a metal door, but fortunately he and the guard upstairs were in telepathic contact, so all I had to do was whip out my identification card, which was enough for him to confirm that I was, indeed, the exact same asshole with all-inclusive orders his buddy had just met upstairs.

The metal door was flung open, and I instantly entered the next century. Special Forces have almost unlimited budgets, and General Partridge's boys had spared no expense when they equipped this ops center. A whole wall was covered with a massive electronic map of Kosovo. It was peppered with lots of tiny blinking dots, some red, some green, and some blue. There were three whole banks of Sun microstations manned by grim-looking men who hovered earnestly over their keyboards. Another wall was lined with high-tech communications consoles, where about ten communicators sat very alertly with special headphones on their ears. It looked like AT&T's global nerve center, only all the workers in this room wore battle dress and natty little green berets. Well, everybody except me, of course.

I stood for a while and watched and listened to the bustling activity. Like nearly all the ops centers I'd been in, most of the business was conducted in low decibels. There was this constant, low hum of voices and computer keys being mashed and radio messages being received. Every now and again, somebody dashed across the floor, either carrying a message to some other part of the cell or coordinating some activity. A hulking monster wearing sergeant major's stripes sat at a big wooden desk in the middle of the floor. Although there were a fair number of officers present, it was clear that this sergeant major was the big boss of this machine and its many moving parts.

After a while, he glanced over and saw me standing observantly in the corner. I apparently aroused his curiosity. He kept glancing over for the next five minutes, until he finally got up from his desk, went to the corner, fixed himself a fresh cup of coffee, then walked over. That's when I noticed he'd fixed himself two cups of coffee. I also noticed his hands. They were so big and beefy that the coffee cups looked like a couple of thimbles.

His hands matched the rest of him. He was a big, rough-looking man who obviously had had his nose broken at least a few times. He had an enormous, ugly head that seemed to be connected directly to his shoulders, because his neck was the size of a tree stump. He had the standard Special Forces crew cut, and floppy ears that made him look sort of elephantine. A tall man, too, maybe six foot three, with broad, ponderous shoulders.

He squinted at my nametag and the JAG emblem on my collar, then broke into a wide grin. "You the same guy doing the investigation?" he asked.

"Yeah. Thanks," I said, quickly grabbing a coffee cup from his hand before he could decide he didn't want to talk with me and wandered off in search of someone else to hand the coffee to. This made it too awkward for him to try to move on without making himself appear to be my personal errand boy.

His nametag read Williams, and I said, "I take it you're the ops sergeant."

"Yup. Welcome to my kingdom."

"My compliments, Sergeant Major. Looks like a pretty tight ship."

"We try. Gets a little kinky when you're running U.S. teams, KLA teams, and trying to keep watch on the bad guys at the same time."

"Thank God this ain't a war, huh?"

"Say that again." He chuckled. "If we'd fought this way in the Gulf War, the Iraqis would still be grilling hot dogs in Kuwait."

"That bad, huh?"

"Christ, a little girl with one leg could fight a better war than this."

"How many teams are there?"

"Right now, we've got nine U.S. teams inside Kosovo. Then there are sixteen KLA units."

"You've got nine SF teams and another sixteen with the KLA?"

"No. There are nine KLA teams operatin' with our guys and another seven KLA units without A-teams."

"I didn't know there were KLA units operating without Guardian Angels."

"We call 'em GTs . . . uh, graduate teams."

"Graduate teams?"

"Yeah. Every KLA unit that goes in starts with baby-sitters, till they've done three or four successful missions. Then we cut 'em loose. We still supply 'em, and a few have liaison cells, but they operate more or less independently."

"They any good?" I asked.

He took my arm and ushered me over to the huge electronic map on the wall. He looked it over for a moment, then pointed toward a blue dot located in the northeastern corner of Kosovo.

"Red dots are Serbs, green dots are our guys, blue dots are KLA. That's GT team seven there. One of the first teams we formed. Nearly every man had at least a tour in the old Yugoslav army. The commander was an infantry major."

"They're pretty deep inside," I remarked.

"We try to keep the rookie teams as close to the Macedonian border as we can. That way, they get in over their head, it's a short walk out."

I stared up at the dot that represented team seven. "That a good team?"

"Very damn good."

"What have you got them doing?"

"As we speak, they're pinpointing targets for the flyboys. We issued 'em some laser designators. See that line right there?" He pointed at a string of blinking red dots that were aligned from the northeast to the southwest. "That's the Serbs' main supply route. About half the Serbs' ammo and supplies come down that artery. Team seven's got guys positioned all along it. They heat up the targets with the lasers every time we've got an F-16 that's got a few extra bombs or missiles to unload."

"Very impressive," I said.

"Yeah, well, they're the exception. Most of these KLA teams

aren't worth pissin' on. Most haven't done a damn thing since we put 'em in. You send 'em orders, and they call you back and complain that it's too hard, or they say they're doing it, but when you get the recce photos, you find out they didn't do a damn thing. Waste of food and ammo."

He kept studying my face as we talked. He had that perplexed look some people get when they're trying to remember something.

I said, "So tell me, Sergeant Major, how well do you remember Akhan's company?"

"Ah, a damned shame, that one," he said, rubbing his jaw thoughtfully.

"A good unit?"

"Never really had a chance to find out. Great scores in training, but they got wiped out before they ever had a chance to strut their stuff."

"Yeah, I heard they ran into a real butcher's mart at that police station."

"Yeah, a nasty business, that was," he issued forth without the slightest hint of genuine remorse. Then the corners of his mouth twisted up, and his head canted to the side. "Hey, you ever been to Bragg?"

"Years ago. I was assigned there back when I was in the infantry."

"Yeah, I knew I seen you before."

"Five glorious years in the 82nd. Ooorah!" I said.

He lowered his voice. "Right, and I was Columbus's first mate on the friggin' *Santa Maria*. You don't remember me, do ya?"

"Nope, I'm afraid I don't."

He winked. " 'Course, you don't. I didn't recognize your name 'cause the outfit didn't use names when we screened. We just gave you all numbers, so's to make sure there was no favoritism or command influence. But I never forget a face."

I looked at Williams and tried to place him. The voice was

somehow disturbingly familiar, as were the eyes, but I couldn't recall from where, and that worried me.

"Sorry, Sergeant Major, you've got the wrong guy. I never heard of the outfit."

His smile broadened. "Remember the POW camp? Remember that big, surly asshole wearing a hood that kept kickin' the crap outta you?"

This I remembered all too well. The outfit had a six-month-long test you had to pass in order to get in. About one in every twenty applicants managed to survive the ordeal. One of the passages the outfit expected all recruits to endure was two weeks in a POW camp that was about as brutally realistic as they could make it. For some reason, this huge interrogator who was working the hard sell developed a very nasty affection for me. He liked me so much, he made sure I got one-hour personal workouts with him every day. When he was done, I had two fractured ribs, a broken nose, and two missing teeth to remember him by.

"You were that prick?" I asked.

"Hey, no hard feelings." He chuckled. "That was my job."

"A job, huh? Well, you certainly seemed to enjoy it."

That brought another chuckle. "Part of the job, too. We were supposed to make it look like we were having balls of fun, 'cause they figured that would scare the crap outta you guys."

"It did," I said very earnestly. "I dreamed about you for years."

I didn't mention that they were nightmares, but I was sure he got the point.

"Well, you were a tough little bastard. You shoulda broke and told me what I wanted to know. You'd of saved yourself a lot of agony. And it sure didn't help, you being such a wiseass all the time. Did you know all those sessions were taped?"

"I guess I missed that. A guy gets a little preoccupied when he's being bounced off walls and punched silly. You were very good at keeping my attention."

"Yeah, well, there was one of those little tiny cameras in the corner ceiling. Every night, Colonel Tingle, the camp commandant, would review the tapes, and he'd get all over my ass for letting you mouth off at me that way. I told him after that first week you weren't gonna break, but he kept scheduling you to come back." He shook his head as though he were remembering some disastrous blind date. "You know, you being such a tough motherfucker, that's what got you into the outfit. As I remember, you couldn't shoot worth a shit."

"Never could," I admitted.

"So you left the outfit and became a lawyer?" he asked.

"Yeah. After five years, I decided I needed to preserve my mental health."

"Hey, got that. I was there six years; probably one or two too many. That POW training thing was my final fling. They let me go after that."

"You've been here ever since?"

"Yeah, it's not a bad unit. Ain't the outfit, but then, nothing else is."

"I guess. Anyway, we're both a little old for that stuff now."

I walked over to the wall of communications consoles, and he followed me over.

"You're in contact with all the teams inside the zone?"

"Yep."

"I guess the teams have to make daily sitreps, don't they?"

"Twice a day. One at first light, one at dusk. That's why we have ten of these communications consoles. That way, we can handle the load and collect all the sitreps together."

"Anybody ever miss?" I asked.

"Once in a blue moon. Not our guys, though. They never miss. It's the KLA guys, they get sloppy sometimes."

"What do you do when you don't get a timely sitrep?"

"Try to initiate contact. We've never had to go beyond that, 'cause so far it's always worked. If we still couldn't get contact, we'd get a bird up immediately. And if that didn't work, we'd get a recon team in there, right quick."

"Why wouldn't you just wait till the next sitrep time to see if they establish contact on their own?"

He looked at me like that was a spectacularly stupid question. "Come on, you know this shit. Those sitreps are their only lifeline. Miss even one and we start moving heaven and earth to find out what happened."

"Were you on duty when Sanchez's team was in the zone?"

"Part of the time, but I gotta tell you, Major, paesan to paesan, we've been told to watch what we say to you about that."

I figured that Sergeant Major Williams and I had shared some pretty intimate times together. I mean, a certain amount of repartee develops between a beater and his beatee. So I pressed my luck.

"Who told you that?"

The smile had left his face, and he began shaking his head. "Can't really say. But you better play this real smart. Don't go actin' like the same stubborn shit I remember. Might not have seemed like it, but that POW camp was just kid's play. What's goin' down around here's for keeps."

Just at that moment a fella with a full bird on his collar, who looked like he just bit into a big, saucy lemon, walked over to join us. He glanced at me like I was the guy who had just deflowered his virginal daughter, then grabbed Williams by the sleeve.

"Excuse me, Sergeant Major, we've got another update to send to team four. Would you step over and join me?"

The colonel dragged Williams to a corner, then the colonel's forefinger started doing a tap dance on Williams's chest. I could see Williams's feet shuffling, and I guessed he was getting his ears cleaned out pretty good. I can't really say that bothered me all that much. I mean, the guy once spent two weeks beating the doo-doo out of me, and I don't care what he said about it being just a job and all that. When someone spends about twenty hours turning you into pulp, you can tell whether he sees it as work or sport. Maybe that's why he left the outfit after six years. Maybe the outfit sensed he was going over the edge. If they'd asked me at the time, I would've sworn he was so far over the edge that he'd hit the pitch-black bottom.

At any rate, the watchdogs were on to me, so I knew I wasn't going to get any more help here. I retreated quietly and thought about Williams's warning. There were lots of ways to interpret it. Maybe the word had been put out to stay away from me because I was investigating some of their brethren, and everybody wanted to make damn sure they did nothing to help put some of their own guys away. From a technically legal standpoint, that was a large-scale conspiracy to commit obstruction of justice. From a human standpoint, it was an understandable, and in some ways even admirable, fraternal response.

The hitch was that added warning about this being for keeps. I mean, at right about that moment, a big, bloated corpse was packed in a container of dry ice, on the back of a C-130, winging its way to Washington. I'd call that "for keeps."

I reached down and fingered the .38 caliber that rested in the holster on my hip. The time had come for me to actually get some ammunition for this thing. On the other hand, given my deplorable marksmanship skills, I'd probably stand a better chance if I just threw the damn pistol at anyone who was coming after me.

Chapter
☆☆ 17

The fellow waiting for me back at my office looked like a spook. Maybe it was all those James Bond movies. Or maybe it was all those spymaster novels that were the rage during the cold war, but sunglasses and trench coats had become the shibboleths for anybody connected with intelligence collection. Now just how an NSA guy expected to be perceived as a daring spy was beyond me. I mean, give me a break. NSA guys and gals don't do secret missions or any of that crap. Hollywood sometimes portrays them as furtive skulduggers, but that just goes to show what happens when you give guys like Oliver Stone a camera and a license to interpret the universe. The NSA folks are terrestrial gazers. They rely on satellites and fancy airplanes with lots of odd gizmos to do all their work. Still, I guess you can't fault them for wanting to exploit that spurious image Hollywood has created for them. I mean, it's a cheap way to have a little sex appeal.

At any rate, this guy was sitting in a chair beside my office door, trench coat slung across his lap, *Washington Post* splayed open, just trying his damnedest to look like some nonchalant, hotshot, dashing operative. Actually, he pulled it off pretty well.

He was a handsome guy with slicked-back blond hair, grayed nicely at the temples, and by his build I'd say he and the NSA gymnasium were fairly well acquainted. Most NSA folks look like clerks with wide, flat asses. That's what comes from sitting all day and peering at the world through a satellite aperture.

"Hi," I said as I walked past him.

The newspaper was instantly closed, he popped out of his chair and followed me. "You're Major Drummond?"

"Last time I checked," I said.

He trailed me into my lair, where I got myself situated behind my desk, and he got his self situated in front of my desk. Digging his wallet out of his trench coat, he flung it open to show me some kind of ID. He tried to do this swiftly, the way some cops do, but I caught a glimpse of the letters NSA before he slammed it shut with a quick, violent swinging motion. I wondered if this guy was on steroids.

I said, "I guess you got my request."

"The home office back in Maryland got it. They asked me to make contact with you."

"Good. You've done your job well. We're now in contact."

My wiseass manners were lost on this guy. He said, "I always do my job well. And you're in luck, Major. We did have a satellite focused on Zone Three during the period in question."

"Great. When can I have the pictures?"

"Well, I'm afraid that's going to take a while. Zone Three is a large area. In fact, nearly two hundred square miles. There's a great deal of human activity inside that sector. We've requested Tenth Group to provide us the coordinates of the base camp, and the exact location of the ambush. Once we have those, our analysts should be able to do the cutouts. You want film or stills?"

"Both. I'd like to look at everything you've got and see what I can tell myself."

"Suit yourself."

"Do your people know I'm in a hurry?"

He said in a very condescending way, "Of course they know. Everybody wants our stuff in a hurry. In case you hadn't noticed, there's a war going on just north of here."

There was something about this guy I didn't like. I didn't like his eyes, which reminded me of a couple of pale blue marbles stuffed inside a pair of narrow sockets. There was no life in those eyes, only color, like they were artificial. But there was something else. I couldn't put my finger on it. There just was something.

I said, "I didn't know you guys were directly supporting Tenth Group."

"Sure."

"And you've got a facility here at Tuzla?"

"Located right beside the Air Force's C3I facility. It's just a small setup, but it's a secure facility. You can view the shots there."

"What if I want to take pictures out?"

He broke into a knavish smile. "Uh-uh. That's not gonna happen."

"Why not?"

"Because they're too highly classified."

"Look, Mr. . . . uh, I didn't really catch your name."

The smile changed to a half-assed smirk. "That's because you weren't meant to. Just call me Mr. Jones."

I said, "Damn, that's real original."

He said, "Yeah, I'm a real clever guy. Ask anyone."

Now I knew what I didn't like about this guy. My office was pretty tiny. There was barely enough oxygen for one pushy wiseass, which meant he was crowding my airspace.

I said, "So what happens if I decide I have to include some of your satellite shots in my investigation packet?"

"That's your problem. They're not leaving my facility."

"Am I gonna have to push this up the line?"

"Push as far up as you like, buddy. These shots were taken

by a brand-new experimental satellite, with capabilities I'm not about to describe to someone like you. The President himself couldn't order me to release those pictures."

I brooded over that a moment. "How do I get hold of you?" I finally asked.

"You don't. I'll get hold of you when we're ready."

"You're stationed here?"

"Yep. They called me from home station this morning and told me to assist you. Just be a good boy, and we'll make this as painless as possible for both of us."

"Gee, thanks. I'm really looking forward to working with you," I said as he walked out the door.

This guy really bothered me. His eyes bothered me. His manners bothered me. You know what bothered me more than anything, though? The *Washington Post* tucked under his arm. And that silly trench coat. It hadn't rained in Tuzla in days. The sun was out and was baking everything in sight. I walked out and found Imelda, who was busily reviewing the transcripts we had taken back at Aviano.

"Hey, Imelda, do me a favor."

"I don't do favors," she grumbled. "I only follow orders."

"Right. Then do me an order. Call Washington and find out what the weather's been like the past twenty-four hours."

"How come? You planning on takin' a trip yesterday?" She cackled, and I had to admit it was one of the funnier things I'd ever heard her say. I guess part of me was starting to rub off on her. Unfortunately, it was the bad joke part.

"Actually, my car's parked at Andrews Air Force Base," I told her, "and I just remembered I left the window open. Oh . . . one other thing."

"What's that?"

"Where are you storing our case materials at night?"

"Those cabinets over there," she said, pointing at three large gray military-issue file cabinets.

"Requisition a safe immediately. You, or one of your assistants, sleep next to those cabinets till it gets here."

Her eyebrows went up a notch or two, but she was a smart lady. She didn't ask.

I went back into my office and called my big new buddy Wolky. I very nicely told him I was hereby requisitioning the services of two of his strapping military policemen to stand guard outside my building's doorway every night.

A moment later, Imelda came in to inform me it had been raining torrentially in Washington the past twenty-four hours. Reagan National Airport was closed. Dulles International was closed to everything but emergency flights. The rain, however, had miraculously missed Andrews Air Force Base, so my car was safe. She frowned deeply when she reported this. In Imelda's world, any idiot stupid enough to leave his car windows open deserved ruined electronics and mildewed seats.

The truth was, though, my car wasn't really parked at Andrews. I was just wondering how Mr. Jones got here so promptly. That smug, deceitful little liar. He didn't walk down the street; he took off from Andrews.

But why did he fly all this way? And why was he so secretive about his name? And why that spurious lie about being stationed here? People who make their living gathering and peddling secrets eventually become secretive by nature, but Mr. Jones was stretching things a little.

I pondered this until there was a knock on the door, and I looked up to see my two CID buddies, Martie and David, anxiously waiting to be invited in.

"Please," I said, standing up and walking over to shake hands.

Martie said, "Hi, Major. Hope we're not bothering you."

"No, no bother at all."

"Good. David and I thought we'd stop by and maybe discuss a few more things with you."

"Sure."

They threw themselves into a pair of seats and spent a moment getting organized. Martie's face was kind of cold and detached, while David looked like he had a couple of big hemorrhoids that were bothering him terribly. These are what professional crimebusters call clues. Their moods had changed since this morning.

Martie said, "Have you seen copies of the two articles published on the front page of this morning's *Herald*?"

I admitted I hadn't, so he handed me a couple of pages that had obviously been faxed to him. The first was a headline banner about Jeremy Berkowitz and his murder. It was a nice piece, exalting him as one of the nation's foremost military experts, a courageous, dedicated journalist, and an all-around saint of a guy. It was the kind of puffy eulogy journalists always write about one another, ending with a long, tear-jerking paragraph about everything Jeremy did for the world, and how much that world was now going to miss him. That kind of stuff. Somehow, I managed not to break into sniffles.

The second piece was the final story Berkowitz filed, the one about my investigation. Only it wasn't even remotely the story he told me he was going to write. This was a very shallow, vague thing about how the investigation was still ongoing, how the investigators were working tirelessly to complete their job, how the facts were slowly unfolding. I tried not to show my surprise.

Martie was now angled back in his chair with this real ambiguous expression. "That the same piece he told you he was going to write?" he inquired, and not in a friendly way, either.

This is one of the problems with CID guys. They have real short memories. This morning I was his best buddy, and by evening I'm being treated like the Boston Strangler.

I calmly said, "He never told me what he was going to write."

"But you said—"

"I said he seemed very excited. I said he alluded that he had an inside source. How the hell would I know what he was going to write?"

"Your office staff says Berkowitz spent over ten minutes in your office. This morning you gave us the impression that he barely stopped by, only briefly, to confirm a few details."

"And I stand by that. We also engaged in a little harmless chitchat about things in Washington."

"Like what?"

"Like how the investigation is being perceived. I believe he mentioned that the White House is very interested."

"And that was all you talked about?"

"That was all."

"That took ten minutes, huh?" he said very skeptically, then rearranged himself in the chair, bending forward. "Well, we've had the chance to go through his notebook more thoroughly. Your name was mentioned a lot."

"Mentioned how?"

"Let's just say a few of the notations are very curious."

I said, "Curious is an interesting word. Was it curious like 'I think Major Drummond is going to strangle me with a garrote tonight'? Or was it more like 'Drummond is in charge of the investigation and he seems like a real swell guy, and I must make it a point to learn more about him'?"

Martie's face was unreadable. He said, "Somewhere between those two."

Now Martie had never disclosed his rank to me, but I guessed he and David were probably warrant officers. That's the rank of nearly all CID field investigators, most of whom are former military policemen who have gone on to better things, sort of like street cops who become detectives.

The moment seemed ripe for me to try to bully him with one of my tantrums, but I somehow thought that would be a very bad idea. Martie, aside from dressing oddly, was no dummy, and he'd chosen the right way to interrogate me: by dropping one disclosure after another so that I could entrap myself. At that POW camp run by the outfit, this was the favored technique of what they called the soft sell. Truthfully, it is a far more successful method than turning a guy's face into hamburger, because tough guys like I thought I was aren't necessarily smart guys, and the soft sell is a contest of wits.

Of course, Martie had no way of knowing I had earned a master's degree in interrogation, so that left him at a bit of a disadvantage. We were at the point now where I was supposed to be getting very jittery. The textbook responses of a guilty man are to deny everything, but also to become desperately curious about how much the interrogator knows. A fencing engagement results; a bit of cross-probing. This is exactly what the interrogator wants. You unwittingly participate in your own destruction.

I got up and walked to the door. I got it open and was already halfway out when Martie said, "Where do you think you're going?"

"I'm going to find an attorney. I'm sure there are one or two around here somewhere."

This was not what the textbook told him to expect. "Wait a minute," he said, trying to put some iron in his voice.

I said, "Sorry, pal, you got your free minute, and you abused it."

"Hold on, Major," he asked, this time with a slight quaver in his voice. "You may have perfectly logical explanations for everything."

"Oh, I'm quite sure I do," I told him. "In fact, I'm positive I do. But you and I are done speaking."

He gave me this look of wearied impatience, then said, "I'd advise you to sit down and hash this out."

And I said, "Fat chance. We both know what's happening here. Your nuts are in a vise until you come up with a suspect. I'm sorry for your nuts—I truly am—but I don't want to be your suspect."

"That has nothing to do with it."

"Bullshit, Martie. This has everything to do with it."

Martie turned and looked at David, who now looked like those imaginary hemorrhoids of his were positively killing him.

I said, "What will it be? Will you two leave, or should I go find an attorney?"

Martie pondered that a moment, then he and David got up to leave. Martie shouldn't have done that. Very amateurish. If he truly believed he had something that implicated me, he would've told me to go find myself a whole herd of fast-talking attorneys, and let's have a showdown. Obviously, whatever Berkowitz had written about me in his little book was either too nebulous or too untainted for Martie to make even a half-assed case. He was grabbing at straws. He was trying to harass everyone in sight to see what turns up. Shaking the trees, they call that. A good technique, unless there happen to be gorillas hanging around, in which case, it's quite high on the not recommended list.

There was another light knock on the door, and when I looked up, Morrow was standing there looking pensive. Beautiful, but pensive.

She said, "You don't look like you're having a good day."

"Nonsense. They just did the Virginia lottery drawing, and guess what? The winning ticket's in my wallet. Two hundred and fifty million dollars. I was just sitting here wondering what I'm gonna do with all that money."

She entered and sat down. "And what did you decide?"

"Every penny's going to Mother Teresa. Not a penny to anyone else but her."

"Uh, Major . . . Mother Teresa's dead."

"Yeah? Really?" I said. "Then screw it. I'll just spend it all on myself."

"I could see you doing that," she said.

"Yeah, me too. I'm seeing it real clear. Me, a grand house at the end of the Florida Keys, a big three-masted schooner, a fancy red sports car. And what would you do?"

"Me?" She ran a long, slender hand through that thick luxuriant hair of hers as though she had never dreamed of having that much money. I mean, give me a break. Everybody dreams of having Bill Gates's money. Just not his looks.

She said, "I guess I'd buy a nice little brownstone in Cambridge, then open up a charitable foundation."

"Ugh, that's awful," I said.

"I beg to differ. It's a perfectly meaningful way to employ money you didn't earn."

"I'm talking about that Cambridge brownstone. Having all those insufferable, lefty Harvard preppies for neighbors. You'd drown in alligator shirts and Weejun loafers."

"You're behind the times. Diversity, remember? Harvard even lets Republicans in now. Not in any great numbers, certainly, but the odd token here and there."

"No kidding? What kind? Real, meat-eating Republicans? Or, that phony, limp-wristed Rockefeller kind?"

"I even had a skinhead in my law school class."

"A skinhead?"

"Way wacko." She rolled her eyes. "All he wore were those freaky black T-shirts, camouflage pants, and combat boots. He concentrated on constitutional law. He had this plan to graduate, then spend the rest of his life trying to stuff the Supreme Court docket with challenges to various antidiscrimination statutes. Rambo Esquire, we all called him."

"Damn, he sure chose the right place. What's the name of that professor? You know, the one who wrote all those best-selling books and keeps suing the government?"

"Alan Dershowitz?"

"Yeah, that guy."

"Alan actually liked him," she said. "He thought Rambo had spunk and chutzpah."

"You know Dershowitz?"

"Very well, in fact. Alan was my faculty adviser. Also the best lawyer I ever saw. I took both his classes."

"Gee, and I thought I was the best lawyer you ever saw."

I nearly smiled. Of course, I was being sly and disingenuous. I was trying to dispel these troubling doubts about Morrow, like maybe she hadn't really gone to Harvard Law, like maybe she wasn't really a lawyer, like maybe she was a plant who'd been placed here to report on me and keep me in line. Of course, I had the same doubts about Delbert, but I was fast reaching the point where I needed someone to confide in. Lots of strange things were happening, and I felt like I needed a sounding board.

I said, "Do you mind if I unload a few things on you?"

Her being a beautiful woman and all, I probably should have picked my words a little more carefully. She'd no doubt had dozens of men ask her that same question, then start unburdening about the lousy wife that didn't understand them, or the sex life that wasn't working or some such thing. Beautiful women spend a lot of time being confessors to men who want to get into their pants.

She kind of winced. "Okay, Major, if you must."

"First, let's drop that major thing, okay? Sean will do just fine."

From the dubious look on her face, this seemed to confirm her worst fears. "Okay, Sean, fine."

"What I need from you is a sanity check."

This confused her for a moment, since it was obviously not what she'd expected to hear. Unless, that is, by sanity check I was leading up to her playing doctor, and when boys and girls play doctor, then, well . . .

She nodded, and I continued. "Look, I'm feeling very weird about what's happening around here. Yesterday that reporter, Berkowitz, stopped by and asked me a few questions about the investigation. Then, this morning, he's dead. It had all the earmarks of a professional hit, the kind of thing a Mafia pro might do, or maybe a Special Forces guy who's been trained to use exotic weapons."

Lisa was nodding along. "And you think there's some kind of link?" she asked, very cool, very detached.

She sounded just like a therapist. Not that I've ever been to a therapist, mind you. Well all right, when I left the oufit, they had me spend a few sessions with a head shaker. They did that to everybody, though. Honest.

I finally said, "Actually, yes, I do think there's a link. But let me cover some other ground first. This afternoon I had another session with that big ape, General Murphy. I asked him what happened when Sanchez's team missed their daily sitreps. He said nothing. That didn't make sense to me, because one of the purposes of those routine sitreps is to confirm to your head-quarters that you're still alive. So I asked him why no red flags went up."

"And he said?"

"That the ops center usually waits twelve hours until the next sitrep period. Only if the team misses that second report is there a response."

"I could see where that would make sense," she said.

"Actually, it doesn't. You have to understand the urgency of timely sitreps. Especially when you're talking about units oper-ating behind enemy lines. But anyway, I then went to the ops center, just to see what I could find out. I asked the ops sergeant if he remembered any cases when teams failed to make their sitreps. He said KLA teams occasionally missed, but no Ameri-can team had ever missed. Then I asked him what he would do if he lost contact with a team. He said they would immediately push every panic button in sight."

"So we have a difference of opinion between a sergeant and a general."

"Or we have a liar."

"Which is a large leap to a dangerous conclusion."

"Maybe. However, the same ops sergeant warned me that somebody put out the word not to cooperate with our investigating team."

This news at last got something other than an argumentative reaction. "Why would he tell you that?" she asked.

"One of those odd coincidences. He remembered me from when I was stationed at Bragg years ago. I guess it was one of those auld lang syne things."

"And you believe him?"

"I watched a full colonel take him apart just because he talked to me."

"There could be a lot of explanations for that."

"There could, but I can't think of any. Now odd incident number three. An NSA guy showed up here a few minutes ago. He stopped by to tell me we're in luck, that one of their satellites was over Zone Three. He told me he was stationed here but refused to give his real name. Only thing was, he was carrying a *Washington Post* and a trench coat. By the way, it's been raining cats and dogs in Washington the past twenty-four hours. I hope you remembered to close your car windows."

She pulled on her lip for a while and seemed to weigh everything I'd just said. Then she stared down at the floor, then up at the ceiling. She put a pencil eraser against her lip, and I don't know why, I just found that sexy as hell.

Finally, she said, "I'm really sorry. I just don't see any connection between all these things."

"Time and place, Morrow. A journalist gets murdered, a general lies, a unit obstructs justice, and a strange man arrives from Washington. All inside twelve hours. All here in tiny Tuzla."

"Taken individually, any of those things has a variety of possible explanations."

"Or maybe they're like those noxious weeds with a common root, with those long underground stems that make them bloom in different places."

"If you have a fertile imagination."

"Maybe you're right," I admitted. "Maybe I'm just paranoid."

"Do you have some reason to be paranoid?"

"None I can put my finger on. But sometimes in battle, you look at a hill and just know there's something lurking on the other side, something dangerous."

"This isn't a battle, though."

"Tell Jeremy Berkowitz that."

Chapter ☆☆☆ 18

Sleep did not come easily that night. I lay in my bunk trying to fit all these little pieces together, and frankly the best I could manufacture was a Frankenstein-like image: a gangly, stitched-together resemblance of a monster. Only my Frankenstein was missing a few arms and legs, and I couldn't bring it to life. Everything I came up with was too moth-eaten for even me to believe.

Clapper's call came at two o'clock in the morning, and I was still fully awake, so I didn't grouse or grump.

He started the conversation with, "Damn it, Drummond, what the hell's happening out there?" He sounded really pissed, which was another reason I didn't grouse or grump.

I said, "Things are proceeding well. Some NSA guy stopped by today and said we're in luck. Thanks for your help."

"I'm not talking about that. I just got off the phone with General Murphy. He says you're harassing him and other members of his command. He says your conduct has been unprofessional."

"He never mentioned anything to me."

"He faxed me a long list of official complaints. Being disrespectful to senior officers. Threatening senior officers with indictments. Blocking an officer from his defense counsel. Harassing and badgering witnesses. Not to mention forcing your way into an operations center and preventing key personnel from doing their jobs in the midst of a field operation, thus endangering the lives of soldiers in the field."

"Look, sir, all of that's bullsh—"

"He attached a stack of witness statements. Let's see, here's a set from Lieutenant Colonel Smothers and his attorney, Captain Smith. Here's another from Sergeant Major Williams, and a Colonel Bitters. Shall I go on?"

"No, sir, I can ex—"

"Ah, let's not overlook this one. It's from the group chaplain. He says you tried to pressure him into violating his confessional confidences."

"I talked to him, but I—"

"Now, I'm going to ask you once again, what the hell are you doing out there?"

He'd finally given me an opportunity to defend myself, but I was too busy trying to get some air back in my lungs. I felt like I had just dived into a swimming pool filled with big chunks of ice, and my gonads were now somewhere in my chest and heading toward my throat. It suddenly struck me that what I was apparently doing out here was being outwitted at every turn. I'd been framed, literally from the moment I'd stepped onto Tuzla's tarmac. Everywhere I went, and every interview I'd done, someone had trotted along behind me. Or beside me. I'd underestimated the opposition.

Besides, the golden rule of the Army is that rank makes right. It might not be fair, but the whole damn system would collapse unless that rule was preserved and protected.

Not to mention the golden rule of law, which is that he who possesses the most compelling and abundant evidence wins. Murphy had gone to the trouble to manufacture statements and collect witnesses, whereas I had nothing but my word as an attorney and an officer. Such as it was.

I very weakly said, "I'm sure we can clear this up, when we have time."

"You're right. When this is over, there'll be an official inquiry into your conduct. I hope I don't need to remind you that Chuck Murphy might well be the most respected officer in the armed forces. He was first in his class at West Point. He was an All-America tackle and got the Heisman. He was a Rhodes scholar and a war hero. His integrity is unblemished and unquestioned."

By extrapolation, my reputation and integrity obviously had some gaping flaws.

I stammered, "I understand that, b—"

"And another damned thing. The very damn reason we chose a lawyer to head this investigation was to have someone with enough acumen to navigate that legal minefield out there. Remember the 'fruit of the poisonous tree'?"

"Of course I remember," I said. The "fruit of the poisonous tree" is the legal doctrine that says that once the route of discovery becomes tainted by poor process, not only that specific piece of evidence but all that follows in its path becomes inadmissible in court.

He more or less yelled, "You recommend a court-martial now, and the defense will have a field day. You really screwed this up."

"Look, sir, I—"

"Another thing. The head of the Criminal Investigation Division was in here a few minutes ago. He asked me for your military personnel file. He's conducting a background check on you. What in the hell's that about? What exactly is your involvement with Berkowitz's murder?"

"None I know of, General. I told you Berkowitz came to see me the day he died. Two CID investigators have been to see me twice. They said they were bothered by some curious notes in Berkowitz's journal."

"Curious? What in the hell does 'curious' mean?"

"I asked them the same question, but they're treating it like privileged information."

There was this long, tense pause, then, "I'm not happy with your performance, Drummond. I mean, I'm really friggin' unhappy."

"I'm not happy with it, either," I admitted, although for very different reasons than his.

"You just keep your nose clean till this is over. No more complaints from Chuck Murphy. I mean, I don't want to hear another word. Have I made myself clear?"

"Very clear."

"We'll have an inquiry when this is done," Clapper threatened again before his phone came down hard in the cradle, and our conversation, such as it was, abruptly ended. Other than a few "yessirs," and "but I's," I hadn't contributed much.

It was no use trying to fall asleep. I got out of my bunk, got dressed, then walked over to our little wooden building. Two of Wolky's burliest MPs stood beside the door. I showed them my ID and they let me in. Imelda was inside sitting on her bunk, flashlight in hand, reading one of those big, thick books she likes so much. She glanced up when she heard the door bang open and shut and quickly stuffed the book under her sleeping bag. This is a woman who makes the most out of being underestimated.

"Who's there?" She blinked into the darkness.

"It's me, Imelda."

"Oh," she said. "What are you doin' here at this hour?"

I said, "I couldn't sleep. I thought I'd come over and review some law books."

The truth was, I was feeling like such a world-class heel that I thought I'd punish myself, like those fourteenth-century monks who used to horsewhip their own backs in expiation for their sins. Only I chose a more cruel form of chastisement. I was going to read every legal text I could get my hands on.

"This gig's not goin' too good, huh?"

"No, it really isn't," I mournfully admitted. "I think I'm screwing it up."

She sat and pondered that for a moment. We'd probably worked two dozen cases together over the years, and although I respected the hell out of Imelda, we'd never really conversed about the guts of any of those cases. I'd shuffled papers at her and given her chores to do, and she'd stayed busy supervising her clerks and making sure I showed up at court prepared and on time.

"You think they're guilty?" she asked.

"To tell you the truth, I don't know. I suspect they're guilty, but I seem to be the only one who holds that opinion."

"I think they're guilty as a cropa diseased whores in a nunhouse," she said.

In case I haven't mentioned it before, Imelda could get very picturesque at times. I leaned against the wall and crossed my arms. I hadn't come here to have a long discussion with Imelda, but I had nothing better to do. If you've ever read a legal textbook, you'd know what I mean.

"Why?" I asked.

" 'Cause I read all your statements. They're lying. They're lyin' their asses right off their faces. That captain . . . uh, Sanchez, right?"

"That's right. Terry Sanchez."

"Yeah. What I think is that man didn't have the balls."

"I'm sorry. The balls for what?"

"That warrant and those sergeants ran all over his weak ass. Read those statements. Those men were dissin' him bad."

"Maybe," I said, "but what if the Army doesn't really want me to find out what happened out there? What if the Army believes it would be much more convenient to just find them innocent and move on?"

"The Army doesn't always know what's best for itself."

She was sitting there on top of her sleeping bag, hair messed up, wearing a wrinkled army green T-shirt, faded old gym shorts, and white socks. Frankly, she looked like a pretty shabby font of wisdom.

I said, "Thanks, Imelda."

"No problem. Now quit snivlin' and get your ass in gear."

"Yes, ma'am."

I went into my office and shut the door. I could hear the sounds of Imelda pulling open drawers and riffling through files. After a few minutes, she walked in with her arms piled high with folders. She carried them to my desk and dropped them unceremoniously into a large heap. Without saying another word, she left.

I looked down at the stack. She had gathered all the transcripts of the statements we'd collected back in Italy. I rummaged through and found Chief Persico's, then started reading. Then I worked my way through each of the other team members' statements.

By six o'clock I was done. Imelda was right. There was a common theme that ran through all the statements. It was a lack of respect for Sanchez. In Persico's case, it was nearly imperceptible, but it was there. He had heaped praise on his team leader, but he continually referred to the KLA commander as *Captain* Akhan. Sanchez was always just Sanchez.

Sergeant Perrite had been more blunt. There was that comment about Sanchez not knowing how to wipe his own ass without Persico being around to help him. But there was more than that. When Perrite and Machusco detected the Serbs on the hill, it was Persico they reported that news to. And maybe this was why Sanchez didn't have a clue how many flares had gone off or what his rear security element was doing, or what they were seeing. The sergeants in the team were bringing everything to Persico as though he were the team leader, as though Sanchez was only along for the ride.

Now that I knew what to look for, in one way or another, that same thread wound its way through every statement. Delbert and Morrow had not probed very deep in their interrogatories, but the same flavor was there. Here were the Moore brothers, the twins, saying that Persico told them where to place themselves in the ambush. Persico gave them the order to fire and ignited the star cluster that told them when to cease fire. Graves, the medic, saying it was Persico who'd put him in his safe position half a mile behind the ambush, and Persico who instructed him where the linkup site was, in case things went awry and they all had to scatter. Butler, one of the two heavy weapons men, who carried the machine gun, saying it was Persico who checked his aiming stakes, who told him where to tie in his fire, who supervised the laying of the claymores. More of the same from Sergeant Caldwell.

Several times during the interrogatories, I'd asked Persico and Perrite how various decisions got made. Both their responses had been vague or uncomprehending. I should have suspected something right then and there. Persico had assured me that all the operational responsibility was on Sanchez's shoulders, but as I read through the statements there was barely a hint that Sanchez was even present.

Delbert and Morrow came in at six-thirty. I decided not to mention a word about this to either of them. For one thing, both would simply see it as yet another wretched attempt on my part to look for guilt when all the evidence screamed innocence. For another, I didn't want word of this making its way back up the mole's chain. But, more important, the entire progress of the investigation now rested on what NSA's satellite photos indicated. If the pictures showed a team cold-bloodedly murdering thirty-five Serbs, then we now had a fresh line of inquiry. If the shots showed Sanchez's team running for their lives and desperately trying to fight their way out of a deadly noose, then the interesting observation I'd just collected was about as useful as a jockstrap in a girls' locker room.

At eight a woman called on behalf of Mr. Jones. She had a sweet, singsongy voice, and she invited us to the NSA field station for a private showing in one hour. I closed the door to my office and spent my time in the most productive manner I could. I paced back and forth. I walked from wall to wall, then corner to corner, until I got bored with that. Then I just stared at the walls.

I didn't want Sanchez and his men to be guilty, but I had passed the point where I could afford for them to be innocent. Right now, my whole career rested on my being right. Clapper's threat of an inquiry into my conduct was looming like a nightmare. Murphy had timed his attack perfectly. If the tapes showed that Sanchez's team was innocent, then I'd have to pack my bags and be back in Washington. I might be able to procrastinate for a day or two, arguing I had to close up some unfinished business, but right now any official inquiry would be stacked completely against me. Delbert and Morrow would say I seemed obsessed with finding Sanchez's team guilty, despite a screaming lack of evidence. Then there were all these statements from Murphy's boys. I would look like a crazed Captain Ahab, whipping and snarling at everyone in sight, all for the sake of some nonexistent whale. I wouldn't be court-martialed, but my odds of practicing any more law in the Army were about as good as betting on a three-legged horse at Saratoga.

At a quarter till nine I went and collected Delbert and Morrow. We found our way to the Air Force's C3I facility, and a guard directed us to a small metal building off to the left. There was no sign to identify it as an NSA building, I guess because they didn't want anyone to know they were here.

Two uniformed guards stood at the entry, which, if you think about it, kind of defeated the whole purpose, because if you were into practicing a little espionage and you saw an unmarked, heavily guarded building right near the C3I facility, well, that might tend to make you a bit suspicious about what was inside there. All that brainpower, and these guys couldn't figure out how much smarter it would be to position the guards *inside* the building.

At any rate, the guards obviously expected us, so we flashed our identity cards, and I showed the fellas that obnoxious set of orders the Secretary of the Army had provided me, then they ushered us right in.

There was a second doorway inside, constructed of heavy-gauge metal, and we had to push a buzzer. There was a camera in the ceiling corner, and someone inside probably peered through at us before there was a humming sound and I pushed the door open.

A woman, I guessed the same woman who called earlier, was waiting for us.

"Hi, I'm Miss Smith," she said with a perfectly wooden smile. She had precisely aligned, gleaming white teeth that indicated either magnificent genetic breeding or a wonderfully talented family dentist.

It struck me that everybody who worked at NSA was either named Jones or Smith, or some other monosyllabic name. I mean, why couldn't they all go by Gwyzdowski, or Petroblaski? Then at least you couldn't really tell if they were tossing off aliases. Unless, of course, you ran into a whole flock of them all at once.

At any rate, Miss Smith could give the ever-impressive Miss Morrow a tight run for the money in ye olde looks department. The difference was that Miss Smith was wearing a very short skirt and a nice clingy blouse that made it more amply clear what you'd be biting into. The lovely Miss Morrow had all her wares camouflaged inside a set of baggy battle dress, although I must say that greens and browns and blacks went quite well with her complexion.

I said, "Very nice to meet you, Miss Smith. I assume you work with Mr. Jones?"

"That's correct. I'm his administrative assistant."

"Well," I said, "welcome to Tuzla."

"Oh, thanks," she said with that same shiny smile. Apparently Miss Smith also had just arrived from Washington.

"So where do we go?" I asked.

"Here, follow me."

She led us to the back of the small office and, voilà, there was a set of steep stairs that took us down into an underground compound.

Like a good tour guide, she talked as we walked. "We had this constructed underground because we had to shield the walls with lead lining. Modern microwave listening devices allow a sophisticated eavesdropper to read everything that passes through a computer. We, of course, have the most modern, shielded computers, but we still like to play it safe and get as much protection as we can."

"That's very smart of you," I said, then mumbled, "like wearing two Trojans when you make love."

"Yes, well, it's expensive, but it's worth it."

"And what kind of strange things do you all do in this special facility?"

I was staring at the back of her blond head and couldn't see her expression, but she didn't answer for a very long moment. "Mostly target analysis for bombing," she finally informed me, although she didn't sound all that sure.

"Do you control any assets?"

"None that I know of."

We had now reached the basement floor, and I sped up to walk beside her as she led us down a long, narrow passageway.

"That's odd," I remarked. "Someone . . . maybe it was Mr. Jones, mentioned that the U-2s are controlled from this facility."

"Oh, yes, of course that's right. I'm sorry, I'm just an administrative assistant. I'm really not the person to ask about these things."

"Au contraire. You've been very helpful," I said, and she smiled at that, too. Miss Smith smiled a lot, I noticed. And she lied a lot, too.

We had reached another large metal door, and she deftly flicked a plastic card through a doorlock, then pushed open the door. Mr. Jones was seated at the end of a long table, coffee cup in hand. He had traded in his dark suit and tie for more casual garb. In fact, he was dressed much like Berkowitz had been, duck-shooting vest and all. To me, he looked pompous, but like I said, he was a handsome guy with a lot of muscles. He stood up and walked around the conference table, while I introduced Delbert and Morrow.

Jones did a quick, automatic handshake with Delbert, then a long, lingering, smiley one with Morrow. I might've been imagining things, but when he said "nice to meet ya" to her, it sounded like it came from the bottom of his heart, or maybe it was from somewhere closer to his groin. Whichever.

Then he looked over at me, and I was instantly reminded that we seemed to instinctively dislike each other.

"You mentioned you wanted to see the raw footage, Major. What we've got are thermals taken from seven hundred and fifty miles up. These are cutouts, of course, taken from a much larger panorama, then blown up about nine hundred times. Because they're thermals, the shots are grainy. You can't identify the figures."

"You didn't have any photographic satellites over Zone Three?"

"Turns out we didn't. For reasons that are none of your business, we've been limiting Zone Three's coverage. Thermal matches the requirements Tenth Group was requesting, so that's it."

"Then there are no actual photos in your archives?"

"Great deduction there, chief. Don't worry. I'm sure you'll be very satisfied with what we have."

Jones invited us all to have seats, and I noticed that he positioned himself right beside Morrow. I therefore positioned myself right beside the lovely, still smiling Miss Smith. Poor Delbert was left to position himself right beside, well . . . right beside poor Delbert.

The lights were dimmed by somebody in the rear projection booth, and then the film started. What we saw was all green, variously shaded, with a few tiny dots in brighter, almost translucent green. The particular group of dots we were looking at were gathered in a fairly small clot. One or two figures were moving around, but the rest were still. There were seven dots collected together, and two more some distance away.

Jones had a notepad in front of him, and he did the narrating.

"This film was taken at one o'clock in the afternoon of the fourteenth. The grid coordinates correspond with the position Tenth Group gave us for Sanchez's base camp. We assume that what you're seeing here are afternoon activities in a base camp. Weapons cleaning, maybe eating, the usual base camp activities."

He pointed a finger at the two green dots that were separate from the others. "See those two dots right there? We believe that might be Sanchez's security element."

We watched more of the same for two minutes before Jones said, "This tape runs for another fifty-two minutes. If you'd like, Major, we'll run the whole thing, but all it contains is more of the same."

"No, this is good enough," I told him. "What have you got next?"

"Glad you asked. The next film was taken on the seventeenth. I don't want to ruin the suspense, so I'll ask the projectionist to go ahead."

A silent moment passed as the projectionist changed tapes. I felt like drumming my fingers on the table or whistling, or

leaping across the table and strangling Mr. Jones. I settled instead for sitting perfectly still. It wasn't easy, but I'm a very dis-
ciplined guy.

Finally, a new flash of green tones appeared on the screen,
and it took a minute to sort out what we were seeing. This one
had a hell of a lot more of the small, bright green dots, all of
which were moving, some slowly, some more quickly. I watched
for two minutes and felt my heart land somewhere in the pit
of my stomach.

Finally, the equitable Mr. Jones stood up and walked over to
the screen. He began using his hands to point toward this and
that as he said, "For those who are unfamiliar with our technology, these smaller green dots are personnel. The larger, brighter dots, like this one right here, are from stronger heat sources.
In this case, they correspond to automobile engines."

Delbert asked, "Where is Sanchez's team in that mess?"

"Good question. I wouldn't have known the answer myself
if I hadn't called and talked directly with the team of analysts
who did this work."

He turned around and whipped a laser pointer out of one
of the many pockets in his field vest, flicked it on, then flashed
its tiny red beam at a small line of slowly moving green dots.

"Count here, and you'll recognize there are seven dots. If you
run this tape at hyper speed, then you realize they're moving
in a single file. Our analysts were thrown off at first, because
they were told to look for a group of nine men. Eventually, an
infantry officer on our staff mentioned that the team might've
posted a rear security element."

Jones's little red pointer shifted position to show a pair of
little dots located some distance behind the bulk of Sanchez's
team. "We think this might be Sanchez's rear security element.
Although they're only two inches away on this screen, in true
ground measurement they're about a quarter of a mile back."

Morrow said, "That must be Sergeants Perrite and Machusco."

"If you say so," Jones remarked, awarding her the kind of smile that said, "Good girl. I still want to sleep with you." He continued: "Now, if you'd like we can watch this tape for another forty-nine minutes, or I can explain what you're looking at."

"Explain," I said, feeling sick.

"Oh, before I do, one other piece of good news," he announced with a lofty smile. "We also have audiotapes taken the same day from some of our other assets. They were sent in code, and the language is Serbian, but our analysts decoded and transcribed them for us."

He paused for a moment to let the drama of all that sink in.

"What we have here is a massive manhunt in progress. All told, nearly seven hundred Serb troops were involved. A Serb recon unit reported the sighting of an American A-team at"—he paused and looked down at his yellow pad—"Let me see . . . at two fifty-eight in the afternoon. Immediately afterward, Serb militia radio traffic got very busy. Mobilization orders went out to various units in what we call Zone Three. The Serb militia obviously don't call it that. They refer to it as the Fifteenth Divisional Command region. It took them a while to get all these units in place. The Serb militia in Kosovo operates in a very decentralized fashion, with small units located across large areas."

"Why is that?" Delbert asked.

"Several reasons. One, they don't face any large ground threats that would force them to keep their units concentrated. Two, they wouldn't want them concentrated anyway. By spreading out, a single division can exert control over a much larger geographic region. Third, we believe our bombing campaign has forced them to spread out, so there are no large, inviting formations for our planes to hit."

"Go on," I said, trying to sound interested rather than miserable, which was exactly how I felt.

"Right. This tape we're watching was actually taken around 10 P.M. I guess that's about eight hours before the ambush. As you can see, Sanchez's team was pretty well hemmed in. It's actually a miracle they made it out. By the way, our analysts overlaid maps of the area on this film, and these right here"—he paused to sweep his red dot and make a line on the wall—"are two intersecting roads where Serb vehicles appear to be moving to establish a block."

I said, "Can you show us where the ambush took place?"

"Be happy to, pal." His little red dot moved to a position along one of the lines where he had indicated there were roads. Then he said, "No satellites were overhead at the time of the ambush, but we did get another pass the next day, when Sanchez's team was nearly to the Macedonian border. Wanta see it?"

"No, not really," I sourly replied.

The light flipped back on, and Morrow and Delbert were both beaming like children under a Christmas tree.

Jones looked at me with a real wiseass grin. "Guess it all came out the way you wanted, huh, buddy?"

I wasn't his buddy, and I had an almost irresistible impulse to make that clear, but all I said was, "And I'm still not allowed to take any tapes out of this facility?"

"Nope. They'll be stored in the archives back in Maryland. If anyone wants to view them, they can see them there."

I looked at Delbert and Morrow. "Any questions for Mr. Jones?"

Delbert said, "No, I think it's pretty clear-cut."

Morrow turned to Jones. "Did you get any audio transcriptions of the Serb response to the ambush?"

"Actually, we did. It was kind of nutty. We've got a transcript of a unit reporting the discovery of the bodies. Then there's another transcript of the Fifteenth Division headquarters ordering all units to halt in place and await further instructions. That's all we got, though."

"And how do you interpret that?"

"What we guess is that once the Serbs found out Sanchez's team could bite, they got a lot more cautious, real quick."

Morrow was nodding like, yes, of course, that's exactly what happened. I wanted to strangle her, too.

She then said, "No more audio interceptions? Isn't that a little odd?"

Jones nodded at her like this was a really brilliant question and, oh, by the way, he still wanted to sleep with her. "Not really," he said. "The Serbs know we listen in. When they want to hide things from us, they stop transmitting and start using messengers."

She said, "But you have a copy of the transcription when the ambush site was discovered?"

"Want to hear it?"

"Please."

He riffled through a stack of computer printouts, then culled one out. "Okay, here we are. The sender's call sign was Alfa 36, and the receiving station was Foxtrot 90. We haven't been able to identify Alfa 36, probably a militia company, but Foxtrot 90 is the headquarters for the Fifteenth Division. The message went like—"

"Hold it," I said. "Read it verbatim."

He shook his head at me—a clear sign he didn't want to sleep me with me—then looked down at the page. "Okay. It was a series of four transmissions. First transmission went, 'Foxtrot 90, this is Alfa 36. Report that there has been an ambush at grid 23445590.' Now second transmission: 'Alfa 36, this is Foxtrot 90. Describe condition.' Now the third transmission: 'Foxtrot 90, this is Alfa 36. Seventeen dead, thirteen wounded, five living.' Now the fourth transmission: 'Alfa 36, this is Foxtrot 90. Hold in place and await further instructions.' "

He looked up and said, "That's it. No more audio interceptions between those two stations after that."

You could almost hear Delbert and Morrow gasp. There were still eighteen living Serbs when the ambush site was discovered.

Ergo, Sanchez and his men must not have killed the survivors. *K-chunk!* The two of them just won the daily double.

Morrow shot me a triumphant look, then asked, "You said it's common for the Serbs to go to radio silence when they have sensitive orders to pass?"

"Right. The Serbs have a great deal of experience trying to elude our intelligence capabilities. In the early years of Bosnia, we used to listen in all the time when they planned their massacres and mass rapes. We made tapes of it, and a lot of our stuff got used as evidence in the Hague tribunals. It was unfortunate, really. We protested, because we didn't want to expose our capabilities, but the President overruled us. Pretty soon, every time they planned an atrocity, they made damned sure not to talk about it on the radios." Then he paused and looked at us curiously. "Why? Is there something here I should know about?"

Morrow looked at me and I gave her a nod of permission.

She said, "There sure as hell is. Somebody went around that ambush site and put bullets into the heads of the survivors."

Jones took a heavy breath, then looked down at the table. "No shit? Their own men? Why would they kill their own men?"

Delbert said, "To create an atrocity to pin on American troops."

Jones nodded as though everything just fell into perfect place. "Those bastards! Yes, that would fit. No wonder they stopped transmitting."

After that, there really wasn't anything left for me to say. The daily double had become the trifecta. Morrow and Delbert could not resist giving me the occasional triumphant leer, and good form required that I smile back and respectfully acknowledge that they'd been brilliantly right where I'd been miserably wrong. Unfortunately, good form never was my forte. I just glowered and sulked.

Jones began quietly murmuring with Morrow, and Miss Smith decided I was no longer good company, so she got up and walked around the table and initiated a similarly low-key conversation with Delbert. It was as if they were having a winner's convention, while I stewed in loser's melancholy.

Finally, I got up and showed myself out of the NSA facility. I could've skulked back to my office, but instead I wandered around the Tuzla compound for an hour or so. I did a lot of thinking during that hour. I thought about how stupid I'd been. I thought about what I was going to do after Clapper banned me from ever practicing military law again. I thought about what life was going to be like selling cars on one of my father's car lots. I guess I deserved it.

One of the first lessons you learn in law school is to trust facts, and only facts. Avoid deductions, spurn instincts, and run like hell every time a hunch comes within ten feet of you. Every law school professor tells you that, in one way or another, on the very first day of class. I'd done just the opposite. I'd done a swan dive off a circumstantial highboard and it turned out there was not a single drop of evidentiary water in the pool.

Chapter ☆☆☆ 19

By the time I got back to my little office building, I must've looked pretty doleful, because Imelda's girls all started offering me coffee and asking if there was anything they could do for me. I was quite touched. Before I knew it, I had three cups of steaming java and was sitting in my office, twiddling my thumbs and wondering what in the hell to do next.

The truth was, the only thing left to be done was to finish the report. Then I'd climb on an airplane and go face Clapper's tribunal. Imelda and her tribe had already typed up the transcripts of the interrogatories. Delbert and Morrow had already prepared and proofed all the supporting documentation and evidentiary indexes. Really, the only work that remained was to prepare the final statement that laid out our conclusions and recommendations. I thought about doing it myself; I just didn't have my heart in it. Besides, Delbert and Morrow would figure I was infringing on their victory dance.

Then it struck me. The coroner's report. I asked Imelda to put me through to Dr. Simon McAbee, and about a minute later she stuck her head in and told me to pick up the phone.

"Hey, Doc, Sean Drummond here."

"Hello, Counselor."

"Listen, I owe you a big apology. I should've called two days ago. Our due date got moved up. We're going to need your results tomorrow."

"Oh, well, that's really no problem," he assured me. He had one of those voices that dripped with prissy efficiency. "I finished three days ago anyway."

"Good," I said.

"If you don't mind my asking, what's the outcome? Curiosity, you know."

"We're recommending against court-martial."

"Ah, that's a great relief, isn't it?"

"Yeah, sure," I lied.

"So how did you account for the bullets in the head?"

"The Serbs did it themselves. There's no doubt about that. We found definite proof that there were still survivors when the first Serbs arrived at the ambush site."

"Well, very good," he said. "It would sicken one to believe that American soldiers would do such a hideous, barbaric thing."

I was already getting tired of Simon McAbee's voice. Like lots of doctors, there was this pedantic echo to nearly everything he said. I guess I could understand that from doctors who deal with living beings. But a pathologist? Besides, I was in a really black mood. I was preparing to wrap up our conversation when some impulse made me ask, "Hey, Doc, one thing."

"Yes?"

"Remember I asked you to see if you could estimate how many of the Serbs would've died from wounds other than head shots?"

"Right."

"Were you able to do that?"

"I made an estimate. Let me see . . ." he said, and I could hear the sound of papers being shoveled around. "Ah yes, here. Perhaps twenty-five of them would have died as a result of the wounds received previous to the head wounds."

"Twenty-five?" I asked.

"Well, I wouldn't want to be held to that number. I mean, I didn't have the bodies here to examine them properly."

"Does that mean twenty-five who would've died eventually?"

"Oh goodness. Maybe I misunderstood what you wanted. Twenty-five of those men would have died almost instantly. Certainly others would've died afterward. Too many variables in those cases to make reliable judgments, though. Quality of trauma care. Time elapsed before they arrived at a proper facility. Adequacy of medical care."

I felt this sudden heavy pounding in my heart. "Doc, listen. I need you to be perfectly clear. Are you saying that twenty-five of those men were killed instantly?"

He paused for a moment, and I nearly bent the corner of my desk.

"Instantly, no," he finally said, and my heart rate started to settle back down.

Then, after another moment, he clarified. "I would state it like this. Twenty-five of the Serb bodies were inflicted with such catastrophic trauma that they would have expired within three minutes of receiving their wounds. There were four others who would be borderline, but you warned me that the exact number of deaths inflicted by Sanchez's men might be a contestable issue in court. I therefore didn't include those four. With proper first aid, a few of them might've lingered longer."

I didn't say anything for a long time, until McAbee finally said, "Major, are you still there?"

"I'm here, Doc."

"I apologize if I prepared the wrong estimate. Just tell me what you want, and I'll work all night if I have to. I'll bring in extra office—"

"No, Doc. You did just what I asked. You're sure of your numbers?"

"Of course. I even erred toward the safe side. It's quite possible, in fact very likely that twenty-seven or twenty-eight died almost immediately. Judging by the wounds, it was a hideously violent ambush."

"Again, Doc, tell me you're positive of your numbers."

I could hear his voice getting more exasperated. "Major Drummond, I'm a graduate of Johns Hopkins School of Medicine. I've been a fully functioning pathologist for sixteen years. I think I can recognize when tissue damage is severe enough to cause imminent mortality."

"Thanks," I said.

I hung up the phone and sat there, stunned. Well, okay, maybe not stunned, but in that general proximity. I was certainly mystified. Jones had said that when Alfa 36 arrived at the ambush site, it called its division headquarters and reported that there were seventeen dead and still eighteen survivors. Yet, according to McAbee, twenty-five of the thirty-five Serbs should most definitely have been dead. That would've left, at most, only ten survivors. Depending how it went with the three or four questionables, maybe less than ten survivors. Maybe only five or six.

Say that Alfa 36 reached the ambush site right after Sanchez's team pulled out. Maybe that accounted for the difference. I tried to think that through. Sanchez's team opened the ambush by detonating the two mines buried in the road. That might've killed the driver of the lead truck and maybe a few of the men in the back. Then Sanchez's men began raking the column with M16 and machine-gun fire. Willy-nilly, the Serbs piled out of their vehicles and scrambled for cover behind them. Then the daisy chain of those deadly claymores went off. All of this happened in that first frightful minute.

In ambushes, that opening minute is the height of mayhem. It's when most of the blood is spilled. And remembering the corpses I'd seen back at the morgue, a very large number appeared to have been shredded by those claymores. Then according to Sanchez and his men, another five to seven minutes were spent trading bullets back and forth. Figure a few more Serbs might've been killed during that exchange. By that time, though, the Serbs were mostly behind cover and were furiously returning fire. Sanchez's men would have been hunkered down, firing back more sporadically, less accurately. Plus, with Perrite on security, and Graves, the medic, back in the rear, Sanchez only had seven shooters at the ambush site. The number of casualties would've dwindled to a trickle.

McAbee was sure that twenty-five, and maybe even twenty-nine of the Serbs would have been dead within three minutes after they received their wounds. He was the expert. He knew which organs had to be smashed, which arteries severed, and which limbs obliterated before human brains and hearts started putting up out-of-business signs. That made it physically impossible for Alfa 36 to have arrived at the ambush site in time to find eighteen survivors.

So what in the hell was going on here? A tough question with only two possible answers. Either McAbee was the most incompetent idiot to ever graduate from Johns Hopkins or I'd been duped. Cleverly and professionally duped. The transcripts of the Serb radio transmissions had to be fakes. And if those were faked, well, then maybe . . . no, probably . . . no, definitely, the satellite films were fakes as well. Mr. Jones with the marble eyes had somehow managed to orchestrate a bit of high-tech chicanery.

There was a very unsettling problem with that scenario, though. Mr. Jones wasn't a freelancer. Mr. Jones was here because General Clapper had officially requested NSA to assist my investigation. And Mr. Jones had the authority to waltz in and sequester the use of a fully functioning NSA field facility. And Mr. Jones had the resources to create false satellite images. I mean, I'd seen my share of satellite images, and the ones I just saw sure as hell looked like the genuine article. On the other hand, computer graphics being what they were these days, two expert analysts with a Sun microstation and CorelDRAW probably could have fabricated that product.

I wanted to kick myself for being such a gullible dumbass. I should have seen it. The con job was too perfect by half. First came that trumped-up explanation that no photographic satellites had passed over Zone Three, only a thermal imaging collector that spit out all those vague, unidentifiable little green dots. Then only two sets of film, both of which verified everything Sanchez and his men claimed. Then, voilà—Jones and his people just happened to have discovered those intercepted transcripts that just happened to solve the last great mystery about how those corpses got all those nasty little holes in their heads.

Of course, Jones could not have done this without help from someone inside my team. He knew every pressure point of our investigation, every area of doubt, every unresolved mystery. Well, all of them except one—the body count. But then, no one knew that I'd asked McAbee to prepare that particular article. Back at the morgue, McAbee and I were alone when we spoke about that. Delbert and Morrow were off in another corner together, comparing notes. Therefore Jones and his people had probably applied that old tried-and-true, well-studied maxim that for every man killed in battle, there are usually one or two wounded. Jones just split it right down the middle and made it one survivor for every corpse. Only problem is, when it comes to ambushes, particularly one with a devilishly well-prepared killzone, that ratio has a tendency to get badly skewed.

But where did knowing all this get me? The answer is it got me closer to the alligator pond than ever before. I had no proof. If I confronted Mr. Jones, he'd scratch his head and say, gee, old buddy, that's really odd. I didn't do the work myself, you know, so why don't I get on the horn and check the numbers with the old home office. Then someone back in Maryland would simply say, oops, how awfully embarrassing. One of our simple-minded clerks made a stupid mistake when she transcribed those Serb transmissions. Drummond was quite right: Alfa 36 reported twenty-five corpses.

Besides which, I now knew there really was a conspiracy. I hadn't been imagining things. How big a conspiracy I had no way of knowing, but all of a sudden, those dark, steely-eyed power brokers in Brooks Brothers suits were dashing through mazes inside my skull again. Not that I took any satisfaction in that. The problem with this being a conspiracy was that there was no one I could trust. Clapper? He was the guy who sicced Jones on me. Accidental? I don't think so. And if I had reason to suspect him, then what I felt about Morrow and Delbert was beyond suspicion. I'd already convicted them in my mind. Well, I'd convicted one of them. Which one, though?

Was it Delbert, who came up with the bright idea to start checking around for satellite shots in the first place? I mean, how in the hell did he think of that? His specialty was criminal law, not strategic intelligence.

Or was it Morrow, who'd asked all the right questions for Jones to unfold his spiel? Her performance reminded me of those wonderfully contrived dialogues Ed McMahon used to have with Johnny Carson. Gee, Johnny, yuck, yuck, and why do you think the Serbs stopped transmitting right at that particular moment?

All of which meant it was now time to take inventory. What stake did I have in this investigation? No stake. It was another job. Simple as that.

What did I care if Sanchez and his men murdered thirty-five Serbs? Other than the families of those men, did anyone care what really happened? It was war. Men got killed. Nobody said they had to die in fair ways. There were no Marquis of Queensberry rules in battle. Besides, who knew what those thirty-five

Serbs did before they died? How many rapes, how many massacres, how many towns and villages had they ethnically cleansed?

But let's say, just for the sake of argument, that I decided I wanted to be stupid and get to the bottom of this. Where would I start?

I guessed that I'd start by buying myself a little time. Then I'd buy myself a little space to maneuver. Then I'd begin wondering who Mr. Jones and Miss Smith really were. Who sent them here? And why?

Then I'd wonder who really killed Jeremy Berkowitz. Maybe Berkowitz knew there was a conspiracy. Maybe he tried to break one scandal too many. Maybe he got too close to the truth, and Mr. Jones, that marble-eyed prick, decided it was time for him to go. That sounded like complete hogwash even to me, but as long as I was ruminating, I might as well fit a few long shots in there. I mean, I'm part of the television generation. I'd read all those Robert Ludlum books, and Oliver Stone might be nuts, but I still loved his flicks.

Then, of course, back to the basic question I was supposedly sent here to answer: What had really happened out there with Sanchez and his men? The one thing Jones's charade accomplished was to confirm that it was something terribly rotten. Where there's smoke, there's fire, and where there's a cover-up, there's a sin. Usually a really big, really smelly sin.

Chapter ☆☆ 20

By 1 P.M. Delbert and Morrow still hadn't returned to the office. I was glad. It gave me time to think. Time I badly needed.

In the Navy, they yell "clear the decks" and "batten down the hatches" whenever they're about to go into combat. Sort of like your father punching you on the arm and asking if you have one of those shiny little wrappers in your wallet before your first date. Or your mother asking if you're wearing clean, fresh undershorts every time you grab the car keys. Proper preparations take many forms.

My two colleagues waltzed into the office together at quarter past one, chattering happily, just all too pleased to have spent most of their day with a couple of sterling physical specimens of the opposing sex. After passing the rest of the morning with Mr. Jones and Miss Smith, I guessed they'd both shared a leisurely lunch with their new, or old, NSA chums. Whichever.

Imelda was smoldering. She had this stern notion of duty, and long, unaccounted-for absences were damned close to a mortal sin. I heard her demand to know where they'd been all morning. As usual, Delbert was too pumped up on his own garlic to either fib or just outright humbly admit guilt. I could hear

him arguing, then trying to tell Imelda it was none of her business. That boy had a death wish. He might be right about it being
none of her business, only being right never worked where Imelda
was concerned. She was the one who decided what was her
business and what wasn't. Whenever she chose to butt into my
business, for instance, I just moved aside and made room for her.

I chose this moment to walk out of my office and into the
building maelstrom. I was sorely tempted to sit back and enjoy
the fireworks, but that didn't fit into my freshly devised scheme.
It was time to clear the decks, batten down the hatches, check
my wallet and underpants. Whatever.

"What the hell's going on here?" I barked.

Imelda's feet were spread wide apart, her fists were clenched,
her lips were fluttering, and a trail of angry black smoke was
leaking out of her ears. She was in her full Mount Vesuvius mode.

Delbert pointed a shaking finger at her and, in a very prim,
very outraged voice, he declared, "Major Drummond, this specialist has been disrespectful to me for the last time. I'm filing
charges."

"You're doing no such thing," I yelled.

More meekly, he said, "She's been demanding to know where
we've been. It's none of her business."

"There's where you're wrong, Captain. I've been harassing
her all morning to find out where you were. You and Captain
Morrow have been AWOL."

Imelda looked curiously over her shoulder at me. I hadn't
once asked her where they were.

"I'm sorry," Delbert said, "we were with Harry and Alice."

"Harry and Alice? Just who the hell are Harry and Alice?" I
demanded.

Morrow, who looked absolutely baffled, said, "Mr. Jones and
Miss Smith."

"Those two assholes? You spent half the day with those two
assholes? Was this social or professional?"

"A bit of both," Morrow said, boldly and bravely admitting the truth. Well, the truth don't always set you free.

"Get your asses in my office," I coldly ordered. "And don't even let me find you in a relaxed posture when I get in there."

That line was one some old drill sergeant had once used on me, and I'd always wanted a chance to try it out.

They traded quick, fearful glances, then scurried away like chastened children. Imelda was checking me out, and I gave her a wink. She smiled and winked back. She never did like those two.

I went over and fixed myself a cup of coffee. I took my time. I slowly added sugar and cream. I took forever to stir. Let Delbert and Morrow stew, I figured.

Finally I walked back into the office and fell into my chair. I took one or two leisurely sips from my cup, just to remind them who was boss. I always hated bosses who lollygagged while I waited. It's such a naked display of power. Heh-heh-heh.

I stared icily. "Think this investigation's over?"

Morrow, thinking she'd defuse this with smooth gallantry, said, "Sir, we apologize if we've caused an inconvenience."

I coldly said, "I didn't ask that, Captain. I asked if you think this investigation's over."

Delbert gulped and took his turn. "Sir, well, uh, after this morning, uh . . ."

"What about this morning?" I asked with a nasty scowl.

This brought another round of panicky glances between Delbert and Morrow. You could almost read their minds. Wasn't this dork listening during this morning's session? What is he, dense?

Delbert finally blurted, "Well, uh . . . yes, frankly."

"So everything's wrapped up?"

Morrow's brow was furrowed and she was studying my desktop as though maybe the answer to my question was lurking inside my inbox, or maybe lying on my blotter.

I said, "Captain Morrow, what was the exact chronology of events between the fourteenth and the eighteenth of June?"

"Chronology, sir?"

"Don't they teach chronologies at Harvard? You didn't think we were going to turn in our report without a detailed chronology?"

"Uh, no, Major." She nodded like, woops, yeah, gee, you're right. A chronology; what kind of a half-assed packet would it be without one of those?

See, that's another of those silly little things about the Army. When a senior officer comes up with a perfectly insipid suggestion, the rules dictate that it be treated like Einstein's theory of relativity.

"And Delbert," I yapped, "isn't something else missing?"

"I . . . uh—"

"Don't be hasty, Delbert. Think, now. What else?"

"You mean aside from the chronology?" he asked, trying to buy time.

I said, "Duh!" I couldn't believe I said that. I detest that phrase. It's so infantile, so obnoxious.

He blushed. "Perhaps a few more interviews wouldn't hurt."

"Of course we need more interviews. Thick is always good in government work. Shows we worked hard. Shows we're diligent. We *do* want the powers that be to know we worked *hard* and we're *diligent,* don't we?"

"Uh, yes, sir, of course. And I suppose we could check around and see if any other teams had to use force," he said, getting into the spirit of this thing.

"You're grabbing at straws, Delbert. What about the rules of engagement?"

"Rules of engagement?"

"Right. Shouldn't someone fly to Bragg and find out what the inventors of this operation intended? See if an ambush was a permissible act of self-defense."

"Why, yes, I see what you mean," he said, stroking his chin like I was the smartest guy on earth.

Of course he saw what I meant. In addition to all his other flaws, this boy was so sycophantic he could suck the bark right off a tree.

"Good, we're all in agreement," I announced. "Morrow, get your ass back to Aviano. Build a chronology. Delbert, your butt better be on an airplane to Bragg tonight. Don't come back without an answer to my question."

They both reeled back in shock. But which of them was most in shock, I asked myself. Tough call there. Morrow's eyes grew wide, and Delbert looked like he'd been punched in the stomach. I still couldn't tell which one was assigned to watch me.

"Move fast," I barked. "Only three days left."

"What are you going to do?" Morrow asked. It was either a very nervy question or she was the one who had to report back to her superiors on my activities. Hmmm.

Either way, she'd asked for it. "I'm writing the closing summary," I announced, mustering as much arrogance into my tone as I could manage. "I considered letting one of you two write it. The only problem is, it has to be perfect. Can't risk any amateur mistakes, can we?"

Morrow clearly wanted to howl at that one, but she bit her tongue. "And what position are you going to take?" she asked.

"Isn't that obvious? Now move it, damn it! Both of you! Don't let the door hit you in the ass!"

That was another timeworn statement, but it served its purpose admirably. They were gone in less than two seconds. Both of them would be gone from Tuzla before the cock crowed, or fell asleep or whatever cocks do when it gets dark. Right now, they'd both be dawdling on the street outside this building, scratching their heads and trying to decide what just happened. They'd figure I was a sorehead about being proved wrong. That much was true, only I hadn't been proved wrong. I'd had my pocket picked. They'd figure that like every other typical senior officer, I was taking out my bitchy, foul mood on them. They'd figure that now I wanted to cover my ass by polishing the packet and writing the summary myself, as though I had believed in innocence all along. These were all things your average senior officer would do.

And whichever of the two was the mole would report back to Mr. Jones or General Clapper that I'd caved in, that we were just wrapping things up. Then the mole would climb on an airplane and be out of my hair for at least a day or two. I felt pretty proud of myself. What a smart guy you are, Sean Drummond. See how easily I could forget about being the biggest sucker at Tuzla Air Base?

I picked up the phone and called my old buddy Wolky. I thanked him for lending me his guards. I told him they were no longer needed. He was profusely happy. Ever since Berkowitz's murder, he was being required to provide guards for every journalist in the guest quarters. To make matters worse, the murder of one of their brethren had drawn them like flies. A whole flock of fresh, inquisitive reporters were now in Tuzla, which, Wolky complained, was stretching his meager resources to the breaking point. Only too glad I could be of service, I told him.

I walked out of my office and nodded at Imelda. She left her desk and followed me out into the street. I looked around a few times, then indicated for her to walk with me a while.

"What do you want?" she asked.

"I'd like you to go to my tent and get one of my uniforms. Remove all the patches and sew on sergeant's stripes. Then get a nametag from one of your assistants and sew that on."

Imelda said, "What's this about?"

I said, "Imelda, I'm over my head. I need your help."

Her tiny brown eyes got tinier, and I laid it all out. I didn't like dragging her into this, but I couldn't see that I had any other choice. For one thing I couldn't sew. For another, I was going to need a great deal of assistance and a worthy co-conspirator. She listened attentively, nodded occasionally, blew bubbles with her lips a few times, but did not seem the least surprised.

"One of those two legal aces has been rattin' on you, huh?"

"At least one. Maybe one or two of your girls as well. Every move I've made has been watched and reported from the second I got off the plane. I'd guess our phones are bugged. Maybe the office also."

She considered that a moment. "I can get that checked."

"Please don't. Let whoever's listening think everything's normal. They have to believe they won."

She agreed in her characteristic way, mumbling something under her breath, which could have been "Great idea. You're really one hell of a smart guy" or "Friggin' A." Whichever.

I went to the mess hall for a belated lunch. Any long-serving veteran will tell you there's a trick to eating in Army mess halls. You have to be very, very imaginative.

The mess hall was a long, narrow wooden building, jammed with blocklike wooden tables and chairs. The extent of interior decoration was a few plastic plants someone had sprinkled around and a bunch of Army recruiting posters on the walls. The recruiting posters mystified me. I mean, who exactly did they expect to recruit in an Army mess hall in Tuzla? At any rate, this would not work at all. I decided the recruiting posters were actually Rembrandts and a few Degas, because the mess sergeant—I mean the Paris-trained chef—was a man of eclectic tastes. The plastic plants became towering tropical ferns that wound their way along the walls, with long, winding stems that had wrapped themselves around the nonexistent mahogany ceiling beams. We were doing tropical paradise restaurants today.

Three shifts of hungry soldiers had already tromped through, so the pickings were slim. I slid my tray along a metal railing and took a dried-out salad with brown edges, a carton of lukewarm milk, and a slab of some kind of meat that looked like mottled liver. A cook wearing a dirty white apron lazily watched, and I chose not to ask about the meat. I decided to call it grilled pepper steak, to go with my lobster salad, and the milk would be an exotic coconut cocktail the local natives devised.

I found a table and sat down to eat. I took the first bite of that meat. It had the texture of overcooked leather, and this was when my imagination faltered. I suddenly found myself wondering where my law school classmates were eating. About a year before, I had gone to lunch with a guy I hung around with named Phil Bezzuto, who was already a partner in one of those big D.C. firms. He took me to one of those glitzy power restaurants on Wisconsin Avenue, where rich and famous people were sprinkled about at various tables, feeling oh so superior because they could all afford hundred-dollar lunches that they tried not to spill on their thousand-dollar suits and hundred-dollar neckties. No imagination required at that place. All the tables had white linen tablecloths, crystal glassware, and the kind of super-fancy plates that actually break when you drop them. Phil was rubbing it in real good. When it came time to pay the bill, he flashed his firm's card and told the waiter to put it all on the expense account. Not that he couldn't afford to pay it himself. He told me he was pulling down 300K a year with an almost guaranteed 30 percent bonus. I was making just short of 50K and the Army has this thing against bonuses. Expense accounts, too. He was doing real estate law, and the things he feared most in life were paper cuts or running into some road-raged driver on the beltway. Then again, for all I knew, Phil's gleaming new Mercedes 300SL was bulletproofed.

This was the kind of self-pitying, self-indulgent, wistful melancholia I wallowed in as I ate my mystery meat and sipped warm milk from my carton. There weren't many soldiers left in the mess hall, but the few remaining stalwarts occasionally glanced over at me and then mumbled quietly among themselves. I didn't feel very welcome.

I plopped half a bottle of greasy Italian dressing on my brown-edged salad and began thinking about marble-eyed Mr. Jones and the lovely Miss Smith. The Army teaches that before you go into battle, you must know your enemy. Right now, the enemy knew me, whereas I knew next to nothing about them. Well, I knew their lousy aliases. And I knew that they supposedly worked for NSA. I knew Jones was a cocksure wiseass. I knew he was a ladies' man, and shame on Morrow for not seeing through him right away. I knew Miss Smith had startling blue eyes, pouty lips, long legs that tapered into slim ankles, big boobs—about double D cups was my guess—wore nice clothes, and smelled like an expensive French perfume. When it comes to females, my skills of observation are uncannily sharp.

As things stood at that moment, those two were my best leads. If I could find out who they were, then maybe I could find out who sent them and exactly what the hell was going on here. I finished my salad and walked back over to the dessert section of the serving line.

The only dessert left on display was something that, from a distance, resembled brown pudding. I studied it more closely and decided it looked even more like something squishy and moist that came out of a dirty diaper. Even a fertile imagination like mine couldn't turn it into chocolate mousse. I decided I'd had enough culinary treats this day and went back to work.

Chapter
☆☆ ☆ 21

At six o'clock, I was in position across the road from the NSA facility. I was hiding behind another wooden building and watching the entrance. Miss Smith, now more fully known to be Alice Smith, walked out and smiled brightly at the two guards, both of whom smiled back right nicely, then followed her with their eyes as she moseyed down the street. She had a very nice mosey. One hip this way, one hip that way, and this very encouraging jiggle up top.

Staying behind the row of wooden buildings, I set off in her direction. I caught glimpses of her between the buildings as she continued her journey.

At the end of the dusty street she went left. So did I. She kept walking past another seven or eight buildings, then turned and walked through the entry of a small, one-floored wooden building. A printed sign over the entryway read NO MALES. I deduced this to be some kind of women's dormitory or barracks. I made a date inside my mind to maybe pay her a visit later, then sprinted back to my hiding place across from the NSA building.

Only about five minutes had passed, so I hoped Mr. Jones was still at his desk or conference table or whatever. Lots of bosses work later than their employees, and I assumed by the way they had treated each other that morning that he outranked Miss Smith. Another forty-five minutes passed. I paced back and forth. I daydreamed about Miss Smith's walk. Mosey, mosey, jiggle, jiggle. Finally, about a minute before seven, Jones emerged. He ignored the guards and headed off in the opposite direction from the way Miss Smith had taken. He had a jaunty walk, almost a swagger. We walked about five minutes before he also hooked a left into a wooden building. God bless the Army for marking everything in sight. This one had a big sign, written in large, bold letters that read VISITING GENERAL OFFICERS' QUARTERS.

If our Mr. Jones was a government employee, he was a hefty one, since Army general officers are very finicky about who they allow as neighbors. Why this is, I don't know. Maybe they all like to get together at night and dance around naked. I waited around for three minutes and watched to see if I could tell which lights went on inside which room. I saw nothing. Jones's room had to be on the back side of the building.

Among the many useful skills we were taught in the outfit was breaking and entering. They even brought in some ex-cons to put us through the paces. I ended up working with a guy named Harry G. No last name, just Harry G.

Harry was what my grandfather would call a grand piece of work. He was short and squat, much like a fireplug, bald as a billiard ball, and had this pair of sparkling little black eyes. When he laughed, he sounded just like a horse with a hernia. He'd only been caught once, he informed me, even though he had burgled thousands of places. The government knew he had managed to steal a fortune and threatened to do an IRS audit to add to his legal woes, then prosecute him for tax fraud on top of burglary, unless he agreed to cooperate. Since Harry always worked alone, he figured they couldn't make him rat out anybody. Any kind of ratting, in Harry G's book, was a capital offense. But since he had no partners to turn in, he therefore agreed.

The deal was this. In exchange for agreeing to train government agents in his skills, he was allowed to stay free. Oh, and he had to promise to stop stealing. Harry said, hey, what the hell, he was already worth millions, so why not? It would give him something to balance out the ledger when he met The Maker, as he put it. Maybe give a little back to the country that had given him so much. He had about ten more of these worthy justifications, and I thought they were hilarious at the time.

I spent a month with Harry. Two days on disabling burglar alarms, three days on picking locks, five days on safecracking, et cetera, et cetera. When Harry was done with me, I could break into and hot-wire a car in one minute flat. I could do a reasonable second-story job on a well-protected home, and get past most any safe manufactured before 1985. That was the year the government had forced Harry out of business, and he ruefully admitted that he hadn't kept up with the new technologies.

I went back to my tent and lay down for a nap. I set my alarm for one o'clock, then fell asleep. When the alarm went off, I dressed in running shoes and a pair of Army sweats, which were as innocuous as green berets around here. I grabbed my black gloves, a knife, a poncho, and cut eyeholes in my Army-issued black ski cap, then tucked those in my waistband.

It was dark, and very few people were out and about. I jogged as though I were a late-night fitness addict. Since this was an Army base and lots of folks pulled night shifts, late-night runners were a common sight. Nobody paid me any attention. I got to the Visiting General Officers' Quarters and did three swift laps around the building. I saw nobody, and nobody saw me.

I quietly went through the front entrance and into a hallway. There were four doors, two on the left and two on the right. I immediately ruled out the two nearest doors, because both had windows that faced the front of the building, and I hadn't seen any lights go on when Jones entered his room. This left the last two. I had a 50 percent chance of hitting the right one.

I walked down and stood by the doorway on the left. I let two minutes go by to give my eyes a chance to adjust to the darkness. Then I bent down and studied the lock. It was a simple two-way tumbler. As Harry used to say, a piece of cake. I took out a straightened paper clip and went to work. Harry had taught me to insert the end of the clip and start feeling to the left. Once the end of the clip struck the first tumbler, spin it quickly counterclockwise, then withdraw it quickly. Harry would've been proud. I hit it on the first try.

Then I stayed where I was for a full minute. Picking a lock makes noise, so I waited to see if I could hear anyone stirring inside the room. If I did, I was prepared to sprint out of the building and call this one a dead end. Finally I twisted the knob and quietly entered, carefully pulling the door shut behind me.

The room smelled like perfume and I felt a sudden stab of fear. Maybe Jones had lined up some company for the night. It took me nearly a minute to work my way across the room to the bed. A lumpy figure was under the blanket and I could hear light snoring. Only one set of snores, though. A uniform jacket was slung across the desk chair, and I got out a small penlight and studied it. There was a single star on the collar, and the nametag read Jackson.

I put two and two together; the first two being the perfume, and the last two being her name. General Wanda Jackson was in charge of the military post exchange system. I guessed she was visiting here to check on the service being provided to our boys and girls in the field. It took me another full minute to work my way back to her door. I turned the interior locking mechanism, then slipped out, pulling the door closed behind me.

I waited two minutes, then went to work on the next lock. It took me four tries this time. I was glad Harry wasn't there. He would've chewed my ass till it bled. I slipped in, closing the door behind me, and whiffed the air. This odor was much more satisfying. The room reeked of men's cologne, which meant it was almost certainly Jones's lair. Soldiers in the field, even general officers, don't wear cologne. But civilians who think they are ladies' men almost certainly do.

I stood for a moment and listened to Jones's breathing pattern. He was a quiet sleeper, which was not a good omen since quiet sleepers are very often light sleepers. I worked my way over to his desk. It was a tiny room, but I moved very slowly and very delicately, so it took me a full two minutes. I knew what I wanted; it was only a matter of finding it. Quickly and without bashing into anything.

My hand pawed softly around on the floor until it hit Jones's briefcase, which was located right between his desk and the headboard of his bed. I squeezed it and felt it. It was smooth, maybe suede, or maybe a very fine Italian or Spanish leather. I lifted it up and left the way I came in, making sure to leave the door unlocked.

I walked out the entrance and stretched as though I were preparing to jog, while I searched both sides of the street. Nothing. Not a soul anywhere in sight. I then ran across the street and dodged between two buildings. I had a poncho stuffed inside my waistband, and I pulled it out, whipped it open, then got inside it, using it like a little tent. I got on my knees and placed Jones's briefcase on the ground. Then I pulled out my penlight and inspected my haul.

The briefcase was locked. It had one of those little combination locks, only, unfortunately, not the cheap type found on most briefcases. These were made of solid brass, three tumblers, with ten numbers each. Mr. Jones had spent a lot of money on this briefcase. Too bad for him, because I didn't have the right equipment to get into it without damaging the mechanism. So be it.

I took out my knife, made a hole, withdrew it, and flipped it over, then used the serrated edge to cut a long slit along the bottom edge of the case. Then I kept sawing along the next edge.

I took some joy in destroying Mr. Jones's obscenely expensive briefcase. You have to take your victories where you find them. That done, I reached inside and felt around. There were a few papers and folders, but I figured that Jones knew better than to store any classified materials in his room. Besides, what I was looking for was smaller. I finally felt a tiny booklet and pulled it out.

I opened it up and there was Jones's handsome face inside his passport. The name wasn't Jones, though. It was Tretorne; Jack Tretorne, to be exact. I flipped quickly through the pages. Jack was a busy traveler. The passport had been issued only a year and a half before, yet nearly all the pages were already filled with visa stamps and entry permits. All the ones I saw were for European countries, the majority of which were Balkan states. It was not an official passport of the type commonly issued to government employees. It was a common, garden-variety passport. That might mean something, and that might mean nothing. As a result of the terrorist scares of the seventies and eighties, lots of government employees in sensitive jobs were encouraged to travel with civilian passports. That way, when Abdul the 747 hijacker began walking up the plane row collecting passports and looking for candidates to shoot and dump on the tarmac, he wouldn't be able to discriminate.

Since I'd already had to break into his briefcase, I decided to keep his passport. It might come in handy, but even if it didn't, now Tretorne would have to go through all the hassle of getting a new one. I rather liked that idea. I had ruined his briefcase, and now I was stealing his passport. Then I began rummaging around inside the briefcase again. This time I was fishing around to see if I could find a small plastic card. It took a while, but I finally felt a hard plastic edge inside one of those little compartments they put inside these fancy briefcases.

I pulled it out and flashed my penlight on it. There was Jack Tretorne's handsome face again. Only this card did not show his name, only a long number and the name of the issuing agency. Oh, and of course, it also proudly displayed the shield of the Central Intelligence Agency. This was the identification card Jack used to get in and out of that big complex in Langley, Virginia. An NSA factotum, my ass.

I decided to keep his ID also, before I put everything away and walked back across the street to the Visiting General Officers' Quarters. I went back down the hallway to Tretorne's room, entered quietly, and made sure I moved just as stealthily back over to the desk. I gently set the briefcase back down on the floor, right where I found it, with the side I'd cut open flat against the desk, where I hoped it wouldn't be noticeable.

I then made my way back out, this time turning the inside locking mechanism on the doorknob so the door would lock when I closed it. I hadn't noticed Tretorne carrying his briefcase when he first came to see me two days before. Nor had he carried it with him the evening before, when I followed him back to his quarters. I hoped he was the type who didn't use his briefcase every day. I didn't want anything to make him suspicious yet.

I decided to give Miss Smith a pass that night. It seemed highly likely that she was also a CIA employee, and I really didn't care what her real name was.

I raced back to my tent and changed into battle dress. Then I went to General Murphy's headquarters building. The sergeant who was pulling night duty asked me what I wanted. I whipped out my fancy orders and told him I needed a private office with a secure phone. He showed me down the hall and let me into the office of the operations officer. Then he used a key to open up a special metal cabinet that contained another special key that would convert the phone to secure. He handed the key to me, warned me not to mess anything up, and left me alone.

Colonel Bill Tingle was a living legend in the Special Operations community. It was widely rumored he was the real-life guy John Wayne portrayed in that sappy 1968 movie *The Green Berets.*

Tingle was long past mandatory retirement age, but a special committee of Congress just automatically extended him on military duty every year. For all I knew, he had over a hundred years on active duty. He'd been a full colonel during the Vietnam War and was the mastermind behind the San Te raid, which was a heroic attempt at a helicopter assault deep into North Vietnam to free a bunch of our POWs. The raid went off without a hitch, but for one inconvenient little detail. Unfortunately, the North Vietnamese had removed all the POWs from the camp a few weeks before. As a result, the raiders went in and killed a bunch of bad guys, but returned empty-handed. It was an intelligence glitch-up, but other than that, everybody agreed the raid itself was a stunning masterpiece.

After the war ended, it was Tingle's idea to form the outfit, and he'd remained on board ever since as the official adviser. It was a young man's game, so outfit commanders came and went, but old Bill Tingle was always there, like the cornerstone of a building. Even after I left, I always made it a point to call Tingle at least once a year, and we were on each other's Christmas card lists. I think he found it terribly amusing that an outfit guy left to go to law school and become a JAG officer. Bill Tingle hated lawyers.

I dialed a special number that all outfit vets were required to carry around in our wallets. If we ever suspected our former association with the outfit was at risk of being exposed, we were supposed to call that number. A male voice answered and said, "Ling Hai's Chinese Takeout." This was the outfit's screening service, and I said, "I'd like to talk with the bull, please." The bull was Bill Tingle's code name.

I heard some switching noises in the background, then this deep, gravelly voice said, "Tingle." I can't remember ever seeing Bill Tingle without a lit Marlboro in his lips, which accounted for the fact that he sounded like Darth Vader chewing on marbles. On the other hand, him being the toughest man anyone ever saw, maybe he was born that way.

I said, "Hey, sir, Sean Drummond here."

"Drummond? Drummond? Ah yeah, the dumbass who quit and went to law school."

"Right, sir. Same Drummond. Listen, I need a big favor."

"Favor? Then I'll give you the number for May's escort service. Old May'll do you a favor you'll never forget."

Tingle had a lousy sense of humor. I laughed anyway. "Sir, if you don't mind, we have to go secure."

Tingle grunted, then we went through the laborious process of using the special keys to change our phones from unsecure to secure. The secure mode scrambled a perfectly human voice and made it sound like Tingle sounded normally. You can only imagine what it did to Tingle's voice. Made you think you were talking to the guy who ran hell.

It took about thirty seconds, then I said, "Listen, I think I'm in real deep shit, and I need some help." Raw candor was always the best way to deal with Tingle.

"All right, spill it, Drummond."

And I did. I spilled everything that had happened, right down to breaking into Jones's room and stealing his passport and ID. He listened to it all and said nothing for a moment.

Finally he broke the silence. "Don't know nothin' about it."

"I didn't think you did. That's not why I called."

"Why did you call?"

"I need to find out more about this Jack Tretorne guy."

"And you figure I can do that?"

"Yes, sir. You've got all kinds of contacts up there. Maybe you can find who I'm up against."

There was a long silence for another moment. I heard Tingle cough a few times. On a secure phone, it sounded like little mines detonating in his throat. He really needed to quit smoking.

He finally said, "All right, Drummond. By the way, you ever hear of Operation Phoenix?"

I said, "Vaguely. One of those Vietnam things, wasn't it?"

"Right. Look it up," he ordered me. "I'll get back to you."

"Colonel," I said, "if you don't mind, that's not a good idea. I think my phones are bugged. I'll call you."

"Whatever."

"By the way, I ran into another outfit vet out here. A Sergeant Major Williams. Remember him?"

"We've had three Williamses come through the outfit. Of course, one died. Mogadishu, I think. Yeah, it was Mogadishu. Poor bastard."

"This one's still kicking. He worked the POW hard sell when I went through screening. He told me you kept having him kick the crap out of me."

"Ahh, that asshole. You stay away from him. He's a bad egg."

"Really?"

"One of them white supremacist nuts. Was even helping train some group of goombahs in the backwoods. Williams was a real wacko. That's why we booted him out."

"How'd you find that out?" I asked.

"Ah, we tapped all of your phones. Bet you never knew that, did ya?"

I instantly tried to recall every phone conversation I had ever had when I was with the outfit. "No, sir," I managed to croak.

"Oh yeah," he said, "I heard every word you ever said about me, Drummond."

"Well, you know. The heart grows fonder and all that crap."

"Okay, Drummond, get back to it. And watch your ass, boy. Don't forget. Read up on Phoenix."

I hung up, returned the secure key to the duty sergeant, and walked back to my tent. Then I lay down and got three more hours of sleep before I showered and shaved, got dressed again, and went to our little wooden building.

Imelda was still asleep on her cot by the file cabinets when I came in. She could've had one of her girls do the guard duty, but that wasn't Imelda's style. I tiptoed over to the coffeemaker and prepared a pot. Then I went into my office and waited till it was percolated. Imelda awoke while I was pouring a cup.

"Fix two," she growled.

"Cream or sugar?"

"Black. Bone black. That cream and sugar, that crap'll kill ya."

"Yes, ma'am," I mumbled. I quickly maneuvered my shoulder to block her view as I added a third spoonful of sugar to mine.

While Imelda crawled out of her sleeping bag I carried the two cups over, politely turning around to give the lady some privacy. After a minute I heard her stomping her combat boots on the floor, and I turned back and handed her the coffee. Then I hooked a finger and indicated for her to follow me.

I sat at my desk and began writing on a legal pad while asking, "So, how'd you sleep?"

"Good as can be. You?"

"Like a baby. Went to bed early and got the first full night of rest since we got here," I said, holding up what I'd written on the page.

It read, "Research this: Operation Phoenix."

She shrugged her shoulders. "Good. Maybe you won't be such a grumpy asshole to my girls anymore."

I wrote out: "Vietnam era. Might find it on Internet."

I said, "Today, what I'd like to do is work on the summary statement. I told Delbert and Morrow I'd write it."

"Yeah, okay," she said, also nodding her head at what I wrote on the paper.

"You know how I like to do these things. I'll be wandering in and out all day, trying to compose my thoughts."

"You don't need to tell me, Major. I know how you like to work."

"Good. Thanks, Imelda."

"No problem," she said, wandering back out of my office.

In the interest of authenticity, since I couldn't be sure whether one or more of Imelda's girls was informing on me, I quickly began scribbling out a long, rambling statement about how Sanchez and his men were completely innocent of all charges. I wrote fast and didn't worry about syntax or literary refinement. It only had to be convincing enough that if anyone checked, they would believe I was doing my part in the whitewash.

I scribbled for two hours, then there was a knock on the door. When I looked up, Martie whoever and David the wimp, my two favorite CID agents, were standing there.

"What?" I said.

"Could you spare another moment of your time, Major?" Martie asked.

I decided to be politic. "Sure. Can I get you coffee?"

"No thanks," he said as the two of them entered and sank into the chairs across from my desk. "We've already had half a dozen cups. I'm jittery as hell."

Their haberdashery had not improved in the past two days. Today Martie was dressed in a checkered suit, with a checkered shirt and a checkered tie. He looked like a walking chessboard done in three shades. David wore a more conservative chintzy-looking blue blazer, a dark blue shirt, and a garish tie covered with pastel-colored flowers that looked as if they were exploding. He reminded me of a hybrid between a mobster and Bozo the Clown. These guys were hard to take seriously.

"How's the investigation going?" I asked.

"Oh, you know. A piece here, a piece there. These kinds of things, you rarely find a golden nugget that breaks it all open. Usually it takes a lot of small clues."

"You took the footprints, right?"

"Yeah. They're back in the lab in Heidelberg."

"Anything else interesting in Berkowitz's notebook?"

"Tough to tell. You learn a lot about a guy when you investigate his death. Take Berkowitz. The guy was a real slob. Dirty clothes and candy wrappers everywhere. Left notes and scribbles all over his damn room. We're still sorting through it."

"I heard there's lots of new reporters in town."

"A whole army. They're climbing all over the information officer's ass. And you know how the feeding cycle works. They chew on his ass, he chews on mine."

"I guess," I said. "So is there anything specific you want to talk about?"

"Uh, yeah, actually." He looked up and stared at my ceiling. "Just thought I should inform you that I've got two agents in your tent right now. I've got a military judge's order to search your personal possessions and to borrow your running shoes."

I didn't like the sound of this one bit. I took a sip of coffee and tried not to look distressed. This wasn't easy. I was feeling very distressed. I don't know why, I just was.

I gave him a hard stare. "And may I ask why?"

"Just some lingering concerns about a few notes Berkowitz left behind. Don't get all bothered, though. We're just borrowing your shoes to compare them with some molds back at the lab."

"But I shouldn't be concerned?"

"No. It's just standard procedure. We're collecting lots of molds. You never set foot in that latrine, right?"

"That's right," I said.

"Then we'll get you cleared faster than you can say Jack the Ripper."

Chapter ☆☆ 22

One thing you learn when you practice criminal law is that the moment a police officer tells you not to be concerned, start gnawing on your nails. Fortunately, or unfortunately, I didn't have anyway near enough time or attention to worry. I kept writing my opus summary while I waited for Imelda to bring me some materials on Operation Phoenix.

She waltzed back in at quarter after eleven and dropped a bunch of printouts on my desk.

"Where have you been?" I bellowed.

She bent over and began writing on my yellow legal pad.

"Workin'," she said. "I made the supply run, then ran all over this damn post lookin' for printer cartridges."

I watched what she was writing. I said, "Well, I've gotten a lot of work done, and I want someone to start typing."

"And what's with you?" she barked. "Is your ass glued to that chair or something? You can't tell those clerks to type?"

She straightened back up and I read what she had written. "Found on Internet. To be safe, used supply room terminal."

"Okay, okay," I grumbled. "Just take what I've finished and get it typed."

She collected my stack of yellow pages and departed. I grabbed the printouts she left behind and dug in. It took nearly thirty minutes. There was a lot of stuff on the Internet concerning Operation Phoenix. There were extracts from history books. There were testaments from guilt-ridden veterans who were participants. There were some wild ramblings from anti-war groups who made reference to it in fairly negative ways. Some of the articles made for pretty fascinating reading, and some made you wonder if everyone who posted things on the Internet had all their marbles.

Operation Phoenix was a secret operation run jointly between the CIA and the Green Berets during the Vietnam War. A secret pact was made between the two that actually bypassed the military chain of command. Neither the Joint Chiefs nor General Westmoreland even knew it was happening.

It was a classic counterinsurgency operation where the CIA penetrated a number of communist cells that were operating in South Vietnam, then the Special Forces did the nasty work of eliminating the suspects. Some of the material Imelda got off the Internet said the Green Berets only killed a few dozen operatives. Others claimed they killed thousands. Killed them without trial, without proof, just knocked off whoever the CIA told them to take out. The sterile euphemism they used was "sanctioned."

I guess I was too engrossed in trying to study the anatomy of my high school cheerleading squad to have been paying attention, but the operation got exposed sometime in the early or mid-seventies, just as the war was winding down. Then there was a mad rush by various congressional investigating committees to help the Army sort fact from fiction, to borrow General Partridge's phrase. The word for what the Green Berets were doing was assassination. The words for what the CIA was doing was playing God. It was a war, but the people being summarily executed were South Vietnamese citizens, thus technically our allies. That's a pretty vital distinction.

I saw immediately why Bill Tingle wanted me to research this. I mean, it made a lot of sense. Here was Jack Tretorne, aka Mr. Jones, masquerading as an NSA employee while he helped cover up a possible massacre committed by a Green Beret team. You couldn't escape the parallels. Still, it struck me as beyond stupidity. Operation Phoenix had apparently led to an explosive scandal, and I just couldn't believe that the same folks who did it the first time would turn right around and try it again. That's like Ford Motor Company trying to reintroduce the Edsel.

Besides, this was not a war. At least, technically this was not war. There were no communist cells being infiltrated, no suspects being assassinated. This was a NATO police action, or whatever silly word was being used to describe an attempt to coerce the Serbs by bombing the crap out of them. As simple as that.

On the other hand, there was the murder of Jeremy Berkowitz. Maybe Tretorne told General Murphy to "sanction" him. As bizarre as that sounded, everything going on here struck me as bizarre. So why not? Tretorne seemed to me to be exactly the kind of guy who would order someone killed in cold blood. There was no sign of life or moral gravity in those eyes of his. And, if a man would help engineer a cover-up, then he was already breaking some very serious laws. What was a few more?

I decided I needed to be cheered up. All morning I'd been working out another scheme, and I decided its time had come. It was time to do some flushing, as they say in quail-hunting circles.

I left the office and walked back over to the NSA facility. The guards passed me through to the inner sanctum, I pushed the doorbell and looked up and stuck out my tongue at the camera in the corner. Sometimes I wonder how I ever made major.

A moment later, the door made that humming sound, and I pushed it open. Miss Smith was waiting. I gave her a shy grin, and she returned it with one of those wonderfully plastic smiles she must have perfected at some northeastern preppy college. She reminded me of a thousand cheerleaders I used to lust after.

"How are you today?" I asked.

"Fine."

"That's nice. I hope this isn't inconvenient, but I need to talk with Mr. Jones again."

"Follow me," she said, and I studied her lovely sway as she led me back through the building, then to the stairway in the rear. We went down the stairs again, and I noticed that her hair roots were brown, not blond. The more I learned about this woman, the less real she seemed.

We reached the conference room at the end of the hall again, and Miss Smith's long, manicured fingers very elegantly slid her little plastic card through the lock slot, then she pushed the door open. There were about five men in the room, all sitting around the table, with Jack Tretorne at the head. Aside from Tretorne, it looked like a nerd's convention. There were lots of thick bifocals and pocket penholders and short-sleeve white shirts. These were NSA employees, no doubt about it. They had that certain charisma.

Tretorne had on his duck-murdering vest again. He looked badly out of place, like a jock at a software programmers' convention. He glanced up and the room fell quiet. If I were a courteous guy, I would've said, "Excuse me. I'm obviously interrupting, so why don't I just leave and you can call me when it's convenient for you."

I didn't say anything; I just stood there. Tretorne's marble eyes studied me, but I had no idea what he was thinking. Then he looked around the table and said, "If you all can please excuse us for a few moments, Major Drummond here is working on a very critical project, and I must speak with him. Alone."

The nerds all got up and began filing out of the room. Finally, it was just the three of us, and Miss Smith closed the door.

"Hi," I said.

He got right to the point. "What do you want?"

"I just need a few minutes. I'm preparing our summary, and I have to get a few questions answered. You understand, right?"

I collapsed into a chair before he could answer. I looked over my shoulder. "Miss Smith, would you be a good girl and fetch me a cup of coffee? Three sugars and just a small dose of cream."

The lovely Miss Smith's face turned instantly ugly. "I don't *fetch* things, and don't call me a *good girl*."

I smiled. "Oh, I'm sorry. I thought you were Mr. Jones's administrative assistant."

I could see Jones nodding his head furiously for her to do what I asked. She pouted for about two seconds, then whirled around and walked back through the door.

I said, "Boy, has she got an attitude. How do you put up with that?"

Jones's eyes were studying me very coldly. It was a little like being examined by that mechanical camera upstairs. "She's all right," he assured me. "This isn't the Army, Drummond. We fetch our own coffee around here. Now, what do you want?"

"Well, remember yesterday when we looked at those films, and you read those radio transcriptions?"

"Of course I remember."

"Good. I'll need some kind of verification that all that was authentic. Also, you mentioned that the films will be stored in a file at NSA. I'll need some kind of reference or name for that file."

"I can get you that," he said. He smiled. This was all so easy.

"Gee, that's great," I said. "One other thing. I'm gonna need your full name, social security number, and where you work at NSA."

Oops, it was not so easy anymore. The smile was instantly replaced by a deeply perplexed look as he said, "Why?"

"Well, since you wouldn't let me have the films or transcripts, you know, them being too sensitive and all, I have to cite you as a material witness in my exhibit. This is a highly controversial incident we're investigating. The findings are going to be closely scrutinized. I can hardly write that I met with some jerk from NSA named Jones and leave it at that. I mean, how many Joneses are there at NSA? Must be a thousand or so, wouldn't you guess?"

Tretorne's jaw, I noticed, became very tight. There was very little body fat on his face, and right at that moment, those two little muscles just below his ears were ticking like time bombs. My obnoxiousness was breaking through the iceberg.

Just at that moment, he was saved by the bell. Miss Smith traipsed back through the door with my cup of coffee in hand. She gave it to me, and I took a sip. It was cold as ice, and she must have added half a jar of cream and at least ten large spoonfuls of sugar. The girl had spunk. I liked that.

I cranked back my neck and drained the whole thing. "Ah, just the way I like it. Thanks, honey." Take that for spunk, bitch.

Miss Smith tried to take this in stride, but I noticed that she stomped a little as she worked her way around the table and took a seat near the opposite end. Unfortunately, Tretorne had recovered his composure.

He leaned across the table and, in a tellingly reasonable tone, said, "Listen close, Drummond. I'm not going to be listed in your report. Let's get that clear. My work requires me to do sensitive work, and I cannot risk being exposed. Just use the name of the NSA chief, Lieutenant General Foster."

I grinned. "Hey, don't sweat it, Jonesy, old pal. My report's going to have 'Top Secret Special Category' stamped all over it. You won't be exposed. Besides, General Foster had nothing to do with this."

A tinge of red was working up Tretorne's neck, and his face was becoming flushed. "He knows all about it, Drummond. Just do what you're told."

You could tell by his tone that Tretorne was a guy who was used to giving orders and getting his way.

My smile got even wider. "Gee, I really can't, old buddy. Look, if it'll make you more comfortable, I'll list your name and employment data in a special annex that's eyes only to the Secretary of Defense and Chairman of the Joint Chiefs. Can't get more accommodating than that, can we? See, the thing is, Jonesy, you're now part of my investigation. You invited yourself in the moment you walked into my office. I mean, surely you knew that."

"No, I didn't. And I still don't believe it."

"Suit yourself," I said, getting up and preparing to leave.

"Where are you going?" Tretorne demanded, now even more perplexed.

"I'm going to call a military judge. I'm gonna tell him to write me a court order addressed to the director of the NSA that gives him six hours to release your name and job data." I was assuming that Jack Tretorne was not an attorney and wouldn't know whether I could do that or not.

"That wouldn't be a very good idea," he muttered in a very menacing tone.

"Why, Mr. Jones, you're not threatening me, are you? There is another way I can handle this. I'm pretty damned sure I can also talk that judge into issuing a writ against you and your agency for withholding evidence critical to a criminal investigation. Hell, maybe I'll ask the judge for both."

This issue of law, Tretorne obviously thought he knew something about. "You can't bluff me," he snarled. "That's been tested in federal court a million times. Nobody can force the government to release classified data."

"You're right," I said. "But you're also a little confused. All those cases involved civilians without security clearances requesting the release of classified information. I represent another government agency. Also, the information I've requested is going to be enclosed in a classified investigation packet."

He was still sputtering something when I closed the door behind me. Another law of war is to keep the enemy off balance. God knows he got his share of agony out of me the day before, and I wanted Tretorne to feel what it was like to sweat for a change.

I was sure he would immediately get on the phone to the lawyers back at the CIA to ask them if I could accomplish everything I'd just threatened. They were lawyers, though. They would defer. All lawyers, everywhere, always defer. In civilian firms, lawyers never answer anything right away because then they'd lose the opportunity to pump up a bunch of billable hours. In government agencies, lawyers never answer right away because they're bureaucrats and on general principle never do anything right away. Besides, they like to minimize risk by meeting with lots of colleagues, so they can make sure the blame for wrong answers gets spread around.

What Tretorne would eventually learn was that I could get the writ for his name, but CIA and NSA lawyers could fight it and keep it in limbo for months, long past the point of relevance. He would also be told that no military judge can compel another government agency to hand over sensitively acquired, classified information. Regardless, it was going to be a while before he got this confirmed, and I wanted to see if I could force his hand.

I went back to the office and returned to working on my phony screed. At four o'clock I went back over to General Murphy's headquarters building and asked an eager-looking captain if he could please find me a secure phone in a private room. He led me down the hall to the adjutant's office, who was off visiting troops somewhere, got me the secure key, and left me alone.

I called the Chinese takeout again and was put right through to Colonel Bill Tingle.

I said hi, we did the shift to secure mode thing again, then Tingle said, "Found him."

"I can't thank you enough, sir. Who is he?"

"Tretorne's a GS-17 in Operations."

A GS-17 is like the equivalent civilian rank of someone between a two- and three-star general, and Operations is the half of the CIA that does field work.

"Wow," I blurted out, because I couldn't think of anything even halfway clever to say. I felt like that proverbial fisherman in the small wooden boat who's just realized he's hooked a three-ton man-eating shark on his line.

He added, "He's in charge of field operations for the Balkans. Career man, too. Not one of them political Pudleys."

I had no idea what a Pudley was, but that was the word Tingle commonly used to describe anyone he didn't like. Most often, I'd heard him use it to describe lawyers. Like years before, when I told him I was leaving the outfit to become a lawyer, and he screamed, "You wanta stop bein' a hardcock to become a goddamn Pudley?"

I said, "Did you learn anything else about him?"

"He's got a good rep. A can-do guy. Also, he went to West Point. Guess he did his few years, then got out and went to the Agency."

I said, "Very interesting. By the way, I read about Operation Phoenix."

"Don't believe the half of it. Believe the other half, though. That really happened."

He was in Vietnam then, and was wearing a green beret, so I assumed he probably had firsthand knowledge about the whole thing. He may even have been part of Operation Phoenix. I didn't like the thought of Bill Tingle, who was something of a personal hero of mine, assassinating folks, so I did what I always do when confronted with unpalatable facts. I instantly decided he didn't do it.

I said, "Any chance that's what's going on here?"

"How the hell do I know, Drummond? I'm here, and you're there."

"I just thought there must be some reason you wanted me to look it up."

"Look, son, I've been in the Army since 1950. You have no idea how stupid we can be."

"Okay," I said, "I can't thank you enough, sir."

"Right. Hey, another thing. You see that Williams asshole again, tell 'em I said to get fucked."

"Will do, Colonel."

"One more thing. Think before you act, boy. Sometimes what looks bad is really good."

"Right," I said, then he hung up.

Bill Tingle was a coarse, crusty old fart, but you don't get to be old in his line of work by being stupid. "Think before you act" was always good advice. Of course, that required that you have time to think, which was something I didn't.

Chapter ☆☆ 23

I went back to the office and exchanged my battle dress for the uniform Imelda had sewed new insignia on. My new nametag and rank declared me to be Sergeant Hufnagel. Harold, I decided; I would be Sergeant Harold Hufnagel. Say that ten times real fast and see what happens.

Specialist Hufnagel was the legal clerk who looked a bit like a saber-toothed tiger. I figured I couldn't get her or me into any trouble by borrowing her name. If someone took undue interest in me, they could turn this base inside out looking for a male sergeant named Harold Hufnagel, and we'd both be safe and clear.

I left and walked over to the supply room Imelda had staked out as her unofficial communications center. I asked if I could borrow the phone. The private on duty said sure. I called the Tenth Group's information office. A sergeant named Jarvis answered.

I said, "Sergeant, this is Barry McCloud at the day desk of the *Washington Herald*. You got any of my reporters out there?"

"Right, sir," he very politely said. "Two to be exact."

"I'm trying to get hold of them. We had their numbers here,

but some dumbshit on the night shift misplaced them. Would you do me the kindness of telling me where they're staying, and what number I need to use to get hold of them?"

"Uh, sure," he said. I heard him tapping some computer keys, and assumed he was accessing some file. "Got 'em right here," he announced.

"Great, I'm ready to copy," I said.

"Gee"—he chuckled—"that's exactly how we say it in the Army. Ready to copy."

I wanted to kick myself. "Uh, yeah, sure. I'm an old vet myself."

"Oh really? Who were you with?" he asked. He was a really friendly sort of guy.

"You know, here and there. You got those numbers yet?"

"Yeah, sure. Okay, Clyde Sterner's in room 201. You can reach him at 232-6440. Janice Warner's in room 106, same number, only put a three at the end. Dial the same extension you used to get Tuzla."

"Great, thanks," I said, then hung up.

Let's see, which one should I call? Sterner or Warner? I flipped a coin and it came down heads. Clyde Sterner it was. Then I dialed the number for Janice Warner's room. Like I was going to call a Clyde over a Janice.

An intriguingly soft voice answered, "Janice Warner."

"Hi, Miss . . . uh, is that Miss or Mrs. Warner?" I very slickly asked.

"It's Miss. What can I do for you?"

"Name's Sergeant Harold Hufnagel. Harry, to my friends. I knew Jeremy Berkowitz."

"That's nice, Sergeant. I knew Jeremy, too."

"Yeah, well, he was a swell guy. A real sweet guy. Damn shame what happened."

"No, Jeremy was not a swell guy. Nor was he a sweet guy.

He was a rotten prick, but you're right about it being a damned shame what happened. Is there some reason you called?"

I liked this girl. "Yeah, actually. I might know something about what got him killed."

There was this long pause before she finally said, "It sounds like you and I should get together."

"Yeah, I'd like to," I said, "I really would. But there's complications."

"I'm sure we can find some way to work around them."

The hook was in. "See, Miss Warner, the thing is, the Army doesn't like buck sergeants talking to reporters. Especially about sensitive stuff like murder."

"I see your point," she said.

"We'd have to meet in secret."

"Why don't you just come to the Visiting Journalists' Quarters? I'll sneak you in."

"Uh-uh. They got guards on your building. They might catch us. Then they'll take my name and I'll be in front of the colonel's desk within an hour."

"Okay, then, what's your idea?"

"Meet me tonight. Nine o'clock, by the entrance of the mess hall. And come alone, or you'll never see me."

She said, "Okay. Oh, and Sergeant Hufnagel, I'll be armed. I'm a really good shot, too. Get my drift?"

"Yes, ma'am. Farthest thing from my mind."

Her voice might've sounded soft and pleasant, but *she* sure as hell didn't sound soft. I had this sense that Miss Warner was going to be an interesting package. If she showed up wearing one of those duck-shooting vests, I was going to blow my brains out.

There were two more hours before we were supposed to meet. For want of anything better to do, I returned to my hiding place across from the NSA building. I stood there and watched for over an hour. A few of the nerds I'd seen earlier in the conference room passed in and out, but there was no sign of Mr. Tretorne or Miss Smith.

I was just getting ready to call it quits, when who should walk out of the entrance but that unmistakably tall and handsome hero, General Murphy. A Special Forces captain held the door, then fell in to walk beside him. His aide-de-camp, I guessed. Murphy had to have been inside the building at least an hour and a half. Now what would draw him to this facility, much less keep him inside that long?

Maybe he was there to view satellite films and radio transcripts. Not likely, though. Lieutenants and captains do that kind of scut work, not brigadier generals. Much more likely, that bastard was in there meeting with Tretorne. Maybe he was there picking up new lists of people to be sanctioned. Or maybe they were talking about me. Hell, maybe I was on the list to be sanctioned.

But that would really be stupid. I mean, how would the Army and CIA explain the murder of the chief investigating officer of the Kosovo massacre? Were they that stupid? Worse, were they that desperate? No, I decided. Right now they thought they had me right where they wanted me. Well, except for the threats I'd made to Jones. But would they try to kill me for that? Anyway, there was no more time to ponder those lofty questions because it was time to go meet Janice and see if her voice was the only interesting thing about her.

I jogged and got there twenty minutes before nine. I found a spot about three buildings away, where I could safely observe. I watched the cooks file out and lock up the mess hall at 8:45 P.M. as they did every night. This left the building entirely abandoned, which was precisely why I chose this time and place. It made it easier to see if Miss Warner was bringing company. Maybe I was being overly scrupulous, but I didn't want to join Jeremy Berkowitz, stuffed in a container of dry ice on the back of a C-130.

At nine o'clock exactly, I saw a slender woman dressed in

civilian attire stroll leisurely toward the entrance of the mess hall. No sway to her walk, just a straight, unassuming gait. She stopped under a light and leaned against the wall. Her hair looked long and black. She wore jeans with a short leather jacket. I was so glad she didn't have one of those vests. Now I didn't have to shoot myself.

I began doing a complete circuit around the mess hall, checking the alleys and sneaking around to see if anyone was watching. Nobody. Then I walked to the corner of a building located about forty yards from the mess hall.

"Miss Warner!" I yelled.

She glanced over and I meandered slowly to the nearest street. She followed me. When she finally caught up, I started walking and she fell in beside me.

"What was that about?" she asked.

"Can't be too careful these days."

"Do you have something to be afraid of?"

"Well, you never know."

"Where are we going?"

"I thought we'd just walk. Good for the health," I said, inspecting her face for the first time. Sharp, perceptive eyes. Pronounced cheekbones. Wide lips. A thin, willowy body. She looked like that girl in your high school class who got straight A's, but was too detached and intellectually sophisticated to go out with a jock. I'd never gotten to know that type well.

She said, "Where are you taking me?"

"Nowhere special. This your first time at Tuzla?"

"Yes. This isn't my beat."

"What is your beat?" I asked.

"West European politics and economics."

"Um-hum, but you're here to cover Berkowitz's murder?"

"Partly. Clyde Sterner and I have been thrown into the breach to cover what Berkowitz was working on, at least until the paper can get a replacement out here."

"Anything interesting?"

"Yes, actually."

Well, in a few moments, I intended to make it even more in-teresting. I said, "Do I take it you and Jeremy weren't friends?"

"Let's just say we had different philosophies on reporting."

This sounded interesting. "What's yours?" I asked.

She studied me with those perceptive eyes for a few sec-onds. "I don't believe in paying my sources. If that's your game, you've got the wrong reporter. Try Sterner. He's got an expense account just like Berkowitz."

"Actually that's not what I'm asking for."

"Then what are you asking for, Sergeant?" she asked with an indulgent look.

"I'd like the same deal I had with Berkowitz."

"Which was?"

"We traded information," I said. I didn't think it necessary to admit that this only happened once or that I'd lied and tried to set him up. Why bore her with small details?

She stopped walking and eyed me even more suspiciously. "Why would a sergeant be interested in information? Who do you work for, Hufnagel?"

Miss Janice Warner had a very quick mind, and this was ex-actly the deduction I'd hoped she would draw. I gave her a big, broad smile. "Look, we're not at that point yet. Are you ready to talk the deal or not?"

"What if I'm not?"

"Then I find myself another reporter. The smell of a corpse has brought fresh new flocks. There's scads of 'em around here these days."

She considered that a moment, but from the expression on her face I wouldn't say she was fully committed. At least, not yet.

"Okay, continue," she said.

"The way this works is you're going to give me a little information. Then I'm gonna give you a little information. Play me right, and I'll give you a story that stops hearts."

"I'm nobody's dupe, Stupnagel."

"Hufnagel. Harold Hufnagel," I said. I loved the way that rolled off my tongue. "But you can call me Harry."

"Are you an MP?"

"Ah-ahh! You're not allowed to probe."

"How do I know the info you have on Berkowitz's death is legit?"

"Because I was one of Jeremy's inside sources. I gave him a big story, then he got garroted."

She was nodding as I spoke. "That it?" she asked, somewhat dubiously.

Give her credit for trying. "Come on, Miss Warner. In or out?"

She stopped and examined my face. I couldn't tell what she was thinking. Like I said, she had these real perceptive eyes, which meant they took a lot in, but emitted nothing.

"All right, we'll try it," she said. "You give me one piece of information, and I'll give you one piece. Right?"

This reminded me of the game little boys and girls always like to play. You show me yours and I'll show you mine. I'd tried it once. When I was six. Only this little girl talked me into showing mine first, then she laughed and ran away and told all her little friends what a stupid dunce I was.

"Nope, you first," I insisted, still smarting from that old memory.

"Is there some specific area you're interested in?"

"In fact there is. I happen to know that Berkowitz was on to something big. Why wasn't there any hint of that in his final story?"

"I'm not sure what you're talking about. Berkowitz was working several different story lines."

"Come on. Don't be cute. The Kosovo massacre."

She seemed genuinely bewildered. "He sent a dispatch back to the paper the night he died."

"That's right," I said. "But the next day's story was an empty puff piece. Last time he and I talked, he told me he was going to break something big."

She seemed to be reappraising me, as though our discussion had just taken an unexpected turn and ended up on uncertain ground. "Was that where you were helping Berkowitz? The Kosovo massacre?"

"Maybe," I said.

She canted her head sideways. "I don't know what happened," she said. Then she added, "Let me check with the paper on Berkowitz's last dispatch. Sometimes the editors cut a lot out."

I shook my head like I wasn't buying it. "Your editors wouldn't take a pass on something that big."

"You never know," she said. "Editors can be maddeningly arbitrary. Maybe they didn't think his sources were complete or reputable enough. Berkowitz had a reputation for hip-shooting."

"Okay, you do that," I said. "But do it quickly."

"Why? Are you in some kind of hurry?"

"I have my reasons. Now, my turn. Berkowitz believed there was some kind of conspiracy here. Now I'm gonna give you a name. Jack Tretorne. Ever hear of him?"

She shook her head, and her luxuriant black hair shook all around, catching flecks of light. "Can't say I have," she said.

"He's a big muckety-muck with the CIA. He's been spending a lot of time here at Tuzla working directly with the Green Berets."

"And this is supposed to have something to do with Berkowitz's murder?"

"It's related," I assured her.

"And what am I supposed to do?"

"Maybe shake the trees to find out a little more about Tretorne and what he's up to. Be careful when you shake, though. You know what they say about shaking trees with gorillas in the branches."

"That it?" she asked, eyeing me speculatively.

"For now, yes. I'll get hold of you again tomorrow morning. When I call, I'll say I'm Mike Jackson and your order is ready. I'll give you a time to pick it up, which means meet me at the mess hall entrance at that time. Got that?"

"Sure, fine," she said, but the way she said it, she evidently thought I was maybe a little weird or extravagant with my secret passwords and clandestine meeting places. Well, she didn't know what I knew.

We were only a block from the reporters' compound, so I left her there and headed back to my tent. I was beginning to get my traction. I now had an unwitting ally—the best kind of ally for this kind of fight. The CIA thrives on secrecy. Its worst enemy is the threat of public exposure. A guy like Jack Tretorne would shrivel up and die if he was yanked out of the shadows. I'd just sicced Janice Warner and her paper on his trail, which was bound to make his life a little more miserable. Hopefully a lot more miserable.

I really was curious to learn why Berkowitz had never filed the story I gave him. It had to be a key piece in the puzzle. The plot that was taking shape in the back of my mind went something like this: Tretorne somehow learned that Berkowitz was on the verge of breaking the conspiracy story. Maybe Tretorne got tipped because the *Washington Herald* filed an inquiry with the CIA back at Langley. I'm no expert in the ways of modern journalism, but I am under the impression that newspapers generally offer the chance of rebuttal or comment to someone before they slice 'n' dice them on the front page. Or maybe Tretorne had NSA eavesdropping on Berkowitz's electronic transmissions, maybe even his computer, and learned of it that way. Anyway, Tretorne then had Berkowitz "sanctioned," and faxed the *Herald* a planted story under Berkowitz's name.

The only thing that confused me was that Janice Warner sounded completely clueless about what was happening around here. When I mentioned the Kosovo massacre, she seemed genuinely confused. Maybe Tretorne had succeeded in throwing her paper off track. Since Berkowitz never got his real dispatch filed, the *Herald* had no idea what he'd discovered.

When I got back to my tent, I noticed that my possessions had been rifled through. The CID guys had been benevolent enough to try to put everything back where they found it, but a few things were out of place. Also, my running shoes were gone. Such are the terrific inconveniences I had to work with.

Chapter ☆☆ 24

Clapper called at two that night. I began to suspect something insidious in these late-night calls. Maybe this was part of the conspiracy: to try to make me so groggy and miserable that I'd be willing to buy any line of baloney just to get this over with and get some rest. Very devious, those guys.

Clapper said, "Where are you? Are you getting it wrapped up?"

"Dotting a few i's and crossing a few t's," I answered, trying to sound confident.

"I had a call from General Foster over at NSA. He's furious. He said you're making trouble for one of his employees, a Mr. Jones. What's this one about?"

I should have expected this. I said, "I'm just trying to make him get reasonable. He's the same guy who showed us the tapes and transcripts. Only he won't let us have any copies. Too sensitive, he says. I told him I could live with that as long as I had his name and section so I can refer to him in my report."

Clapper said, "You should be able to get by perfectly fine without them. This Jones character is apparently in a very sensitive job. General Foster offered to let us use his own name."

"Boss, it's a chain of evidence thing. Only in this case, I'm not allowed to even touch the evidence. You know the rules. You've got to establish the chain of evidence."

This was an entirely specious line of legal reasoning, but it sounded proximate enough to the real rules of evidence that it might be true.

At any rate, Clapper blew right through it. "If you're going to recommend against court-martial, it's irrelevant. It won't be tested in court. Damn it, Sean, just use Foster's name."

I said, "Sir, I'm the investigating officer. I don't care if it won't be tested in court. I don't do shoddy work. You can advise me on this, but you can't order me."

There was the sound of a set of lungs being emptied on the other line. Clapper was ordinarily a very even-tempered fellow, but major generals don't generally take it kindly when junior officers remind them of their limits.

"You're already facing an inquiry into your professional conduct. Let's not make this any worse."

"Sorry, General, but I have to do what I think is right."

"Have it your way," he said before he hung up, sounding very pissed off.

I hung up the phone myself, then pushed the stop button on the tape recorder I had turned on the moment he identified himself. Recording a phone conversation without the willful consent of the other party is a moderately serious violation of the federal statutes. I really didn't care, though. I didn't plan on using the tape in court, where it would be inadmissible anyway. But I knew the boys in the editorial office of the *Washington Herald* would love listening to it, if things came to that. Besides, they—whoever they were—weren't playing fair with me. So why should I?

On that note, I slept soundly until I felt a rough hand shaking my shoulder. I blinked a few times, until I was able to get my lids to stay up. Not up very far, but enough that I could squint and just make out vague shapes. Martie whatever was hunched over beside my cot and peering into my face. Behind him were two real big shadows that I guessed were military policemen.

"Please get dressed and come with me," he said.

I struggled out of my sleeping bag and sat up. "Are you going to explain what this is about?" I asked, searching around for my battle dress and combat boots.

"When we get to my office."

"Are you arresting me?"

"I'm taking you into custody."

I felt very groggy, and decided not to speak again until I had a cup of coffee in my hand and the caffeine was doing its magic. I got dressed quickly, then stood up and staggered along behind Martie. A military policeman walked on each of my flanks. I noticed that Martie was dressed in the same cockeyed checkered outfit he'd worn the day before. He must've worked through the night.

The time was three in the morning, so the streets were still dark and empty as we headed to his office. I kept a wary eye on Martie and his escorts. For all I knew, they were working for Tretorne or Murphy. In fact, the more I thought about it, the more this seemed like a perfect pretense to perform one of those nasty "sanction" things on me. They'd take me to some dark, secluded part of the compound, then pop me in the back of the head. On the other hand, they hadn't handcuffed me, and I took that as an encouraging sign.

It wasn't until we got to the MP station that I relaxed. I shouldn't have though. What Martie had in store for me was better than taking me into the woods and shooting me.

"Sit down, please," he ordered once we were gathered around a table in an interview room. He then read me my rights. This was something I'd done to suspects a number of times, but you get tight in funny places when the words are recited to you.

I heard him out until he asked, "Do you wish to retain counsel at this time?"

This is always the critical question. I had no idea what I was charged with. I had no idea if I was even going to be charged. I decided that a lawyer probably wasn't going to do me any more good than I could do for myself. I mean, I'm a lawyer, right? Of course, it's exactly that kind of solipsistic thinking that gets a lawyer in deep shit. When it's you the police are questioning, you lose the ability to make the kind of cold, disinterested, dispassionate decisions a hired barrister provides.

Regardless, I said, "Not at this time."

Martie looked at the two military policemen and nodded for them to leave. They closed the door behind them. He then spent a moment just staring at me, I guess to make me nervous. There was a big mirror on the wall, like there is in most interrogation rooms. I figured it was probably one of those two-way jobs with somebody on the other side. Maybe Murphy. Maybe Tretorne. Maybe both of them.

"You have a serious problem," Martie finally said. "Your running shoe matches a print we took from the latrine where Jeremy Berkowitz was murdered."

I said, "That's impossible." Of course, those were the first words out of the mouth of every suspect. So much for my brilliant legal acumen.

He shrugged, then leaned across the table. "Look, Major, if you were in the latrine that night, it would go better if you'd just admit it. Maybe you met him there?"

"I didn't go near the latrine that night."

"You don't expect me to believe that somebody else borrowed your running shoes, murdered Berkowitz, then put them back under your bunk?"

"I don't expect you to believe any damned thing. I didn't go near that latrine, and unless my running shoes grew legs, neither did they."

"Then how do you explain the fact that your shoe prints were there?"

This was a standard technique. God knows, I'd defended enough clients who'd fallen for it. Get me to start building excuses, then tear apart my alibis and try to chase me into a confession.

"I'm not here to explain any damned thing. I never went near that latrine."

He leaned back and began playing with his pen. "There's more," he said.

If this was supposed to make me more nervous, I wasn't biting. I sat patiently and coolly watched him.

He began tapping the pen against his chin. "Among the notes we found in Berkowitz's room was one where you asked him to meet you in the latrine at one o'clock."

My coolness suddenly dribbled away. I now knew I was in very serious trouble. The running-shoe prints could be challenged in a courtroom. There was always the possibility of the crime scene being contaminated by poor procedure or even of contamination at the lab back in Heidelberg. Poor police and lab procedures had bollixed more than one case. There was also the chance that someone with my exact same shoe size and taste in running gear did the crime. An outside chance, admittedly, but I'd built defenses on weaker arguments and prevailed. I mean, I knew I'd never gone near that latrine, so somebody, somewhere, had made a bad mistake. The note, though—that was a slam dunk.

I blurted out, "That's impossible." Oops! There I went again.

"We've had two experts examine the handwriting. It's yours, Major. For Chrissakes, you're an attorney. Do I have to spell it out for you?"

No, he didn't have to spell it out for me. I was being framed. Actually, I was being framed for the second time, if you want to get perfectly technical about it. I didn't know how, but there was no other explanation. I knew I'd never made an appointment with Berkowitz. And I knew I'd never been in the latrine.

I was surprised how tight my lips were when I said, "Martie, I'm done talking without counsel."

He stared at me a few seconds, then stood up, walked over to the door, and knocked. The two MPs came back in, and he ordered them to book me and put me in a cell. They did. First, I was dumbly led to another room where I was fingerprinted, although for the life of me I didn't know why. The military keeps copies of the fingerprints and dental X rays of all personnel in the event they're needed to identify remains. Maybe they just wanted to humiliate me. It worked, too.

My belt and shoelaces were collected, then I was taken to a cell. I knew I'd need a clear head in the morning, so I collapsed onto the bunk and tried to will myself back to sleep. Of course, that never works when you need it to. For thirty minutes I sat there thinking how terrifically stupid I'd been. I'd been too overconfident. I'd overestimated my own cleverness. Worse, I'd once again underestimated who I was dealing with.

I just couldn't figure out how they'd pulled this off. Even if Martie was working for Jones, aka Tretorne, how in the hell had they fabricated such condemning evidence?

I suddenly heard the sound of a lock being opened down the hall. Then footsteps. No lights were turned on, so the hallway and my cell remained pitch-dark. The footsteps stopped in front of the cell.

I could smell the cologne. A good one, too, like scented pines. Very expensive.

"Tretorne, you bastard," I said.

"You look good in there, Drummond," he said.

I said, "Yeah? Why don't you come on in and join me? I'd love a chance to rip your guts out."

He chuckled. "I knew it was you who burgled my room. You have no idea what that briefcase cost. And I really would like to get my passport and ID back. It'll be a real pain in the ass if I have to get them replaced."

Sounding more bitter than I wanted, I said, "Gee, Jack, I'm really sorry. I'd hate to think I've put you out."

"Well, you have, Drummond. You've really pissed me off."

"Then we're even. Let me out of here."

"I'm afraid it's no longer that easy."

"Sure it is, Jack. If I go to jail, I won't take my secrets with me."

"You don't have any secrets. You only think you do."

"Hah," I said. "I know all about what you and Murphy are up to. You frame me, and I'll get the word to every reporter I know. Believe me, I'll find a way. Think about that."

"I already have, Drummond. You think they'll listen to you? No one listens when an accused murderer starts mumbling about conspiracies and frame-ups. Think about it, Drummond. You've got no evidence, and you've got no leverage."

He was right, of course. And that only infuriated me all the more. He moved back and I saw him lean against the wall. His face was completely in the shadows, which only made him appear more sinister.

When he spoke again, his tone sounded suspiciously reasonable. "Regardless, I'm here to make a deal. This will be your only chance. Want to hear it?"

I said, "I've got nothing better to do for the moment."

"Okay. You quit screwing around and do what you're supposed to do on this investigation, and we'll call this thing even. I'll even convince Clapper to cancel that inquiry, and you can get on with your career."

"That's it?" I asked.

"That's it," he said.

"And I'm supposed to just overlook this little thing you've got going with the Green Berets?"

"In a nutshell, yes."

"What about Berkowitz? Am I supposed to forget you did that, too?"

"We didn't do Berkowitz's murder."

Now it was my turn to chuckle. "Horsecrap."

"It's the truth. I don't know who murdered him."

"But you're framing me for it."

"Sure. You've put us in a difficult corner, Drummond. But if you're the leading suspect in a murder investigation, well, you can hardly remain the chief of the investigating team. Nor can you leak to the press like you tried with Berkowitz. Very cute, that."

So that confirmed it: My office was bugged. They'd listened to the whole conversation I had with Berkowitz. They'd listened to everything.

That confirmed something else, too. They had a compelling motive to murder Berkowitz.

I said, "Come on, Tretorne. What was it? Was Berkowitz getting too close? Did he have you figured out? Why'd you have him killed?"

"I'll say it again. I don't know who killed Berkowitz. We didn't do it. I'm not crying any crocodile tears about it, though. He wasn't much of a human being. However, his death gives me the opportunity to get you out of the way."

"You're a real prick."

"I'm not proud of this, but I'm doing it for my country."

I almost guffawed at that one. That line really was the last refuge of the worst kinds of scoundrels. I thought of telling him he sounded just like one of Hitler's henchmen on the docket at Nuremberg, but I'd just be wasting my breath.

Instead, I said, "How'd you work the frame?"

"Easy, really. Everything today is electronic, even police lab work. You'd be surprised to know how easy it is to hack in and change the image of a shoeprint stored in a lab computer when you have the right technology. These NSA people can do miracles."

"And the note they found in Berkowitz's room?"

"A man with all the right credentials planted it in Berkowitz's room yesterday. The right technology can also produce flawless forgeries."

I didn't say anything, so he added, "Look, Sean, don't force us to do it this way. I admire you. I really do. I know all about your time in the outfit. You did some very courageous things, and you've been very dogged in this investigation. But I can't let you damage your country. Don't make this personal."

Back when I was dancing with Sergeant Major Williams in the hard sell interrogation room, every time he hit me, something nasty took control of my brain. I kept mouthing off at Williams, and he kept hitting me harder and doing more and more serious damage to my frail body. I thought about that every night when the day's session was over, and I knew I was facing another one the next day. The rational part of my brain warned me that passive resistance would spare me a lot of pain, but somehow every time they threw me back in that padded room with that sadistic monster, I couldn't help myself. I climbed right back in the saddle, and he drew a little more blood and bounced me off the walls a little harder.

Now I was twelve years older, but was I twelve years wiser? All I had to do was give Tretorne what he wanted. I could get on with my life. Okay, I'd have to live with the fact that I'd participated in a whitewash. Everybody in life has a few blemishes on their record. That's why Catholic priests do such a brisk confessional business. What made me any different? What made me so holy?

I said, "Okay, Tretorne, I'll do it."

He jerked himself off the wall and approached my cell. "You better mean that."

I sounded angry, because I was. "I told you I'll do it."

Even in the dark, I could feel his mechanical eyes studying me.

"Give me your word as an officer," he demanded. He was a

West Pointer, so he'd been trained to believe that an officer's word was an inescapably sacred bond. It was kind of funny, really. He looked right past the irony of forcing me to swear I'd lie on an official report.

"You have my word," I said.

"Okay. In about two hours, General Murphy will come in here and swear you were with him the night Berkowitz was murdered. That'll get you released. But you try to screw me, and I'll have your ass right back in this cell. There won't be any second chance, either."

"Look, I gave you my word. Get me outta here, and I'll do everything you want."

"All right," he said.

Then I heard his footsteps echoing down the hallway again. I was lying, of course. The second I got out of here, I was going to do every damned thing I could to screw Tretorne and Murphy and the whole United States Army. I had no idea what that was, but I sure as hell couldn't get anything done sitting in this jail cell.

You are who you are, and there's nothing you can do to change that. These guys framed me and blackmailed me, and I was mad enough to spit. Only I'd settle for a little revenge.

Chapter ☆☆ 25

At eight o'clock they came to get me. Martie accompanied the military policeman who carried the keys. He had showered and changed, and now he wore a striped suit with a striped shirt and a striped tie speckled with tiny stars. On top of his abominable taste, he was color-blind. It was all red, white, and blue. He resembled a walking American flag.

He looked tired, too, with lank hair and these big puffy dark things under his bloodshot eyes. He also looked mopey. He thought he had his crime solved, then the Army's most respected brigadier general shows up to give me an alibi, and now poor Martie was right back where he started. Only a lot more tired.

I didn't mind one bit, though. I mean, I liked Martie, but not enough to volunteer to stay here and be his culprit.

I went back to my tent, showered, shaved, and put on a fresh uniform. Delbert and Morrow were both back when I walked into the office. Nobody knew I'd been arrested and released. At least nobody acted as if they knew. The mole probably knew but was canny enough to keep it to himself. Or herself. Whichever.

I invited them both into my office. Then we spent an hour

or so hashing through the motions of reviewing what they'd accomplished. The folks back at Bragg had told Delbert that a preemptive ambush wasn't exactly what they'd envisioned when they wrote their rules of engagement. However, they reasoned, the parameters certainly fit as long as you stretched things the right way and as long as the team was under genuine duress. No surprise there.

Morrow had built a lengthy, intricate chronology of events that closely resembled the checkery outfit Martie had worn the day before. She'd produced this twenty-page computer-generated spreadsheet, composed of tiny color-coded blocks for each man in Sanchez's team. It was an amazing piece of work. You could follow their every action for four straight days. I sarcastically mumbled something about how I couldn't tell when they went potty in the woods, and she gave me this dead serious look and assured me she had that in an annex but would certainly integrate it in the master chronology if I thought that was necessary. I had no idea if she was kidding.

When we were done, Delbert and Morrow stood up and started to leave. Morrow suddenly paused at the door and asked if she could speak to me. In private, she stressed. I nodded, and she shut the door and returned to her same seat.

She looked deeply troubled. She paused, then said, "I'm having second thoughts."

"About what?" I asked.

"It's kind of hard to explain. Just a sense."

"A sense about what?" I asked again.

"I no longer think they're innocent."

I shook my head and cleared my hearing. "You're kidding, right?"

She looked me dead in the eye. "No. When I was working with them to construct this Chinese puzzle, I just got this impression that it was a little too fabricated. Does that make sense?"

"I wasn't there," I said in my most maddeningly ambivalent tone.

She stood up and began pacing. "Look, I make my living dealing with guilty clients. Sometimes, you know, you just get a sense. Well, I got that sense."

"And just where was this sense last week?"

"Look, I know. I've changed my mind."

She'd picked up a pencil and was holding it against her lip again. I don't know why, I still found that sexy as hell.

"Look, Morrow, we've got two days to get this done. You saw those satellite pictures. You heard those transcripts."

"I know," she said, still moving back and forth across the front of my desk like one of those ducks in a carnival shooting gallery.

"Well, then, how in the hell do you explain it?"

"I can't," she said. "I just know. All nine of those men were able to perfectly reconstruct the events of those four days."

I said, "Sure. They not only experienced it together, they also had ample time to discuss it among themselves. Get mad at that chunky Air Force jailer of theirs for letting them get away with that, but it doesn't make them guilty."

"Nine men don't remember events with the kind of coordinated accuracy I heard over the past two days. It's like they've been drilled and rehearsed. Like actors in a Broadway play. They never argued with one another. There were no contradictions."

I stared at her incredulously.

She stopped pacing. "There's a clincher, too."

"And what's this clincher?"

"Every man now knows exactly how many flares went off. Both before and after they were detected. Don't you see what's happening here? Even after you ordered that major to keep them separated, those men were somehow allowed to get back together and compare notes. I couldn't find a single point of disagreement."

This really was ironic. Here I'd suspected Sanchez and his

men because they'd walked all over one another on the details, and now Morrow thought them guilty as hell because their stories were so mysteriously identical.

That's when it hit me. That Tretorne. That devious, manipulative bastard. Morrow was the mole. He'd put her up into coming in here with this last-minute change of heart just to flush me out and see if I was going to keep our Faustian pact.

Well, I knew how to handle this. I said, "Look, Morrow, you can't do this. It's . . . well, it's too late."

She wheeled around and her eyes got kind of pointy and narrow. "It's not too late until the packet's signed."

I tried my damnedest not to smile. She was such a charming schemer, but I now had her number.

"And how are you going to explain it?" I asked derisively. "You gonna vote for court-martial on the basis of your sixth sense? Or are you gonna try to explain that the witnesses were too good to be believed?"

"I'll vote whatever my conscience tells me. I've got two more days to decide what that is, and I will not be pressured."

"Hey," I said, "I'm just trying to save you from embarrassing yourself. Delbert and I believe they're innocent. I'm totally convinced of it. In fact, they're heroes. They should all get medals for what they did."

She scrutinized my face, and I guessed she was trying to decide if I was being genuine. I stared back with this look of fiery conviction, the same look I used to give court-martial boards when I was a defense counsel and my client was guilty as hell. Sometimes it actually worked. Sometimes it didn't.

Finally, she pounced very angrily from the room. Tretorne and Murphy would've been very proud of her. A compelling performance right down to the finish line.

I, on the other hand, now had a vital phone call to make. I walked out and told Imelda I'd be back in an hour. I returned to my tent, put on my Harold Hufnagel disguise, then went back

to the supply room. The same private was there, lounging in the
back and listening to some rap group chanting about shooting
and castrating cops. How would you like to be a cop and hear
that tune pounding on the radio? Well, at least they weren't
chanting about lawyers. I asked the private, who was bouncing
to the rap, if I could use the phone again. His head was bouncing, too, so I took that as a yes. I dialed Janice Warner's number.

"Hello," she answered.

"Hi, Mike Jackson here," I said, employing my clever pass-
word.

"Oh, you," she replied. "Is my delivery ready?" I could tell by
her tone that she was having a little trouble playing along.

"Yeah. Can you come pick it up in fifteen minutes? After
that, I'm gonna be tied up for a few hours."

"All right," she said. "I'll be right there."

I then positioned myself about midway between the mess
hall and the Visiting Journalists' Quarters. After about five minutes, I saw her heading my way, and I walked out and intercepted her. I took her arm and we started walking through the
streets again.

She wore khaki trousers, a blue button-down shirt, and the
same black leather jacket. In daylight, new observations came
into play. She had great skin, very white, almost like alabaster.
Her eyes, I now noticed, were nearly black, like her hair. And
she had these thinly arched eyebrows, like curved scimitars. Very
mysterious and very alluring.

"Hi," I said.

There was no warmth in her recognition. "Hello, Sergeant
Stupnagel."

"Hufnagel," I reminded her, "Harold Hufnagel. Harry to you,
though."

She rolled her eyes. "Right."

"So did you get hold of your home office?" I asked.

"I did. They have no idea what you're talking about. Berkowitz never mentioned anything about a breakthrough in his dispatch. Nor did he mention any inside source."

"That's damned curious. I mean, he went off like a whirling dervish the last time we spoke. I can't believe he wasn't gonna write about it."

"I also did some checking on Jack Tretorne. Our reporter who covers the Agency knows him. He's in charge of the Balkans. He's even got a nickname. Jack of Serbia."

"No kidding," I said.

"Nope, no kidding," she deadpanned. "Like Lawrence of Arabia. He's been working Serbian affairs since 1990 when Yugoslavia first exploded. He's got a great reputation, very smart, very capable. They say he's the behind-the-scenes mastermind on nearly everything."

"Makes you wonder why he's here, huh?" I asked, giving her a sly, confidential wink.

She was still looking at me strangely, and I was starting to feel like Mel Gibson must've felt in that conspiracy movie.

She said, "Why wouldn't he be here? There's a war raging just across the border. Maybe if he was hanging around in Nicaragua, I might wonder. In fact, if he wasn't here, I might wonder."

I got this sense she was losing patience with me. I said, "So you're telling me nobody heard Berkowitz mention anything interesting about this investigation?"

"No. But then the Kosovo massacre wasn't really the main attraction that brought him here."

That surprised me, until I thought about it. Then it made perfect sense. Of course. What Berkowitz was really interested in was the conspiracy between the CIA and the Special Forces. Breaking my massacre story might get him some acclaim, but exposing a modern replay of Operation Phoenix—hell, that would get him a seat in the Pulitzer hall of fame. Maybe he'd write a book about it, and they'd make a movie about him, like what happened with Woodward and Bernstein over Watergate. Who would they get to play Berkowitz, though? Dom DeLuise?

Only there was one very vexing problem with this scenario: His own newspaper didn't know anything about it.

At that moment Warner said, "Look, Sergeant Stupnagel, I have to admit that I'm having a little trouble taking you seriously."

I said, "No, you look, Miss Wiener—"

"Warner," she sharply corrected.

"Right, and like I've told you four times, my name's Hufnagel. Harry Hufnagel."

She gave me the kind of look usually reserved for used-car salesmen. Black eyes, by the way, can be very penetrating. She said, "Well, that's part of our problem here. I had the information office run down your name. There's only one Hufnagel in all of Tuzla. She's a legal specialist on temporary duty."

"A rose is a rose by any other name," I said.

"You're no rose. Who are you?"

My first impulse was to lie again. Make up some name like Godfrey Gommeners: I mean, I was getting tired of Harold Hufnagel anyway. But why not tell her who I really was? All the jigs were up at this point anyway, and it wasn't like I could get in any deeper trouble than I was already in.

"Okay, I'm Major Sean Drummond. I'm the chief investigating officer for the Kosovo massacre."

She looked at me curiously, like I'd suddenly gravitated to a whole new plane. "Can you prove that?"

"If you insist. I actually have this military ID card they issued me, but it's back in my tent. I could always take you back to my office, but then I'd get in trouble, because I'm not authorized to deal with the press."

"Then why this masquerade?"

"Because I believe Berkowitz's murder was somehow connected to my investigation."

"And you wanted me to fill in some blanks for you?"

"Actually, yes. That's exactly what I wanted."

"But you didn't want me to get a hook into you? Was that it?"

I acted embarrassed, which wasn't too difficult, because I was. I said, "Look, Berkowitz did a hatchet job on me on the front page of your paper. He also tried to blackmail me. Under the circumstances . . ."

She seemed very disappointed in me. Those scimitar-like eyebrows sliced downward in a deeply disapproving frown. "And you have no solid information about Berkowitz's murder? Do you?"

"I can tell you he was murdered by a pro. I can tell you it had something to do with the story he was covering. And I'll repeat again, I believe it was connected to my investigation."

I decided not to mention that I was also being framed for his death. Or that my office was tapped and that the conversation Berkowitz and I had there might've been the trigger to his murder. After all, I needed her to trust me, and I already seemed to be having a bit of trouble in that department.

She said, "And that's it?"

I said, "Well, what do you think got him murdered?"

She seemed ambivalent for a few seconds, and I hoped her mental coin toss landed in my direction. I gave her my most endearing expression, which, like my look of fiery conviction, tends to get mixed results.

Finally she said, "Major Drummond, I don't know what you're up to, but I'm still having a little trouble trusting you."

I said, "Story of my life. Every pretty girl I ever met says that."

She chuckled a bit, and that took some of the edge off.

"Look, Janice," I said with as much conviction as I could muster, "we're headed in the same direction. I'm an Army officer. I don't like the idea that someone who wears my same uniform slipped a garrote around a reporter's neck. I'm also an officer of the court. Call me old-fashioned, but I believe crime should pay."

She said, "All right, all right. I just don't think I can help you. If we had any idea what got Berkowitz murdered, you'd be reading about it on the front page of the *Herald*. He was covering your investigation. And he was doing the occasional routine piece on the operation in Kosovo. We just don't see any angles there that got him killed."

"Was there anything else?" I asked.

"Well, he was also running some silly investigation on neo-Nazis and white supremacists in the Army. It was a personal passion of his. A crazy thing he'd been working on for years. Berkowitz was Jewish, you know. His grandparents actually died in the Nazi death camps."

Only with great difficulty did I keep a perfectly straight face. "What kind of investigation?"

"This time he was following a trail he had picked up at Fort Bragg. I don't know much about it. Some group of soldiers helping train a bunch of hicks to blow up and burn synagogues and Black churches. Nobody took it too seriously. From what I hear, he was always finding new leads for his story, and they always went nowhere."

"And that's why he was here?"

"According to Bob Barrows, his editor, it's one of the things he was checking on. Remember that string of church arsons about a year back? Berkowitz thought the man behind it might be here."

I said, "You're kidding."

She said, "No, really."

I almost blurted out, "You're not going to believe this. I think I know exactly who he was looking for."

I didn't, though. Partly because my mind suddenly got very busy. It would be an incredible coincidence, but fate owed me a break. Sergeant Major Williams was an expert with a garrote, since all of us in the outfit were taught how to use that ghoulish thing. He'd been thrown out of the outfit for mucking around with a bunch of backwoods, redneck racists. And he had a brutally short fuse and a bent toward cruelty. I could testify to that in excruciating detail. But murder? Yes, I could see that son of a bitch murdering somebody. With a garrote, too. Hell, he'd probably smile as he did it.

Then one more piece of the puzzle suddenly went *kaplunk!* Maybe this was how Berkowitz knew about the existence of the outfit. Maybe he had a source somewhere who told him about Williams, and maybe that same source put him on to me.

My thoughts were interrupted by a now-curious Miss Warner, who grabbed my arm. "Do you know something about this?"

I summoned every ounce of innocence I could. "No, not really. I mean, bigots sometimes slip through our net, but I think you're right. Probably just some crazy idea he had that didn't pan out. I'd be willing to do some checking around, though."

She looked disappointed. The edges of her lips sagged a little, and she said, "I have to admit that the first time you called, I thought this was what it was about. Hufnagel's a good German name, and you said you were a sergeant. I mean, I thought it fit, and—"

As much as I didn't want to arouse her suspicions, I glanced down at my watch and said, "Geez, look what time it is! Listen, I've got to take another interrogatory. Why don't I give you a call, if I find something?"

She was no dummy. Her eyes got even narrower, almost squinty. "Yeah, why don't you do that," she said as I dashed away.

It is an old Army axiom that you should never defecate in your own mess kit, but I really couldn't tell her about my old buddy Sergeant Major Williams. For one thing, she was a reporter, and all I had was a suspicion based on an odd coincidence. A suspicion with pretty strong legs, but still. Besides, I had other plans for my newest revelation.

The neat box Tretorne and Murphy had built around me had suddenly developed a fatal flaw. They'd lose all their leverage

over me if I could prove Williams murdered Berkowitz. I rather
looked forward to that. I still owed Williams for two false teeth
and about a month of pissing blood out of my pummeled kid-
neys anyway. As for Tretorne and crew, I owed them something
special, too. I'd rewrite my investigation summary and blow them
all to pieces. I'd say I had great difficulty getting at the truth because of Tretorne's plotting and Murphy's conspiracy. I'd write
about the director of the National Security Agency, who was in
the cover-up so deep he'd even fabricated false evidence. I still
wasn't positive whether Clapper was in or out. His calls had
been strategically timed, and that was suspicious, but not iron-
clad. Anyway, I'd find some way to take a whack at him, too.

Chapter ☆☆☆ 26

Lisa Morrow was still in a sulky funk when I got back to the office. She was seated at the desk outside my office and gave me a sulfurous look when I walked by. Give the girl credit. She was very tenacious.

I drafted a brief note to Sergeant Major Williams, then asked Imelda to please have one of her aides deliver it to him in the ops center. Then I left and went back to the MP station. Martie and David had been given a conference room in the rear, right next to Captain Wolkowitz's office.

I knocked and someone called for me to come in. All three of them, Martie, David, and Wolky, were seated around a conference table. A large easel had been erected on a flimsy metal stand. On the easel was their own Chinese puzzle, with lots of little boxes filled with scribbled-in names, and lots of intersecting lines that connected this suspect with that suspect and this motive with that motive. It looked to me like a hopeless montage.

About two dozen empty white foam coffee cups were strewn around, and both Martie and David had loosened their ties and rolled up their shirtsleeves. The room reeked from the acrid smell of body odor. And my ever-acute nose also detected a fragrance of desperation. I'd smelled enough of it on my own body these past few days to recognize it.

I said, "Hi guys," and gave them my cheeriest smile. At least somebody around here was getting less sleep than me.

Then I fell into a chair that allowed me to face them. "Any new suspects?" I asked.

Of course, they were not about to answer this question to a man who, only that morning, had been a suspect himself. And maybe still was in their fevered minds; General Murphy's alibi notwithstanding. Martie stared back at me with clouded indifference.

"We're making headway," he said. He didn't sound real convincing, though.

I said, "Oh good. Then I won't waste your time by telling you who the killer is."

Wolky was the first to recover and open his mouth. "Is this some kind of a joke, Major?"

"Actually, no. Did you ever get around to asking the *Herald* what stories Berkowitz was working on?"

"Of course," Martie said. "All they said, though, was that he was writing about the Kosovo operation. They were too worried about disclosing sources and stories in progress to offer specifics. The only reason we knew your investigation was one of his subjects was because of the article he wrote about it. And, of course, you admitted it."

"Well, turns out he was working on a third story, too. He was trying to uncover some neo-Nazi, white supremacist ring."

All three of them were now bent forward, their hands poised on their chins, their eyes wide, and their mouths were hanging open a little. It made a lovely picture.

I added, "It seems a source told Berkowitz that a soldier stationed here might have been implicated in the Black church burnings that happened about a year back."

Martie said, "How do you know this?"

"I have my sources, too."

He started to say something and I cut him off at the post. "Don't even think about it, Martie. I'm an attorney, remember? I can play attorney-client privilege games until we're both toothless old farts."

"So the killer contacted you and asked you to negotiate with us?" he guessed.

"Wrong. But I'm pretty sure I know who the killer is. Even if he didn't do it himself, I'd bet anything he was at least implicated."

Martie turned to Wolky. "You aware of any white supremacist activity here?"

Wolky shrugged his big shoulders and said, "Nope."

This was no surprise because Tuzla was a temporary operational base. The MPs did not have the kind of grip on their population they would have at a permanent installation. Here, units floated in and out on a rotational basis, and their troublemakers passed in and out with them. Still, I was glad Martie asked. Now they knew they needed me.

I said, "Are you ready to hear my deal?"

"Deal? What do you mean, deal?" David asked. It was nice to see he had a voice too.

I leaned back in my chair, locked my hands behind my neck, and plopped my feet onto the table. "Well, for various reasons, your chief suspect is going to require special handling."

David asked, "What reasons? What kind of special handling?"

"You can make the arrest. You will then lock him up in a quarantined cell, and nobody will be allowed to go near him. Someone will be here within a day to take him into custody. He'll be whisked out of here, and aside from whatever assistance you may be required to provide to the people who take him, your relationship with this case will be over. You'll forget all about it."

All three of them were looking at me like I was nuts.

Martie said, "I never heard anything so weird."

I said, "Take it or leave it. If you can't live with it, I'll get someone else to handle it."

"What's so special about this guy?" Wolky asked.

"I'm sorry, Wolky. I can't tell you."

"Who's gonna take him into custody?"

"Guys in dark suits. They'll have special orders signed by the Secretary of Defense. That's all you need to know."

You see, the truth was that the real reason Clapper had once been so agreeable about sending me to law school was because it solved a delicate problem for the Army. The outfit was only one of several "black units" on the Army's rolls. Altogether there are several thousand secret warriors roaming around out there, and anywhere there are thousands of soldiers, guess what you get: troublemakers.

In fact, as you might imagine, that kind of duty attracts some real rogues. You could screen as hard as you wanted, but a few murderers, rapists, thieves, and sundry other lawbreakers always slipped through. When they did a crime and were apprehended, your standard-fare, open court-martial would have exposed not only them, but also the existence of their units. The Army's answer to this ticklish conundrum was to convene a permanent "black court," located at a tiny, secret base in northern Virginia. The military judge who sat over that court had a special clearance. The lawyers all had special clearances. The court was guided by military law, but its existence and its proceedings were every bit as closely guarded as the outfit or any other black unit. There was even a special "black review court," to handle appeals. This, of course, was my unit, where I worked until I was yanked out to conduct this investigation.

Williams, because of his history with the outfit, was going to have to be tried by us. The trail of his crime reached back to the days when he served in the outfit. In any case, he would no doubt threaten to publicly divulge the existence of the outfit, if he thought that would offer him some leverage. It was one of the first resorts of nearly every "black world" rascal who got caught. I could not allow that to happen.

It did not take Martie and David and Wolky long to realize their hands were tied. They talked and argued and bitched for a while, and I deferred every question they asked. Then I explained that, if necessary, I could always get on a phone, and they'd get a call from a four-star officer back in Washington ordering them to obey my instructions. In the end, they took the only recourse that would allow them to end this case and to get some rest. They caved in.

Only we now had to prove Williams did it. I was sure he was our man. Too many angles fit together. The court systems, however, have all those discommoding rules about evidence, and right at the moment that was the one thing we sorely lacked.

I explained as much about Sergeant Major Williams as they needed to know and nothing more. I asked Martie to call the lab in Heidelberg and have them immediately transmit the largest shoeprint that had been collected at the crime scene. Williams was a big boy, about six foot three, and, oddly enough, I had once spent about two weeks staring at his feet. One of his interrogation techniques was to order me to keep my eyes focused on the floor, like a repentant monk. Every time I made the mistake of lifting my eyes, he hammered me on the back of the head. I remembered that he had very big feet. Big hands, too. Big, hurtful hands.

The shoeprint came across the wire, marked and labeled with the size, shoe type, and manufacturer. The size was thirteen, double E. It was an Adidas running shoe, style name Excelsior. Martie told me there was a reporter from the *Los Angeles Times* staying at the Visiting Journalists' Quarters the night of the murder who also wore size thirteen shoes and they had all assumed this was his shoeprint. Since the L.A. reporter was a civilian, they had no jurisdiction to question him or take his shoeprint, and he had returned to L.A. a day later. Martie pointed to where the reporter's name was written into one of the little possible suspect blocks on their jigsaw puzzle. He told me he'd even wired the LAPD and asked if they had any background on the reporter. He was still awaiting a response.

I told him to get on the phone and ask the jurisdictional military judge to issue us a search order to get into Sergeant Major Williams's room so we could get a pair of his shoes. I wasn't hopeful, though. Williams was no dummy. If he'd worn his running shoes into the latrine that night, there was a good chance they would've gotten splattered with blood, and surely he would've been clever enough to dispose of them. We'd at least get his shoe size, though. That was a step in the right direction. Figuratively speaking, of course.

This led naturally to trying to figure out how Williams knew that Berkowitz was on to him.

David suggested, "Maybe Berkowitz's source was double-dealing and put Williams on to it."

This might've happened, but we quickly agreed it didn't seem likely. Why would a source rat Williams out to Berkowitz, then Berkowitz out to Williams?

Wolky suggested, "Maybe Berkowitz actually met with Williams. Maybe he threatened to expose him."

This seemed much more likely. I said, "Was there no mention of Sergeant Major Williams in Berkowitz's notebook?"

Martie said, "None. We've been through every page two dozen times. And every little note in his room. Never saw that name."

I turned to David. "Call the operations officer. Find out if Williams was on duty at the ops center that night."

He ran out, and we bantered about the weather until he returned. The weather was nice, we all agreed. A little hot, but nice. David returned.

"He was on day shift," he said a little breathlessly. "He was in the ops center from six in the morning till six at night, except from noon till one for lunch."

So he was off duty when Berkowitz was murdered. That much fit. There was a knock at the door, then an MP entered carrying a pair of real big running shoes. They looked brand-new, which made it easy to read the shoe size, which was stamped in black letters on the inside of the shoe's tongue. Thirteen, double E's. We all nodded sagely. Brand-new shoes. Um-hummm, we all murmured. And the same size as the mold. Now we were getting somewhere.

Not far enough, though. If there was one other man on this compound who wore size thirteen, double E's, then Williams was home free. And we already knew there was a reporter in Los Angeles who wore thirteen, double E's.

We went back to trying to figure out how Williams discovered Berkowitz was on to him. We decided they either met face-to-face or at least talked to each other on the phone.

We sat and stared at the tabletop for a while. How would Berkowitz have learned where Sergeant Major Williams worked, I wondered. I mean, assume his source gave him Williams's name and told him he was now with Tenth Group at Tuzla Air Base. Berkowitz still would've needed to track him down. Maybe he did what Janice Warner tried with Harry Hufnagel.

I went to the phone and called the information office. That same friendly little sergeant named Jarvis answered again.

I said, "Hey, Sergeant Jarvis, Major Sean Drummond here."

"Good morning, sir. How can I help you?"

"Just answer a few questions. Who handles press inquiries in your office?"

"They come to me first. I sort through them and parcel 'em out."

"So if a reporter calls or sends a paper request, you would see it?"

"That's right. But I only handle the easy stuff. If it's a complicated request, it goes to the information officer, Major Lord. Usually he tasks it out to whoever in Tenth Group has the right expertise to answer the question. Then it comes back to us, and we send the response back to the journalist."

"Okay," I said. "Suppose a reporter wanted to track down somebody in Tenth Group. Who would handle that?"

"Me. I mean, it's no toughie. I just access the group's manning roster and get the answer."

"Do you remember if Jeremy Berkowitz asked you to track anyone down?"

"Sure. He asked me to find you, for instance."

"Good. That's right. Anyone else?"

"Just a second, sir. I keep a record of every request. It's SOP here."

I heard his fingers tapping his computer keys, accessing some file. Then, "Yeah, I've got the list here."

"Could you read it to me, please?"

"Sure. Uh, let's see . . . Colonel Thomas Weathers . . . Major Sean Drummond . . . Captain Dean Walters . . . Sergeant Major Luther Williams—"

"Stop there," I said. "Did you tell him how to get hold of Williams?"

"I did. But he asked me to get hold of him and have Williams call him back."

"And did you?" I asked.

"Yes, sir. I've got it all logged right here. Let's see . . . I called the sergeant major at 1030 hours at the ops center on the morning of the second."

"Very good. Now, I'd like you to put a copy of that file you're reading on a disk and bring it down to the MP station. Don't mention anything to anybody, just do it. Ask for Captain Wolkowitz when you get here."

Sergeant Jarvis was a smart kid, and no doubt deduced this had something to do with the Berkowitz murder. He sounded almost breathless when he said, "Be right there. Only take ten minutes."

In a matter of only a few hours we now had a motive, and we had the makings of a very good circumstantial case. It's amazing how much you can accomplish when you know who the killer is and only have to fill in the blanks from there. Especially on an Army base.

What we didn't have was tangible proof. And what I didn't have was more time to build a better case.

We could prove Berkowitz was here trying to break a story on white supremacists. We could prove, with the outfit's wiretaps, that Williams was associated with a backwoods band of bigots. We could prove Berkowitz made contact with Williams. We could prove Williams had the right shoe size to fit a mold from the murder scene. All this was great. Arithmetically speaking.

What we couldn't prove was that Williams murdered him. No small inconvenience that last point.

It was nearly noon. I turned to Martie. "I need you to provide me a wire, and I need you to call your judge and get me permission to tape a conversation with Williams. You've got proximate cause."

He called the judge and it took about ten minutes before the judge wrote out an order.

The note I had earlier sent to Williams asked him to meet me at 1230 hours at my office. I'd also told Imelda to make sure everyone was gone and that the building was empty.

I figured it wouldn't hurt anything to directly confront Sergeant Major Williams. It wasn't like he could escape. Tuzla Air Base was heavily guarded and, even if Williams could get out into the surrounding countryside, he wasn't going to get far without a passport. It wasn't like he could blend into the population. He didn't even speak Serbo-Croatian.

I asked Wolky to position a few of his best ass-kicking MPs in the nearby vicinity, without their identifying brassards, just in case our man got violent. Williams was about six foot three, and weighed about 230. I'm about five foot ten and weigh only 170. I was always pretty good with my fists, but the laws of physics are what they are.

I then returned to my office to meet the man I was sure murdered Jeremy Berkowitz. Imelda had done her job, and the building was empty. She'd also brewed me a fresh pot of coffee. I love that woman. I got a cup and went into my office.

Sergeant Major Williams swaggered in two minutes late. I went out to meet him, offered him some coffee, he nodded, and I went over and poured him a cup. I owed him a cup anyway, so now we were even. Well, not exactly even, since there was the matter of nearly two dozen excessive ass-kickings I still owed him. He followed me back into the office and sat in a chair across from my desk.

"So what you doin'?" he asked, grinning. He had a cocky manner anyway, but in my case, since he'd once spent two weeks pounding me like Silly Putty, he felt a bit superior.

I said, "I'm leaving tomorrow. My investigation's complete so I gave the rest of my staff the day off, and I'm left with a little time to kill. Us being old comrades and all, I just thought you and I should get together."

He looked at me curiously and took a sip of coffee.

I took a sip, too, then said, "Ever get to thinking about the outfit days?"

"Sure do. Great fucking days. We did some wild-assed stuff."

"Sure did, didn't we? If it wasn't for getting accepted to law school, I'd probably still . . . well . . ." I let that thought taper off. "So, why exactly did you leave?"

"Ah, y'know, you get burned out. Can't live on a high wire like that forever."

I said, "That's funny. I heard different. I heard you got in some kinda trouble back there."

He became noticeably tighter. "Yeah? Where'd you hear that?"

"Here and there. Something about you working with a bunch of bigots down in North Carolina."

I had his undivided attention. He was staring at me hard and trying to figure out what was going down here. "You must be listenin' to the wrong people," he said. "Ain't no such thing happened."

I said, "Did you know the outfit tapped all of our phones? Probably not. Hell, I didn't know it myself till a few days ago."

He leaned back in his chair and drew in a heavy breath. "That legal?" he inquired.

Give the man credit; his mind was racing quickly. He was trying to get a little free legal advice. He wanted to know how the wiretaps would stand up in court if he ever got apprehended for Berkowitz's murder.

"I'd guess the outfit has some kinda court order that allows it," I answered. "Kinda like the CIA is allowed to impose lie detector tests on its employees. Unique privileges for unique organizations."

"Uh-huh," he said. "Well, that was a long time ago."

"Yep, it was," I agreed. "And you probably stopped whatever you were doing when you left."

"I probably did," he said.

I took another sip from my coffee, and he took another sip from his coffee. He knew now this was no friendly, idle chat.

"Hey," I said, "ever meet that reporter who got murdered? What's his name? Berkowitz, right? Jeremy Berkowitz."

His eyes were now very narrow and guarded. "Nope, can't say I ever did."

"That's odd. I met with him the day he got killed. In the morning. He told me he was gonna see you around lunchtime," I lied.

"No shit?" he said.

"That's what he said."

"Well, he never told me, 'cause I never heard of him till he was dead."

"Well, that's the other thing. There's this sergeant who works for the information officer. Guy named Jarvis. I talked to him just this morning. Real pleasant guy. He says he helped line up a meeting between you two."

"He must be lying," Williams growled.

"Actually, he's got an official log to prove it. Seems every time a reporter asks him to contact a member of the command, he's required to log it."

"That right?" he said a little too nonchalantly. He was working hard at repressing his hotheaded nature.

"Yep, that's right. Oh, and another thing."

"What's that?"

I said, "You know, CID stops by here now and again to compare notes. Till now, everybody's been convinced the killing was somehow connected to my investigation. Hell, CID still thinks that. Anyhow, they lifted the footprints of the asshole who killed Berkowitz. He wore running shoes so he could sneak up behind him. You know, we're talking about a real gutless pussy. Never gave Berkowitz a fair chance. Same kind of low-life scum who'd burn a church."

He shrugged, but I knew what he was thinking and feeling. He was once my torturer. Anyone who has ever been tortured for an extended period will tell you that it becomes a strangely intimate experience. You get closer than lovers. The interrogator is trying to measure your physical and mental breaking points, while you're desperately trying to climb inside his head and figure out how to get him to stop hurting you. It's very visceral. You study his every gesture, a shift in his muscles, a change of tone in his voice, a look in his eyes, anything to prepare yourself for the next blow. You learn how to please him, and in my case, how to infuriate him. In an obscene kind of way, I guessed

I knew Sergeant Major Luther Williams better than any man I'd ever met.

I added, "Killer used a garrote, too. Back in the outfit, we always figured that was a real sicko's weapon. You know, like something maybe an angry fag might use. Or maybe one of them sexual deviants. I mean, what kind of guy you figure would kill a man that way?"

"I never thought about it," he said. His knuckles were very white.

"Another thing. From the footprints, turned out the murderer was some big, goofy bastard with splayed feet."

"That right?" he asked.

"Size thirteen, double E. You've got big, wide feet. I didn't mention it to CID yet, but I remember staring at 'em all the time while you were beating the crap out of me. What size you figure you wear?"

"I never went near that latrine," he said.

I said, "Hey, you know, after you left Bragg that rash of child molesting that had been happening in the housing area stopped altogether. All those little boys were safe to go to the bus stop without their parents again."

He was now glaring at me with a very nasty scowl. Like a lot of big men, he did not like being taunted or mocked. One thing I'd learned about him in the hard sell was that he'd get real touchy when it came to sexual perversions. He'd be slapping me around, and I tried calling him all kinds of names. Wasn't long before I learned that faggot or baby screwer, or variants thereof, really hit his funny bone. Like they say, where there's smoke, there's fire. I'd always figured there must be some kind of ugly sexual pathology locked up inside that big skull of his that he either didn't want to admit or sure as hell didn't like to be reminded of. Lots of perverts are like that. Not real comfortable with their own nasty habits.

He said in this very menacing tone, "Listen, motherfucker, I don't have to sit here and listen to yer shit."

I stared at him hard. "Yeah you do. See, this ain't the outfit's screening. Now I'm a major and you're a noncommissioned officer, and I'm ordering you to stay right where you are. Besides, you leave here and I'll walk right over to CID and tell 'em what I suspect about you."

A murderous look crept into his eyes.

"Anyway," I continued, "only damned reason I haven't mentioned anything yet to CID was because I wanted to be sure. But I got to thinking about your feet, and what Sergeant Jarvis told me, and why you were thrown out of the outfit, and the cowardly way Berkowitz was killed, and what a sick, yellow asshole I knew you were, and it all kinda makes sense."

I knew the signs. Because he always wore a mask when he was kicking the crap out of me back at Bragg, I got to know his eyes real well. Right at that moment, they were scrunched with a calculating shrewdness, because he now knew I was the only man on this base who could put all that together. And golly gee . . . well, here we were, all alone in my office building. Just the two of us, just like old times. Only there was no hidden camera up in the corner making films that Colonel Tingle would review later that night. All there was was a tiny microphone under my shirt; of course, he didn't know about that.

"Know what else, Williams?" I chuckled. "I think you probably screwed Berkowitz before you killed him."

He leaped out of his chair and came across the desk, until his face was inches from mine. "I didn't fuck that fat Jewboy," he said.

"If you never met him, how'd you know he was fat?" I said.

I saw the punch, but I couldn't dodge it. Williams hadn't lost his touch, either. I went flying backward, right over my chair, and ended up sprawled on the floor, seeing stars, and hearing this loud ringing sound in my ears.

He shoved the desk aside and came after me. He lifted me right off the ground by my collar. I'd forgotten how incredibly strong he was when he got mad. I felt like a little Raggedy Ann doll. He threw me across the room, and I bounced off a wall. These weren't the padded, cushiony walls he and I had practiced with before. These were the real thing, with hard, unyielding surfaces. It hurt a lot more. Then he ran over and jerked me up by the hair and started punching my head back and forth while I screamed, "You screwed him, you pervert! You sick bastard."

He was now completely out of control, on a rampage like he had been so many years before. He pulled my face right up to his and hissed, "I didn't screw him! I used that garrote so I didn't have to touch the filthy Jewboy."

He threw me across the room and sent me crashing into another wall. I felt something snap, maybe a rib, maybe an arm bone. Everything hurt.

He moved across the room for me. "You fucked up, Drummond. We're all alone here. I'm gonna kill you, and I'm gonna make it hurt."

He made only one mistake. His feet were spread apart when he bent over to jerk me up again. Maybe he was too enraged to watch his technique. Or maybe something deep inside his memory cells programmed him to remember me as a helpless, defenseless hostage. I aimed for his testicles. I felt the wonderfully satisfying sensation of my left heel burying itself in his groin. The thing with a testicular kick is that it does not immediately disable the opponent. A shin kick, a punch in the solar plexus, or a tap on the Adam's apple, all cause an instantaneously overpowering response. It takes a second or two for testicular pain to wind its way up to the brain. Maybe that's because women are right, and there's another, tiny brain in the nearby vicinity that has to process all signals from that organ first.

Worked out fine for me, though. He had me hoisted back up

to his eye level when his higher brain finally got the message that his left testicle was ruptured and his right one was severely concussed. His eyes got real round, and his hands suddenly got real slack and let go of my neck.

He doubled over, completely incapacitated by the pain. I knew the MPs had to be hearing the sounds of our fight, because of my wire, and must even now be running to save me. They should be there any second.

Ordinarily, I am not one to kick a man when he's down. However, I made an exception. I was enraged, for one thing, and bent on revenge for another. My left knee came straight up and ended up in Williams's face. Crunch, I heard his nose break, and his head came snapping back up. My right hand flew into his solar plexus. That blow doubled him back over again. Then my right knee came up, and there was another snap, only this time it was Williams's jaw, or maybe a few teeth.

The door suddenly flew open, and I stepped back. Three real big MPs came diving through the air and jumped on Williams, who was reeling around in a slow, painful dance, but they sent him flying through the air, where he struck my desk and split open the back of his head. Kind of like adding insult to injury. It didn't kill him, but head wounds always cause a fair amount of blood.

That's about the point where I stopped paying attention. Suddenly there was this sharp pang in my left rib cage, and my face felt like it was on fire. Blood was running down my forehead and out of my nose and mouth. When you're twenty-two, you can take a beating like the one he just inflicted on me and end up feeling no worse than you would if you'd just been hit by a speeding car. When you're thirty-nine, you feel like a steamroller just mashed you into the road. I slumped down on the floor and lapsed into a remarkably deep trench of self-pity.

Martie and Wolky walked in while the MPs were slapping metal cuffs on Sergeant Major Williams. They looked around my office and saw a fair amount of blood dripping down the walls where Williams had used me like a basketball, and puddling on the floor, where Williams and I had both given liberally of our precious liquids. They both were smiling, though.

The confession I'd extracted from Williams might or might not be admissible as evidence. I am an officer of the court, and I hadn't read him his rights. A real slick defense attorney might be able to construct a plausible argument that I'd illegally entrapped Williams. If it were me, that's how I'd handle the defense. Williams, however, had assaulted me with the stated intent of murdering me. That much was admissible. I'm a commissioned officer and the Uniform Code of Military Justice takes a dim view of enlisted men trying to murder officers. It also lists another twenty or so different offenses that could be thrown at him, from assault to a few odd zingers like disrespect by apportment, which translates literally as me, a senior officer, saying he had looked at me in a way I didn't like very much. There really is such an offense. No kidding.

Plus, now that Williams had been apprehended, there was time to search for more evidence to support the charge of murdering Jeremy Berkowitz. Not to mention the flurry of charges related to the church burnings. As it was, the additional charges I'd just earned for Williams offered any able prosecutor a lot of material to trade for a full confession.

That's why Wolky and Martie were smiling. I got my fanny whupped pretty good to break their case. All they'd had to do was sit back in the building across the street, sipping their coffee and listening to the sounds of me crashing into walls.

Chapter ☆☆☆ 27

The doctor spent two hours inspecting and repairing the carnage Williams had administered to my body. There were two fractured ribs, not one. And I now sported eighteen stitches, about evenly divided between three different gashes. Williams was being treated in the next room, and the doc jovially told me they had to use a sewing machine on him. I guess he was trying to cheer me up. You know, like one of those "you should see the other guy" things. I didn't need to be perked up, though. My mood actually was fairly frisky.

While the doctor taped and sewed and X-rayed to his heart's content, I spent the entire time thinking about how I was going to handle Tretorne, Murphy, and Clapper. These guys were what my grandfather would call Slippery Dicks. Nothing to do with Richard Nixon, I don't think, because my father and my grandfather both thought Nixon was the second coming. I guessed a Slippery Dick was something like a Pudley, only slimier.

Anyway, I couldn't afford to underestimate them again. They weren't as dangerous as I had thought, since they hadn't murdered Berkowitz. But framing and blackmail and obstructing justice weren't likely to get them on anybody's list for sainthood, either. Also, Tretorne had warned me I wasn't going to get a second chance. He didn't strike me as the type who wasted idle threats.

The first thing I did when the doc released me was make a call back to that little base in Arlington, Virginia. I talked to that special judge they had there. I explained everything we had on Williams and told him we needed a team dispatched to collect our prisoner. He said they'd have someone here within ten hours. They had this real nifty jet that had been seized by the DEA from a Florida drug lord and subsequently got turned over to the Department of Defense. Then, through a little sleight of hand, the jet disappeared off the inventory and ended up belonging to my secret justice unit.

Then I made sure Williams was locked away in his own cell. He had to walk on crutches because his testicles had swollen up nearly as large as billiard balls. He actually looked pretty funny, with his legs splayed apart, trying to walk without his big thighs rubbing against his groin. One thing was for damn sure. He wasn't going to run away.

I made sure the guards at the facility knew they were not allowed to even enter his cellblock. I even made them all wear earplugs, on the grounds that it never hurts to be too safe.

Then I went to Imelda's tent, instructed her on what we were going to do, and we walked together back to our office building. It took nearly three hours before we were done making our preparations.

I left her there and took a walk over to the NSA facility. I went through that same old routine of showing the guards my orders, ringing the buzzer, and staring into the camera. Miss Smith opened the door and greeted me again. I was too sore and swollen to engage in my normal, charmingly obnoxious banter.

She studied the bandages on my head, my black eye, my swollen lips, and the various other bruises and abrasions I'd managed to collect. She didn't look sympathetic. In fact, she smiled. Not that old wooden smile, either. The real thing.

"I need to see Tretorne," I said.

"I'm sorry," she replied, trying to appear clueless. "I don't know anyone named Tretorne. Are you sure you don't want Mr. Jones?"

"Look lady, I want to see your boss, Jack Tretorne, or Jack of Serbia or Clyde Smothersmith-Blakely, or whatever stupid alias he's going by today. By the way, I don't like your alias, either."

She spun around and did this huffy heel-stomping thing as she led me back through the facility, then down the stairs. I was in a fairly ornery mood myself. With a dash of petulance, she sliced her card through the slot at the conference room door, then nearly shoved me into the room. Tretorne and General Murphy were seated together, with a bunch of papers tossed around the table.

Miss Smith's voice came out prudish and high-pitched. "Excuse me, Mr. Jones, General. I'm sorry to bother you. This officer is insisting on meeting with someone named Jack Tretorne. I told him there was no such man here."

She must've thought she was putting me in my place, because a general was here and that was supposed to make me get real shy and timid. Tretorne gave her a swift sideways nod, like get lost. She smirked as she roiled past me, and I became instantly worried for any nation that had people like her in their CIAs.

Tretorne, I noticed, wasn't wearing his duck-murdering vest. In fact, he looked quite natty in a perfectly tailored dark blue serge suit and a stiffly starched white shirt with French cuffs. A pair of big presidential cuff links were poking out of his sleeves, where they were meant to show. Well, I wasn't impressed. Well, actually, I was, but I didn't let on.

I said, "You're together. Great. Saves me another trip."

Murphy said, "What do you want, Major?"

There's a way of enunciating a man's rank that's supposed to remind him of his place. The trick is, you put all the emphasis on that first syllable and depress the rest. Like "What do you want, *Ma*jor?" It's taught in Lesson 101 at West Point, and Murphy had been a good student.

Only problem was, I was past caring. I felt unfettered and seditious. I said, "A little wrinkle has developed in your plan, guys. CID just arrested Berkowitz's real killer."

Tretorne did not look happy to hear this. He toyed with one of those cuff links that had that presidential seal on it, then looked up. "It's irrelevant, Drummond. You gave your word. There were no conditions."

"You're right," I said, "no conditions. Just like when I took my oath to become an officer. No conditions then, either. Or when I took my oath to become an officer of the court. No conditions that time, either. That's two unconditional oaths to one. You lose."

Tretorne said, "Don't do this, Drummond. Force my hand, and I'll just come up with something else. You can't win."

I'd been waiting for him to say this. I'd rehearsed all kinds of great lines to throw back at him, but in the end I decided on a childhood classic.

"Up yours," I said. "You throw your best shot, and I'll throw mine. I only came by to tell you that I'm throwing mine now. I've just written a long statement that exposes everything. Both of you are mentioned prominently. So is Clapper. So is General Foster. If I don't make a call in forty minutes, that statement will be in the hands of the *Herald,* the *Post,* the *Times,* and *Newsweek.* Even your fancy NSA technology can't stop it now."

Tretorne shook his head. "You have no idea what you're doing, how serious this is, what's at stake."

"But I do," I assured him. "You and your big buddy here are out on a limb that's breaking. You're assassinating Serbs and it don't get much more serious than that."

The two of them looked at each other in shock. Murphy was so choked with surprise that he did not even reprimand me for calling him Tretorne's big buddy. West Point would frown on him for letting that one slip by.

"Sit down. Please," Tretorne said.

It was couched more like an invitation than a demand. Well, what the hell, I thought; at least he asked nice. That was my first sign that I was finally winning. I tried my damnedest not to smile.

He waited till I was seated and comfortable, then asked, "What do you *think's* going on here? What we're doing?"

I said, "I *know* what you're doing. You're using Green Berets to murder Serbs. Sort of a modern version of Operation Phoenix. 'Sanction' was the euphemism then, wasn't it?"

"You're wrong," Murphy said. "Dead wrong."

I said, "Is that right?"

Murphy scratched his big head with his big hand. "To start with, Operation Phoenix was the result of an informal handshake between the Special Forces and the CIA. It was done without official knowledge or permission. We're operating with a presidential finding. You know what that means? This operation is fully approved by the President. It's also known within a select committee of Congress."

I didn't expect to hear that. I thought he might be lying, but that proverbial voice we all have in the back of our heads warned me he wouldn't be stupid enough to lie about something like this. It was too easy for me to say, Prove it.

He added, "Also, we're not assassinating Serbs."

I said, "Sorry, I'm not buying it."

Murphy studied me for a moment, then said, "Please step out of the room. Just for a moment. No funny business, I promise. Jack and I need to speak."

I didn't like it, but I did it. I mean, what the hell, I had nothing to lose. Imelda and all four of her assistants were positioned

at various locations around Tuzla, each poised over a fax machine, each ready to push a button. Each had a sealed envelope
in her hand that contained a copy of the statement I'd written
earlier. In less than forty minutes, those envelopes would be torn
open, the electrons would start buzzing, and the cat would leap
out of the bag. There was nothing Tretorne or Murphy or NSA
could do to stop it.

About five minutes passed. The conference room had spe-
cially sealed doors, which I found awfully inconvenient, because
I had my ear pressed to the crack but couldn't hear even a mur-
mur. When the door opened, Murphy waved his hand for me to
reenter. I walked back in and took the same seat.

Murphy said, "Jack and I are going to clear you for this operation."

I said, "Don't think I'm falling for that. I'm not taking any
vows of secrecy."

Murphy nodded at Tretorne and I had the impression they'd
guessed I'd say that. I wanted to thumb my nose at them, or
pull down my pants and bend over, anything that would surprise them. So far, they'd managed to predict every move I'd
made.

Then Tretorne said, "What's happening here is we're losing
a war. We're losing because it's a NATO operation, and the President has his hands tied. Our allies are dead set against ground
forces. All we're allowed to do is bomb."

Like a tag team, Murphy said, "You can't win a war with
bombs. That's why we came up with the idea of building the
KLA. We hoped to use them as our ground element, only they've
been a terrible disappointment. Six or seven KLA units have
done good work, but the rest are completely outmatched. They're
ineffective. Most just stay hidden in the woods, praying this thing
will end. Several KLA teams have been chewed up and almost
all the rest are demoralized."

"That's not a justification," I said. "Assassination's illegal."

"We're not assassinating anyone," Tretorne said, sounding tired. "Guardian Angel is a ruse for an operation we call Avenging Angel. Some of the SF teams we're sending into Kosovo with the KLA are selectively performing the missions their KLA units are supposed to be doing."

"What kind of missions?" I asked.

"Raids, ambushes, interdicting supply lines. Several times, we've learned the Serbs were planning another massacre, and we had them go in and free the Kosovar prisoners. We're very careful, believe me. No assassinations, no vigilante stuff."

"That right?" I said. "Then what happened with Sanchez's team?"

They exchanged more looks, and a lot of wind seemed to go out of their sails. Murphy's face looked like it was trapped in a warp.

He said, "We don't know."

"You don't know?"

"That's right. The KLA company they were with, Akhan's team, all of them were killed. We're still not certain how it happened."

"But Sanchez's team wasn't detected by the Serbs, was it? And they weren't responding in self-defense, right?"

Tretorne said, "We have no way of knowing."

"Bullshit."

He said, "The satellite tapes and transcripts we showed you were forgeries. Somehow, you obviously figured that out. Our real images for those days showed no unusual activity for Sanchez's team. We've got shots of them in their base camp, a few where they're traveling . . . nothing, though, that shows them being detected or chased."

"Then why—"

"Because we couldn't allow Avenging Angel to be exposed," Murphy said.

"I don't get it."

Tretorne was drumming a finger on the table. "When Sanchez's team extricated, they didn't report anything about the ambush. We didn't learn of it until three days later when Milosevic started holding press conferences."

I could hear little pieces beginning to fall into place.

"So you arrested Sanchez's team?"

"Right," Murphy said. "And they gave us the story about being detected and chased. Jack had NSA check their files and there was nothing that substantiated their story. Nothing contradicted it either, though."

"Then why was I brought in?"

"That was decided back in Washington. The massacre suddenly had international attention. We all felt the easiest solution for all concerned was to conduct a genuine investigation. Sanchez's team was sticking with their story, and we were ordered to make it a more convincing tale."

"And where was this decided?" I asked.

Tretorne didn't answer, at least verbally. He simply held up a hand and pointed at his cuff link.

I shook my head. Maybe Oliver Stone wasn't as harebrained as I'd always thought.

With as much disdain as I could, I said, "So you cooked up a deal with Sanchez and his men. They work with you on the cover-up, and they walk away scot-free."

Murphy did not appear the least bit fazed or ashamed to admit it. "That's right," he said, "except you're forgetting one thing. We have no proof they're guilty of anything. Maybe it happened exactly the way they said."

"Really?" I said. "I went to the morgue. I saw the Serb corpses. How do you explain the holes in their heads?"

Tretorne finally stopped tapping the table. "Please believe me, we didn't know about that until you reported it to Clapper. By then, this thing was already in motion."

"But you didn't do anything once you learned of it, did you? You kept right on with the cover-up."

"We had our reasons," Murphy said. "But we're prepared to make a deal with you now."

I looked down at my watch. In another twenty-seven minutes, Imelda and her crew were going to push a few buttons and unleash an army of hungry reporters on these two. They'd probably guessed what I had in store for them. It was a little like a poker game where they knew I was holding a royal flush, and they wanted me to allow them to take some of their cash out of the pot before I flashed my cards. These guys had balls made of brass.

I chuckled and shook my head. "I'm listening."

Murphy said, "We're willing to let you complete your investigation. We won't hinder you in any way. No more games. We'll give you the actual logs. We'll tell you everything we know, and you see if you can find the truth."

I said, "How kind of you."

Tretorne ignored my sarcasm and said, "There's only two conditions."

"And what are those?" I snarled. I mean, where was this guy coming from? Conditions at this point?

"Hold off on going to the press. When you're done, come back and talk with us."

It was a surprising offer, so I took a moment to consider it. Maybe they were just trying to buy time till they could arrange some other diabolical plot against me. If so, they were stupid. They'd just admitted the details of their conspiracy. Okay, maybe it wasn't a flashback to Operation Phoenix, but running a secret war wasn't chump change, either. They'd also admitted their orders came from the White House.

But they weren't stupid men, I reminded myself. God knows, I'd learned that by now. They had to be aware they'd just given me more ammunition to use when I went public and exposed them.

"That it?" I asked.

Tretorne said, "After we talk, if you want to go public, that'll be your option. We won't try to stop you."

I will admit, I was stunned. I had expected that they would look for some last-minute way to shut me up. Maybe this was it. Maybe they were lying their asses off to buy time to find a foolproof solution against Sean Drummond and his goody-two-shoes philosophies. If they were, though, I sure as hell couldn't see it. I could blow the whistle anytime I liked.

It was my turn to test the waters with a few demands. "No more phone taps? No more bugs in my office? No more following me around?"

Tretorne grinned. "You had all that figured out, huh?"

"Yep."

"Done," said Tretorne.

"Oh, and your mole goes," I said. "Morrow climbs on the next plane."

Tretorne's grin became a smile. "You might not want to get rid of her."

"Oh yeah I would."

"She's not working for us."

I cocked my head a little, and he actually chuckled.

"That little shit Delbert?" I asked.

"Floyd Collins, actually. Floyd's a real Army lawyer, too. A very ambitious one, although unfortunately, his trial record nowhere near matches the record you were provided in your folder."

Sometimes you just outsmart yourself. I had thought Delbert, or Floyd, had just seemed too obvious to be the mole.

"Okay, he goes," I said. "I won't have you owning anyone's vote."

"Done," Tretorne said.

"And I'll have to tell Morrow what's going on. She'll have to be cleared, too."

"Okay."

I got up and started to leave. I made it to the door before Murphy said, "One more thing, Major."

I turned around and faced him. That big, handsome face was staring up at me.

He said, "Sometimes those principles they teach at West Point about duty and honor and country, sometimes they clash against one another. The world's not as pristine as West Point makes it out to be. Sometimes you have to decide which of those three is most important. You have to decide which principle you need to sacrifice."

I stared back at him. I knew he was reciting the rationalization he'd employed to justify his own dishonesty in this affair. And it got me feeling real righteous and uppity.

I said, "I didn't go to West Point, so I don't know about all that. I tell you what I do know. I know what makes us different from the Serbs. We don't coddle our murderers. We don't lie to the world when our troops commit a massacre. We wash our laundry in the open. That's duty and honor and country, all in one."

He shook his head in a condescending way, like I just didn't get it. Only he was wrong. He was the one who didn't get it. At least that's what I thought.

Chapter
☆☆☆ 28

A good night's sleep did a lot for my disposition, but I couldn't say the same for my body. My bruises and broken ribs sort of calcified, and the pain seeped down through another few layers of tissue. I awoke feeling terrifically stiff and sore. I limped to the latrine tent, took a long, hot shower, and tried to coax the warm water into soothing my aches and pains. I ended up with crinkly, wrinkled fingers, but my wounds proved impregnable. I was still sore as hell.

Clapper had not made his normal two o'clock call. I guessed he was too abashed to talk with me. Delbert was gone when I walked into the office. He left a note in my message box: It read "Sorry," and it was signed Floyd G. Collins, Captain, JAG. Probably it was best that Murphy and Tretorne sneaked him out in the middle of the night. Probably if I'd seen Floyd I would've done something stupid, like reposition his nose so it stuck out through the back of his head. He lied to me, screwed me, and trampled all over his oath as an officer and a lawyer. I have this bad habit of taking things too personally. Tretorne and Murphy must've figured that out about me.

Morrow was back at her desk, rabidly scribbling something

in longhand. She coldly ignored me as I walked by. I went to the coffee urn and began making a cup. I made as much noise as I could, clanging my spoon against the side of my mug, knocking the coffeepot around, then took several real noisy, annoying sips as I tested my mix of sugar and cream. She kept right on giving me the bone-chilling indifference routine. She was good at it, too. Personally, I'll take the hot, smoldering treatment any day. You can always duck a punch.

I walked over and irritatingly peered across her shoulder at what she was doing. She kept writing. I coughed a few times; loud, obnoxious hacks. She bore down and wrote harder. I clumsily bumped into her chair. She rearranged it and got back to her writing.

I finally said, "Guess you don't want to know what happened to Delbert. Why he isn't with us anymore. Or how I got us a five-day extension."

Then I turned and walked back into my office, closing the door behind me. I stared at my watch. Thirty-six seconds passed before she knocked. Curiosity, it seems, is a far more powerful incentive than anger.

I told her to come in and have a seat, then spent thirty minutes explaining what had really been going on around here while she thought she was innocently trying to get at the truth. Here and there she stopped me to ask a few questions, but mostly she just listened. That gorgeous face of hers traveled through a range of emotions from surprise to hostility, then indignation, then eventually full circle right back to curiosity again.

"Why didn't you tell me about all this?" she asked.

I was deathly afraid she'd get around to asking that. I stared at my desktop.

"You bastard. You thought I was Tretorne's stooge, didn't you?"

"No, I never thought that," I lied and winced. It didn't even sound convincing to me. "I mean, I wasn't sure," I amended. "Besides, what does it matter? We have a green light now."

This was an awful lot of disturbing news to learn in a few minutes, and she needed some time to digest it. She was mad as hell, at them and at me for not trusting her. But she was also a lawyer, and thus was trained to keep her emotions in tight rein.

"Why don't we just hold a press conference and blow the whistle?" she finally asked.

The truth was, there was no good answer to that. If we were smart, that's exactly what we'd do. I'd made a deal with the devil, and only a damn fool thinks you can do that and walk away smiling. Now that Morrow was part of the deal, she had a vote and she was having second thoughts. Maybe it was first thoughts. Hell, I guess I was the one having second thoughts.

I said, "Anyway, we always have that option. They screw with us, we bring the whole thing down around their ears."

She nodded.

"I just don't see where they can get a new angle on us," I insisted. I said that to myself and to her.

She nodded again. "You might be right."

"Aren't you curious?" I added. "Don't you want to know if Sanchez and his men did it?"

"I guess," she said, sounding as if she thought she wanted to but really didn't.

"Well then, that settles it," I quickly announced before she could change her mind. Or I could change my mind.

I walked to the door and called Imelda. She came steaming in and I said, "We've got five more days. Get us a flight to Aviano for this afternoon. If they don't have a flight scheduled, tell 'em I said make one. Also, call Lieutenant Colonel Smothers's office and tell him Captain Morrow and I will be there in an hour."

"Got it," she said.

"One other thing," I said very loudly. "Get someone in here

to sweep this damned office for bugs. I don't want any silly-looking pussies in duck-hunting vests listening in to my conversations."

That reference to vests confused her a bit, but she nodded anyway. I figured that was as good a way as any to put Tretorne on notice that I'd be watching to be sure he was following his part of the bargain.

I was back in fine fettle, dishing out orders and shoving myself around. It felt good, too. The claustrophobia had cleared away. After packing our bags and loading up several boxes with documents, Morrow and I went to see Lieutenant Colonel Will Smothers, Sanchez's battalion commander.

We went to his office, and this time he had his lawyer, the same Captain Smith who had filed a complaint against me. Smith started with a smug smile, till we exchanged some surly looks, the way a pair of antagonized lawyers do.

I looked at Smothers. "No need for him," I said, pointing a digit in Smith's direction.

Smith's face showed his outraged surprise that we were about to start this all over again. He was just opening his mouth when Morrow, to my own vast surprise, said, "Get out of here, Smith. If he needs a lawyer, he'll contact you."

"I, uh, I . . ."

I made a menacing move in his direction. "You can no longer serve as his attorney. I'm reserving the right to cite you as part of a conspiracy to obstruct justice. If you're not gone in two seconds, I'll toss you out that friggin' window."

Smith glanced at the window. He studied my face, with all its swells and bruises. He weighed his options. "I'm gonna call the jurisdictional judge again," he threatened.

"Do that!" I barked. "Be sure to tell him I'll also cite him as an accomplice in the obstruction charge if he makes a move against me."

Smith peered at his client, who frankly was looking at him

to see what to do. They were both looking to the wrong place. Smith finally figured that out and quickly got up and departed the office. He was smarter than I thought he was.

I was giving Smothers an only slightly milder version of my I'd-also-like-to-rip-your-guts-out look. "Party's over, Colonel. Lie or mislead us once, and I'll indict you as a co-conspirator to murder. Got it?"

He nodded.

"Okay, let's go back to the beginning. Tell me about your role in this Operation Avenging Angel."

He looked over at Morrow and she somehow managed to hide those sympathetic eyes of hers. In fact, she looked positively fierce.

"Okay," he said. "My battalion, the First Battalion, we're the avenging angels. Murphy told you about the operation, right? We're the ones chosen for it. I've got one or two teams in every zone. We do the dirty work."

"Why just your battalion?" Morrow asked.

"Because we obviously can't afford any mistakes in this thing, and my teams are the most experienced."

"And does secrecy have something to do with it?" I guessed.

"There's that, too," Smothers admitted. "The less people who know about this, the less chance of a leak."

"Tell us about Sanchez," I demanded.

He looked at me. He sort of shrugged. "You sensed it," he admitted. "I probably made a mistake. Terry's a good guy, a very likable guy, and he needed the job to get promoted. He did great work in the operations shop and I felt I owed him a chance. Unfortunately, it's a different thing, you know, between being a staff officer and being in charge of a team."

"But you gave him the job?" I asked or said or pronounced as a verdict.

"I did." He glumly nodded. "I thought that if I gave him the strongest team in the battalion, things would work out. Persico's probably the best warrant in all of Tenth Group. He's been through some rough shit, and he knows what he's doing. I thought he'd keep Terry from screwing up. His NCOs are pretty tough, but damned good, and Persico keeps 'em in line."

"And Sanchez's performance since then?"

"I guess I'd have to say that on good days, he's fairly mediocre. Not for lack of trying, though. Christ, I wish some of my guys with more talent would put in half the energy."

"So it's a matter of talent?"

"Some guys just do it naturally. Terry has to work at it every minute. Guys like that run scared and his people smell it."

Morrow said, "When Akhan's team were killed, what happened?"

Smothers became very focused. His eyes narrowed and he started rubbing his lips. "That happened on the fourteenth. In the morning, I think. Sanchez called on the radio sometime around noon. All he said was Whiskey 66—that was Akhan's call sign—was that the Whiskey 66 element was at black. You understand that?" he asked.

Morrow shook her head.

"It's a color code we use to describe unit strengths. Green means the unit's at one hundred percent. Red is fifty percent. Black is zero percent. Some of our KLA units have gotten shot up pretty bad, but we've never had a whole company, ninety-five men, go from green to black in only a few hours."

"Did he explain what happened?" Morrow asked.

"Only that they were performing an operation. But that bothered us, because we hadn't approved an operation for Akhan's team."

"According to the statement he gave us, they were attacking a police station in a town named Piluca," I said.

"Well, that's what he said. We had a problem with that, though. Piluca wasn't on our approved target list."

"Excuse me," I interrupted. "What approved target list?"

"We get a list of what to hit. It's screened all the way up the line to the Joint Staff in the Pentagon. The idea is to avoid any kind of screwups."

"And those are the missions you assign to your teams?"

"That's right. No targets of opportunity are permitted in Avenging Angel. Everything's run tight, you know?"

I guess I did know. If the Avenging Angels made a mistake, like the Air Force hitting the Chinese embassy or bombing a column of Kosovar refugees, the ensuing furor would blow the lid right off their secret war.

"Okay," I said, "so Sanchez reported that his KLA company was wiped out, then what?"

"I ordered him to extricate."

I said, "General Murphy told us he was ordered to stay in place."

"That's not right. We considered it, but I was worried."

"What specifically worried you?" Morrow asked.

"Sanchez, I guess."

"What, specifically, about Sanchez?"

"Every time one of our teams train a KLA company, you get this big brother mentality. Not just here; same thing happened in northern Iraq with the Kurds. Bosnia, too. They're just so damned helpless and needy and eager. American soldiers can't resist it."

"So you were worried that Sanchez couldn't control the situation?"

"Two of our other A-teams had their Kosovars get beat up pretty good, and we actually had to stand them down and let the Group psychiatrist and chaplain help them sort through it. A lot of guilt and other powerful emotions get unleashed. It would take a real strong leader to hold it together and . . . yeah, I guess I was worried that Terry couldn't do it."

I gave him a steady look. "The suicide and the attempted suicide, they weren't members of those two other teams, were they?"

He nodded, a painful, jerking motion. "Yes, they were. Like I said, the emotions become very powerful."

"But Sanchez and his team, they didn't extricate?" I asked.

"No, not when I told them to. For two days, they kept reporting heavy Serb activity in their sector. Sanchez said he felt it was too risky to move south."

"And how did you respond to that?"

"What could I do? He was the guy on the ground. I did ask the NSA station here to increase surveillance over Zone Three, so we could get a picture of what was happening."

"And did they?" Morrow asked.

"They put a thermal up for an hour or two each day. The films showed Sanchez's team in their base camp, but there were no signs of unusual Serb activity. Basically, though, we had to believe him."

Now I understood why NSA used a thermal gatherer over Zone Three during those days. They weren't looking for targets that required pictorial analysis. They were looking for human heat sources, like Serb soldiers in the woods.

I said, "So his team finally extricated four days later?"

"Right. But you had to figure it would've taken a day and a half, maybe two days, to make it out on foot. So there were only two days unaccounted for."

"When they got back, did they report the ambush?"

"No," Smothers said, and you could hear a note of anger in his voice. "We debrief every extricating team. They never mentioned it. They just insisted the area was crawling with Serbs, so it took them a while to make it out."

I said, "Then three days later, Milosevic started holding his press conferences, and what did you do?"

"I went to General Murphy. I told him I thought Sanchez's

team might've done it. It was the same sector they were in. It was three days after Akhan's unit was killed. It all fit."

Morrow said, "Back to what happened to Akhan and his unit. Did Sanchez and his men clarify what occurred?"

"It was discussed during the debriefings."

"And what did they say?" Morrow asked.

"They all said Akhan made the decision to attack the station himself. They couldn't stop him. Zone Three was where most of Akhan's men lived. The commander of Piluca's police station was supposed to be a real cruel bastard, and he'd supposedly murdered or tortured some of their family members. It made sense. We've had other KLA units launch off on private vendettas."

I said, "Have one of your people run a copy of the debriefing notes over to my office as soon as we're done."

"Okay."

"Doesn't it feel better to tell the truth?" I asked.

He looked at me strangely. "No, not really," he said. "None of us liked lying to you. But we believe in what we're doing out here."

Well, so much for truth and justice being the American way. I turned to Morrow and she indicated she had no more questions, either. I gave Smothers a long, solemn look. He stared back, clear-eyed, not the least bit bothered by the fact he'd been involved in a massive cover-up, or that he'd lied in an official investigation. This boy would get ahead, I thought to myself. He was a true believer.

We left him there and headed to the airfield, where a C-130 was already revved up and waiting.

Chapter ☆☆ 29

We pulled up to the marble entrance of the same Italian hotel on the hill, and my mouth watered. Morrow and I got side-by-side rooms and stowed our gear. My room had one of those cushy German featherbeds, which made me think God just might love me after all. It also had a minibar. A well-stocked minibar. My body hurt like hell and I stared at the row of tiny Dewar's bottles. Dr. Drummond screamed at me to give that pain what it needed. I fought the temptation and went back downstairs to the lobby.

Imelda and two of her girls took rooms a floor below us and rented a full suite to use for our office. When Morrow and I got outside to take the van to the air base, Imelda and her assistants were still lugging computers and boxes of paper up the entry stairs to the elevator. Imelda was bellowing at them to move their asses, and the girls were giggling at her. They'd obviously figured out her secret. She really was a softie, like one of those dogs that barks a lot but don't bite too hard.

It took fifteen minutes to get to the Air Force holding facility. The same pudgy Air Force major was there to meet and greet us. He was being real deferential and courteous, virtually fawning, I guess because he didn't want to get any dishonorable mention in our report. I treated him coldly, and Morrow followed my lead. Let him sweat.

Morrow and I had spent a lot of time considering our next move. Our first inclination was to start the re-interrogation of the team with Sanchez. We needed one of the nine to break, and he was the one carrying the most baggage. All we needed was one. Like with all conspiracies, once that first man broke, there'd be a chain reaction. We'd pit them against one another, and threaten and make deals until we had the whole story, as well as a slew of witnesses to testify against one another.

But the more we talked about it, the more we persuaded ourselves that Sanchez probably wasn't the right man. He'd obviously made some kind of pact with his troops. And for whatever went wrong out there, he was ultimately responsible, and therefore had the most to lose. It is a prosecutor's maxim: Most to lose very often equals last to confess.

It was Morrow's notion to bring in Persico first. I thought it was a real dumb idea. Well, at first, anyway, but the more I considered it, the better sense it made. In every organization, there're two kinds of leaders. There's the leader appointed by the system. That was Sanchez, the guy with a commission provided by the United States Senate and two silver bars on his collar. Then there's the leader appointed by the men themselves. That was Persico, the guy with Silver and Bronze Stars on his chest. Get him to talk, and the rest would follow.

But there was another reason, too. At some point while in Kosovo, the formal chain of command in Sanchez's team simply disintegrated. That's what Imelda had detected in their statements. Quite possibly, there'd been a mutiny. We were sailing on instinct there, but based on our earlier interrogatories, there'd been no indication that Sanchez was in charge. There had to be a trigger for that. The team probably had doubts about Sanchez all along, but soldiers, especially experienced noncommissioned officers, generally adhere to the arrangements the Army makes. Unless, that is, some dramatic event comes along and persuades them otherwise.

Something had happened out there. Something powerful. I was guessing it occurred around the fourteenth, because that's when the team began acting in odd and mysterious ways. That's when Akhan's company got wiped out. That's when Sanchez got on the radio and claimed they couldn't extricate. That's when the chain of events began that led eventually to a narrow road between two hills where thirty-five men were slaughtered. It was just a guess, but I was pretty sure that was the day Persico took over command of that team.

Morrow and I positioned ourselves in the interview room and began arranging tables and chairs into a rough-and-tumble resemblance of a courtroom. Imelda showed up a few minutes later with both her girls. They began setting up a desktop computer and a court transcription device. Morrow and I had decided to formalize the atmosphere, to make it look as much like an actual courtroom as we could. It would get the witnesses thinking about what lay ahead.

We were finally ready and I sent Imelda to bring in the first witness. It took a few minutes, during which we all sat around nervously and waited.

Finally the door opened and Imelda came through, followed by Chief Persico. She formally announced him, as though she were a court bailiff. He casually, but not at all casually, looked around and studied the new setup. Again, I had the impression of a man checking the field of battle, trying to calculate his odds.

"Please sit down, Chief," I said, indicating a chair we had positioned in the middle of the floor. The chair sat isolated, without the protective comfort of a desk or table.

He sat down, folded his legs, and spent a brief moment study-

ing Morrow, who was holding a tape recorder. Then his gray
eyes shifted to me. "Mind if I smoke?"

He hadn't smoked the first time we talked. The cool demeanor
aside, I guessed that something about this session made him
more nervous.

"If you'd like," I told him.

He reached into his pocket and pulled out a pack of Camels,
unfiltered, knocked a fag out of the packet, tapped the end a
few times on the palm of his hand, then stuffed it between his
lips and lit it. All this was accomplished in a smooth, flowing,
almost instinctive motion.

I said, "Please state your full name and rank for the record."

He blew smoke as he talked. "Michael John Persico. Chief
Warrant Officer Four."

"Thank you," I said. "Our last meeting was merely an interrogatory, an informal exploratory session, to discuss the events
that transpired between 14 June and 18 June 1999. The purpose
of this session is to take your full formal statement concerning
the same time period. Are you sure you want to waive your
right to have an attorney present?"

"I'm sure," he said.

"At your interrogatory, you stated that you and your team
were in Kosovo participating in Operation Guardian Angel. You
were lying, weren't you? You were participating in Avenging
Angel, which involved the performance of combat missions
against Serbian forces in Kosovo. Isn't this correct?"

Morrow and I had decided the best way to handle Persico
was to come barging out of our corner and shock him with our
best punch. We knew now why he, and the rest of his team,
had been such confident, able liars. They had the U.S. government behind them. Who couldn't tell a great whopper when
NSA was building evidence to support you, when the CIA was
fronting for you, when the United States Army was tying the

hands of your listeners? I could tell a perfectly good lie even without all that help.

Persico took a long draw from his cigarette. Aside from that, he showed no visible signs of anxiety or distress. Finally, he said, "I ain't got the slightest idea what you're talking about."

I said, "Jack Tretorne and General Murphy cleared Captain Morrow and me on the details of Avenging Angel. Now, please answer my question, or I will add obstruction of justice and lying under oath to whatever other possible charges we come up with today."

He considered this only a moment. "Okay," he said, "we were part of Avenging Angel."

"Let's deal with another lie," I said. "When Captain Akhan's unit raided the police station in Piluca, was this an approved and authorized operation?"

He said, "No."

"Why did you lie to Colonel Smothers about what happened that day?"

"We didn't lie," he calmly said.

I withdrew the notes of the team's debrief that Smothers had kindly provided. I looked down and pretended to study the sheet.

I looked up. "On the nineteenth, you informed Major Grenfeld, your battalion operations officer, that throughout the day of the thirteenth, you and Captain Sanchez attempted to stop Captain Akhan from raiding the police station at Piluca. Do you still stand by that statement?"

He took another heavy drag, looked around for an ashtray, then flicked his ashes on the floor. Then he turned back to me. "I do," he said. "I tried damned hard to keep Captain Akhan from going after that station."

"You tried damned hard? What about Captain Sanchez?"

"Well . . . he, uh, he tried, too."

"He tried what, too?"

"Look," Persico said, "it was a risky operation."

A nice attempt at evasion, I thought. "Why was it risky, Chief?"

"Kinda obvious when you consider what happened, don't ya think?"

"Right. But you said you tried hard to stop them. You must have had some strong reasons. What were they?"

"The target wasn't approved by Group. Ain't that reason enough?"

"There was more, though, wasn't there, Chief?"

"Maybe."

"What more was there, Chief? Why were you so opposed to that raid?"

"For starters, never go into an operation that ain't well planned. That one wasn't just poorly planned, it was hardly planned at all."

"Not well planned?"

"That's right. Captain Akhan and his guys just wanted to do it. Hardly any recon. No rehearsal. Since it wasn't an approved target, there was no intell prep like we normally got from NSA or the CIA. They just wanted to march down there and kick some ass."

"When Akhan insisted on doing it anyway, why didn't you call Group and report that?"

He said, "That was Sanchez's call. Ask him."

I made an instinctive guess. "Was it because Sanchez wanted them to do the raid? Was that the reason you didn't call Group?"

He hesitated, and that was his first mistake. "You're asking the wrong man," he said. "I ain't no mind reader."

"You and Captain Sanchez discussed it, though, didn't you?"

"All right," he said. "We discussed it. What's your point?"

This was a very smart move on his part. He was unsure how much I knew. Maybe I was fishing, or maybe I was building a house from a blueprint. He was calling my bluff.

There was nothing to do but make another guess. "My point

is that Sanchez wanted Akhan to do the raid, whereas you didn't. When they were all killed, you blamed Sanchez."

I was right. I could see it in his eyes. I was right.

But what he said was, "That ain't the way it went down, Counselor. You're sitting on your ass, here in this nice warm room tryin' to figure things that happened in the heat of combat. You ain't got a clue."

He was angry, and in my mind there could only be one reason why. I said, "Then, afterward, you took control of the team away from Sanchez. Was it a mutiny?"

He reached into his pocket and withdrew the pack of Camels again. He had just ground out his other butt on the floor, but he dug out a fresh one and pounded it on his palm. He hit it so hard he broke it, and had to ditch it on the floor and take out another.

He lit it, then said, "Look, I didn't have no problem with Sanchez. Like I told you earlier, he's a good guy."

I ignored him. "Then Colonel Smothers gave your team the order to extricate. That was around noon on the fourteenth. Sanchez spoke to the ops center at 1800 hours that evening. He said the area was thick with Serbs, and he did not consider movement advisable at that time."

"That's right," he said. "I remember that call."

"Then the next morning, at the 0600 sitrep, he repeated the same message. Then again, at the 1800 hours sitrep on the evening of the fifteenth."

"That's right."

"Who was detecting all this Serb activity?"

"Perrite and Machusco were on security. Occasionally we rotated them out with the Moore brothers, to give Perrite and Machusco some rest."

"So Perrite and Machusco were reporting heavy Serb activity in your sector?"

"Yeah. We figured that after Akhan's raid the Serbs must've

guessed there was a base camp that Akhan's company was operating from, so they were out looking for it."

"Hadn't you already moved base camps, though?"

"Yeah, but not far. We was still in the same sector."

"What kind of activity did Perrite and Machusco report?"

"They saw some patrols, and they heard heavy vehicle activity on some roads nearby."

"Then, on the morning of the seventeenth, they spotted the Serb recon unit that was supposedly surveilling your base camp?"

"That's right. Only it wasn't supposedly."

"How do you know that, Chief? You didn't observe the activity yourself, did you?"

"No, but Perrite and Machusco don't fuck up. If Perrite tol' me we was being observed, we was being observed."

"Why did Perrite report that to you, Chief? Why didn't he tell Captain Sanchez?"

"I ain't got a clue."

"Then you gave the order for the team to move out?"

"That's right," he replied, in the process making another telling mistake. If Sanchez had been in charge, he would've given the order.

"Then you moved throughout the day, until around midnight, when you formed a perimeter and decided to ambush a Serb column."

"We've already been through all this shit, haven't we? My testimony ain't gonna change."

I ignored him again. "One last series of questions and we're done with this session."

"Okay," he said, digging out yet another cigarette. He was smoking them hard and fast. A small cloud of pale blue smoke actually hung on the ceiling over his head.

"The other members all testified that you were in charge at the scene of the ambush itself. You were the one who positioned them, who checked their aiming stakes, who directed the lay and wiring of the claymores. You gave the order to fire. You gave the order to cease fire. I find that very intriguing. You told me yourself that Sanchez was the operational leader."

He appeared confused as he tried to think up a response. His eyes roved quickly across the floor.

Then he said, "Sanchez wasn't feeling all that well. He hadn't got any sleep for two days, so I offered to help him out."

I almost smiled. "That was very good of you," I said. Even better was that he just gave us the hook we needed. I turned to Morrow, and she nodded. She had picked up on it, too.

"Thank you, Chief," I said. "We'll call you to testify again, maybe later this evening, maybe tomorrow morning. I strongly advise you to have an attorney present at our next session."

He planted his elbows on his knees and worked up a very convincing petulant expression. "When we gonna get done with this crap? I spent over two weeks in this shithole and I wanta get out. You've questioned me twice already."

I said, "When you stop lying to us. By tomorrow morning we'll have the whole truth. One way or another."

The petulance receded into a bland look. He stood up and started to walk out.

"By the way," I said, and he turned around to face me. "The deal you had with Tretorne and Murphy is off. I have full authority to recommend whatever I want, and I intend to use it."

He turned back around and kept walking. It was in his eyes, though. He'd just heard the sounds of the walls crumbling down around him.

Chapter ☆☆ 30

Sergeant First Class François Perrite," Imelda announced with great formality and astoundingly clear enunciation. Morrow's head reeled back in surprise. Imelda could speak like the Queen of England herself when she had a mind to.

Perrite had the same cocky, self-assured walk I remembered from before. And again I also noticed how soundlessly he moved, how catlike, as though there were a blanket of air under his feet.

It was my idea to do Perrite next. He was the hothead of the team. He had also been at the center of nearly everything that happened. More important, though, he was very clearly Chief Persico's boy. There was a powerful bond between them, and I judged that to be as much of a strength as it was a possible vulnerability.

I indicated for him to take the same seat Persico had vacated only thirty minutes before. I repeated the explanation of our purpose and invited him to smoke if he so desired. He did so desire and quickly pulled from his pocket a pack of Camels, unfiltered. Among other loyalties, he and Persico preferred the same brand. Smoking buddies.

I stared down at some papers in front of me till he had a cigarette lit and was seated in a relaxed posture. He wore an amused smirk, as though we were all gathered here for his entertainment.

I looked up. "Sergeant Perrite, we've already determined that you and other members of this team have perjured yourselves. We know Captain Sanchez supported Captain Akhan's desire to raid the Piluca station. We know that, afterward, there was a general loss of confidence in his abilities, and Chief Persico virtually took charge of your team. We know your location was never detected by the Serbs. We also know the ambush was not an act of self-defense. It was a deliberate act of retribution."

We didn't actually know those last two points, and we only suspected some of the former, but I thought I'd just toss it all into the cauldron and see what came out. He didn't contradict me, either. Instead he stared up at me, scratched his face, then smiled. "Then what the hell do you need me for?"

"We need to question you about your role in these events."

"Oh yeah."

"Start with when you and Machusco went into Piluca on the morning of the fourteenth. What did you encounter?"

He bent over and used his right hand to stub out his cigarette on the floor next to the three butts Persico had left behind. Perrite had barely smoked it a quarter of the way, so I guessed his real purpose was to bend over and inspect the brand of the crushed butts lying around his chair. Real recon men are curious that way.

When he came back up he said, "Fuck you. I got no reason to answer your questions."

"But you do," I said. "How old are you?"

"Thirty-three."

"Have you spoken with a defense counsel yet?"

"Sure. Some fatassed bitch stopped by. I tol' her to get lost. Like I tol' you before, I don't like lawyers. They give me hives."

"I hope, before she left, she had enough time to explain that once you've been charged with a single court-martial offense, I can add as many charges as I deem fit. The judge at your court-martial will instruct the board to consider each individual charge separately. You understand what that means?"

"No."

Very matter-of-factly, I said, "It means that every charge receives its own punishment. Sentences accrue. Even if you're found entirely innocent of everything that happened in Kosovo, the additional charges I might bring against you—for refusing an order, for disrespect, for obstructing justice, for perjury—will all be weighed and sentenced separately. Is all this clear to you now?"

He nodded. It was a flinty, reluctant nod, but it was a nod.

"See, Sergeant, you're here to bargain years of your life with me. Get your head out of your ass. Think about whether you want to spend your entire middle age watching the world through iron bars."

"Yes, sir," he replied in a way that made "sir" sound like something that needed to be flushed down a toilet, but nonetheless indicated he now knew the stakes.

I said, "Now, again, what exactly did you encounter when you and Machusco entered Piluca?"

He said, "You really wanta know, huh?"

I nodded.

"Okay, then I'll tell ya," he said, although he said it angrily, like I'd asked for it, and I was going to get it. He leaned forward in his chair and put his elbows on his knees. He looked around the room and studied each of us in turn, his head nodding in a sort of derogatory motion, as if we were all unworthy, but what the hell.

Then he stared back at me. "For starters, it wasn't just me and Machusco. Brian Moore came with us, too, 'cause he speaks the local patois. We went in around ten. The place was real quiet, but there was this heavy odor in the air."

"What kind of odor?"

"Two smells, actually. Blood and cordite. And the reason it was real quiet was because everybody left. There was lots of smoke and some of the buildings was still burnin' or smolderin'. There was lots of pockmarked buildings, like you'd see after a real nasty fight. There was cannon holes in some of the walls, made by tank rounds, we figured. I tol' Machusco and Moore we oughta get outta there real quick. I mean, it sure as shit didn't look like Akhan won. But Machusco figured that Chief would just make us turn our asses back around and find out what happened. Knowing Chief, I guessed he was right. So we kept on."

He paused to take out another Camel, which he tapped on his palm, just as Persico had done. Amazing.

"Then what happened," he continued, "was we snuck down some side streets. Moore kept cover for me and Machusco, and we worked our way close to the town square, like they got in all them little Kosovar burgs. That's where the police station was located. Machusco and I got as near as we thought was smart, then dodged into this three-story building. We worked our way to the top. We climbed out a window and got up on the roof."

His hands and arms did a panoramic sweep through the air.

"We could see the whole square and the police station. Saw it real good, too. It was crawling with Serb militia. We could see about ten tanks, old T-34s, all lined up, and the crews were climbing all over 'em, doing post-op chores. We could also see this huge stack of bodies. We had binos with us, so we pulled 'em out, and we studied those bodies. We were near enough that with our binos we could see their faces, you know. There was a few faces that had been tossed on the pile that we didn't recognize. Probably villagers that got in the line of fire. But we recognized most of the faces we saw. Then Machusco elbowed me and pointed at something by the police station. So I looked there. There was this tall pole that'd been stuck in the ground, right by the front door. On top of that pole was this black, dripping thing. It was Captain Akhan's head. They'd chopped it off and stuck it there like a trophy."

He paused to look at us. He wanted us to know it was a terrible, gruesome scene.

"After that," he said, "we climbed back down and got the hell out. We found some tracks just outside of town and followed them. After about three miles we found some villagers who was hiding in the woods. They'd left the town that mornin' after all the shooting was done. They said the Serbs was on a blood rage, and nobody felt safe. There was two old ladies, an old man, and I guess, about three, maybe four little kids. They was all scared to death. We gave 'em some food, and Moore questioned 'em for about twenty minutes. They said the Serbs had brought in a real big unit late the day before, just before dusk, maybe six hundred men, and hid it in various places around town. They parked tanks inside barns, and hid most of the men inside buildings. They spent all night stacking ammunition, running commo wire, building positions, getting ready for somethin'. Then around six in the morning, they told us, the town just kinda exploded. There was shit flying everywhere. The fight lasted about two hours. There was a lot of shooting inside the town, but the villagers said they heard a lot of shit up to the north, too. That was where Akhan's security team was supposed to be positioned, and we figured that was what they was hearing."

I asked, "And what did you judge had happened?"

His face was red, and his anger was beginning to boil over.

"What happened? Pretty fuckin' obvious, ain't it? The Serbs knew Akhan was coming. They was waiting for him. Six or seven hundred men in town. Probably another big force waiting outside, maybe a reinforcement that they used to take down Akhan's security team. Poor bastards never had a chance. They was all butchered. One of the old ladies told us that the last thirty minutes of the fight was just Serb troops roaming around, hunting down the last survivors. They found about ten or fifteen and brought 'em into the town square. They butchered 'em to death with bayonets. She said she'd never forget the sounds of them men screaming."

Something about the way Perrite told the story made it enormously affecting. Maybe it was the coarse, simple way he expressed himself. Maybe it was just the brutal believability and awful sense of what had happened to Akhan and his men. Even Imelda and her girls were all bent forward, fixated on Perrite's agonized face.

Perrite was deeply affected himself. He'd wanted to shock us, but in doing so, he'd had to relive the scene inside his own head. His jaw was tight, and his eyes were gleaming with anger.

I said, "Do you blame Captain Sanchez for that?"

"Of course I blame that dumb son of a bitch!" he exploded. "Bastard was desperate to get something good on his record so he could get promoted. Chief Persico told him not to let Akhan go. He warned him. I even heard him screamin' at Sanchez. He took him off in the woods the day before where he thought none of us could hear, but I heard 'em arguing. Sanchez wouldn't listen to him, though. He kept sayin' it would be a real coup if Akhan and his guys knocked off that police station. It would enflame the whole countryside, he claimed. Dumb bastard."

"When you, Machusco, and Moore rejoined the team, what happened?"

"Well, uh, we went to see Chief first. I wasn't in no mood to talk to Sanchez, you know? Machusco and I felt like beating the crap outta him, or maybe even shooting his dumb ass. So Moore said we'd better go see Chief first. Let him handle it."

"And what did Chief Persico do?"

"He got real pissed and upset. I mean, he never said it, but I knew he'd told Sanchez not to let this happen. Still, Chief felt

real guilty. I mean, that's the kind of guy Chief is. He done everything he could to stop it, but he still felt responsible."

"And did he confront Captain Sanchez?"

"Not that I know of. He might've said something to him
when none of us was listening, but the Chief can swallow a lot
and keep goin'."

"Okay," I said, "let me phrase this differently. Did you detect
a noticeable shift in leadership afterward?"

"No."

"Who was giving you your orders?"

"Sanchez mostly, Chief some of the time. No different than
normal."

"By your own earlier testimony, you said you made all your
reports to Chief Persico. Why was that?"

" 'Cause I couldn't stand talking to Sanchez. I know it's unprofessional and all that, but he got those guys killed. I didn't
wanta go near him. I mighta done something I regretted."

He was lying again, but I couldn't tell how or why. It was
just a sense. Maybe he was trying to cover Persico's ass.

I said, "What can you tell us about the execution of the ambush?"

"Nothing really. Like I told you before, I was half a mile away,
out on the left flank, performing security. I wasn't in on the decision to do the ambush, and I never saw what happened."

I turned to Morrow, but she shook her head, indicating she
didn't want to ask any more questions. I told Perrite to return
to his cell and nodded for Imelda to escort him.

When he left the room, you could almost feel the decom-
pression.

Morrow went, "Phew!" and her eyebrows shot up. "It's beginning to make sense, isn't it?"

"Only up till the afternoon of the fourteenth. What happened
after, that's still murky."

I let Imelda and her girls go out and take a potty break or

a smoke break, or a relax break or whatever their hearts desired.

Morrow and I put our heads together to figure out what to do next. We were at the point now where it was real fluid. The story was cracking, and we had to follow the stream where it led us. With each witness, we'd know a little more about what actually happened, and we'd use that as our start point for the next team member we drew into our confessional web.

Morrow said, "I think we ought to bring Brian Moore back in next."

I thought about that but wasn't sure what he could add. "Give me another name," I told her.

"Okay. Ezekial Graves, the medic."

"Why him?"

"He's got the least to lose. He didn't participate in the ambush."

"That means he also knows the least about it."

"But he can fill in the blanks between the fourteenth and the ambush."

She was right, of course. We went and got a cup of coffee while I idly flirted with her. She wasn't real responsive. Maybe her mind was too preoccupied with what we were doing. Maybe she was still sore over me suspecting her to be the mole.

Ten minutes later, Imelda did her bailiff thing again, announcing Sergeant Ezekial Graves. She was getting better and better at it. I could have sworn she was enjoying her new role.

Sergeant Graves was thin, mulatto-skinned, and handsome. He had large, watery brown eyes, clean-cut features, and a long, narrow chin. The Army chooses soldiers with fairly high IQs for the medic corps. This is one of the things the Army actually does right. Nobody wants a dummy who can't add feeding morphine into their veins, or struggling to remember exactly how to tie off a tourniquet to stem a pulsing artery.

I introduced myself and Morrow to Graves and explained

our purpose again. He seemed a little nervous, although I re-membered that Floyd, aka Delbert, had described him as fairly tough. Of course, Floyd was trying to sabotage us, so maybe that was a contaminated judgment. I had a strong suspicion that maybe Sergeant Butler was the tough one, and Delbert had ac-tually been trying to steer us away from Graves.

I told Graves how much we already knew about what had happened out there, adding the new details we had just learned from Perrite. Then I added my admonishments about truthful-ness, commenting that we didn't think he had much to fear, since he didn't participate in the ambush. By his expression, it struck me that he'd already figured that one out on his own. Like I said, medics are generally pretty smart.

I then said, "Could you please tell us what happened after Perrite, Machusco, and Moore returned from Piluca with their report about the fate of Akhan's team?"

He bit his lip and looked around the room. He was the newest member of Sanchez's team, and he was a medic. That cut both ways. He had the lowest loyalty quotient. But he could also be the one who was trying the hardest to fit into the pow-erful tug of the fraternity.

He stopped looking around, but he began fidgeting with his hands. "I'm not sure what you're asking, sir."

He knew damn well what I was asking, and I guessed he was still trying to sort out whether to reveal anything or not.

I said, "Look, Sergeant Graves, the story is coming out. You can't stop it. The others are coming clean, and it would be a terrific shame if you destroyed yourself for nothing. Now, was there a blowup? Was there a perceptible change in morale, or maybe in the attitude of the team?"

I was trying to pick my words carefully, because some fu-ture defense counsel might claim that I had first told him he wasn't likely to be prosecuted, and now I was discreetly, or indiscreetly, leading him in what to say if he wanted me to lay off him.

He said, "No, sir, there was no blowup. It took a while for the word to get around about what happened down in Piluca. Sergeant Machusco and Sergeant Perrite sort of circulated around and let us know."

"Did they blame Captain Sanchez?"

"Yes, sir. They didn't need to, though. We all knew. A team that small gets to be like a family. Not a lot happens we don't all know about."

I nodded, but didn't say anything. He waited for me to ask the next question but I didn't.

Finally he said, "It wasn't like a mutiny or anything, sir. I swear it wasn't."

I found it interesting that he would choose to jump to that particular denial. "What was it like?" I asked.

"Well, you have to understand, sir, we all liked Captain Akhan and his guys. It was crazy, really. It wasn't like we had a whole lot in common with one another, at least with Akhan's guys. Most of them couldn't speak any English. They were farmers, butchers, shop people, a few schoolteachers. I don't know how to explain it. It was kinda like you might feel toward an overeager puppy. But don't get me wrong; that's not the way we all felt toward Captain Akhan. No, sir. He was different . . . real different from them."

"Different how?" Morrow asked.

"Did you know what he did in real life?" he asked.

Morrow shook her head.

"He was a doctor. A heart surgeon, in fact. Graduated from Harvard Medical School. That's how I got to know him real well. At night, after the training, he'd take me over to the UN medical tents. They were swamped with all these wounded, sick people pouring out of Kosovo, and we'd work there about seven or eight hours every night. I don't know how he did it. He'd get up every morning at five-thirty for the training, and since the training program was only six weeks, we were really busting their asses. When we let them go, usually about five, his men would stagger over to get something to eat, then climb right into their sacks. I mean, they were all exhausted. Akhan would skip the meal and work till one, sometimes two or three in the morning. I don't know how he did it. You had to see him with those people in those tents, though. He wasn't just a doctor. He was like a saint. You'd get some little kid, with maybe a broken leg and maybe some shrapnel wounds, and the kid would be wailing with pain till Akhan got there. He'd talk to the kid in this incredibly soothing voice while he was operating on him, and the kid would stop crying and just let him do it. None of the other doctors had that touch."

Graves stopped for a moment and you could see he was in some kind of private reverie.

He finally said, "I mean, Captain Akhan, he didn't even have to be here. His parents had immigrated to the U.S. a long time before. Did you know he was a U.S. citizen? He had a wife and three little kids, a house in Boston, and he worked in some big hospital there. When this thing blew up, he parked his life, paid his own fare, and got over here. The UN folks wanted him to work in a camp hospital full-time. He refused. He figured that was the coward's way out. He didn't know anything about soldiering, but he was smart, and everyone naturally looked up to him."

Graves's face had by this point become a study in human agony. It was evident that he, like Persico, had developed a very deep affection for Captain Akhan.

Then Graves said, "I'm sorry. It's hard to describe sitting here in a room with you all, but he was . . . well, he was different than anyone I ever met. It's just hard to put into words. It was like he emitted some kind of strength. You had to like him. Everybody liked him."

I opened my lips to ask another question, but he cut me off.

"No," he said. "People didn't just like him. People sort of loved him. I did. The other guys in the team, even Machusco and Perrite, who're pretty tough, we all loved him. Even Chief, I think. I mean, the Chief doesn't show a lot of emotion. That's not his way, but whenever he and Akhan were together, there was some kind of a special bond there. It really made no sense. I mean, Chief's a soldier right down to the bone, and Akhan was really a doctor at heart. You wouldn't think they'd be that close."

"So what happened?" I asked. "If it wasn't a mutiny, what did happen?"

"Uh . . . I guess we all just decided we weren't going to follow Captain Sanchez anymore. Nobody said anything. It was just a feeling. We didn't mutiny, though, sir, I swear."

"But the effect was the same?"

"Yes, sir, I guess it was. It's odd, though. Even Captain Sanchez seemed to be part of it. Does that make sense?"

"No. Please explain it."

He looked down and studied the floor, and his face became perplexed as he tried to find the right words. "He just sort of faded out. He was there, but he stopped giving orders. Maybe it was guilt, I don't know. Chief just sort of filled in the gap and started giving orders."

I said, "Then you spent a day and a half in your base camp, right?"

"That's right, sir."

"What was the team doing during all that time?"

"Waiting."

"What were you waiting for?"

"I don't know exactly. I mean, I'm a medic, and I'm the new guy, you know? If they were sick or hurting, they'd talk to me, but nobody wanted my opinion on operations. Perrite and Machusco and the Moores kept going out on their patrols, while I guess they were all trying to think about what to do next. I mean, after what happened to Captain Akhan and his company, none of us wanted to slink back home with our tails between our legs."

"Was your camp detected by the Serbs?"

"Not that I know of. We pulled up stakes about two days later. I remember, because that was the morning Sergeant Caldwell cut his foot with an axe. He was chopping firewood and opened up a deep gash. I had to stitch him up."

"How did the ambush come about?"

"I don't know, sir. I just remember that on that night, we pulled into a hasty perimeter. It was late and we'd been moving all day. Then the word went around to start checking ammo and cleaning weapons for a fight. Since I'm a medic, I didn't have to clean my weapon or check my ammo, so I dozed off. Sergeant Caldwell woke me when it was time to move. He wanted me to give him some more aspirin, because his foot still hurt and we had to start walking again."

I looked at my watch. It was seven o'clock and none of us had eaten since breakfast. I wasn't particularly hungry, but the golden rule of the Army is that you have to feed your troops. I thanked Sergeant Graves for his insights and asked Imelda to please escort him back to his cell.

Morrow and I then walked out together. We didn't say much until the van delivered us back to the entrance of the hotel. I guess we were both sort of entombed in our own thoughts. Until this point, we'd been handling a legal case with evidence and elements of proof and all the other cold, rational pieces that lawyers are trained to delve into. Now the fragments of an immensely human tragedy were coming together before our eyes, and that has a tendency to leave one disturbed.

"Dinner?" I asked.

"Who's buying?" she parried.

"That depends."

"On what?"

"If we treat this like a date, I'll buy. If it's more in the line of a business meeting between associates, my hands are tied, and we go Dutch. Some guy left a tablet on a mount somewhere and it's carved in stone someplace near the bottom: Thou shalt only pay for dates that show some promise of conquest."

"Dutch it is," she said, leaving me thoroughly dispirited as she headed up the stairs.

I got changed faster than her and rushed downstairs and got us a table. A good one, too, right in the corner, right beside the big picture window that looked out over the plains below. There were twinkling lights as far as the eye could see.

I didn't spend any time studying the landscape. I guiltily and swiftly knocked down two long and tall glasses of scotch and decided not to mention that I'd started before her. My ribs hurt, though, and I owed them a nice surprise. I even had the waiter carry off the evidence before she joined me.

He was just escaping with the glasses when she glided through the entrance. If this wasn't a date, she was a little over-dressed, or underdressed, or both. She had on this short, clingy blue skirt that stopped about five inches above her knees and a perfectly lovely blouse with what is politely termed a plung-ing neckline. Suddenly, you could see just about everything she'd been hiding under those BDUs these past few weeks. I almost gasped, but I'm too cool for that, too. I limited myself to some heavy panting and a long, filthy, ogling stare.

I wondered what she was up to. Maybe she was trying to show me what I was missing out on. Like, hey, this could've been yours, all yours, if only you hadn't suspected me of being Tretorne's stooge. Or maybe it was some subliminal impulse in-side her, like she was out to prove that Miss Smith back in Tuzla wasn't the only one with what my grandfather would call a great set of gams. Now, I did know the precise meaning of the word gams, and Morrow had a perfectly sterling set, I assure you. Ever so long, ever so slim, tapering down to this wonderful pair of slender little ankles. A nice set of uptoppers, too. That was an-

other of my grandfather's favorite words. I knew what uptoppers were, too.

Her walk across the dining room attracted a flock of attention in the form of lots more ogling stares. Two Italian gentlemen even rushed over to pull back her chair. She sat down, said
thank you very pertly, then both the men sort of stood there
gaping, like nobody knew what to do next. I caught one of them
peeking over her shoulder at her uptoppers, and I gave him an
evil stare. He smiled at me, then retreated. The other man stood
there until the waiter came to take our orders. Then it got a little crowded and he finally ambled back to his table. Some lady,
I guess his wife, was there, and she started yammering at him
in Italian.

I said, "Nothing like making a low-key, unobtrusive entrance."

She smiled politely and blushed a little. "I had nothing else
to wear. If I don't get to a laundry soon, I'll be out of clean underwear, too."

I thought of ten cleverly lascivious retorts to that, but this
was a business meeting between associates, no matter what my
libido was screaming at that moment.

"No sweat," I assured her, patting her arm like any good senior officer who's concerned for the welfare of his troops. "It
gets to be a problem, I'll just loan you some of mine."

She giggled kindly at that. "So, should we get a bottle of Chianti?"

"Go ahead," I said. "I've got two broken ribs and a body that's
screaming for some genuine medication." I looked up and winked
at the waiter. "I'd like to start with two scotches, straight up."

She said, "A glass of Chianti, please."

Then there was this long, awkward silence. She smelled absolutely stunning. It wasn't that sweet lily of the fields crap, either, but something much more pungent. Something musky and
naughty.

It's damned hard to think of something intelligently businesslike to say when you're staring at a beautiful woman whose uptoppers are peeking out her shirt, your nose is getting hard from her smell, and your mind's off in a boudoir wildly cavorting between some silk sheets.

Finally, she said, "Who do you want to start with tomorrow?"

I very reluctantly retreated from the boudoir and thought about that a minute. "Why not Sanchez?"

"You don't want to wait until we know a little more?"

"What's left to know?"

"Was there a mutiny? The ambush, whose idea was it? Why did they really do it? Why did they shoot the Serbs in the head?"

"And just who's going to tell us about all that?"

"There are still five others we can pick from."

"I just have this sense," I told her, watching the waiter walk across the floor with our drinks. "The fastest way to all that is through Sanchez, and I think we have enough to get him to open up."

The glasses were deposited on the table and I tried not to appear too desperate as I grabbed the first scotch, which was actually my third scotch, and knocked down a huge slug. Before I knew it, the glass was empty. They were the big, tall kind of glasses, too, and the bartender wasn't one of those awful cheaters who waters things down. For some reason, my ribs had started to ache like hell. Must've been her perfume, I thought.

She was twirling her glass of wine with her slender fingers. "It's a terrible story, isn't it? It really touches your soul."

"Yep," I said, feeling the effects of that third scotch right quickly. "What did you expect, though? Did you really think we'd discover nine evil men who got together and decided to commit an atrocity?"

"No. I've just never handled a case like this. It's confusing. Not very black and white."

"But it is. You're wrong, because they were wrong," I said, starting on the next glass and hoisting up two fingers at the waiter to rush over with some reinforcements. "One of the reasons the Army insists on iron discipline is situations just like this. Officers are human, too. They screw up, and when they do, their men see it. The structure, the discipline, they have to remain. Persico's an old soldier. He knew that. Hell, they all knew that."

"I understand all that," she said, still twirling her wineglass, "but Sanchez got all those men killed. I know what the rules say, but I can also see why those men didn't want to follow him anymore. Besides, it sounds like he stopped giving orders. Almost like he went into a walking coma."

My glass was now empty, and the waiter was there with the two fresh ones. I smiled at him quite happily.

Morrow said, "Are you all right?"

"I'll be fine," I assured her. "Just administering a little painkiller. Look, there's going to be plenty enough blame to go around for everyone. Smothers never should've given Sanchez the job," I said, taking another huge swallow. "Sanchez should've gutted it out when things went south. His men should've supported him. Even Hollywood knows that. Did you ever see *Mutiny on the Bounty*, or *The Caine Mutiny*? Great movies, both of them. Remember that scene with Captain Queeg, this battleship commander in World War Two, sitting there on the stand rolling those ball bearings around in his hand, ranting about who stole his strawberries? It was Humphrey Bogart at his best, playing this hard-nosed son of a bitch who rode his men mercilessly, and his first officer sympathized with his men and ended up undermining him, until it resulted in mutiny. The lawyer got the first officer off, then in the final scene he told the first officer he disgusted him, because what he did really was wrong. The system has rules and everybody has to obey them."

"Strange words coming out of you," she said as I got a good firm grip and hoisted down some more scotch.

"What? Because I act like a wiseass? Because I don't seem

to have a lot of respect for the system? Don't kid yourself, Morrow. I was raised an Army brat," I said, pausing only long enough to inhale a little more painkiller. "I've never shoved a bite of food into my mouth that wasn't paid for by Army dollars. I saw my father go off to war three times. When the Army ships your father away to the other side of the world, and he's being shot at, you do a lot of thinking about the Army and what it means. I actually got shot at a few times myself. That's also been known to make one think about it, once or twice. I believe in the Army and all its silly rules. Doesn't mean I like them, but God knows, we've won a lot of wars. We must be doing something right."

Morrow was wearing a look of surprise, and I realized that I was drinking way too much and was letting my mouth get way too carried away. My ribs still hurt like all hell, though, so I kept wading through the glass in my hand. Besides, it would be a damned shame to let a perfectly good scotch go to waste.

She took a sip from her wine and studied the bruises and swells on my face. "You've had a difficult few weeks," she said.

"I'm not complaining," I answered, wondering if I should stick up my finger to get the waiter to bring two more. The waiter was actually sweating from running back and forth. People from other tables were staring at me.

"Do your ribs still hurt?"

"I think sho," I admitted.

She giggled a little.

"What?" I asked. "Wassshh so damned funny?"

This was when I first noticed that my ribs hurt so much that they had made my tongue swell. Until that instant, I never knew my ribs were connected to my tongue.

"We'd better order dinner quickly and get some food in your stomach," she said, flashing those wonderfully sympathetic eyes.

This was also about the same moment when I realized that eating had just gotten a little beyond my reach. I looked down at my silverware and there were at least ten forks. Which one would a polished gentleman choose, I wondered.

I said, "Mmmnydnodmebok," or something like that.

Morrow stood up and came around the table. She took my arm, and she was really strong, because she hoisted me out of that chair like I was a fluffy pancake. She wrapped my left arm around her shoulder and led me out of the dining room. My left hand was dangling right across her left uptopper, and her naughty perfume tickled my nose. I wanted to give that comfy uptopper a gentle little squeeze, but my body was way past the point of listening to my brain.

She leaned me against the wall in the elevator, and I stood happily humming some song as we sped up to the third floor. Once we got to my room, she actually dug around inside my pants pocket until she found my key. Then she led me over to the bed. This was the moment I was waiting for. She thought I was intoxicated. She thought I was a harmless, incapacitated, drunken eunuch, too scotched out to raise ye olde noodle. Heh-heh-heh. I lunged toward the bed, tugging her along.

I said, "Youydod a jummbock," and it was a real good thing she couldn't understand a word I said, because what I'd just invited her to do was something nice girls don't usually do.

The next thing I knew, the alarm on the nightstand next to my bed was howling at me, and I could hear someone pounding on my door. I rolled out of the bed and stumbled over and opened it. That damned Morrow had changed out of that fetching skirt and was back inside her BDUs again. Now how had she done that so fast?

She brushed past me and headed for my bathroom, while I stood there feeling stupid. I looked at the alarm clock. It read 7:40. I had set it to go off at six. I heard the shower go on, and Morrow went over to the phone and called room service. She told them to send up two American-style breakfasts and stylishly offered them a ten-dollar tip if they had it here in ten minutes.

She put the receiver down and said, "You've got five minutes to shower and shave. Don't walk out of the bathroom naked, either. Army rules dictate that higher officers shall not display their Pudleys to lower officers. It wouldn't bother me, but you're the one who loves Army rules."

Damn, so that's what a Pudley is, I thought, as I lurched toward the bathroom. The shower felt great and my ribs only ached a little. Dr. Drummond and his scotch cure had accomplished another medical miracle. I emerged from the bathroom fully dressed about seven minutes later. Morrow was at the door paying the bellhop for our breakfasts.

I couldn't help myself. "Where'd you learn about Pudleys?" I demanded.

"What?"

"Pudleys? Where'd you learn that word?"

That made her giggle a lot. "At that private girls' school I went to. That was the word we used for . . . well, you know. Only for little ones, though. Big ones we called Humongos."

I thought about that a moment. I took a bite of eggs and wetted it down with a little coffee. "I don't have a Pudley," I insisted.

"Be that as it may," she said, smiling, "we're going to be late, so eat quickly."

"Okay," I grumbled. "Just remember. I don't have a Pudley. Maybe I'm not a Humongo, but damn it, I'm no Pudley."

"Eat," she ordered.

"Maybe I need to wear different pants or something," I mumbled.

She was still smiling when we went out and caught a sedan to the air base.

Chapter ☆☆☆ 31

Terry Sanchez looked thinner. And more gaunt. There were dark, hollow pockets around his eyes, so deep it actually seemed as if his eyeballs were sucking in all the skin around them. His eyeballs themselves looked like brittle crystals that could shatter at any minute. He shambled when he walked, and his arms hung limply by his sides. I had the sense of a man who was rapidly deteriorating.

I pointed at the chair in the middle of the floor and asked him to be seated. He slumped into it and stared at me with a blank expression. I repeated the same explanation I had used the day before, taking care to update our understanding of what had happened in Kosovo.

His eyes were wandering around the room as I spoke, and he appeared too listless to be fazed that we had learned so much about the terrible events that occurred out there.

I paused, but before I could continue, Morrow suddenly said, "Terry."

He looked up at her. Her voice became very soft, mellow and soothing. Almost like a violin playing a lullaby. Or maybe more like a concerned mother talking to a hurt child.

"Terry, we know now what happened out there. We want to hear your side, though. Do you understand what's happening here?"

He stopped gazing around the room and looked into her eyes. "Yes."

"Good," she said, offering him a gentle smile. She was taking over the interrogation.

"It's important for you to know we haven't made any judgments yet. Things like this are never black and white. You were under terrible pressures. You were trying to do what was right. We want to hear your side."

He was now staring into her eyes, as though they were a life raft he wanted to climb into.

She continued. "We're going to ask some difficult questions now. The cover-up has fallen apart. Jack Tretorne and General Murphy just want us to find the truth. The other members of your team have all been truthful. It's your turn, Terry. Okay?"

He nodded, but his eyes stayed glued to hers. It was almost like he was mesmerized. I knew in that instant that I could never do what Morrow was doing. She sensed that Terry Sanchez was drowning. She sensed that his insides were seething with turmoil, that he required a sympathetic listener or else he would just fall to pieces. Sympathy is not my strong suit.

"Good, Terry. Why don't we start with the decision that led Captain Akhan to raid the police station in Piluca?"

He licked his lips a few times, and I thought of a man who was stuck in a desert and was staring at an oasis off in the distance. His only company the past few weeks had been the same men who obviously detested him for whatever he'd done out there. Some part of him had to be begging for the chance to explain himself to someone who wasn't there. Morrow expertly sensed that.

He said, "I know what you've been hearing from the others about that. They're wrong, though. It's not the way it happened."

Morrow said, "Then please tell us what did happen."

He said, "Akhan begged me to let him hit that station. A lot of his men lived near Piluca, and they were begging him. I guess he wasn't strong enough to say no. He wasn't really a soldier, you know. There was a Serb captain named Pajocovic. He'd terrorized that town for a year. A number of Akhan's men had lived there. Some of them had family members who were tortured or killed by him. You see why they wanted to hit that station?"

"Of course," Morrow said. "It makes perfectly good sense. But it wasn't on the approved target list, was it?"

"I told Akhan that. I swear I did, but he said the target list didn't apply to him and his men. He said that list only applied to my team. He was right about that, you know."

"Yes, Terry, according to the rules, he was right. Did you want him to raid that station at Piluca?"

"Sure. I understood what his men were feeling."

"Then—"

"No, wait," Sanchez said, almost coming out of his chair. "You have to understand. Nobody understands. My mother and father, they're from Cuba. They came over in '61, with the first big wave. My father, he was recruited by the CIA to go back. He was on the first wave to hit the beach. His friends were dying all around him, but he fought for three days. He fought until the American ships that brought him there pulled out and abandoned them. Then the American planes left and there was no hope. The Bay of Pigs, you remember it? My father spent three years in a Cuban prison. We finally traded some tractors to get him and the others freed."

Morrow was following along with more gentle nods. She bent forward and rested her chin on her hands, as though everything he was saying made perfectly good sense. Frankly, he was rambling. I thought his mind was becoming incoherent.

"You understand?" he continued. "He didn't blame them though. It was his country. That happened to my family. I knew how these Kosovars felt. The others, the rest of the team . . . they didn't, you see? These men weren't fighting for America. They were fighting to free their own homeland. We can't tell them what to hit and what not."

It suddenly struck me that Terry Sanchez was stretching desperately. The Bay of Pigs and what was happening in Kosovo could not be more different. Faced with overpowering guilt, his mind was trying to construct a rationalization, any rationalization that would absolve or soften what he had done. Not an atonement, but an escape.

Morrow said, "Was Akhan's operation properly planned?"

"Sure. I went over it with him for two days. I told him we couldn't lift a finger to help him, because it wasn't an approved target for us, but I told him everything to do. I even had Akhan send three men down to town the day before. They checked all over. All they saw was a bunch of drunk Serb police lounging around. It should've been easy."

"Then what happened, Terry?"

"I don't know for sure. Nobody knows for sure. What I think happened was one of Akhan's men was a mole. It's happened with other teams, you know? The Serbs send spies into the camps to be recruited in the KLA. I think that's what happened here. I think one of his men tipped off the Serbs. That's not my fault, you see? They were waiting for him. I told him before he went down there that if he got in trouble, we couldn't lift a finger to help him. He understood that. It wasn't my fault, you see? I told him."

Morrow was in her full sympathetic mode, nodding and pursing her lips, but Sanchez wasn't through. He was speaking louder now, almost frantic.

"That's what the men in my team couldn't get through their heads. You see that, right? I didn't get Akhan killed. I didn't make him go down there. I didn't order him to do it. Whoever told the Serbs he was coming, he was the one who got Akhan killed.

I just let Akhan do what he and his men wanted to do. You understand that, right?"

"I understand," Morrow said. "What happened when Perrite and Machusco and Moore returned from Piluca?"

"What happened?" he said. "What happened was they all turned against me. None of them liked me much anyway. They never did, not from the day I took over the team. Persico, Perrite, Machusco, Caldwell, and Butler, they'd all been together over ten years. The Moores had been there six years. It was like trying to join a family, only I didn't have the right blood."

"Was there a mutiny? Did they approach you? What exactly happened, Terry?"

He finally broke eye contact with Morrow. He looked over at Imelda and her girls as though he were seeing them for the first time. Then he started rubbing his legs with his hands. Not a massaging motion, but a slow, methodical stroke with his fingers stiffened and his palms wide open. It seemed unconscious and mechanical.

"What happened was Persico took me off in the woods. He told me what the recon team found in Piluca. He spoke real quiet, but he was accusing me. You know what I mean? He was staring at me like I was some kind of monster. Like it was my fault."

He paused for a moment, but the leg rubbing continued.

"They all loved Akhan, you know? Something about him. I don't know what it was, but they worshipped him. I think they believed I deliberately set him up to die. Like maybe I was jealous. That's stupid, though, you know? He wasn't even a soldier. Besides, I liked him, too. I wouldn't have done that to him. When we came back out of the woods, they were all looking at me that way. They started avoiding me."

Morrow said, "But there was no overt mutiny?"

"Not like you might see on a ship maybe, not that way, but it was a mutiny. Yeah, it was a mutiny. I knew they weren't going to do what I said anymore. You know what I mean, right? They weren't gonna let me lead them. We were in the middle of enemy territory, and there wasn't anything I could do. You see that, right?"

Morrow said, "Terry, at 1200 hours you reported to Colonel Smothers that Akhan's team was black. He then directed you to begin extraction. At the 1800 sitrep that night, you reported that there was too much Serb activity in your vicinity to safely extricate your team. You reported the same thing at the 0600 sitrep the next morning, and the 1800 sitrep that evening. Why did you report that?"

The spectacle of Lisa Morrow soothingly taking him through this journey, and of Terry Sanchez mentally crumbling, had so thoroughly captivated my attention that it actually took me a moment to realize the timely brilliance of her question. If it had in fact been a mutiny, why had Sanchez conspired in the effort to keep the team in Kosovo? Had someone held a gun to his head?

"Persico told me to."

"I'm sorry, Terry, I don't understand. Chief Persico told you to say what?"

His leg stroking got a little more frenetic. "Yeah."

"No, Terry, what did Chief Persico instruct you to report?"

"Oh, sorry," he said, appearing confused. "He told me to buy us some time."

"Why, Terry? Time for what?"

"Time to set it up. Time to do it."

"But you were ordered to extract. What more was there to do?"

"Well, you know," he said, still avoiding her eyes.

"No, Terry, I don't know. Please tell me."

"Get Pajocovic."

"Pajocovic? Wasn't he the station commander in Piluca?"

He glanced up at her, as though she was already supposed

to know this. Unless I missed my guess, Terry Sanchez's mind was getting very, very mushy.

"Yeah," he said with an expression of vast impatience. "Who else do you think we ambushed?"

Suddenly, an avalanche of missing pieces came tumbling into place. The column they'd ambushed wasn't picked for its size, it was picked to punish the man who killed Akhan and put his head on a stake.

Morrow never stuttered or blinked an eye. "So you and Chief Persico kept the team in the base camp while Perrite and Machusco went back out and searched for this man Pajocovic? Is that what happened?"

"That's right. Only I sent Moore out, too. I came up with the idea that the only way to make this halfway right was to do what Akhan set out to do in the first place. The only problem was that Pajocovic and his unit had left Piluca. We had no idea where they went. So I sent Brian Moore back out with Perrite and Machusco. They snuck into a few local villages and asked around. Pajocovic was known by everyone in our zone. The Hammer, everybody called him. Moore kept asking people if they knew where the Hammer was. Finally, some old man told him that he was with his unit in a little village named Ishatar. That was how Pajocovic operated. He'd sometimes go to local villages, spending a day or so terrorizing the citizens, then he'd go back to his station in Piluca. That's when I decided what we were going to do."

"I'm sorry, Terry. You said *I* decided. Do you mean Chief Persico decided, or you both decided?"

"No. I mean I decided. Persico came to me, and I said this was what we were going to do."

"I see," Morrow said.

"Right, so we moved off and I set up an ambush on the road between Piluca and Ishatar. We moved in the night before, around midnight. That gave us plenty of time to set up. Then I waited and—"

"Terry," she interrupted him. He stopped and blinked a few times.

She said, "Would you like a glass of water?"

He was still rubbing his legs. "Uh . . . yeah, sure. Please."

Morrow filled a tumbler, then walked around the table and handed it to him. I thought she'd just made a major blunder, interrupting his flow at the crucial moment. She then went and got a chair and moved it to a position directly in front of him. She sat down and leaned forward so their faces were nearly together. He looked into her eyes again.

"How are you doing?" she asked.

"Okay, I guess."

She said, "Terry, you have nothing to prove to us. We're just trying to get at the truth. God knows, we're not judging you. We're lawyers. We've never been through what you went through."

She reached out and laid a hand on his hand. "Just tell us the truth, okay?"

He kept staring into her eyes, the way a small, frightened child looks at his mother. "Okay," he said.

"Who was making all these decisions, Terry? It wasn't you, was it?"

"No," he said, "it was Persico and Perrite."

"And what were you doing?"

"I did whatever they said to do."

"Did you try to stop them? Or did you encourage them?"

This actually was a very crucial question because it went to the heart of who bore legal responsibility for the murder of the Serbs. I think Sanchez was past caring about the legal niceties, though. His mind was trapped in a desperate effort to construct a plausible alibi it could sell to itself. His mind was swimming in shame and scrambling for some internal clemency. I think in a strange, remorseful way, he wished he had ordered the ambush, because that might have afforded him some residue of honor.

"I let them do what they wanted to do," he finally mumbled.

"What happened at the ambush?"

"Well, there was a lot of traffic on the road. We stayed there until nearly eight. Perrite was off on the flank, between us and Ishatar. He had night-vision goggles, you know? He was watching for the vehicles from Piluca. Pajocovic's vehicles had his station's name marked on the side, and it was written in Serb, and Brian Moore had written out the words on a piece of paper for Perrite so he'd recognize the right column."

"Then what happened?" she asked, still with her hand on top of his.

"Around eight, he gave Persico the signal they were coming. Persico was controlling the fires and he waited till the lead vehicle got right over the two antitank mines planted in the road. The explosion sent this big truck catapulting in the air. I remember watching it flip, end over end, like a little Tonka toy." His hands fluttered through the air to show us how the truck flipped. "It was really a sight, you know? Then we opened up. It lasted only seven or eight minutes, then we left."

Morrow got up and walked back to her seat at the table beside me. Nobody said anything for a moment. I thought about everything he'd said. Everything made sense now. Well, maybe not everything.

I said, "Terry."

He looked at me. I tried to sound as gentle and comforting as Morrow had been.

"Someone went through after the ambush was over and shot the Serbs in the head. Was that you?"

He looked at me in shock.

"No," he said.

"You're sure?" I asked.

"I swear."

"Do you know who did it?"

"None of us did. I was shooting, just like everyone else. But as soon as Persico shot off the flare to order us to cease fire, we all stopped. Then we all left and started running for the rally point, a mile or so behind the ambush site."

I said, "And were there still some Serb survivors?"

"Yeah. I never lied about that, you know? There were still a few down there firing back at us."

I was confused. This made no sense. If there were still survivors firing their weapons when the whole team was headed for the rally point, then who shot them in the head? We all grew quiet. I stared around at the walls for about a minute and tried to think what else to ask.

Imelda suddenly lifted herself out of her chair and approached Morrow and me. She got to the edge of the table, then leaned toward us as though we were judges and she was a lawyer seeking conference in a courtroom.

She whispered, "Ask him how long the Serbs was still shooting. Just ask him that."

Then she returned to her seat. I looked quizzically at Morrow, and she stared back at me.

I said, "Terry, can you remember how long you heard the Serbs still shooting, after you and the rest of the team were headed for the rally point?"

He rested his chin on his hand and placed the elbow on his knee, then stared down at the floor. He might've been Rodin's *Thinker*, only there was no purity of contemplation, only anguish on this man's face.

"A while," he finally said.

"How long a while?" I asked, finally realizing what Imelda might have figured out.

He rubbed his hands over his face. "I don't know, maybe two minutes. Then there was this pause, then we could hear it off in the distance again. But we were getting farther away, and the terrain was hilly, and it sounded like little pops echoing through the hills. Might not even have been shooting, you know?"

"Assume it was. Why do you think they were still firing?"

"I don't know. I guess maybe because it was an ambush, and we were pretty well hidden in our positions. Maybe they thought we were still there."

"Okay," I said.

Morrow said, "Terry, now there're only a few more questions left. How are you doing?"

"All right," he said, but he looked terrifically relieved to know this was almost over. He'd gone back to that odd leg-rubbing motion.

"When you all got back to Macedonia and were debriefed, why did you decide to lie?"

He suddenly looked pathetically uncomfortable. So uncomfortable, in fact, that he didn't seem willing to answer.

That's when I knew. I said, "Terry, did you make a deal with your team out there?"

He kept staring at the floor and was rubbing his hands on his legs a little more frantically, and I finally figured out why he was doing that. His conscience was impelling the motion. He was trying to rub the guilt off his hands, or erase it from his soul.

"Terry, please answer. Did you make a deal with your team?"

He mumbled something, but I couldn't make it out.

"What?" I said.

"Yes, we made a deal."

I said, "Is that why you went along with the ambush, Terry? Is that why you bought them the time with Smothers? You wanted them to do that ambush, didn't you? You knew it was a violation of orders, that if they killed Pajocovic and his men they'd be facing court-martial when you all made it back. You knew that if they did that, they would have as much to hide as you? You knew, then, that the team would cover for you, because they needed you to cover for them."

He kept staring at the floor, and that was an answer in itself. I looked at Morrow, and she stared back at me. There was nothing more to be gained by talking with Terry Sanchez. We now knew everything he knew. We knew everything, except the most crucial thing. Who killed the last of the Serbs?

Chapter

☆☆☆ **32**

After Imelda escorted Sanchez back to his cell, we all desperately needed to take the edge off. I ordered everyone to take a break. Imelda and her ladies went off in search of a coffee machine. I asked Imelda to notify the Air Force warden that I wanted to see him. And I asked her to bring back two cups of coffee, one for Morrow and one for me.

Morrow and I were a little dazed. Most trials don't have all the pathos and theatrics and emotional hysterics that are depicted in all those TV and movie courtroom battles. The truth is, what happens in the courtroom is rarely a battle; it is far more like watching water become ice. Most trials are as well-orchestrated as a Kabuki dance. They bore you almost to death. A smart lawyer knows to always get a good night's sleep before a court date, because of the stifling somnolence and the fact that judges can get pretty cranky when you nod off in their court. That is, if the judge is awake to catch you. Everything's tightly scripted, because the last thing any lawyer wants is to have his witnesses up there freewheeling it. While a little spontaneity might make for a more interesting trial, lawyers aren't looking to be interested. They're looking to win. Besides, even most of the uncoached folks who climb up onto a witness stand aren't real interesting, because most folks just aren't. In fact, they're less interesting than they might normally be because the lawyers and the judge are making them speak factually, devoid of the lively opinions and exaggerations that lend a little spice and spunk to ordinary conversation. About everything that needs to be sorted out gets sorted out long before the case gets to court, so there are rarely any surprises.

Add to that, one of the rules of being a lawyer is to never, ever utter a single-syllable word if a more stuffy, five-syllable word can suffice. And displays of emotion are anathema, something that's cleaved out of you by the second year of law school, or else you're not allowed to proceed. I mean, just think about how many really interesting lawyers you ever met in your life. Don't think it improves when you put two or more together in a room.

That was the world Morrow and I inhabited from day to day. A world of few surprises, sparse drama, a tedious world where your emotions are almost going in reverse. We were both a little startled and disoriented. We felt like someone who had spent their whole life riding a tricycle on backcountry roads, then suddenly got thrust behind the wheel of a twelve-cylinder Maserati on an L.A. freeway.

It's one thing to have suspicions about what happened out there. It's another thing altogether to have a witness flesh it out for you, firsthand, in full-blown emotional Technicolor. Particularly a witness who's afflicted with gangrene of the soul. There's a stench to gangrene, and it gets into your mental nostrils and lingers there a while. We both sat quietly at the table for a few minutes. Then Morrow pulled out her trusty pad of yellow legal paper and began making notes.

I watched her write for a few moments, then said, "About that Pudley thing this morning, I'm sorry."

She giggled a little, but it didn't sound like her heart was in it.

I added, "I'm also sorry about last night. I drank too much. I didn't do anything . . . uh, you know . . . like, anything too forward when we got to my bedroom, did I?"

What I hoped she'd say was, well, yes, actually you did. A very naughty thing, too, and you did it four or five times, you animal, but the truth is, I enjoyed the hell out of it, and I sure hope you do it again.

Instead, she said, "Don't worry. You were snoring before you hit the bed."

I said, "Yeah. My ribs were hurting like hell."

"It wasn't your ribs," she said, still writing.

"Yeah it was."

"It was your conscience."

"No it wasn't," I lied. "It was my ribs. These ones," I said, pointing at my side.

"You're not as absolute as you like to pretend," she said, still jotting notes. "You like these men. They're just like you and that bothers you. Admit it."

I thought about that a moment. I'm not the deep, introspective, sensitive type. Every attempt I ever made to fathom my own psyche, I just ended up like one of those rats lost in a maze of twisted turns and dead alleys. But okay, so they were a little like me. Maybe a lot like me. The difference was, I'd never mutinied against my senior officers, I'd never let my troops do something I could later blackmail them for, I'd never cut deals with my troops, and I'd never murdered a bunch of wounded men. Those, to me, were fairly gaping distinctions.

She put down her pen and turned to me. "You know, you're the right man to head this investigation, but you're also the wrong man. You've shared some experiences with them. No ordinary lawyer, like me, could ever have hoped to comprehend what happened out there. For the same reason, though, you can't look at them impartially."

I stared back at her. This sounded a little too much like psychoanalysis to me. That was Morrow's problem. The reason her eyes were so damned sympathetic-looking was because she was so damned sympathetic, and she was probing here for a fresh customer.

I said, "Was that why you wore that dress last night?"

"What?"

"That was it, wasn't it?" I said. "The skimpy dress, that sexy nectar you rubbed on. You thought I needed to get my mind off it. You thought I needed to be saved."

She blushed ever so lightly. "Well, didn't you? The way you were drinking? Did you really think I didn't know you'd put down a couple before I even got there? Your breath reeked."

"My ribs hurt," I said.

"Your ribs, my ass," she said. "You should see your face when these men are testifying. You're completely absorbed in it. This is too personal for you."

Fortunately, Imelda and her ladies walked back in at that moment, because my lips were just parting, and I wasn't the least bit sure even I wanted to hear what I was about to say. Imelda approached our table with two cups of steaming java. Mine had been prepared just the way I liked it, with just enough coffee to legitimize my addictions for sugar and cream.

I grabbed Imelda's sleeve before she could return to her seat. "Hey, Imelda," I whispered.

"What?"

"You ever hear of a Pudley?"

She sort of snorted once or twice. "Hell, who ain't never heard of Pudleys. Why? You a Pudley?"

"Absolutely not," I insisted. "I'm more like a Humongo."

"Um-hmm," she said, walking back to her chair. It wasn't one of those "um-hmms" like yep, you sure as hell look like you're packing a Humongo to me. It was the other kind of "um-hmm."

Morrow was grinning when, fortunately, there was a knock at the door and she had to force herself to stifle it and appear like a sober, buttoned-down attorney.

The door opened and the chubby Air Force warden stuck his head in. He had this awfully tentative expression on his face, as if he was deathly afraid of me.

"You beckoned me, sir?" he asked.

"Damn right! Get in here," I bellowed, and he nearly bounced through the doorway. He approached our table, walking gingerly, like a man with pins sticking through the soles of his shoes.

I said, "Is there a psychiatrist on this base?"

"Yes," he said. "There's one over at the base hospital, in the flight surgeon's office."

"You get him over here today. I want him to spend time with Captain Sanchez. Also, I want you to institute a suicide watch on him. You do have procedures for that, don't you?"

He nodded vigorously.

I bent forward and peered intently into his face. "Haven't you noticed that he's experienced a very severe weight loss?"

"Uh . . . no, I hadn't noticed."

"But surely you've noticed that he's very depressed?"

"No, I, uh, I hadn't noticed that, either."

"Then listen closely. If he manages to kill himself or loses even one more ounce, I'll see that you're charged with gross negligence. Do I make myself clear?"

"Uh, yes, sir . . . or, er, yes, Major."

"Get out of here," I said.

He scurried quickly away and his overweight butt shook like Jell-O.

I'd just done the best I could for Terry Sanchez. I wasn't sure it was going to help, though. When a man walks all over his own image of himself the way he had, something dies inside.

Sanchez was rotting away from the center, because he had compromised nearly every principle he believed in.

Most of the fault for that lay on his own increasingly skinny shoulders. But some of that fault fell on Smothers and Murphy. Smothers, because he allowed his sense of personal loyalty to overrule his judgment and gave Sanchez a team. He never should've done that. It was one of those all-too-common instances of doing something for all the right reasons with all the wrong consequences. It was a disservice to the men, because Sanchez wasn't up to leading them. It was a disservice to Sanchez for the very same reason. He was bound to fail.

Murphy's blame came from another source altogether. He had allowed his group to continue its policy of treating the First Battalion like it was some kind of privileged private men's club. An exclusive old-timers' club. Since Persico and his sergeants all felt handpicked and had all been together for so many years, and those bonds had been calcified by so many shared experiences, any newcomer, even a newly appointed team leader, was likely to be treated like an unproven outsider. The sergeants and warrants in the First Battalion were all convinced they were something special. They had isolated and blocked out Terry Sanchez. When that sense of isolation was compounded by the pressures of a combat situation, it became too much for the human spirit to bear. Particularly when that spirit was a little frail and pappy in the first place. The result was the pitiful picture of Terry Sanchez we had just seen.

I would bet that if we went back and interviewed the men who had led that team before Sanchez, we'd hear echoes of the same tale. In fact, I'd bet we'd find the same thing in a lot of the teams in First Battalion. The old-timers' club. There were probably a lot of accidents waiting to happen out there.

I looked over at Imelda and asked her to get Chief Persico.

Chapter

★ ★
 ★ 33

Persico had disregarded my advice. He did not return with a lawyer. He walked into the room alone, and I had to wonder about that. Surely he knew we were closing in on the truth. Surely he knew there was a fairly strong possibility we were going to take the whole damned proverbial book and stuff it down his throat.

I said, "Chief, please have a seat."

He took the same chair and casually hiked his right leg over his left. You couldn't help but notice the yawning contrast between this gray-haired, leathery, self-assured man and the simmering, leg-rubbing wreck that was left of Terry Sanchez. If I were a sergeant in that team, there'd be no question which one I'd want to follow, either.

I said, "Chief, I want to be frank with you. You are facing possible charges of multiple counts of murder, failure to obey orders, inciting mutiny, obstruction of justice, lying in an official investigation, and a long host of lesser charges. I advise you from the bottom of my heart to have counsel present for these proceedings. I am willing to suspend this hearing, if you wish to take the time."

He sat perfectly still. "I don't want counsel."

"That's your right. If at any point you change your mind, though, we will halt the proceeding so you can obtain one."

He said, "Can we get on with it?"

"Of course."

Before I could say anything else, he said, "Mind if I start with a few points?"

"If you'd like."

He studied me carefully. "Major, I see you're wearing a Combat Infantryman's Badge and a combat patch on your right sleeve. You were in combat, right?"

"Right."

"Where?"

"I was with the 82nd in Panama and the Gulf," I answered, which was technically true, since the 82nd Airborne Division was in both places while I was there with the outfit.

"Were you in leadership positions? Were you in the field?"

"Yes," I answered, which was also true because like Sanchez I was a team leader.

"You get shot at any?"

"A fair amount," I admitted.

"Good wars, weren't they?" he asked, breaking into a grim grin.

I said, "I suppose the politically correct answer would be to say that there's no such thing as a good war, but as wars go, I guess they were pretty good. Short, lopsided, and we won."

"Goddamn right," he said, nodding and watching my face very intensely. "I was in the Gulf, too. Didn't do Panama, though. Did Haiti, Mogadishu, Rwanda. Also spent a shitload of years in Bosnia, doing this and that. You missed all those, didn't you?"

"By that time, I was in law school or the JAG Corps."

"Yeah," he said, nodding thoughtfully. "Me, Perrite, Machusco, Caldwell, Butler, the Moore brothers, we done nearly all those together. The Moore brothers, poor bastards, they joined too late for the Gulf. Never gotta taste of what it feels like to get a sweet war under their belts. Only thing they've ever done is float through all these endless shitholes we've been doin' ever since. They don't even know what it's like to win, you know?"

He paused for a moment and his gray eyes roved around the room, taking in each of our faces. He paused for a moment at Imelda's face. She quietly nodded. He smiled at her, then nodded back in some kind of private acknowledgment.

Then the smile evaporated and he faced me again. "Can't tell you how many refugee camps we've been through since the Gulf. You kinda lose count. I swear I've seen a hundred million miserable faces with those empty-looking eyes all those refugees got. Maimed kids, raped women, orphans, mothers who just lost their babies, men too ashamed to look at their families 'cause they let this happen. Christ, you get tired of it. They send you into these things, and you're supposed to just . . . well, you know? I mean, they call these things humanitarian operations, but a real humanitarian would go in and knock the crap out of the bad guys, wouldn't he? A real humanitarian wouldn't stand around putting Band-Aids on 'em after they got hurt. A real humanitarian would keep 'em from getting hurt in the first place. Don't ya think?"

"Chief," I said as kindly as I could, "we're not here to debate the righteousness of our national policies. We're here to consider what happened in Kosovo between the fourteenth and eighteenth of June."

His voice was cool, almost matter-of-fact. "You wanta know, then listen. 'Cause this is what happened. I mean, it's a head game, isn't it? You wanta know what happened, you gotta climb in and share some headspace with us. Anyway, you do enough of these things, you eventually reach a point. Maybe it was 'cause of Akhan. Any of the others tell you about Akhan?" he asked.

I nodded.

"Yeah, well, I doubt what they said did him justice. Christ, I can't do him justice. I seen some fine men in my time, but I never saw one who could touch him. God, I would've followed that bastard myself. Didn't know crap about fighting, you know. Really had no business at all being out there. The guy was a brilliant doctor. I mean, he was really gifted, you know. I heard some of the UN docs talking about him. They talked about him like he was just Jesus Christ, a guy who could do miracles. Only thing was, Akhan refused to stay back in some hospital tent tending the wounded when others were out fighting. He wanted to be one of those real humanitarians, you see?"

He looked me dead in the eye. "Christ, I wish I knew the words to describe him. I mean, I'm not real educated or nothing, and I can't make you picture him. But you gotta picture him if you wanta know what happened."

He was getting more animated, maybe out of frustration that he couldn't find the words, or maybe just from the excitement of thinking about this extraordinary man. I'd met a few men like that. Not many, but a few.

"He was young," he continued. "Early thirties, I'd guess. A handsome guy, tall, thin, with sunken cheeks, but this special calmness in his eyes. Can you see that in your head?

"Thing is," he continued, "Akhan never should've gone down to Piluca. Sanchez egged him into it, though. I mean, I saw it building when we was puttin' 'em through training. Everyone just admired Akhan, you know. Christ, you just couldn't help yourself. And Sanchez? Well, he just couldn't get anyone to respect him. A bunch of the men in Akhan's company talked a lot about this Serb, Pajocovic. They had all kinds of stories, so we all knew they really hated him. So Sanchez started goading Akhan about how he probably shouldn't go after him, even though all his men wanted to, 'cause it might involve a little bloodshed. I mean, he started on Captain Akhan even before we took 'em into Kosovo. He was trying to shame him, you know, 'cause the way this Avenging Angel's supposed to work is the KLA aren't supposed to do the tough crap. Being with 'em was like our cover so we could do the hard ones. But I knew Sanchez was jealous of Akhan. I mean, Akhan just had this easy way with men, you know? He was a natural. Sanchez had to work hard at it, and he still didn't measure up. I think he wanted Akhan to try some hard things, so he would fail. That make sense? I mean, Akhan had the talent, but he wasn't trained to do it. Sanchez didn't have the right stuff, but he had the training. You see what was going on there?"

"It makes sense," I said.

He looked over at Imelda again, and she nodded at him again, her face taut but also proud.

"Anyway, when Perrite and Machusco and Moore came back from Piluca, everything kinda came apart. I don't think Sanchez wanted that to happen, you know? All of 'em getting killed that way, that was more than he bargained for. It's what he set in motion, though, wasn't it? I took him off in the woods and told him about what Perrite and the guys saw, and he started crying. I mean, he bawled like a little kid. The rest of the team didn't handle it real well, either. If this wasn't the Army, the men probably would've taken Sanchez into the woods and lynched him. It really was a sorry thing he done."

"Did you tell Sanchez he couldn't lead the team? Was there an organized effort to keep him from doing his job?"

"No," he said, appearing very disquieted. "But I didn't fix it, either. I knew what was happening. I just didn't want to. Don't blame the men. They didn't have nothing to do with it. It was my fault. I just didn't make 'em follow his orders anymore. And I didn't make Sanchez keep doin' his job, neither. I mean, he nearly always needed a kick in the ass anyway, but this time I saw that he lost his guts, and I just let him be. You understand? I didn't do it. I didn't want to do it. You wanta charge someone with mutiny, you charge me. I guess I mutinied."

I said, "When did you decide to ambush Pajocovic's unit?"

"That morning. Right away, really."

"Why? Why didn't you extricate when Colonel Smothers ordered you to?"

He reached into his breast pocket and pulled out the Camels. He looked up at me. "This still all right?"

"Sure."

He withdrew one and tamped it down, staring at his palm. He lit it and inhaled heavily, allowing the smoke to sit inside his lungs before it filtered slowly out his nose. He spent a long moment chewing on his lower lip. Then he answered.

"That's why you gotta understand what it feels like to do all these humanitarian missions. It does get personal. They can bring in all these shrinks to tell you not to hold on to it and all that psychobabble, but it gets personal. I mean, we're soldiers, not doctors, you know? Captain Akhan's head was on a stake, like some kinda trophy. This guy Pajocovic was a real murderous bastard. He'd killed and tortured hundreds of people. Maybe thousands. However this Kosovo thing ends, he'd of just walked away from it. Look what happened after Bosnia and Rwanda and Haiti. The dead got buried and forgotten, and the murderers went on with their lives."

"So you decided to execute him?"

He stared at the smoking tip of the cigarette. "Yes, sir, that's exactly what I decided to do. I don't regret it, either. The men just did what they were told to do, so don't charge them. I was giving the orders. They were only following 'em, just like the book says they're supposed to. They didn't do nothing wrong."

I said, "Somebody did, though, Chief. Somebody went through and shot the Serbs in the head. Can you tell us who did that?"

He still stared at the tip of the cigarette. He did not even blink. "Yeah," he said. "I did it."

I felt something stick in the back of my throat, and I had to take a moment to swallow and catch my breath. These were the last words I expected or wanted to hear.

I finally asked, "How, Chief? How did you do it?"

"Easy, really. Most of the Serbs were dead or wounded from the ambush. I gotta tell you, Major, as ambushes go, it was a pretty good one. Real lethal, real quick. I waited till there was only three or four still firing before I shot off the star cluster for everyone to cease fire. Then I ordered everyone to head for the rally point. They all got up and started running, only I gave 'em all a little head start, then I went in a different direction. I worked my way over to where the road curved and crossed there. Then I ran up the hill on the other side of the road. The last of the Serbs were huddled behind their vehicles, still shooting at the hillside where our team had been. They had their backs turned to me. It was kid's play, really. I shot 'em. Then I went down and put bullets through all their heads."

"Why, Chief? Why did you do it?"

"Ain't it obvious? Maybe one of those guys down there still firing back might've been Pajocovic. Besides, after what they done, I wanted 'em all dead. And I guess I didn't want any witnesses left."

The room suddenly became very quiet. He calmly finished smoking his cigarette. He dropped it on the floor and ground it out, turning his heel four or five times to make sure it was completely extinguished. The physical metaphor was very powerful and very persuasive.

I said, "Okay, Chief, that will be all."

He stood up and actually saluted me. I saluted him back, then he dropped his hand and turned and looked at Imelda for a very long time. She stared right back. Real soldiers, the professionals, can almost smell each other. Then he marched out and closed the door on a room full of stunned and saddened people.

I turned to Morrow, and her eyes were real moist. I looked at Imelda and she was staring back at me like I was the biggest maggot that ever slimed the earth. I guess Chief Persico was the last man anyone wanted to have done such a despicable crime, and it helped everyone to blame me for having made him confess.

There were some very pent-up feelings inside this room, so I ordered everybody to take a twenty-minute break. Even Morrow got up and left the room. I was left in isolation at the small table we had set up. Something was stuck somewhere back in my dark recesses, some missing piece, and I was trying like hell to dredge it up. I stared at the floor for a very long time.

Fifteen minutes passed before Morrow reentered. She was carrying two cups of coffee.

"Thanks," I mumbled as she put one in front of me.

She fell into her chair and groaned. "God, this is awful."

Hard to argue with that, I thought, only nodding. I wasn't feeling real talkative.

She said, "Thank God it's finally over. Except for deciding what to do."

I said, "It's not over, Lisa."

"It is for me. We've got enough evidence to make our recommendations. I don't want to sit here and rehash this with every member of the team."

"I don't intend to, either," I said. "Only one more to go."

I got up and went out to find Imelda. I told her what I wanted her to do, then I returned to the interview room and quietly waited till Imelda's girls came filtering back in and took their seats.

Two minutes passed before the door opened. First, Imelda came through, then Sergeant François Perrite.

"Have a seat," I told him.

He did, although more nervously this time. He broke out the cigarettes immediately and began tamping a fresh one.

I said, "Do I need to remind you of your rights again?"

"No, I know my rights."

"You can spare me your feelings toward lawyers this time,

but are you sure you don't want counsel, Sergeant? I would seriously advise you to have a lawyer present."

"Nope. There's enough fucking lawyers in this room already."

"Nobody would argue with that," I admitted.

Then we looked into each other's eyes a moment, and he knew that I knew.

I said, "Chief Persico just left. He took responsibility for everything. He said he was the one who made all the decisions, who led the quiet mutiny against Captain Sanchez, who decided to execute an ambush, who ignored the order to extricate."

He was quietly nodding as I detailed this.

"Of course, Sergeant Perrite, you bear most of the responsibility. You were the one who came back and tried to incite the men against Sanchez. You knew they didn't like him anyway, and you stoked the fuel. It was your idea to kill Pajocovic, wasn't it? Yet Chief was in here trying to cover for you."

He didn't nod or acknowledge a word, only watched me and listened.

I continued. "Then he confessed that he was the one who went around after the ambush and shot the Serbs in the head. He said he sent everyone else to the rally point, then he snuck across the road and dispatched the last survivors. Then he went down to the site and administered the coup de grâce."

Perrite was now staring at the end of his lit cigarette, much as Chief Persico had sat and stared at his only thirty minutes before. It was uncanny. Perrite admired the man so much he even affected the same mannerisms.

I said, "The problem, Sergeant Perrite, is that you and I both know he didn't do that. Don't we? He was trying to save somebody he cares deeply about, and I only hope to God that man cares as much about him."

I paused for a moment as he continued to regard his cigarette.

Finally I said, "He was trying to save you, wasn't he?"

Perrite stayed frozen, still staring at that cigarette for what felt like eternity. I had no idea what he was thinking, because I had no idea how a man like him thought.

Then he nodded dumbly. He was perfectly willing to lie right down to the end, but he was not willing to let Persico take the rap for his crime.

"That's right," he finally mumbled. "I did it."

"Tell us what happened."

"You wouldn't understand," he said.

"Try me. Maybe I would."

"No, you're not really soldiers, you and that other lawyer up there," he said, waving dismissively at Morrow. "You got no idea what it's like out there. The way you feel about the other men in your team, how you stop thinking when the bullets are flying, how you just do whatever you feel like."

Suddenly Imelda jumped out of her seat and walked over and stopped right in front of him. Her body was very tense, and her fists were clenched tightly.

"I've heard enough of your shit, Sergeant. You don't know what you're talking about!" she yelled. "See that damned combat patch on the major's right arm? See that Combat Infantryman's Badge on his chest? What you don't see is the three Purple Hearts and two Silver Stars, and the Distinguished Service Cross he earned, too. Know why he's a lawyer? He spent six months in a hospital recovering after the last one. They wouldn't let him stay in the infantry after that. Don't you go thinking you've got shit to tell him about what it's like out there, Sergeant. Now, act like a damn soldier and answer that man."

Perrite stared up at her and Imelda glared down at him. How she knew about that was beyond me. My citations and awards were inside a musty drawer somewhere, because they were given for operations that nobody knew happened, and nobody was supposed to know happened. Besides, who cared what combat awards lawyers got? But then, Imelda was a sergeant and you may remember my earlier warning that sergeants could be very devious when they wanted to find things out. Make that ditto for Imelda.

Perrite looked at me. He was not only a Special Forces soldier with all the macho baggage that carried, but he was also a Cajun. This added a whole mix of spices to the ordinary Special Forces macho culture, so Imelda had just leveled the playing field a bit.

"That true?" he asked.

"I guess so," I admitted.

He pondered that a moment, then he made up his mind. "Okay, Major, I was off on the flank, like I said. I heard the ambush go off. I heard the shooting for seven or eight minutes. I got curious. You know what that means, right? Bein' on security, you always wonder. You wonder if your friends are gettin' killed, if your guys are winnin', if things are goin' to shit."

He paused and looked up at me.

"I knew I shouldn't, but I crossed the road and worked my way down, till I was behind the Serbs. I got there just as Chief gave everyone the order to beat feet. There was still some Serbs down there, maybe three or four, still shooting. So I decided to . . . well, you know, I decided to . . . kill them, I guess."

"Why?" I asked.

"I dunno. I just felt like it."

"No. You must've had a reason."

"Okay. Maybe because I wanted a piece of the action. And maybe because Chief should've made sure they were all dead so there were no witnesses."

I said, "And maybe you wanted a trophy?"

He looked at me in alarm.

I said, "When Captain Morrow and I viewed the corpses in the morgue in Belgrade, one had no head left. Was that Captain Pajocovic's body?"

He turned his eyes away from mine. "I dunno. Mighta been

his body. Maybe his head got blown off by the claymores. That happens sometimes."

"No, Sergeant, I don't think so. That head looked like it had been hacked off, like maybe with a bayonet. You cut his head off, didn't you?"

He began fidgeting and suddenly looked nervous. I finally had it all figured out. Perrite was a Cajun. He lived by the old Cajun code of an eye for an eye and a tooth for a tooth. Cultural stereotypes often do happen to be valid. Pajocovic had decapitated Akhan, so Perrite returned the favor in kind.

"What did you do with it, Sergeant?"

He still refused to answer. But he didn't have to. I knew the answer to this one too. Perrite would've wanted his hero to be proud of him, just like a hunting dog brings its trophies back to its owner.

"You brought it to Chief, didn't you? You wanted him to see what you did, right?"

He sort of straightened up in his seat and he dropped the cigarette on the floor. Unlike Chief Persico though, he did not grind it out. He stomped it out.

"That's right, that's what I did."

"And what did he do?"

"He got real pissed. He tol' me not to say anything to the others, and he ordered me to bury the head."

I said, "Thank you, Sergeant Perrite. You may return to your cell."

Imelda got up and escorted him out. He still had that same jaunty walk.

Chapter ☆☆ 34

It was the last time I ever planned to show those guards my orders, to grin stupidly into the camera, and to wait for Miss Smith to open the door. Only it wasn't Miss Smith who opened the door this time. It was a man, and he was much older than Miss Smith. I knew his real name, too. It was General Clapper.

We stood and looked at each other stupidly for a moment before he thrust out his hand. "Sean, how are you?"

"Pretty crappy," I admitted.

Then he shook hands with Morrow and she admitted how she felt pretty crappy, too. That's not the word she used, though. She said abysmal, or some variation of that, because she's too much of a lady to admit she felt like shit.

Clapper then led us through the facility and back down the stairs to the conference room in the lead-lined basement. Someone had given him a passkey for the door, and he slid it through the little magnetic reader, then swung the door open and we all walked in.

The long conference room table had acquired an abundant audience. Tretorne was there, of course, and he was back to wearing that damned vest he seemed so fond of. Murphy was there, of course. So was his boss, General Clive Partridge, who had all four of those heavy little stars weighing down his shoulders. And so was the White House man who had briefed me before I came out here. He at least was wearing a nice conservative suit and was too modest to try to pretend that he was a field agent. His name was Parker, and he didn't look happy to be here. None of them looked happy to be here. Hell, Morrow and I didn't look happy to be here. It was just a great big room filled with unhappy people who were unhappy to see one another.

Morrow and I had made a promise, though, and we were keeping it. We'd worked around the clock the past three days, dissecting the evidence and testimonies, considering every legal angle and alternative, arguing back and forth, often wanting to scratch each other's eyes out, until we built the packet we intended to present.

Clapper walked around the table and took the seat next to General Partridge. The table had been artfully arranged so that all them were seated on one side, and there were these two empty chairs positioned in the middle of the other side. These, obviously, were intended for Morrow and me. Well, I knew a little about arranging furniture to achieve a certain psychological effect, and I wasn't about to feel the least bit threatened. We were way past the point where some silly little game was going to manipulate our sensibilities.

I led Morrow over and we both sat down. I glanced at her and she appeared as exhausted as I felt, but she also looked calm and unperturbed. After what we'd been through, the fact that a few of the most powerful men in our country's national security establishment were seated across from us didn't seem to bother her in the least.

We spent a few moments digging through our legal cases and withdrawing our findings. We had made only ten copies, each numbered and stamped with the words TOP SECRET: SPECAT. Morrow, being by some order of magnitude the lowest-ranking personage in the room, got up and placed a copy in front of each of the men on the other side of the table.

I said, "Gentlemen, these are our findings. If you'd like, we can pause for twenty minutes to give you time to read them. Otherwise, Captain Morrow will orally present our conclusions."

General Partridge, being the highest-ranking man across the table, and also the man who ultimately had to decide whether to convene a court-martial or not, made the call.

"Tell us what you found."

Morrow looked at me, and I nodded for her to proceed.

She cleared her throat once or twice and her eyes swept across the line of faces on the other side of the table. Then she began.

"On the morning of 18 June, at approximately 0800 hours, Captain Sanchez's A-team did willfully execute an ambush that resulted in the deaths of . . ."

She spoke for nearly twenty minutes. I was real proud of her. She was organized, succinct, and never strayed an inch from the facts, just like a Harvard-trained lawyer's supposed to do. She explained everything that occurred, from the assumed betrayal and massacre of Akhan's company, through the attempted obstruction of justice. The men across the table sat stone-faced and listened without interrupting even once.

I watched their faces and tried to imagine what they were thinking, what they felt, how they were reacting to the story Morrow was so skillfully unraveling. It had not been an easy case to break. Winston Churchill once described the country of Russia as "an enigma, inside a mystery, wrapped inside a puzzle." What we had been up against was a cornucopia of conspiracies, a convoluted jumble of conspiracies wrapped inside more conspiracies. It was too many layers of collusion and connivance, starting with Persico trying to hide the fact that Perrite had murdered the survivors, to the team making a deal with Sanchez to cover one another's misdeeds, to the men across the table attempting to subvert our efforts to find out what had really happened. It was all such a hopeless mixture of motives and compulsions that I still wasn't convinced I had it all sorted out.

Morrow finally finished. There was a moment of fretful silence.

General Partridge reached into his pocket, took out a pack of cigarettes, and I'll be damned if it wasn't a pack of Camels, unfiltered. He extracted one, tapped it gently on his palm a few times, then lit it. Simply amazing. General Murphy got up and went over to a side table, opened a drawer, and fetched a glass ashtray for his boss. Smoking was strictly prohibited in all military and government facilities, but nobody in that room had the balls to remind the meanest, snarliest four-star general in the whole United States Army that this rule applied to him, too. I sure as hell didn't.

Partridge then stared at me. "So what do you recommend, Major? What do I charge, and who do I charge?"

I said, "Why don't we deal with the most serious charge first? The charge of murder."

"Go on," he said, his eyes watching me through a veil of smoke.

In my most lawyerly tone, I began. "The issue of murder becomes very complicated, mainly because when we began this investigation we were deliberately misled into believing that the role of our teams in Kosovo was essentially that of noncombatants, except in instances of self-defense. Only later did we learn of Operation Avenging Angel, and that Sanchez's team was actually in Kosovo for the express purpose of performing offensive combat operations. Since Sanchez's team had the legal authority to perform offensive operations, we concluded that the ambush conducted on the eighteenth of June was a tolerable act. It follows that the ambush was not an act of mass murder. It was, however, a willful disobedience of orders, since

Colonel Smothers ordered the team to extricate, and since the orders the team were operating under strictly disallowed attacks on targets of opportunity."

Partridge said, "Noted." Nothing else, just that.

I continued. "Sergeant Perrite's initial attack on the remaining survivors was not murder, either. It was a case of willful disobedience of his orders. Also, he abandoned his post in combat, which you're aware is an added offense. He crossed the line from those infractions to murder when he purposely dispatched the wounded Serbs. He committed multiple acts of first-degree murder and one act of mutilating a corpse. Exactly how many murders he committed is impossible to ascertain. We have included copies of the coroner's findings in your packet. A minimum of three. As many as ten."

"Noted," Partridge said again.

I said, "The act of mutiny is again a matter of extraordinary complexity. The Uniform Code of Military Justice defines mutiny as a deliberate and organized attempt to usurp the authority of the designated leaders of the unit. Over the centuries, there have been many test cases involving multiple variations of mutiny. Captain Morrow and I did as much research as our limited time and resources permitted. We will not bore you with the details, but we found no case in military law that precisely mirrors what happened inside Captain Sanchez's unit. More able or experienced jurists might argue with our finding; however, our considered judgment is that Captain Terry Sanchez willfully abrogated his responsibility to lead the unit, and that Chief Michael Persico took the commendable step of performing his duties. There seems a strong possibility that had Sanchez not voluntarily relinquished his leadership, there would have been a mutiny, but Sanchez's own passiveness preempted this offense."

Partridge flicked an ash in the ashtray. "Noted."

I said, "There are a host of lesser offenses, which are described and dealt with in your packet, but there are only two additional serious offenses left to be considered."

"And what are those?" Partridge grunted.

"Conspiracy to obstruct justice, and perjury."

"Okay," Partridge said. "How do you two lawyers wanta deal with those?"

"On these two charges we confront the most serious complications. The team's conspiracy passed through many evolutions, beginning with the joint agreement to make false reports to Colonel Smothers, to their calculated failure to report the ambush, to their willful misleading of Colonel Smothers's debriefing officer. But then the United States Army *and* the government of the United States became party to the conspiracy. The interests of the government to protect the cover of a secret war corresponded with the team's need to cover their crimes, and an overt bargain was reached."

"Noted," he said.

I drew in a heavy breath. "General, were you party to or knowledgeable of this agreement?"

"I was," he frankly confessed.

I said, "Then it is your duty to disqualify yourself from this case. You must cede your authority to decide on our recommendations."

I expected Partridge to leap across the table and rip out my throat when I said that. Morrow and I had discussed this issue for many hours. We guessed that Partridge was a co-conspirator, making him as much a criminal as any man in Sanchez's team. He could no longer pass judgment on their crimes. Nor could any of the other men seated on the far side of the table. For that matter, it seemed entirely likely that the entire chain of command above Terry Sanchez, possibly up to and including the Commander in Chief himself, was implicated in the crimes we'd uncovered. Quite possibly, no one in the existing chain of military command could decide on this case. A mass recusal was in order. It made for an interesting precedent, Morrow and I had decided during one of our more academic interludes.

Partridge merely smiled. His Camel pack was lying on the table and he picked it up and carefully placed it in his pocket.

He said, "Okay, Counselor, you done? You said all you wanta say?"

"Yes, sir."

"You're right, Drummond. In front of these witnesses, I hereby relinquish my responsibility for judging your recommendations. You've done a great job, son. You've shown real courage and character and intelligence. Your father would be proud of you. Hell, I'm proud of you."

I said, "Thank you, General. I'll be sure to tell my father when I see him next."

This time he smiled when he said, "I told you before, Drummond, don't blow smoke up my ass."

"No, sir," I said.

"Now, it's time for a little more off-the-record guidance. You ready to listen?"

"Yes, sir."

"How many counts of murder you recommending?"

"Maybe ten counts, sir. But only one man to be indicted."

"So, only one man. That's this Sergeant First Class Perrite. Is that right?"

"That's right, sir."

"Then aside from this Perrite, none of the rest of them men in that team are guilty of any serious offenses. I mean, we could prosecute Sanchez for gross dereliction of duty, but what would that prove, huh? He's crazy as a loon already. And we could hit some of the others for various misjudgments, but then we'd look like a bunch of niggling, vindictive pricks, wouldn't we? So all that leaves is all these conspiracy charges, and if you're gonna make one charge of conspiracy to obstruct or perjure, or whatever the hell, well, then you're gonna have to make hundreds of charges that go in every which direction, all the way to the moon. I got all that straight, Counselor?"

"Yes, General. I'd say you have the whole picture."

He leaned back in his chair. "And Tretorne here, and Murphy, they told you that if you wanted to go public with this thing, then we won't stop you. That right also?"

"That was the deal, General."

He nodded. "Well, a deal's a deal, son. So it's up to you to decide."

"Thank you, sir."

He chuckled. It was a humorless chuckle. "Don't thank me, Drummond. God, don't thank me, boy. I just put the biggest heap of shit on your plate you ever smelled. You thought about what's gonna happen if you go public?"

"I believe I have, General. I think it will incite a considerable scandal."

He sort of chuckled at that, too, only this chuckle was sort of like the way parents do when their three-year-olds say something cute. Not something worldly or intelligent, just cute.

"Hell, Drummond, if that was the worst of it, none of us woulda got in your way in the first place. Scandals come and scandals go. A few souls go to jail or spend a fortune paying for lawyers, but these days even that ain't all bad. If their scandal's big enough, they write a book or get some movie rights before they're even outta jail. Then they buy themselves a nice place in Malibu or Hilton Head and spend the rest of their lives being shuttled around with first-class seats and getting paid twenty thousand a shot on the speaking circuit. People just can't get enough of hearing these pricks babble on about their sins. Don't think there's a one of us on this side of the table who's afraid of some pissant scandal."

He chuckled some more as he turned to the White House man. "Hey, Parker, how many scandals you had to handle for our beloved Commander in Chief?"

Parker chuckled with him. "I don't wish to sound disrespectful, General, but the man attracts scandals like a wool suit
attracts lint. Every time he closes a door in the White House,
we all wince and wonder what he's up to next."

Partridge turned back and faced me. "See, son, don't think
Tretorne or Murphy or I did this 'cause we're afraid of some
scandal. You been through any the camps while you were here?"

"We have."

He nodded his approval. "Good for you. Right now we got
nearly one and a half million Kosovars in our camps. One and
a half million of these poor bastards whose only hope is us. You
go public, this whole operation to get them back their homeland's gonna fall apart. This thing's hanging together on a thin
thread anyway. The Russians are accusing us of genocide. Our
NATO allies hate us for making 'em do this. We shamed most
of 'em into it. They find out we're running a secret ground war,
they'll pull the plug faster than you can spit. The Italians won't
let us fly off their soil anymore. The Brits might hang in, but
there'll be nothing to hang on to. Think Congress will let us
hang in? I don't. And I'm the one who's spent a lot a time up
there dealing with those guys. Hell, it might even cause NATO
to fall apart. Don't think the French won't make a run at it."

I sat and listened to every word.

"It's up to you, Drummond. Do what *you* think is right. Milosevic's probably got tens of thousands of murderers and rapists
and every other assortment of criminal on his rolls. Most of 'em
will never see the inside of a courtroom. But you go ahead and
pit this one soldier, this Sergeant Perrite, you pit his fate against
the fate of one and a half million Kosovars. You decide if going
public's worth giving Milosevic a victory in this thing. You decide if you're willing to destroy the lives of millions of people
so we can get a chance to punish one man for killing some bastards who probably deserved to die anyway. Think about how

just it would be for those millions of people to lose their country over some joker named the Hammer."

He got up and walked out of the room without saying another word. Until this moment, Morrow and I had enjoyed our worm's-eye view of the world, thinking we were on a mighty crusade to right a terrible wrong. Now we were glued to our seats, too stunned to move. The other men stared at us.

I suddenly felt a tidal wave in my stomach. I quickly blurted out, "If you gentlemen will please excuse us, Captain Morrow and I need some time together."

Before we left, I turned and looked at General Murphy. He could still look me dead in the eye, and without the slightest hint of guilt or shame. He didn't smile, though. I'll give him credit for that. He didn't rub it in.

He and Tretorne had sucked me in one more time. I really had made a bargain with the devil.

Chapter
★★★ 35

There are times in life when the wrong thing to do is actually the right thing to do. Maybe vice versa, too. I don't know. I haven't gotten around to testing that theory yet.

I looked across the courtroom and knew I had my hands full. The ten members of the court-martial board all had their eyes riveted on the defense counsel, who, to my vast dismay, was very skillfully presenting an incredible opening argument. I was the prosecutor, of course, though right at that moment I wished I could crawl into the defense counsel's shoes. The legs of my case were being ripped out from under me.

I turned around and looked anxiously at my senior legal assistant, Imelda Pepperfield. She merely shrugged a little, rearranged her gold-rimmed glasses, and gave me a stern glare. If I was looking for sympathy, I had sure as hell turned to the wrong corner. Imelda might even have been the one who originally invented that timeworn phrase about "sympathy" being found in the dictionary between "shit" and "syphilis."

I had thought my case was fairly airtight. One of those open-and-shut things. Another sure victory under the belt of that brilliant legal scholar Sean Drummond. The facts were irresistibly simple. A sergeant assigned to one of the Army's black units, in this case a special communications unit that performed some pretty nifty work using communications gear that the American public couldn't even imagine existed, got caught making illegal use of his credit card.

Unfortunately for both him and the government, it was an Army-issued Visa card. He'd used it to purchase a car, a camera with a zoom lens, some very expensive clothes, even a set of golf clubs. Now the golf clubs, that really took chutzpah. His unit commander discovered the fraud, had him apprehended, then turned him over to us for trial. My caseload had been staggering as a result of the month I'd spent working on that Kosovo thing, but the prosecution was assigned to me anyway. No problem, I figured. I did the preliminary work. I tracked down copies of his receipts. I prevailed on the clerks who handled his purchases to give me positive identifications on videotape, which the judge allowed me to introduce as evidence.

Airtight, right? The very nature of the goods he'd purchased damned him. Any idiot could see that he'd milked his government card for personal gain. The only thing left was to explain all that to the board of officers and sergeants. As was always the case in this court, every board member was selected from a black unit. That was a defense counsel's nightmare, because folks who go into "black" work tend to be pretty hard-nosed and unforgiving. I figured I'd entertain them with a brief but trenchant opening statement, show them my tidy little pile of evidence, and voilà! One more sniveling bad guy headed upriver for his misdeeds.

Unfortunately, the defense counsel wasn't going along with my scenario. She was up there prancing in front of the board, flashing her arms around, and building this perfectly outrageous defense. She claimed her poor client suspected two officers in his unit of engaging in espionage. He made the purchases, she claimed, to complete a disguise he intended to use to try to prove it. Once a month, she claimed, these two traitorous officers met with their foreign contact on a local golf course where they played as a trio. This was where the money and information changed hands. Her client, she claimed, only bought the car so they wouldn't recognize his own car. He bought a used car at that, a rust-covered, nasty-looking, beaten-up old 1969 Ford Mustang that cost only four hundred dollars. It wasn't even a convertible, she emphasized. He'd also purchased a false mustache and a wig to go with the golf clothes he bought, to complete his disguise. And the camera with the 400X zoom lens? How else was he expected to record the money and envelopes changing hands?

The board members were nodding their heads right in time as she made her points. She even whipped out a charge card receipt to prove he had purchased the fake mustache and wig, in addition to all the other apparent luxury artifacts she accurately predicted the one-sided prosecutor planned on presenting during displays of evidence.

I mean, you've got to be kidding. I never heard such a scandalous, contemptible, flimsy defense in my legal career. Why didn't she just say he was making the purchases and reached into his wallet and accidentally pulled out the wrong card? He meant to use his own Visa. That's a good defense. Hell, it was the exact same defense I'd once used in a similar case. My poor client got convicted, but it was still a good defense.

Unfortunately, the board members were all captivated by her sympathetic eyes, not to mention her other physical charms, which I have to admit were quite considerable. And the one thing she had going for her defense was that it was so dazzlingly unbelievable as to be completely plausible.

When she finished, Morrow flashed her most winsome smile at the board members and you could almost hear their hearts flutter. Then she turned and smiled at me. Only my smile wasn't like theirs. Mine was more like the way a lion might smile after a particularly delicious meal. Or maybe *before* a particularly tasty meal. Whichever. I've never been sure how those two smiles might be that much different anyway.

She and I had obviously decided not to go public about Sanchez and the conspiracy. The truth is, you just can't trade the fate of one man against the fates of a couple million lost souls. All that philosophical blather about ends not justifying means aside, this was one of those times when the ends did justify the means. The reason for laws in the first place is to protect entire societies, and one and a half million Kosovars are a society. And Perrite? He was just one man. At least that was the conclusion Morrow and I came to before we threw in our towels and enlisted in the conspiracy.

Clapper very generously gave us another three-day extension, during which we rewrote our report and completely absolved Sanchez and his men of all crimes. We cited Tretorne's cooked-up satellite shots as proof that the team merely acted in self-defense. And the coroner's report? Somehow that never got included in our packet. I think Imelda might've lost it somewhere, like in a burn pile. Wasn't like Imelda to lose things, but hey, everybody makes a mistake sometimes.

We threw ourselves into the whitewash whole hog. The Serbs responded just as Delbert, or Floyd, or whoever that asshole was, had predicted they would. They convened a big press conference and complained about the fact that all their troops had been shot in the head, too. Well, Morrow and I held our own press conference and said there was compelling NSA evidence that this was a contemptible attempted frame job by Milosevic. A few reporters got the gripes over that, but Milosevic had spent so many years telling so many whoppers that he didn't have much credibility. It actually was sort of a delicious irony that, for once, we were the ones lying about murder. As much as I believe in justice for all, the victims who suffered and died at the hands of the Hammer and his boys hadn't gotten any. Or maybe this was their justice.

Chief Persico got another Silver Star, and a few of the other team members got Bronze Stars. Right on the White House lawn, too. I liked Persico anyway, so I didn't mind all that much. Terry Sanchez got moved to the psychiatric ward of a VA hospital somewhere in southern Virginia. Last I heard, they had him in arm restraints so the blisters on his thighs could heal. And Sergeant Perrite? They pulled him out of the team and took away his green beret. That was one of the only two concessions I demanded before I began splashing whitewash at the government's behest. Perrite still had two years left on his current enlistment, and I talked them into reclassifying him into graves registration, where he'll spend the next couple of years digging holes and filling them with bodies. It might be a lot less than he deserves, but who knows? It might make him think.

When I meet my maker someday, I'm fairly confident I'll be able to square all this up. I mean, I'm a lawyer. I'm a damned good one, too. I've defended weaker cases and prevailed.

What did I learn? I guess I learned that Murphy was right. Sometimes those principles of duty and honor and country clash against one another in pretty ugly ways. You can't always make them fit together. You've just got to decide which one to throw overboard.

I went to Clapper and extracted one other tiny tribute in return for blemishing my previously pristine principles and integrity. My special legal unit had just lost one of our two defense counsels, a good one, too, who'd left the Army to seek his fortune and fame in one of those huge Washington firms that hibernate in those big, regal glass towers. I don't know what got into his head. Well, actually I do. It was those damned unlimited expense accounts and mouthwatering bonuses. Just think of what he'll be missing, though.

Anyway, we needed a replacement and I made Clapper agree

to give us Morrow. Right at this moment, though, I felt a strong tinge of regret. I looked at the faces of the board members, all of whom still had their eyes glued on Morrow's shapely gams. How am I supposed to compete with that? I mean, give me a break. The guy bought a car and clothes and a fancy camera and a full set of golf clubs, all so he could expose some of his officers for selling secrets to the enemy? Morrow's been watching too many of those Oliver Stone movies.

But the last and final truth was that I kind of wanted to keep her around. I mean, she has those incredibly sympathetic eyes and occasionally they come in handy.

In any case, by now you probably have figured this out about me: I don't give up easily. Someday soon, maybe right after I kick her ass in this trial, I'm going to prove to the lovely Miss Morrow that I'm not a Pudley. Maybe I'm no Humongo, but I'm no Pudley. Metaphysically speaking, of course.